J. ALBI

IN THE DAWN'S EARLY LIGHT

2007

In The Dawn's Early Light

ACKNOWLEDGEMENTS:

The facts about Admiral He are true and can be found in abundance on the Internet.

I thank the following people for supplying this information about this great man and his achievements.

Michael L. Bosworth *The Rise and Fall of 15th Century Chinese Seapower*
http://www.cronab.demon.co.uk/china.htm

Siu-Leung Lee, Ph.D. *Chinese Mariner Zheng He* [Cheng Ho] March 16, 2002
http://www.chinapage.com/history/zhenghe2.html

The seafaring tale in Chapter Four is my version of one originally spun by Secretary of the Navy John H. Dalton during a speech he gave at the Seattle Rotary Club Luncheon on 6 August 1997. (http://www.defenselink.mil/speeches/1997/s19970806-dalton.html)

The Navy Hymn: "Eternal Father, Strong to Save" The original words are by Rev. William Whiting of the Church of England. More history can be found at: http://www.history.navy.mil/faqs/faq53-1.htm

Cleve Backster's book *Primary Perception* http://www.primaryperception.com/ and his business webpage: http://www.backster.net/generalinfo.htm

U.S. Census Bureau: http://www.census.gov/
City-Data.Com: http://www.city-data.com/

Abraham H. Maslow (1908–1970) was one of the great humanists of our time. His ideas have advanced the concept that the nature of the individual human is basically good. That if left to our own choices, we will choose the right and best path for not only ourselves, but for the family and community in which we live. Maslow introduces you to his Hierarchy of Needs in chapter five of his book *Motivation and Personality.* I highly recommend this book for anyone who wishes to expand his or her knowledge of Maslow's ideas and concepts.

Ripple: (wine) was produced in the 1970s by Ernest & Julio Gallo Winery of California. It was an inexpensive fortified wine with a sweet taste and high alcohol content.

To The Many Youth That Have Been Part Of My Life, In Whose Hands Our Future Rests. You Are The Inspiration For This Book. To The Ladies Who Have Shown Me The Female View Of Life And The Elders Who Have Shared Their Wisdom. I Thank You For Enriching My Life. And To Joshua Richardson, You Are Not Forgotten And Are Definitely One Of The Above Youth. May You All Enjoy Your Great Adventure Called Life.

In Remembrance:

Of Mary Dyer, My Eighth Great-grandmother, A Quaker Who Was Hanged On The Boston Common On June The First In The Year 1660 Because As She Said, "My Life Not Availeth Me In Comparison To The Liberty Of The Truth."

Of My Fellow Veterans Who Have Gone On Before, Those Who Still Carry On, And Especially For Those Who Suffer Still From The Wounds To Mind, Body, And

Spirit. It Is My Hope That We, Whom They Served, Will Embrace Them In Their Daily Lives.

The USS Constitution In My Story Was Named After The Oldest U.S. Navy Ship Still In Service. You Will Find A Description Of The Ship At The End Of The Story Before The Epilog.

AS THE DAWN ONE

As the sun rises above the horizon the light of dawn announces the new day...

On the USS Constitution CVNX-911, Pacific Ocean in the Year 2012:

Many have written of the calm before the storm, but even this was too eerie for words. There was no sound, no wind, not a ripple on the ocean, which was flat as glass as far as the eye could see. Even the ship seemed suspended there, like a dead carcass awaiting her inevitable fate. Her mighty engines had remained silent for hours now. The environmental systems, computers, radios, every electrical device, all stopped as the ship's electrical pulse vanished in the blink of an eye.

She was completely lifeless, and most of her crew wandered aimlessly about the main deck like trapped fleas. The crew was trained to respond to every imaginable type of crisis, from attack to violent acts of nature, but this was beyond them, like a non-event. Nothing had happened. Everything just stopped working. And this was the dawn of a new day.

When it had all started they were left in a complete dark silence. The mid-watch had just come on and the OOD (Officer of the Deck) had confirmed all was secure. The captain was asleep in his cabin and the XO (Executive Officer) was sleeping in the cabin on the bridge, since one of them had to be there whenever the ship was underway. The seas were calm, the sky was clear, the stars were bright, nothing was in sight, and there were no contacts on the instruments. They had been alone; steaming at flank speed in the open ocean to deliver a large box marked TOP SECRET. Even the Marines guarding it seemed bored as they opened a deck of cards. They were five days out of port headed for an undisclosed delivery point, known only to the civilian now pacing the open bridge.

Most of the crew wondered if the man could speak. He had come aboard and handed the captain a sealed letter and showed him his identification. He silently watched as his box was loaded and secured. Once the Marines took up their station at it, he vanished to his cabin. Since then he arrived at meals and wandered about the ship like a silent apparition, but that night he was holding vigil on the open bridge.

Most of the crew had been aboard as she was scheduled to leave for sea trails in forty-eight hours. Two civilian workers doing last minute work had to stay onboard to finish and accepted this quirk of fate philosophically and settled in to enjoy the cruise with overtime pay. The crew was used to odd assignments, and this delivery mission was better than an ill-defined combat mission. It had also spared them having to play the sea trail games to test all the shipboard systems. It was just a simple cruise in good weather.

Harry Haul had finished installing the new transceiver. The other civilian, Bob Cybernaut, had the new software running on all the ship's systems, which interfaced with this new equipment. To test its full integration, Bob loaded some of his son's computer games and gave the whole crew access to them. It would be a better test than the real thing and keep the bored crew busy on this cruise to nowhere.

Bob had headed to his cabin in Officer's Country and drifted to sleep to his favorite music. Harry had procured a beach chair from one of the crew and was lying on it wrapped in a wool blanket on the bow under the stars. As Harry got comfy he wished for a cold beer and a good woman. He knew he'd get neither. Instead his thoughts turned to a pond far away. He could almost hear the soft chatter of boys and the loud snoring of the adults sleeping in their snug, warm tents. He quietly drifted off to sleep with his pleasant memories of the past.

The OOD sat down with his coffee, checklists done, watch relieved. All was quiet and he decided to ignore the silent man on the open bridge. His four hours would fly by and he would go back to bed. Even the bridge crew was quiet tonight as they watched their instruments. As he read the master computer console he noted the date and time readout: 01-04-2012 00:09:11. Before his brain could fully register the date, a blinding flash forced his eyes closed. Instantly his hand shot up for the blast shield and slammed it down in place. The others followed suit just as they had many times in practice. He heard no alarms and searched to see the master console, but could not.

Assuming he was flash-blinded he called out to the bridge crew who all reported a loss of sight too. The closest man stumbled to the sleeping cabin to wake the XO. With his sight returned and before the XO could get there, the OOD knew they had real trouble. He could still see the bright stars, but none of the equipment was working. He grabbed the emergency flashlight for a better look and found it too was dead even though he had checked it only minutes before.

On the bow, Harry stirred and smiled up at the stars. As he took a deep breath of the fresh salty air his brain sensed something was wrong. Odd, he could hear nothing as he rolled on his side to look back at the ship. Sticking out his hand he laid it on the deck. His eyes popped wide open. He felt no vibrations coming from the hull—the ship was dead. His bare feet hit the deck as he wrapped the blanket tighter with one hand and grabbed his shoes with the other. He ran to the bridge.

The XO, Cdr. Tu Secondary, had assumed command and went down the checklist once more getting the same sad results. A runner had brought Capt. Bill O. Right to the bridge and he watched the end of the process in stunned silence. Suddenly a dark robed figure appeared on the bridge. Its arm reached up and a flame shot to life making the whole scene even freakier. Once they all realized their torchbearer was Harry and not the Grim Reaper, they doubled their efforts. The reports started coming in on the emergency telephones, which normally lay unused, but now made their hopeless situation even more obvious.

Captain Right set watches around the deck to look out for other ships and handed out flares to use as warning signals. With the XO on the bridge he called a meeting for all his senior officers on the flight deck. He needed answers and fast. It didn't take long for all division officers to report that nothing was working and they had no idea why. Harry and Bob assured the captain that none of the new enhancements or programs could have shut down all the redundant systems onboard, let alone drain every battery and shut down all the reactors. Whatever happened was not possible by any known means and brought the meeting to a long silence when Captain Right asked for solutions.

Meanwhile, below in the hanger deck, the bored Marines had gone to full alert, with weapons ready. They quickly set up a defensive perimeter around the box and readied for the worst. Lieutenant Brice barked orders and checked positions until she was sure they could protect the box they surrounded. She moved through the darkness like a cat even though her night vision goggles hung useless. They knew something was very wrong for all the electronic gear to fail at once, but their training emphasized self-reliance, and they'd fight with just their hands if it came to that. But their biggest challenge came in keeping the blind sailors from walking into them in their search for light. They soon boxed themselves in with crates and equipment, building a fence of sorts around the box they guarded.

Slowly, the situation got quieter as the milling sailors found safe places to gather and wait in the dark. Even a little sense of control returned, but it was short-lived. As Lieutenant Brice sat to wait for orders, her attention was drawn by a soft humming sound coming from behind her. It was coming from in the box.

Her first thought was what if it was a weapon that had armed itself? She sent a runner to tell the captain and the box's guardian.

Lieutenant Brice knew this was dangerous for both the guards and the wandering sailors. She remembered from her first security sweep of the hanger deck around the box that an emergency generator was about two hundred feet forward of their position. Leaving her senior Marine in charge, she and the radioman headed for the generator. Finding the generator's batteries dead, they were about to go back when she recalled that some emergency field generators had back-up methods to start them. She searched with her hands and finally found a small access door and opened it. Inside she felt a small pull-start engine that could start the generator. She primed it the best she could and pulled the cord. On her third try it came to life with a deafening roar on the silent ship. The control panel lights on the big generator came on. There was light.

On the deck above, the meeting had fast run out of ideas other than to wait for the dawn's early light so they could see. The only sure thing was the navigator's report that he knew exactly where they were from the stars. Although Captain Right did not feel very reassured standing on the deck of the most powerful ship in the U.S. Navy, knowing it was totally dead in the water.

A sudden load noise echoing from below brought Harry back to full alert. It almost sounded like someone had started a lawn mower. His mind flashed to the emergency generator he had to move his equipment around and he bolted from the group like a man on a mission with Bob in hot pursuit.

It only took a moment for Captain Right to issue orders and follow with his engineering officer. As Harry descended the ladder to the hanger deck, he could see a faint glow and headed for it like a bird dog. He arrived at the generator to find Lieutenant Brice fighting with a lock on the main access panel door.

"I've got a key," Harry said to her and ran to a nearby container box. He returned with a large ballpeen hammer in hand and received an approved smile from her on his choice of keys.

The captain arrived to find Harry and Lieutenant Brice working to start the generator while Bob read the instruction manual to them. Lieutenant Brice asked the captain if he got the message. The runner had not found him. She told him about the humming and had the radioman guide him to the box so he could hear for himself.

Above, the runner crashed into the meeting and soon turned it into chaos with his news. Some men were ready to abandon ship, others went to hunt down the mysterious guardian of the box, and a few daring souls headed for the humming box.

Soon, the emergency generator roared to life, and the engineering officer gathered men to deploy lights, so the hanger deck started to reappear from the dark gloom. Along with the ship electricians they were soon running cables, so they could start the ship's auxiliary diesel generators. Lieutenant Brice decided to return to her men guarding the box. Since she had explained the box dilemma to Harry and Bob while they worked starting the generator, their curiosity had gotten the best of them. So as Lieutenant Brice headed into the dark they followed.

They arrived as the strange man-in-black was telling Captain Right he could not touch the box. Although its humming was harder to hear over the generator, it was still obvious. A ship's electrician suddenly put some light on the scene and illuminated the captain and the man-in-black standing nose to nose. He was now telling the captain he was in charge and they all had to get away from the box. The man-in-black had not noticed Harry and Bob standing on either side of him, looking at him like he was nuts. He had just started on a new series of threats and was slipping his hand into his jacket when he felt Lieutenant Brice's gun press painfully into the base of his skull. He froze and several Marines took him into custody.

Captain Right smiled at Lieutenant Brice and said, "Thank you."

A very thorough search revealed no key, codes, or other means of entry to the box on the now naked man-in-nothing. After the Marines suggested he could have a refreshing swim in the Pacific with some hungry sharks, the man started singing a new tune. Unfortunately, his owners did not trust him with the means to enter the box.

"Well, I'll open it," Harry said in disgust. Then he turned toward it with Captain Right, Lieutenant Brice, and Bob.

Bob stepped a little ahead of him and grabbed his hammer. "You'd better give me that. Remember I'm the electronics wizard here."

As Captain Right and Lieutenant Brice watched Harry shrugged and said, "Go for it."

After examining the keypad and its blinking red light, Bob leaned back, let out a sigh, and whacked the bottom side of the pad with the hammer. The cover popped open and landed on the floor with a clatter. The red light was still blinking as Bob returned the hammer to Harry. A small screwdriver appeared in Bob's hand like magic and he started dismantling the keypad. Shortly, he had wires everywhere and started adding his own jumpers to the mix.

Suddenly, the panel started beeping. The red light went out. Everyone held his or her breath as the hum continued unchanged. Suddenly a green light appeared, and clicking and whirring sounds came from the door. Bob moved back just in time as the door swung open.

Lieutenant Brice ordered her explosives man, Sgt. J.P. Smith, to join her as she followed Bob in. Harry and Captain Right brought up the rear. They found themselves standing in a brightly-lit empty room about the size of the box. On the right side of the wall opposite the door was a screen, keyboard, and two scanners, but nothing else. The five stared in amazement.

Harry said, "It isn't humming in here."

Before they could come up with any other ideas, a face appeared on the screen and demanded their attention.

The stern looking woman on the screen said, "I'm Acting Commanding Officer Dr. Whosh and you've invaded my ship." Before Captain Right could reply she continued, "You're not supposed to be here, but under the circumstances I must make decisions which my standing orders do not adequately address. Captain Right, would you kindly keep that civilian from doing further damage with his hammer?"

"Yes," Right said, "but I want some answers."

Harry stood there looking somewhat sheepish with the hammer in his hand.

Dr. Whosh said, "I understand your problem, Captain Right, and will let you in, but we must close the outer door first for the interlocks to work."

Lieutenant Brice moved close to the captain. "Sir, you should stay outside with your command. This may not be safe."

They all turned as the engineering officer walked in. Cdr. Alex Albright seemed at a loss for words as he looked at the screen. He looked at Captain Right then at Lieutenant Brice and back to the screen.

"What's our status, Commander?" asked Captain Right.

"Sir, the electricians have the auxiliary generators started, but it will take five hours to restart the reactors. We'll have auxiliary lights, emergency systems, and our backup engine online in an hour. All watches report no contacts and we are drifting at two knots on a heading of 250 degrees."

After a very short pause, Right said, "Commander, I'm going in this thing to find out what happened. Tell the XO to get her underway to the nearest port, which should be Pearl Harbor, ASAP. Transmit requests for assistance as soon as the radios are up. If this box does anything, anything at all that you think will endanger our ship while I'm inside—" He looked at Dr. Whosh and back to the commander—"throw it overboard."

"Yes, sir."

"She says we have to close the outer door to go inside. The XO is now in command."

"Yes, sir."

The commander left and Captain Right looked at Lieutenant Brice. "Close the door."

She pressed the close button on the inside of the door. It shut and sealed. With all their eyes on Dr. Whosh, she said, "Just a moment, please."

Noises started coming from the blank wall and Lieutenant Brice then realized she was standing in an air lock. After a few nervous moments the wall started sliding open. Harry's curiosity propelled him through the door first with Lieutenant Brice leaping after him. Sergeant Smith followed with Bob and Captain Right bringing up the rear.

They hardly noticed the door close behind them. They all stared at the room they'd entered, which looked like it came off a submarine with various diving suits hanging on racks. The room itself was four times larger than the entry.

Harry looked at Lieutenant Brice and asked, "Is this some kind of diving bell?"

A voice from the far side of the room answered, "No, but this room can have a similar function."

They all turned and saw the woman whose face had been on the screen standing there in a blue jumpsuit. "If you follow me, I'll take you to our dining area where you can be comfortable while I try to explain."

Harry turned to the captain. "I think the senior man goes first."

Captain Right smiled and joined Dr. Whosh. Harry and Lieutenant Brice fell in next, with Bob and a nervous Sergeant Smith at the rear as they walked through the looking glass into "Project Wonderland."

A man in a black jumpsuit shut and sealed the door after they'd all entered the next room. He fell in behind Bob and Sergeant Smith, smiling and nodding at both of them. That he was friendly and unarmed made Smith feel more at ease. At the end of the passageway they came to another set of doors. Dr. Whosh pressed a button, which opened to reveal an elevator. They all stepped in after Dr. Whosh, and the doors shut.

Harry looked at Lieutenant Brice and asked, "Is it just me or is this shipping box much bigger on the inside?"

Captain Right turned and looked at them. "I'm glad someone else noticed that."

They all turned as one to look at Dr. Whosh who smiled and had a mischievous twinkle in her eyes. A chuckle came from the back of the elevator.

Whosh glanced in that direction saying, "General Rabbit, this is no laughing matter. The president may have us both shot, and them as well. I think today we've violated at least a dozen standing orders, not to mention the breach of security letting them in here."

Rabbit retorted, "They could have just dropped us in the ocean. Some day someone would have found whatever was left of us."

"That's not funny either," replied Whosh. "You military men are all alike. You'd rather die with a secret than adjust to new circumstances. Besides, these two civilians have a higher security clearance than you do."

Before anyone could ask what she meant, the elevator stopped and the doors opened. She slipped into the corridor and led them to a large room, which was obviously a well-appointed dining area. Several others were waiting and came to attention as she led the group in. She pointed out to a large table.

As soon as everyone was seated, Whosh said, "I guess I should start by introducing my crew. As I said before, I'm the acting commanding officer in charge of Sand Box 4, which is part of Project Wonderland. The man you've already met is our security chief, General Peter Rabbit." She indicated the older man to her left in the black jumpsuit. "This young man is my communications officer, Commander Scott O'Rielly." She pointed to the young man in a blue jumpsuit. "And just joining us is our engineering officer, Captain Alice Furreal."

As everyone turned to look, a tall redhead strode into the room. Unlike the others she wore a red jumpsuit and walked to the head of the table to stand next to Whosh. She scanned the seated people and announced to all, "I'm Alice. Welcome to Wonderland." Then she looked straight at J.P. Smith. "You know, J.P., you're ten years late for our date."

J.P. recognized the voice at once and tried to crawl under the table, remembering well the high school prom he missed years before and the date he had ended up jilting by not showing up.

"It's nice of you to bring him, Lieutenant Brice, even if Sand Box 4 has very few explosive toys that would require his talents," said Alice.

Rabbit gave Alice a long look and laughed. "Perhaps, Alice, he can disarm you for us."

Before Alice could retort, a tall man in green stooped in the doorway to speak into the COM panel. "Cookie, could you bring us some drinks and food for our guests?"

"Right away, Doc," came the reply.

Whosh continued. "And the man in green is Doc Bones, who obviously could not find anything to do with himself in sickbay, so he is conspiring with Cookie, Ensign Blanch Chablis, to meet all of you."

And with that a tall blond wheeled in a cart with drinks and delicious looking snacks. "Hi. I'm Cookie. I'm pleased to serve you."

Whosh smiled. "As soon as you all help yourselves, we can get started now that our crew's information sources have joined us."

Doc slipped his arm around Cookie while grabbing a drink and said into her ear, loud enough for all to hear, "What can we do now that she knows about us?"

After everyone had munchies and a drink, they settled down to hear the rest of the story.

"This is Sand Box 4, part of Project Wonderland," Whosh began. "We have a crew of about one hundred and can carry a research or security team of twice that number for long periods, up to a thousand for short jumps. About half of us are on board. The rest are to meet us in Hawaii. I'll skip trying to explain why Sand Box 4 is larger inside than outside—because it even boggles my mind. Basically we are a time machine. Our government has had this technology since before I was born. I've no idea what our mission was about, only where you were taking us. You were supposed to deliver us to Guam. By our best estimates we are about one hundred miles short of Hawaii."

Whosh looked questioningly at Alice, who said, "Your ship is no longer adrift and is making five knots on a course for Pearl Harbor. Your reactors should be online in an hour and then you'll have full power. There are no ships or planes on the horizon and I figure an ETA there in five hours."

After a pause, Whosh picked up the explanation. "We've no idea what caused the event that occurred on your ship—or what happened to us as well. All of our equipment that could cause such an event was shut down. As far as we know, even if they were fully operational, we could not have moved your ship. Our best fix says it is now the year 1421."

Harry was the first to recover. "Boy that was some nap I took up on your deck, Captain! Dr. Whosh, can we get back even if you've no idea what got us here?"

Dr. Whosh replied, "Alice has started to bring us up to full power, but it's slow going without part of my crew. When we get to Pearl Harbor, Sand Box 4 should be able to make the jump back to our base timeline. Our full crew should be waiting there so we can get all systems online. But so far we have no idea how to move your ship."

Captain Right said, "Some of my crew is there too. Can we get them to the ship?"

"Yes, but we have an even bigger problem. If I contact General Black at the Pentagon, I may be ordered to abandon your ship and all its crew here. The sand boxes are so secret that few inside of the CIA know of them and I fear they would sacrifice your ship and crew to keep their secret. We've all talked this over and believe we should stay with you until we find a solution. We believe it's far too dangerous to just abandon your ship here, especially since we don't know how or who got us here."

Right asked, "John Doe who came aboard with your box and gave me the sealed orders, is he one of your crew?"

Rabbit laughed. "No. That little CIA creep is our minder and it's our good fortune that the locator chip inside him has stopped sending its trace signal. Your crew seems to have him well in hand. Perhaps you could have him gift-wrapped and we could leave him in Hawaii. I think he needs a vacation."

"Can we return without the CIA knowing?" Right asked.

"They must already know your ship is gone. Especially if your crew and ours vanish from Pearl, they'll have a big clue," said Alice. "We could jump to Commander Dew North's home; he's our navigation officer and then get our people while we're there. Another odd thing is that Sand Box 4 has a trace signal. It's built so we can't tamper with it. Like Doe's chip our trace beacon has also stopped working."

Rabbit added, "You're going to make a great spy, Alice, but we'll have to be careful, and we should report so they can't hang Whosh. Like after we're gone."

As everyone scattered, Captain Furreal paused at the hatch and looked back. "Lieutenant Brice, you take good care of Sergeant Smith. I'm not done with him yet."

Lieutenant Brice smiled back and snapped a very professional salute. "Yes, sir, Captain. I'll bring him back in one piece so you can debrief him at your leisure."

After much talk of the pros and cons a plan was formed. Dr. Whosh headed for her command center with O'Rielly to ready the Sand Box for full operation. Lieutenant Brice, Sergeant Smith, and General Rabbit headed for the hanger deck to get the Marines ready for their new assignment as the Sand Box security team. Captain Right followed on their heels enroute to his own bridge to start preparations for their arrival at Pearl Harbor, Hawaii. Alice, Bob, and Harry headed to engineering to bring the Sand Box up to full operation. Cookie and Doc were off to bring the crew up-to-date.

While Whosh issued orders to the command personnel, O'Rielly slid into the seat at the main communications board.

Looking at his watch officer, he asked, "Is the Constitution still transmitting?"

"Yes sir."

"Good. Give me a secure link."

The watch officer's fingers raced over his panel. "You have it, sir."

"This is Commander Scott O'Rielly, from Sand Box 4. Acknowledge and identify, please."

On the Constitution there was a moment of utter silence and a look of disbelief on the ship's radioman's face. "Sir, we have contact—with Sand Box 4."

The XO sat down next to the radioman, wondering if he should question what the lad had said to him, but decided not to—he wanted to talk to someone, anyone who might have answers.

"This is Commander Tu Secondary, the executive officer of the USS Constitution on secure link."

"Good, Commander, your Captain Right will be returning to your bridge within a few minutes and can give you a full— well, as much of an explanation as we know about our situation. You can have your radioman stop transmitting on all those other frequencies, since as best we can figure the radio has not been invented yet. No one can hear you except us. I'll have my watch officer set up full secure data and voice links. If there are any problems, your man Bob Cybernaut is down here with us to help work them out. Right now he's in engineering with Harry Haul and our engineering officer, Captain Furreal or Alice, as she prefers."

Secondary replied, "Our men are already at it. Captain Right just returned, so I need to brief him on our status."

"Good. I'll be here if you need me," said O'Rielly.

Secondary reported that they should be at the entrance to Pearl Harbor in about an hour and they had contact with Sand Box 4. He gave a full engineering update and then inquired, "What did that O'Rielly mean by the radio has not been invented yet?"

Right smiled. "Get all our senior officers in Ready Room One for a briefing in ten minutes. Grab yourself a front row seat, Tu—this will blow your mind."

Washington, D.C. [a long time in the future] in a Large Office in the Pentagon:

"What do you mean the satellites can't find that aircraft carrier?" screamed Gen. Benedict Black. "They don't just disappear! What about the box trace signal? They can't turn that off. John Doe has an implant tracer. What about his? And where is Hardash?"

"Sir, General Hardash is flying into Guam in a Gulfstream and has ordered Sand Box 2 flown there on a C-130 with a fighter escort. The carrier and the trace signal both vanished at the same time, and we've got two Navy ships and a sub headed for that location at top speed. We've had search aircraft over that location for hours and they've found nothing. Spysat had the carrier on visual eleven minutes before it went under a cloud—the cloud vanished and the ship was gone—while they were watching it. As for Doe he went with the ship. And sir, the White House has been calling. The president wants to talk to you," assistant Woozy finished as he tried to back farther away from the general.

"Tell him I'm busy—too busy for some dumb twit who knows nothing! And you can tell that damned Banker the same thing! This is my game and no one is going to mess with me and get away with it. Call the joint chiefs. I want a meeting today. I want answers!" Black screamed at the retreating Woozy.

Oval Office, White House:

"Well, gentlemen, can anyone tell me how we lost an aircraft carrier?" asked President Puritan White.

After a long silence, President White's top aide, Dr. J.J. Flash, dared to venture, "No one, Mr. President. We have called the Navy, Air Force, NSA, and even the CIA. Spysat that was tracking the ship visually lost it. It just vanished without a trace. The Navy is headed there at flank speed. The search planes have been there for hours."

"Do you expect me to tell the press that story?" White asked with a look of pure frustration on his face. "Even the Russians and Chinese have called to ask if I need help! Am I to become the world's fool eleven days after taking this office? Gentlemen, get out of here and come back with answers! Hold all calls—I'm going to have lunch with my wife. She's the only sane person left in Washington and *she* never loses things!"

USS Constitution, Ready Room One [about 1421 and not meaning hours]:

The room was full of all the senior officers and division heads. Most had brought along their top staff to take briefing notes and many volunteers whose curiosity had become irresistible. Most were having hushed conversations while waiting for the captain's arrival.

As Captain Right entered the Ready Room, the XO yelled, "Attention on deck!" Everyone attempted to stand, but before most had done so they heard the captain's voice.

"As you were," replied Right. "We have a lot to talk about. First of all this briefing is ears only and above Top Secret, with a need to know. I'm sure it has a spook classification beyond any we know about in our world. That ugly box the Marines have been guarding, that we're supposed to deliver to Guam, is part of Project Wonderland. That box is called Sand Box 4 and is under the command of Dr. Whosh. We met with her staff of officers for a briefing."

As the crew settled down once again, the room had become silent except for Captain Right's voice, and all eyes were glued to him as he continued.

"First of all, they have no idea what happened, how it happened, or why. They do agree that our current location is near Pearl Harbor. However, they've told us that it is 'NOW' the year 1421. Yes, I said 1421 and, as O'Rielly told Secondary, the radio has not been invented yet. They know this because Sand Box 4 is a time machine. I was told we've had time travel since before I was born."

Right paused to let what he had said sink in. He took a fast sip of water. "Since they didn't cause the ship to jump to the current date, they've no idea how to get the ship back. What Dr. Whosh has proposed we do is let them retrieve their crew and ours from Pearl Harbor. Their ship will travel back to Pearl Harbor of 2012 and then return back to us. She and her head of security, General Rabbit, have suggested that we do this in secret to prevent them from getting orders from the Pentagon to abandon us here. This would mean we could never go home." Right paused for a few moments to let that sink in and could see as he looked around the room that the seriousness of their situation had sunk in. He looked at his officers and said, "I think you'll all agree it's in our best interests to work with them to find out what is going on here."

Pearl Harbor, Hawaii [the future]:

In the Officer's Club, Admiral Flagg Staff downed his whole drink and stared at the glass. "I've never lost a whole ship and without a clue. Even the spooks have no idea." The admiral's years were showing and he looked very tired. His wife, Stella, sitting next to him at the table gently placed her hand on his arm.

She asked, "Isn't there anything we can do?"

Cdr. Topper Bird, the ship's air boss, who was across the table, offered, "I'm calling all my people together at 1100 hours tomorrow to give a briefing—at least I can tell them what I don't know."

Staff looked up from his empty glass. "That's a good idea. They must be very worried. Can you have the ship's crew and those civilian spies there too?"

"Yes, of course," answered Bird. "The head spy, General Hardash, is flying himself to Guam on a Gulfstream, but I can find their senior man, a Cdr. Dew North. He has a home on the island somewhere."

"That would be good," replied the admiral. "I should talk to all of them and maybe by then I'll think of something to say."

On a hill overlooking the Pacific Ocean in a beautiful tropical paradise a tall man held his wife and stared out the sliding doors at the blue ocean under the clear sky. They had just got up, he in his shorts and she in a sexy teddy. As Tracy looked up at Dew's far off look, she said, "Hey, they'll find them—they can't lose a whole ship for long with all that spy stuff in the skies." Trying to move him along she added, "We should eat. James and Chrissy are already outside exploring the yard."

With a deep sigh, Dew nodded his agreement and held Tracy tighter.

Ready Room One [a long time ago]:

The plan was outlined in the meeting of those officers present. Captain Right called the meeting back to order and got everyone seated. He explained that the XO would brief them on the plan of action.

Commander Secondary moved to the front of the room with clipboard in hand to explain the plan. "First the navigator will have to find us a safe place to anchor. It's important the ship doesn't move while Sand Box 4 is gone. Also our current charts may not be accurate for the way Pearl Harbor used to be—or should I say is now. The box's navigation officer, Commander North, is one of the people waiting at Pearl Harbor. He has a home up in the hills overlooking the ocean. The Sand Box's plan is to go there so they won't be seen on the navy base. We hope we can do this in one trip. I'm told the box has a large cargo bay and should be able to hold all our crew. The captain's gig will be put in the water as soon as we get to the bay. We'll send up one chopper to do recon and back-up. While we're at anchor if we can get fresh food from the native islanders, we will. So we need a full away party with an armed Marine escort."

As the XO finished he asked, "Any questions?"

The engineering officer, Cdr. Alex Albright, stood to speak. "Can we trust these spies in the box?"

Captain Right got up, joined his XO, and answered, "I think so. They didn't want to abandon us. They could just land that thing in the middle of base security and forget us."

The intel officer, Lieutenant Kurious, stood at the side of the room to ask, "Sir, is it a good idea to bring more of our people here when we don't know how to return our ship to 2012 where we started?"

He replied, "Well, if the box can get them here, it can get them back. The real question is about the ship. We can't just abandon our ship here. It's much too dangerous. Besides, this is my first big command and I would rather come home with the ship with which I was entrusted." There were no more questions, so Right said in closing, "Ok, everyone is dismissed— let's go make history."

As the Constitution started her approach to the entrance of Pearl Harbor, she slowed to a crawl. The captain's gig was manned and in the water to find an anchorage for the ship. Two choppers were ready on the flight deck with complete flight crews and Marine escorts. The second one was a back up in case there was trouble. Armed watches were set all around the ship to prevent boarders. Sand Box 4 (SB4) was ready. Captain Right felt bad about leaving his ship, but knew he had the best chance of getting Admiral Flagg Staff to follow their plan.

"Set sea and anchor detail and hold your position," Right ordered.

They could already see small fishing boats stopping to look at them. The chopper lifted off the deck and headed for the shore, and the gig headed for the center channel into the harbor. Natives seemed to appear in every open space of shoreline along the waterfront and stared in amazement. The chopper quickly made the full loop on both sides and found no dangers, just stunned natives.

The gig sounded the deep-water channel and relayed the plot and depths back to the ship's navigation computer. With no tugs to guide the big ship, the captain only took her in far enough to get out of the wind and waves. As soon as they were in a safe distance, he had the two forward anchors placed to keep her in center channel. Then he had lines run from the stern to either shore and secured there. A small group of Marines set up camp at both of these locations to keep the curious natives at bay.

All was set; the ship was secure or at least as secure as he could make it. Right gave his final instructions to Secondary and left him with orders to take good care of his ship. And with that he joined the others in Sand Box 4 for his second adventure in time travel. Before the box made its leap, Bob had installed a small device in the radio room. He explained that he had no idea how it worked, but Commander O'Rielly said it would help with communications. Bob and Harry were busy helping Alice keep everything running. Everyone else was at his or her stations. Whosh was at the command console, O'Rielly at communications, Alice at navigation, Harry on engineering, and Bob was observing.

Off the Ship —Into the Garden, Back to the Future:
Whosh saw all green lights. "Com check?"
"Com green," answered O'Rielly.
"Engineering check?"
"Ready here," said Harry.
"Nav check?"
"Nav green and we have a GPS lock," replied Alice.

Now Whosh made eye contact with Alice, "Alice, do your magic."

Alice's hands flew over the keyboard and the screens started reporting new readings and progress reports. At last she stopped, leaned back in her seat, and looked over all the readouts one more time, then turned and announced, "We're here."

With that the floor tilted a little under them as Sand Box 4 settled into its new parking spot. As if by explanation, Alice said, "Tracy's garden was the clearest spot—but the dirt is a little soft."

O'Rielly quipped, "I hope the door opens."

Whosh pointed at Alice. "You're going out first and if you survive we'll send out Rabbit and the Marines. All systems on stand-by and let's go visiting."

Chrissy North, a mature, fashion-conscious teen, was busy arguing with her younger brother, James, about breakfast when the large, ugly box appeared in the middle of their mother's garden. As if it was a normal every day happening, Chrissy said, "Mom's going to be mad."

James was more curious. "Let's go check it out."

Right then the door of the box opened and their Aunt Alice stepped out to find the kids looking at what was left of the garden. Chrissy smiled and gave Aunt Alice a hug, asking if she'd dropped in for breakfast too. James found the Marines streaming out of the box behind Aunt Alice far more interesting and decided he should get permission to play with these new strangers. Chrissy and James ran ahead of Aunt Alice into the house and found their parents embracing in their sleepwear in front of the window staring at the ocean.

Chrissy said, "Mom, Aunt Alice is here for breakfast and you're going to be mad, because she messed up your garden."

James, not to be out done, said, "Dad, can I go play with the Marines Aunt Alice brought to visit? Are they staying for breakfast too?"

Tracy and Dew North turned and stared at their children in disbelief. Then they noticed Alice sheepishly standing in the kitchen. Behind her through the open door came Dew's boss, Dr. Whosh, and a female Marine. Alice, for once at a loss for words, stood silent.

Whosh said, "Hello, Tracy. Sorry about the garden. Alice needs more practice at driving, which is why we're here to collect Dew. I'll try to explain as soon as we can get organized." She turned and looked at Alice. "Alice, you've never told me he was that cute," she said, looking back at the mostly naked Dew.

Lt. Charly Brice chimed in from the other side of Alice. "If your hot sister doesn't cover up some, I'll have to hose down my Marines with cold water."

Alice remained sheepish, Dew turned very red, and yet more people kept streaming into the house. Tracy was about to have a hissy fit when J.P. Smith walked in the door. That refocused her shock.

Tracy asked, "Oh my god, Alice, where did you find him?"

"Oh," Alice replied. "He's one of Charly's boys," pointing at Lieutenant Brice.

Tracy swiped the afghan off the couch and wrapped it around herself. Then she grabbed Dew and dragged him toward the bedroom saying, "We need to get dressed before you talk to your boss."

As soon as the amusement had died down, Chrissy and James refocused all the adults on the fact that they wanted breakfast. Cookie, who was not supposed to be part of the landing party, appeared and had the children lead her to the kitchen. Outside, the Marines and General Rabbit had set up security. Those near the outer edges or off the Norths' property wore civilian clothes to hide their true purpose.

Bob and O'Rielly had already started playing with the phone and high-speed Internet links, plus set up an untraceable satcom link. This caught James' interest. Chrissy had taken note of Charly, a very well armed and obviously in-charge woman. Everyone was busy putting his or her rather complex plan into operation.

When the Norths returned, Whosh smiled at Tracy and said, "If you have a seat, I'll try to explain."

"But Doctor, she's not cleared," Dew protested.

Rabbit, who had come in the house, laughed. "I cleared her a long time ago because of you and Alice—about all you can't tell her is how the box works and even though I'm cleared for that, it makes no sense to me."

Tracy asked, "You work with all these people and Alice too?"

Sheepishly, Dew replied, "Well, I know most of them."

As they all got comfortable around the dining room table, Whosh started her tale. "You see, Captain Right was taking us to Pearl Harbor on his ship, where we were to meet Dew and our crew, Right's crew, and some of the Air Wing who had missed the ship's departure. I guess you could say we had an incident, which we can't explain and we just arrived in Pearl Harbor about two hours ago. The only problem is that it was Pearl Harbor as it was in the year 1421." Now she had Tracy's full attention, but she moved on before Tracy could speak. "The box outside is my ship, Sand Box 4, and it's a time machine. It's part of Project Wonderland, and Dew is my navigation officer, Alice my engineering officer. Cookie, you've met. Peter Rabbit here is my head of security and external research. Charly and that J.P. person sort of joined us on Right's ship. O'Rielly there is my COM officer and Bob is a civilian electronics expert who was fixing Right's computers. And I can't forget Harry, our other civilian and engineering expert. I'm told he can make anything work and, in fact, I think he already borrowed your van to run some errands. Dew, Right needs to meet with Admiral Staff and we need to get our crew onboard, but Rabbit and I fear if we report in to the Pentagon, they'll order us to abandon Right's ship and crew where they are in 1421. So we can't make any official appearance."

Dew's brain had finally caught up. He pointed out that he and Cdr. Topper Bird were to meet at Admiral Staff's home at 1000 hours. Then they, with all three crews, were to meet at the Enlisted Men's Club's large hall at 1100 hours.

Dew said, "I can drive Captain Right and you to the admiral's home for that meeting. You can explain all this and then we can decide how to pull this off."

Right put in, "The admiral is well guarded after someone tried to assassinate him."

Rabbit added, "And after he talks to you he'll need it even more."

Brice said, "Rabbit and I will be your escorts."

Right and Dew looked from her to Rabbit and knew better than to argue.

"Then we have a plan," said Whosh.

Tracy, whose brain had been working overtime, decided it was time to put her finger in this pie. "You're not taking my husband off in any time machine without me!"

She was all ready for an argument, but Dr. Whosh said with a big smile, "I wouldn't dream of leaving our cultural anthropologist expert behind, Dr. North. You, Dew, and the children can have Hardash's suite. Bob has some excellent educational software and Harry will teach the children as well how Sand Box 4 works."

Tracy, realizing all her great arguments were now totally useless, did the only thing left to do. "Why thanks, Doctor."

The mention of Hardash jogged Dew's mind. "What about the trace beacon? Shouldn't they already know you're here?"

Everyone started to laugh.

Whosh said, "No problem, Dew. Whatever or whoever zapped us and Right's ship fried the beacon. It also got the biochip in John Doe, who'll be taking a vacation here in Hawaii. As for Hardash, he's going to miss the boat again and if he does show up, he'll be very lucky not to get a tour of a volcano."

Rabbit put up both hands and said, "Hey, I got the right to remain silent."

With Dew driving, Dr. Whosh riding shotgun, Captain Right in the middle of the back with Lieutenant Brice on one side and General Rabbit on the other, they headed to meet the admiral. Tracy with Alice's help packed up what she, Dew, and the kids needed and moved into Hardash's suite on Sand Box 4. Cookie called a cleaning crew and sanitized the Norths' home so well the spooks would find nothing. Bob was driving Tracy's van into town with O'Rielly along for the ride. They pulled into the airfreight parking lot and took in a small box. Bob filled out the shipping form and paid the man cash.

The address on the box read: Mr. Robert F. Cybernaut, 411 Nooseneck Hill Road, Greene, RI. The sender's address was Mr. B. Jorge, SM, 911 Main Street, Whitmore Village, Hawaii. The note inside read:

Dear Fern,
I found this while on vacation and thought it would be very
enlightening. The "Mysteries of the Mind" have taught you
much truth. So take this and practice the Native American art
of invisibility Al showed you. Uncle Harry sends his best.
Bob.

Meanwhile, Harry had borrowed a neighbor's very expensive car and one of Rabbit's men borrowed a van. Harry backed into the driveway and two Marines in civilian clothes appeared carrying John Doe. As they climbed in the back with Doe between them, a third man placed Doe's jacket and a couple of very illegal weapons on the front seat. He then drove off toward a secluded area with the van following. Pulling up by a phone booth he turned and handed the car keys to the Marines, who put them in Doe's pocket.

Harry got out, leaving the car to be found with John Doe. He then opened the booth door. With no one in sight the Marines brought the drugged Doe and placed him on the floor of the phone booth. Harry then dialed 911 and dropped the phone on Doe. Shutting the door, they all climbed in the van for the ride back. The driver dropped them off at the Norths' home and returned the van where he'd found it. Bob and O'Rielly greeted them in the driveway. All headed back to the box to get it ready for passengers.

Admiral Flagg Staff's home 1000 hours:

Dew pulled up to the security gate and stopped. He could see Bird's red sports car parked in the yard. The female security officer in a blazer and slacks stepped up to the driver's window and looked in at Commander North and his passengers.

The guard said, "Commander North, you have unexpected company with you."

Suddenly two more security officers appeared in full body armor on either side of the car. "Would you all please step out and identify yourselves?"

She stepped back and it became obvious she now held a weapon in her hand. Two more security officers appeared from behind the wall with heavy weapons at the ready. While North slowly got out, Whosh got out and walked right up and got in the lady's face.

"Look, Ensign Shela Smith, I'm too old to be a terrorist and I want to see your damn admiral and his wife Stella, now!"

Brice stepped out and stayed between the security officer and Captain Right. Rabbit climbed out slowly and opened his jacket, so the security officer on his side could see his weapon, and held up his ID.

The security guard barked, "We've got a spook here with a mark eleven laser."

Everyone got tense, except Rabbit, who just smiled at the alarmed guard. Smith found herself up against the gate with a firm hand holding hers with the gun now pointed toward the ground. Dr. Whosh smiled in her face asking, "Did I forget to say please?"

The guard facing Brice found himself on the ground with a .45 under his chin. Dew leapt in front of Right and everyone sort of froze in place.

A large, well-dressed man strode out into the turmoil and yelled, "At ease men!"

Everyone relaxed—a little.

He pulled Dew away from Right and said, "Thank you, Commander. Most spooks do not protect sailors. I take that as a good sign. Bill, I didn't expect to see you and sure hope this means you're here to tell me you haven't lost your ship. I can see you've arrived with an impressive security force of your own."

Admiral Staff stepped over to Brice and smiled. "Lieutenant, please do not break him—good men are hard to find."

As he rounded the car, he stopped. "It that you, Peter? Now I know this is going to be a good tale," he said, putting his arm around his friend.

As Staff and Peter got at the front of the car, Staff exclaimed, "And Amanda, I thought you had vanished years ago! Please be nice to my security chief. She's young and still learning."

Rabbit looked at the admiral and then Whosh. "You really have a first name?"

"Yes, Peter, and you can be a good security chief and forget it," replied Whosh.

"She's your boss?" Staff asked.

"It's a job," replied Rabbit. "Now let's all go get inside before the neighbors notice."

Stella Staff met Amanda Whosh at the door. Greatly surprised at seeing her old friend, they hugged before entering the house.

Topper Bird now joined the group and snapped a salute at Bill Right. "Old man, you didn't go down with your ship."

Bill said, "She's not down yet, just a little lost in Pearl Harbor."

Stella directed them to the dining room where they all took a seat at the table. They all settled down for the story of a lifetime.

The admiral leaned back in his chair and said, "Well, Bill, just what is going on?"

"Sir, as you know, I left to make a delivery to Guam and was supposed to stop here for all the personnel who missed our sailing. About three hundred miles from Hawaii, in the middle of the night, the Constitution lost all power and we were dead in the water. Thanks to Lieutenant Brice and a civilian named Harry Haul we got an emergency generator going and with that jump-started the ship. We've no idea what happened or who caused it. The cargo I was carrying to Guam was a box. Lieutenant Brice noticed it was making humming sounds. She and the rest of us were afraid the damn thing was a bomb. Its caretaker, John Doe of the CIA, wouldn't tell us anything and even threatened me. Lieutenant Brice took that badly and locked him up. Meanwhile Harry and Bob Cybernaut, another civilian, broke into the box, which is where I met Doctor Whosh and her crew. It's known as Sand Box 4, part of something called Project Wonderland. And the darndest thing is the box is a time machine. She explained to me that they weren't operational when the event took place. We somehow made a leap through time to about the year 1421.

"This morning, about four hours ago, I anchored the Constitution in the beginning of what will become Pearl Harbor. Doctor Whosh and her crew brought us here to Commander North's home. His sister-in-law, Captain Alice Furreal, is the box's engineering officer and knew right where it was located."

Captain Right continued his explanation to the wide-eyed group. "Dr. Whosh and General Rabbit believed that if they reported in to the Pentagon officially, they'd order her to abandon my ship and crew where they are, so we've come to you for help. Dr. Whosh has assured me we can get all three crews in her box and return to the Constitution. Once there, we'll work on finding out who did what and how to get her and the rest of us home."

Whosh looked at her friend and said, "We also need someone to explain to the president because we believe he has no knowledge of Project Wonderland. As I recall, Stella, you know his wife. The president must know about the black ops (government operations that officially do not exist) games that are afoot."

Stella said, "Oh, Amanda, I've been looking for some excitement in my life and this sure sounds like fun! Captain, you just make sure to bring my husband back in one piece."

Right nodded to Stella. "Captain Staff, I promise to take good care of the Admiral." He'd called her captain as a sign of respect, knowing she was retired from the Navy.

The group had sat totally still listening to Captain Right's every word. As his tale ended, their minds slowly caught up.

Admiral Staff was the first to speak. He looked from Bill to Dr. Whosh and finally asked, "Amanda you're in command of a time machine. Do you agree with everything that Bill just said?"

Amanda smiled. "It's all true, Flagg, and we've no idea who moved your ship through time to where it's now. Nor how it was done. And more than that, the black ops people we've been working for are up to things that are not in our nation's best interests."

Admiral Staff nodded. "Ok, Bill. Here's what we'll do. You get Amanda back to her ship and get ready. I'll send along two of my security force. They're Navy SEALs. I'll send two more to Washington to mind Stella's back. I'll get her a flight that the spooks won't know about. Then North, Bird, and I'll go to that meeting. We'll get them all under a security alert and mobilized to your location before anyone knows what's up.

We'll call it operation Cook Out. In case anyone asks, we're just going to North's house for beer and ribs."

They all headed out. Stella left for the Naval Air Station and a Navy cargo plane. The admiral and crew went to the EM Club meeting, and the rest headed for the box. Rabbit made them pit stop at a package store enroute and they filled the truck with cases of cold beer.

At the EM Club 1100 hours:

Ensign Smith had preceded Admiral Staff and company to the Enlisted Men's Club. She found the senior officers, got the three groups organized, and had a complete list of all personnel in hand when the admiral strode into the hall.

Commander Bird yelled, "Attention on deck!"

The hall went quiet as the admiral crossed the floor. The large room was clear of furniture for the regular Saturday night dances. It was crowded with many different uniforms and even some in civilian clothes. With all present facing forward, he stepped up to the podium with Bird and North.

"At ease. I am Admiral Staff and in command of the overall deployment of the USS Constitution on her current mission to deliver Sand Box 4. Sand Box 4 personnel, your senior officer in charge here is Commander North, standing on my right. Air Wing 119, you're with Commander Bird on my left. Ship's personnel are under my command until we join Captain Right.

"Our mission is so classified that it is considered need-to-know. We will all be leaving for immediate deployment. Base transportation will take you to pick up your gear and then deliver you to our departure zone for further transportation. Needless to say, our mission has become far more complicated than when we started. You will all be given a full briefing as soon as we get aboard. If anyone asks where you're going, you may tell them you have had a change of orders and are going to Commander North's home for a cookout and reassignment. Would the senior officers please come forward for a quick briefing?"

He then had Ensign Smith explain all the transportation arrangements and asked if there were any questions or problems.

A harried looking woman with three children walked through the crowd and looked at North. "Sir, I'm Chief Patty Sparks. I work for Captain Furreal as an electrician I have nowhere to leave my children because my husband just abandoned us. This was the best job I've ever had, but I can't go." She stood there holding her youngest daughter, Sue.

Her teenage daughter said, "Why can't we go, Mom? We'll behave, I promise."

Commander North looked at the tall teen that had stepped forward. She was as tall as her mother and a head taller than her younger brother. North asked, "What's your name?"

"Krista Sparks. This is my brother Fred, and Mom's holding Sue."

"Well, Chief Sparks," said North, "I'm not so sure Alice can do without you. I think Krista is right. My wife, Tracy, insisted on going with us and we're taking our two teenagers. So I don't see a problem, do you, Admiral?"

"None," Admiral Staff replied.

"Well, then, Chief, just see Ensign Smith. She'll get you all onboard."

"Thank you, sir, you won't regret it," said CPO Patty Sparks.

Five-year-old Sue smiled at North. "I promise too."

And with that the Sparks family headed across the hall to Ens. Shela Smith.

Admiral Staff saw one of his intel officers pulling a reluctant female toward him.

"Looks like you have a problem, Lieutenant Kurious?"

"I'm sorry, admiral. We shouldn't even be bothering you and normally I'd never do so. This woman that I've dragged with me is my wife."

Before either man could speak again she said, "I'm Lt. J.G. Merry Kurious, Naval Intelligence East Pac, Sir."

She looked more than a little embarrassed by bothering a senior officer during a briefing.

"Did Admiral Snoopy send you here to spy on me?" Staff asked her.

"Oh no, sir," Merry replied, "He doesn't even know I'm here and I never thought to tell him I was coming. It was sort of a last minute decision."

"Then why did your husband have to drag you over to see me?" asked Admiral Staff.

Lt. Vary Kurious tried to say something at this point, but Merry just kept on talking. And since he was used to her always babbling on, he kept quiet and let her explain their predicament.

"I really didn't want to trouble you with our problem, but I'm stuck on this island, unless you can help me. I came with Vary so we could have a brief honeymoon and we were robbed the first night here." Merry took in a deep breath and continued, "They stole everything. I mean everything we'd left in the room while we'd gone out on the balcony. We were enjoying the magnificent view of the beach and the sun setting over the ocean. You can imagine how shocked we were when we saw we had been robbed. We were plain dumb, not realizing that it could happen to us. They took our credit cards, money, ID cards, and my plane tickets home. I can't even get a military hop home without my ID."

Knowing how to settle this problem for these young officers, the admiral asked, "How good is your wife at intel, Lieutenant Kurious?"

"Oh sir, much better than me," he replied.

So the admiral asked, "Well, Merry, do you get seasick?"

"No sir," said Merry.

"That's good. How would you like to go help us find your husband's missing ship?" asked Staff.

"I could do that, sir?"

"Yes," replied Staff. "I'll even let you report whatever we find to Admiral Snoopy and that should make him forget we ran off with you."

Both Lieutenant Kurious and his wife said, "Thank you, sir."

"See, Ensign Smith," said Staff. "She'll take good care of you two."

With that the happy couple ran off to find Ens. Smith.

The admiral turned to North. "Since we are done here, North, I think we should get to your home and see this Sand Box 4 of yours."

"Good idea, admiral," replied North.

At the Norths' Home:

The admiral, North, and Bird arrived to find everything in order and that the crew was being loaded into the box as fast as they arrived. A driver returned the admiral's car to his home, and North led the two men into Wonderland to, of course, meet Alice. After the grand tour, North delivered them to Cookie and Doc Bones in the dining hall. North then headed to his own duties as it would be his job to return them to the USS Constitution in 1421. When Dew arrived at the command center, Alice thanked him for rescuing Patty Sparks and her three kids.

Soon, the last of the crew was accounted for and in the box, and they locked down to go. Rabbit had given the last of the beer and a fifty dollar bill to the last Navy driver. Each driver got a case of beer and fifty bucks—oh yes there would be a party in Pearl tonight! Peter, J.P., and Harry were the last aboard after they finished their beer.

Peter smiled into the COM panel. "We're all aboard and locked down," and with a very professional salute said, "Take us out of here, Amanda."

And he got a smile back as she ordered, "Rabbit's in the hole, Alice. Give Dew full power. When you're ready, Dew, make your jump."

"We are traveling, ETA five minutes," reported Captain North.

"COM has gone dark. Burst transmission was away before jump and receipt received. We are standing by for reentry to normal time," reported Cdr. Scott O'Rielly.

"Engineering is green," reported Alice.

Navy Cargo Plane Flying Toward the West Coast:
Three ladies sat huddled in the back of the plane, getting as comfortable as such accommodations would allow. They had all done this before, but this time they were officially not there. In fact, their scheduled flight would not leave Hawaii for three hours and, of course, they would board that flight or at least so it would appear. The pilot radioed in that they were hitting head winds and losing time. He then let the plane drift down below the radar and changed course so he would be about

twenty miles north when he came to land. It was not long after landfall that he found the small private airport and headed in for a landing. He taxied up to a Lear jet that had just started her engines. The pilot went back and escorted his three guests off the plane.

The older lady smiled and said, "Thanks for the ride, flyboy."

He returned the smile and saluted. "My best to the admiral."

He then waved to the familiar private pilot, who had come to collect the ladies, then got his plane back in the air and headed to its scheduled refueling stop.

The Lear was sheer luxury after their ride from Hawaii and all three women thanked their benefactor.

"My pleasure, ladies. It's not every day I have an admiral call and ask me to play secret agent with his beautiful wife," said the pilot.

And from behind him a female voice chimed in, "And it's a good thing for you, your co-pilot is your wife. Stella's two gorgeous young bodyguards might just have their way with you."

"I'm glad you warned me, dear, since they look so innocent for a pair of Navy SEALs. Anyway, Stella, we'll be at our home in Moultonborough, New Hampshire, after we drop you off, if we can be of any further help to our country. It'll be about three hours until we land at Greene Airport in Rhode Island. A ride will be waiting for you there," explained the pilot.

With that he left the ladies to their comfort and headed their plane west with all due speed. The three hours flew by as the plane pulled to a stop near the Air National Guard hanger and the waiting car. On the side of the car, it said "Navy

Recruiter," and by the time they were driving away, the plane was in the air enroute to the Moultonborough Airport.

The male driver drove them straight to the airport short-term parking lot and pulled in beside a medium-sized car. He opened the trunk and helped transfer the luggage. He handed Stella the keys and pointed out that the paper work was in the glove box.

Stella said, "Thank you, Chief."

Stella tossed the keys to Master Sergeant Amy Hunter and climbed into the passenger side. Staff Sergeant Sky Lonewolfe climbed into the back seat and got comfortable. Five minutes later they were on I-95 South. Sky had her computer open and soon announced that they should take the exit on to Route 3 North in Coventry.

Sky said, "The pizza shop where Fern works is on the left."

"He does delivery?" asked Amy.

"Yes," Sky replied without removing her eyes from the screen. She went on to described Fern's car and read his tag number SM369. Amy stopped the car just before the pizza shop and waited.

"I've got him leaving to deliver," said Amy as they pulled into traffic and followed his car.

"Good," said Stella. "He doesn't need to be seen with us."

Amy followed Fern until he stopped, pulling in behind the parked car as the young man ran in the house with the pizzas. Amy got out and waited by his car.

When he returned, he said, "Ah, miss, you're sitting on my car."

"Yes, I am." As she moved close to him she put her arm around him while leading him to their vehicle.

"We want to talk to you," said Amy.

"Oh my God. You have a gun," Fern noted.

"Yes, and a very big gun for bad boys who don't listen," said Amy as she slid him in the back seat. Sky was still intent on her computer, and apparently took no notice of him.

Stella turned sideways and looked over the back of the seat. "Well, hello, Fern. I'm Stella. I guess you could say your fairy godmother."

Fern's eyes were big as he said, "Look. I'm sorry I didn't mean to hack that government computer."

Sky looked up for the first time and straight into his eyes. "Yes you did and those fools at NSA haven't got a clue how you did it."

"Oh God, I'm busted," said Fern.

"No," said Stella. "We're sort of friends of your dad's. The lady with the big gun is Amy Hunter and that's Sky Lonewolfe. I guess you could say we're the good guys and want to keep you safe from the bad guys. Your dad has sent you a very complex device airfreight that he thinks you'll be able to figure out. He thinks you can make it work. The bad guys, however, would like to have that device, which is why we stopped by to warn you of the danger."

Stella continued, "Now we have to go to Washington to see the president to tell him what's going on. Not a safe place for you. But I can leave you some money and we can come back afterwards if you need us." She handed him an envelope as she finished speaking.

Sky asked, "Can you memorize things?"

"Yeah, I have a photographic memory," replied Fern.

"Good, memorize all this." And she turned her computer so he could read the display.

As he read, he asked, "Where's my dad and what's he got to do with that missing ship?"

"Your dad is still on the Constitution, and if you get that device he sent you to work, you'll be able to tell the president and us what is going on and where they are now," replied Stella.

"The phone numbers I get, but why do I need to know how to use a stun gun?"

Sky reached in her bag and pulled out the stun gun and handed it and a spare battery to Fern. Sky smiled. "Just in case the bad guys get too close and, by the way, all that conspiracy stuff you've read is true. You'll be ok. You're smarter than they are, and don't forget to call."

Stella asked if he had any questions. Fern looked down at the stun gun he was holding, then at Sky, then Amy, and asked Stella, "Am I dreaming?"

Sky and Amy both leaned closer and kissed him on either cheek. Then in perfect stereo they both said, "NO. You're wide-awake."

With that, Amy let Fern out to return to his car and what had been a normal life. He said, "Boy, that pizza will be cold. Probably get fired."

Stella asked, "How much you got there?"

"About fifty dollars," Fern said.

She pulled a hundred dollar bill out and handed it to him. "Deliver it for free. Give this to your boss and tell him a customer sent him a tip. Besides, I think you're about to become a civilian consultant like your father."

They sat and watched him drive off and Amy asked, "You think he'll be ok?"

Sky laughed. "Oh, yeah, as soon as his brain catches up with what just happened. That boy's got NSA running in circles."

Stella said, "Well let's go see the president then."

A Phone Booth in Hawaii:

It was a quiet day in Wahiawa as Patrolman Alfrado Villa drove the black and white toward the edge of town. Sgt. Sanders Brother was just finishing his coffee as the radio came to life.

"We have a 911 call from the phone booth on Route 99 with no one answering. We'll have an ambulance standing by," said the dispatcher.

Villa hit the lights and siren. This was the pranksters' favorite phone booth and they had made this trip many times. In less than two minutes the booth was in sight.

Sergeant Brother grabbed the mike. "This is 11. I have a visual, and there's a car at the booth. Roll the ambulance."

Villa pulled past the car and stopped next to the booth.

Brother once more spoke into the mike, "We have a man down in the booth."

The officers converged on the booth, pried open the door, and stopped at the reek of alcohol.

Brother looked at Villa and said, "I think this is one for the EMTs and you better take notes."

The ambulance had hardly stopped when the two EMTs joined them. As Villa and Brother held the door, they pulled the man out onto a board. Villa stepped into the booth and spoke into the phone with the 911 operator so she could hang up the line.

The medic yelled over, "He just seems drunk, he's got no ID, his clothes are all inside out, but there is a set of car keys."

Villa took them and headed for the car. Brother headed back to their cruiser to run the plates. When the owner's driver's license ID picture came up on the screen and was very obviously of Chinese decent, they had a new puzzle. Brother

they could all return home. A senior staff meeting was set for right after breakfast and once they had a plan, there would be a full briefing after lunch.

It was a peaceful night and many walked the flight deck enjoying the stars. Tracy and Chrissy were watching a rather bright star but could not figure out which one it was, so Chrissy called to her father. "Dad, which star is that?"

He turned and walked over to join them and found them staring at each other. Tracy was the first to recover and said, "It was right there and then it vanished."

"Oh, that's not a star, Chrissy, that's Venus. It must have gone behind a cloud," Dew replied.

"Oh, thanks, Dad," said Chrissy.

Those at the morning meeting came up with a plan and arranged personnel to implement it. Admiral Staff would take normal command of the Constitution and the Air Wing. They would weigh anchor after breakfast the next day and head for Guam where there might be some answers. Dr. Whosh and Captain Right would head a team to find those answers. General Rabbit, Commander Bird, Captain Furreal, Harry Haul, Bob Cybernaut, Dr. North, Ensign Smith, Lieutenant Junior Grade Kurious, and Lieutenant Brice would begin the quest for answers.

After lunch, the entire crew was briefed and the new mission set before them. Last-minute arrangements were made. Food was acquired and stored. Systems were checked, and the rest of the day was R and R for all nonessential crew.

It was a great day to enjoy nature. And that night everyone had fresh food from the island. Bob and Harry were strolling across the flight deck under the stars and heard Chrissy say to her mother, "There's that star again, and should we ask Dad?"

Tracy replied, "No, dear, it will just vanish again."

Harry and Bob stopped next to them. They too saw the blinking star. Harry commented, "Just like Al's stars up in the mountains where we take the boys camping."

Bob smiled at the thought. "You two must be special. They don't shine for everyone."

They wandered off leaving the two women staring at each other knowing now that other people could see them too.

"You know, Bob, it was a night like this and I was sleeping up here when all this started," said Harry.

"I never thought to look up," said Bob.

Lieutenant Brice appeared with some of the older children and said, "They wanted to see the stars, but I don't know one from another."

Bob said, "Come on kids, I'll show you," and they left Harry and Lieutenant Brice to their own devices.

"Lieutenant Brice, do you have a first name?" asked Harry.

"Why, yes I do. It's Charly. I'd love it if you would show me some stars." She put her arm around him as they strolled into the warm night.

Greene, Rhode Island, in the Home of the Cybernauts:

"Hey, Mom, I'm home," said Fern. "You'll never believe what happened at work today. These three ladies..." He stopped as he saw the airfreight box on the kitchen table.

"Came for you today. I guess it's from your father, but they got the name wrong and Mr. Jorge is not in Hawaii. I saw him today at the store," said his mother. She was going to ask about the three ladies, but Fern was busy opening the box. So she went back to cooking dinner for her sometimes-present brood.

"Mom, this is weird," said Fern. "Dad never writes like this, but those ladies—they said he sent me a device because he thought I could figure out how to use it."

He handed the note to his mother, who now forgot about food and could smell a good mystery brewing.

Dear Fern,
I found this while on vacation and thought it would be very enlightening. The "Mysteries of the Mind" have taught you much truth. So take this and practice the Native American art of invisibility Al showed you. Uncle Harry sends his best.
Bob

Kate Cybernaut said, "Fern, this is weird. He and Uncle Harry are working on that ship they say is missing and never arrived in Hawaii. Why did he say he's Mr. Jorge? Your father never addresses you as Robert. Wait a minute. Tell me about those three ladies."

Fern said, "They followed me to my first pizza delivery and they invited me to get in their car. The older lady in the front seat said she's my fairy godmother and she is going to see the president. They paid for all the pizza I had, so I could give it to the customers for free because it got cold. And the one in the back seat, Sky Lonewolfe, had this neat computer and had me memorize contact information and how to use this."

He pulled out the stun gun Sky had given him and showed it to her. He continued, "And the other one, Amy Hunter, was carrying a big gun. And they knew about me hacking NSA's computer. At first I thought they were going to bust me, but they just laughed. And the older woman gave me an envelope." He pulled it out and put it on the table.

"They gave you a stun gun?"

"Yes, and a spare battery."

"And they knew your father sent that to you?"

"Yes," answered Fern, "They said I could figure it out, but had to stay away from the bad guys."

"Like becoming invisible?" his mother asked.

"That could be," he said.

He started looking over the device once more, while his mother opened the sealed envelope. Kate counted out twenty one hundred dollar bills and a paper that had three names, a phone number, and a digital address (Captain Stella Staff, MSgt. Amy Hunter and SSgt. Sky Lonewolfe—USN SEAL Team assigned Admiral Flagg Staff).

"Fern, there is $2,000 here," said his mother.

"And this thing is some kind of high-end laptop with an odd-looking antenna," said Fern.

His mother grabbed the phone and dialed a local number.

A man answered and she recognized the voice. She asked, "Have you ever heard of a woman named Capt. Stella Staff?"

"Yes. I worked for her a long time ago when I was in the Navy," he replied. "She married Admiral Staff who just announced we had a ship missing from his home in Hawaii. Today, I heard he's missing, too, with a whole bunch of men from the Constitution."

"Would she go see the president?" asked Kate.

"His wife, Snow, served in the Navy with Stella and they're friends," he answered.

"So if she told Fern to do something, would it be important?" asked Kate.

"The way people keep vanishing and knowing her, yes," he replied.

"Did you know Bob and Harry are on that ship?" asked Kate.

"No, but you and Fern be real careful. Something big is going down," he warned.

"Thanks, Benjamin, and give my love to Susan," said Kate.

"Mom, this is amazing," Fern said. He was sitting at the table where he had been working with the computer his father had sent him. "There is a manual on a DVD and besides being a computer, it's a transceiver. What did Mr. Jorge say?"

"He said you should do exactly what she told you to do. Because he knows that older woman personally," said his mother. She sat down beside him, looking more closely at the laptop. It was strange looking, now that Fern had pointed out its other functions.

Then she continued. "That woman's husband is the admiral who vanished today with about five hundred men from the ship your father is on."

"I'll pack and drive up to the mountains," said Fern.

"Give me your keys, and you take my new SUV. You may need it more than I do," she said. "And don't forget to come back. It's bad enough with your father missing. And I think I'll go stay with Aunt June until you can come home," she added.

"Mom, take Dad's old laptop and plug it in, I'll write to you," said Fern.

After they both packed, they hugged and said good-bye in the carport as one headed north and the other west.

The next day a black Suburban pulled up in front of the Jorges' home. When he answered the door and found two men and a woman dressed all in black, he stepped outside and shut the door. The leadman flashed his ID, but Jorge was faster and snatched it right out of his hand. It was a valid NSA ID or at least a very good fake. He gave it back.

"How can I help you?" asked Mr. Jorge.

"We want to know why you sent a package from Hawaii to a kid name Robert Cybernaut?" asked the leadman.

"I didn't send anything from Hawaii and haven't been there in years. If you call Captain Pearce at the VA hospital in Providence, you'll find I've been there every day for the last month helping to install new lab equipment," said Jorge.

While the two men kind of stared at him, the woman stepped away and made a call on her cell phone.

"Do you know this Cybernaut boy?" asked the leadman.

"He's one of the older Scouts in the Venture Crew and it's hard to know them all with over fifty boys in the troop," replied Jorge.

"Any idea why someone in Hawaii would send this kid a box?" asked the man.

"Well, they're all into the Internet. Maybe he bought something from eBay online," replied Jorge.

The call was over and she didn't look too pleased. "What he said was confirmed."

"Sorry for bothering you, sir," said the leadman as he turned to leave.

Jorge watched them drive away and thought to himself, *Hide well Fern, the scum of the Earth is looking for you.*

As he went back in his wife asked, "Who was it, honey?"

"Salesmen, dear. I told them we just filed bankruptcy and couldn't afford them," he replied.

She gave him an odd look and said, "In a Suburban with government plates? Must have been selling fertilizer. We have an abundance of that, dear."

USS Constitution sailing west from Hawaii enroute to Guam:

With Admiral Staff taking charge of the ship, it freed Captain Right to join the Research Group that was looking for answers and solutions. Dr. Whosh headed the group, which was divided into three areas of investigation. The first was the Science Team looking for how the ship was made to disappear and reappear in 1421. The team was made up of Dr. Tracy North, Doc Bones, M.D., Cdr. Scott O'Rielly, Ltjg. Merry Kurious, and Bob Cybernaut. The second was the Engineering Team looking for what technology could move the whole ship, and consisted of Captain Right, Capt. Alice Furreal, Cdr. Dew North, and Harry Haul. The third was the Security Team trying to find out who could cause this event, and was composed of Gen. Peter Rabbit, Commander Bird, Lt. Charly Brice, and Ensign Shela Smith.

They met each day mining for information, trying new ideas, testing equipment, and comparing notes with the other teams. Concrete answers were very few, but a lot of possible answers were being eliminated off the lists and new ideas were being considered. The box's data uplink was tuned to the frequencies in the unit Fern had in his backpack. The question was, if Fern could get this portable unit programmed to make the leap across time.

Chief Sparks spent her free time minding the children and seeing that they all worked on their home schooling. Beyond that, Patty taught them many lessons around the box and the ship. Everywhere she took them she found eager teachers willing to share their skills and knowledge. So they learned how to cook, run a laundry for thousands, make electricity, how reactors work, weather, radio, navigation, history, and a good dose of the basics in time travel. Their curiosity was endless and they often asked questions the adults had not thought to contemplate, as when Chrissy wondered why that star that some people couldn't "see" wasn't on the star charts of the computers on the Constitution or Sand Box 4. Why did Uncle Harry and Uncle Bob find it so amusing that others couldn't "see" this star and who was this mysterious Al who did know about such things? Ah, it would seem other minds were forming a fourth research team.

Chrissy and Krista found Uncle Bob's computer lessons most enlightening. While their younger siblings kept Krista's mother busy, they went on a cyber search for a boy named Fern, whom they were sure could tell them more.

The teams broke for lunch. Shela Smith and Tracy North were eating in the ship's mess hall when Alice joined them to report her science lesson with the children had gone well. Even five-year-old Sue Sparks got into the hydrodynamics of water and got James' head out of the clouds by showing him how to make rain. But suddenly, Alice's cheery mood became sober. The girls looked in the direction of Alice's stare and saw J.P. had just entered the mess hall. He stopped and reversed direction when he saw them, with a look of sheer panic on his face. Alice got real quiet and stared at her food.

With a sad look on her face, Shela reached across the table and laid her hand on Alice's, then said in a soft voice, "I need to tell you a story. My father is the reason John didn't take you to the prom. He forbade him to go and took away his car keys. He told John you weren't good enough for him and that he'd marry better than you. John spent that night in his room crying." She paused to a take deep breath. "I know. I held him all night. He didn't even go to graduation. As soon as Father gave him the keys back, he left for college in Boston and never returned until he graduated. John came home proud from MIT with a doctorate in quantum physics and thought Father would be proud, too. Instead, Father yelled at him. Told him he was stupid. That he had wasted Father's money and should have gotten an MBA so he could work in the family business. John said nothing. He just hugged me and said goodbye. It was years later in college that I found out he had joined the Marines and trained in the most dangerous field he could find. And damn it, he's the best they have! I know. I've seen his records. I used the admiral's computer and clearances to keep track of him."

By now all three women were in tears and the whole mess hall had taken on their mood. Alice was the first to pull herself together, and she took Shela in her arms, hugging her. When she finally let go, she stepped back, looked straight into Shela's eyes, and said, "Thank you." She then turned and strode out of the mess hall like a woman on a mission.

Alice found J.P. having lunch in Sand Box 4's dining hall with Harry, Charly, Cookie, and Bones. When he saw her enter, he started to stand to make an escape, but Alice was faster. She heaved him up against the wall, pressing her whole body to his, and kissed him so hard he almost passed out.

Alice backed up and announced, "You're coming with me."

Breathlessly J.P. replied, "Yes, sir."

To which she retorted, "I'm NO sir, I'm Alice, and don't you ever forget that, John," as she continued to drag him out of the room.

Harry said, "Well, Cookie, they must have served something interesting in the mess hall."

To which Charly smilingly said, "You want to bet on that, sailor?"

Doc added, "I guess I should start giving talks on contraception to my female patients."

Cookie moved a little closer and smiled at him. "Me first?"

And with that the dining hall became emptier.

At 1300 hours Dr. Whosh stopped chatting with Peter and took her seat at the head of the table. Everyone soon found a chair and was about to start a round robin update of his or her progress when Alice strolled in with J.P. in tow. She stopped at the opposite end of the table from Dr. Whosh, who smiled. "Nice of you to join us, Alice. Hello, J.P. I'm afraid Peter and Harry are out of beer at the moment."

"Actually," Alice chimed in, "I brought him along for his brain and think he would be a good addition to our group and would like to formally introduce, Dr. John P. Smith who earned his doctorate in quantum physics at MIT."

"Well," said Whosh. "Welcome Dr. Smith. We certainly can't be wasting your brain on demolition when we have so much to build here."

Harry pulled out the chair next to him and said, "Have a seat J.P. and don't worry. Peter and I have the still almost done in Bones' back room."

"Harry, you're ruining my plausible deniability," quipped Whosh. "And if Alice will sit down, we can get to work."

As Alice took a seat, Shela and Tracy sat smiling like two Cheshire cats, who obviously knew the rest of the story. And so the meeting continued on exploring the new and analyzing the old with a new voice added.

Pentagon 'years' later:
Gen. Benedict Black was staring at his bank of computer

screens in disgust. When his assistant knocked and walked in, Black growled, "Where's Hardash?"

"He's in Sand Box 2, sir. They left our time almost as soon as they had the box off the C-130," answered Woozy.

"Have Maj. Raul Mercenary come up here. I'll send him to Guam to sort this out so I can get this back under control. What else do you have for me?" demanded Black.

"Sir, we got an encrypted transmission from Sand Box 4," said Woozy.

Black practically leaped on the smaller man. "What did it say? Where are they?"

"The transmission came from the area of Hawaii—our time," replied Woozy.

"That's where they went," Black fumed.

"It was from Dr. Whosh, the acting commander of Sand Box 4. It states that personnel, ship, and box have survived the incident, which they believe may have been a lightning strike. It goes on to say they are having some stability and communications problems and hope we get the message," said Woozy.

"I got it, all right," barked Black. "I should have let Raul fix her years ago! Did it mention Doe? Is he in charge there?"

"No, sir, we have nothing new on him. But we did get word some drunk, under the name John Doe, was admitted to the psyche unit of the hospital in Hawaii by some patrolman named Villa." said Woozy.

"Why are you telling me this, you fool? That is standard procedure for those dumb cops. Anything else?" asked Black.

"Just one thing, sir. A Colonel Jorge, who is on our 'watch list', sent a package from Hawaii to a kid in his hometown in Rhode Island. Our people interviewed him and he denied being in Hawaii, which was confirmed by a Captain Pearce at the VA hospital in Providence. The colonel suggested the kid just bought something from eBay on his computer and maybe used his name," explained Woozy.

"You've got nothing better for me than some busybody colonel and a snot-nosed kid with a computer?" asked Black.

"No sir, that's all we have so far, but we're still looking, sir. We did search North's house. All they found was a trampled garden and three beer cans with no prints," said Woozy.

"Did they check DNA, you fool?" demanded Black.

"I don't think so, sir, but I'll check. And Dr. Warbucks Banks called again looking for you and said to remind you who pays for your toys," said Woozy.

"Send up Raul. Maybe I'll have him go answer Banks. Now get out of here!" yelled Black.

He stomped back to his bank of screens and reached in the drawer for a bottle of pills. He tossed a bunch in his mouth and washed them down with the whisky he had been drinking.

White House, President's Dining Room (same time):

"Mr. President, sorry to disturb your meal, but I have a secure Top Secret encrypted eyes-only message," announced his COM officer.

President White got up and reached out for the communiqué.

The COM officer stepped back and said, "It's not for you, sir. It's addressed to Captain White, sir."

"See, dear, they still remember me," Snow said as she took the folded paper from the COM officer and thanked him. Then she smiled at her husband and said, "No peeking, dear."

The COM officer said, "I think I should leave now before you ask me to break my security oath," and headed out the door.

The two Secret Servicemen guarding the room had all they could do to keep a straight face. Snow read her note and finished her coffee while her husband did his best to act like he had no interest in her message.

"Well, dear," she said, as she got up from the table, "It seems like we're going to have company, so I should go get ready."

And as she walked out the door, she stopped, leaned back in around the Secret Service agent and said, "Oh, dear, that boat you were so worried about was at anchor in Hawaii when this note was sent. See you for supper, dear." And she promptly vanished.

The president's chief of National Defense had walked in the room moments before the president's wife left with her message.

"Mr. President, how does she know that?" asked Gen. Jack Frost.

"She just received a secure Top Secret encrypted eyes-only message," answered White with a laugh. "So, what good news do you have for me, Jack?"

"Sir, Admiral Staff who was supposed to be on the Constitution has disappeared with the five hundred service personnel who were waiting for the ship at Pearl Harbor," said Jack.

"Gone, Jack? Like, no trace?"

"Yes, sir, it appears they all went to a Captain Dew North's house for a party and none of them were ever seen again."

"This does not make sense, Jack."

"I know, sir."

"So let me make sure I have this right. One of our largest boats, which was on a mission too secret for me to know about, just disappeared enroute to Hawaii. And now all the crew that was waiting, as well as the admiral in charge, are gone, too? And then someone sends my wife a message I can't read, saying that this boat is anchored in Hawaii. Have I got it right so far, Jack?" asked White.

"Yes, sir, I'm afraid you do. If it will make you feel better, sir, I'll instruct the COM staff to not deliver your wife's messages when she is with you," he offered.

"Great idea, Jack. What I don't know won't hurt me—maybe."

They headed to the Oval Office to get on with the day's work.

State Police Lab, Honolulu, Hawaii—2012:

Sgt. Sanders Brother watched with great interest as the lab crew in white uniforms searched every part of the car, inside and out. Then they started dismantling it piece by piece. When they were done, there was an impressive list of items found and none were factory additions.

Captain Kid walked in and joined Sergeant Brother, who was reading the computer printout of what the lab boys had found. He handed it to Kid and commented, "Not your average pimp, Captain, or drug dealer either."

Brother said, "It's a well-equipped 2011 white Lincoln Town Car, four-door, with 1421 miles, Hawaiian plate AGT007. It has a high performance engine and transmission with full-time four wheel drive, bulletproof panels, half-inch steel plate under, with high impact glass, nondeflatable tires—solid core—and a drop box under the trunk with tire spikes. They found a Mack 10 machine gun with silencer, thirty rounds of 9mm, a laser pistol, fully charged, Uzi machine gun, sawed-off 12 gauge—in the glove box of all places. Then there was the box of twenty incendiary and hand grenades, five cans of knock-out spray, ten body bags, and a pair of red silk panties."

"Let's go meet Mr. Moon Sung who owns this thing. The SWAT team is enroute and the detectives have his place under surveillance already," said Kid.

"Sounds like fun," said Brother. "How is Villa doing with the shrinks?"

Kid started to laugh. "This guy must've had some good stuff because he's still claiming to be John Doe."

They drove by the house in an upscale neighborhood. It all looked very peaceful. But on a closer look, they saw that two detectives were parked across the street and talking to the postman. A telephone truck was parked around the corner with the man up the pole in the bucket. The man looked like he was busy fixing the phone lines. Also in the bucket was a TV screen and controller, which adjusted the small telephoto camera to see a close-up of the house. The fake telephone man spoke into his mike to the control van sitting down the street.

On an even closer look, they could see the SWAT team moving in through the shadows to the house. A man at the back door jammed the alarm, picked the lock, and a group of men silently slipped through the door. They moved from room to room and found no one downstairs. As they headed for the stairs, the lead man signaled to stop. He found a stair sensor and beam indicating a booby trap. The men brought in a well-padded ladder. As two men held it, the others climbed up past the sensors. They found the first bedroom door open and heard snoring.

They checked with a mirror and the man was asleep on his back under a sheet. The team leader aimed his rifle at the man as the other two moved to either side of the bed. One pressed his 12 gauge under the man's nose, while the other held his gun on him.

The team leader in a firm voice said, "Good morning, sir. You are under arrest."

The eyes popped open, but the man did not move.

The officer continued, "We have warrants for you and to search the house."

The third man moved into the room and pulled the top sheet off of the suspect. They cuffed him and got him off of the bed. As they moved him to the stairs to start down the man spoke for the first time, "There is a claymore on the stairs."

"Get bomb disposal in here," the team leader spoke into his mike.

An hour later the stairs were clear.

Captain Kid and Brother were waiting when they brought Moon Sung out, still very naked but cuffed and now chained. As soon as he saw Kid, Sung announced, "I have diplomatic immunity, I want to talk to my embassy."

The SWAT team leader asked, "What should we do, Captain?"

"Get him underwear, pants, shirt, and socks. Put them all on inside out, and then put him in a straight jacket. Have the medic sedate this madman and then deliver him to the psychiatric ward of the hospital. He can join John Doe number one. If Sung's house is like his car, we should have a gold mine. I've already got the lab team standing by, so they'll be here soon," explained Kid.

Kid's phone rang and he answered it. After a few minutes of exchanging information and instructions, he hung up.

"That was the lab," said Kid. "The computer boys chased down John Doe. He's for real, well, may be. He works in Washington for a research group and seems to have three life histories. I've got to get back to headquarters. Sandy, you better head for the hospital to back up Villa. If the dummies in D.C. figure out we got him, things could get hot. Add to that, we just had Admiral Staff and five hundred servicemen, all connected to that missing aircraft carrier, vanish without a trace. Even the admiral's wife, Capt. Stella Staff, disappeared with two SEAL team bodyguards. Something big is cooking here. When you set up security, use as many of the SWAT team as you need. Once we know a little more we'll interview the Does, but if they are for real, I doubt we'll get much from them."

Brother scratched his head. "The old days when we were in Army Intel was never like this. Good thing Villa was a Ranger. It could get messy. Have you got enough men so we could vanish too?" asked Brother.

"I think so. What do you have in mind?"

"Remember that abandoned underground WWII bunker?" asked Brother.

"Sure. Do I feel a vacation coming on?" replied Kid.

Kid then headed back to the lab while Brother road shotgun in the ambulance. John Doe no. 2 was sleeping peacefully in the back. At the hospital, Brother took Villa down to the cafeteria, while two of the SWAT team minded the Does. Brother filled in Villa about the stash in the car, the arrest of Moon Sung, and Doe no. 1 having three life histories. He also explained that they might need to get out of there to a secure location. They went down to the SWAT tactical unit in the parking lot and rearmed themselves. Both exchanged their police uniforms for hospital scrubs and found that white lab coats hid weapons well. They posted a fully equipped SWAT team member in each room. They opted to not put a uniform outside the rooms, as they would just become a target.

Brother grabbed a clipboard and kept moving around. Villa made himself at home in the nursing station, with the security camera and controls for the ward's locked doors. It was hard to say whether Villa or the staff enjoyed his presence more. And so they waited.

I-91 North Vermont:

Fern drove nonstop and was making good time with little traffic in the middle of the week. He was glad his mother had let him take the SUV. It had more room and the four-wheel drive would be helpful when it came to finding a parking place out of sight. It also had a power port to plug in the computer to extend its operating time and he had a solar panel that could charge it as well. The sign ahead was for St. Johnsbury, so he drove down the exit. At the third gas station where the price was reasonable he pulled in to fill up. He saw they had the strong military spare gas cans for sale. He took one and filled that too. The attendant gave him directions to a good local restaurant as he paid with cash. He left with the spare gas can tied securely in the back and headed for the restaurant where he had a great meal, tipped the waitress well, and got a large coffee to go.

Fern drove for a half-hour before he turned off the paved road. He knew right where to go as he had been in this area many times with the Scouts. The place he was headed to was private land, where forest rangers and fish and game wardens wouldn't bother him, and next to the national forest. The owner knew him, and the Scouting decal in the back window would identify his mother's SUV as friendly even if he wasn't around. It took another thirty minutes on the dirt roads, across a field, up a logging road in four-wheel drive to the turn that led to the campsite by the river, which had a three-sided shelter. He pulled in on the far side of it and parked.

The shelter was open in the front and faced south so it got the sun all day. A sandy beach on the small river was about forty feet away. A fireplace with cooking area was on one side of the shelter's front and a picnic table on the other. The shelter had eight bunks and a table with two chairs.

Since Fern was tired, he pulled out his sleeping bag and got comfortable in the shelter. He sipped his cold coffee, listened to the babbling of the river over the rocks, and stared at a clear sky full of stars. For a while he watched a very bright star twinkle in front of him and was soon sound asleep. In dreamland, he explored the matrix of his mind, wondering where his new adventure would lead. The star twinkled on like a shining beacon watching over the night.

Pentagon, General Black's Office:

Black had just hung up the phone from listening to Warbucks Banks for twenty minutes. He pulled out the whisky bottle and didn't bother with a glass. His secretary buzzed him to announce Major Mercenary and his research assistant were there to see him.

"Send them in!" he barked at the intercom.

The major led the way into the office.

"Hello, Raul, have a seat. So what have you got, Woozy?" demanded Black.

"Sir, I think we have found John Doe. The police in Hawaii ran a fingerprint check to ID a John Doe, so he must be the man I told you about them holding in a hospital. Here is the full report, sir."

"Have you found anything else, Woozy?"

"No, sir, but we are still looking."

"Then get out of here and find something useful, you twit." Black waited to speak again until after the office door closed. Then he said, "I have some work for you, Raul. Take the next flight out. I want you to find Hardash—I want to know what's going on in Guam and how he lost Sand Box 4 to that old woman, who appears to be in bed with the Navy. On your way, stop in Hawaii and get rid of this problem."

He handed Raul the report Woozy had brought him.

"If I find the bitch and her general, shall I take care of them, too?" asked Raul.

"Yes, and if you get a chance, the admiral and his Constitution can join Davy Jones, as well."

"Anything else, my general?" asked Raul.

"If you do all that, you can retire a rich man," replied Black.

As Raul rose to leave, he said, "But that would not be any fun. I was born to this life. It's my destiny to be a living sword."

As the door shut behind Raul, Black smiled and downed another swig of whisky. *Now I'll get action* he said to himself.

USS Constitution, Westward Bound in the Pacific Ocean, a 'long' time ago:

The Science Team had racked their brains for days and the best theory was that an electromagnetic field or time bubble had been generated around the whole ship. They had the most questions about the government having been time traveling for years and kept Dr. Whosh busy answering them. Bob got it the best, as it was just an extension of his technical world— a short leap from cyberspace to moving objects and people, rather than digits on the Internet. Tracy and Merry asked the most and led the group into very deep questions on the effects time travel had on the world and the moral values guiding its use. They examined all the computer data. While the box's "drive" systems were off-line when the event happened, all of its monitoring equipment was working and recorded the event in detail. They all believed an unusual event had happened and were eager to hear a technical explanation of the events which had delivered the ship to 1421.

The Engineering Team started by bringing Captain Right, J.P., and Harry up to speed on the equipment involved and how it worked. Their first conclusion was that the box's "drive" was off and so could not have moved anything, let alone the ship. Its systems were designed to only extend the field it generated to at most a half an inch beyond the skin of the box. The field that the box's instruments measured surrounded the whole ship. The resonant frequency signature of the field was different from the field the box generated. It was a purer and stronger signal, as well. And perhaps the most disconcerting finding was that the field was projected around the ship, not from within it. Unfortunately, the box's equipment had never been set up to locate an external source, since it was always assumed it would come from within the box.

They also examined if the box's equipment could be modified to extend the field around the ship. Unfortunately, the field coils that were part of the box were aimed inward. The ship's power could be used to boost the field strength, but without changing the focus of the coils, that would not solve the problem of moving the ship. However, they did not give up hope because obviously it was possible. Someone had moved the ship, and the field came from outside the ship and box. So the question became one of whether it was a matter of rearranging the equipment they currently had or if they needed to design a new level of technology.

The Security Team came to the conclusion that their technology was not capable of focusing a field bubble around an external object and then shifting the field to move an object. This was bad because it meant that they had not caused the event. Luckily, the level of knowledge needed for this technology rapidly narrowed the group of others who possibly could do it. England, Canada, and Australia were all working with them. The first on the list was the Russians, one of the European Nations, China, and maybe the Israelis or Japanese. At a joint brainstorming session, Harry raised the question of an off-planet intelligence. Most thought that if that was true they should have met them by now. J.P. ended the session by pointing out that many of the group, including himself, had been totally unaware of time travel until he walked into the box for the first time.

J.P. then asked, "What if they don't want to meet us?"

After a long silence, Whosh decided they needed to take a break and regroup.

Hawaii, Locked Psyche Hospital Ward:

Kid stopped by about 2100 hours to update Brother and Villa, as well as make plans for interviewing both "Does" the next morning. As the three men sat in the staff lounge, Kid told them his grandson's Scout troop was now camped at the old bunker and having a blast cleaning it up and exploring. He told them that Sung's house had been a gold mine and the lab boys would be months chasing down leads. There was equipment to make passports, almost five million in U.S. dollars, plus ten other currencies. There was a virtual arsenal of weapons, with three crates of missiles, as well as a whole bank of computers with high speed links and enough spy gear to be the western branch of NSA.

"I have a helpful doctor coming to assist us tomorrow," explained Kid. "You guys get a good night's sleep. I'm headed to the coffee shop to talk with this doc, so see you in the morning."

With that Captain Kid headed out across the street, Villa headed for the nursing station to wait for 2200, when their relief would arrive. Brother got coffee for the two men guarding the rooms where the Does were asleep. Brother chatted with the guards when he delivered the coffee.

The ward was shaped like a V, with most of the patient rooms on the other side. The nurse's station and main lock access door were in the middle of the V. Interview rooms, lounge, and four rooms were on this side. The Does were in the two inside rooms, while charts and nameplates said they were in the outside rooms facing the street. At this end of the wing was another locked door for the doctors and staff to get to the main part of the hospital.

It was late and Brother went across the hall to the empty room, with the dummy of Doe in the bed to see what it looked like outside. It was very quiet out there too. So he decided to heed nature's call before his ride home. He turned out the light and shut the locked door behind him. He walked right across the hall to the bathroom.

He was about to drop his pants when he heard the locked door at the hospital end shut. That seemed odd as the doctors were gone and the staff did not change shift until 2200. He had just decided to take a peek when the first explosion shook the building. When he opened the door with weapon in hand, the first thing he saw was smoke billowing out of the room he had just visited. Farther up the hall, he saw a man in full tactical gear heading past the doctor's office toward the nurse's station. Brother saw Villa swing over the counter and open fire as he stepped into the hall to do the same. But before he could, the second explosion almost knocked him off his feet as the door for Doe no. 2 went flying across the hall and embedded in the opposite wall. In the two inner rooms the guards were reacting to the first explosion. They threw their patients on the floor and put the mattresses on top of them. They then made as small of a target as they could of themselves and aimed their assault rifles at the door to the room. They were already talking to each other and Villa. Brother was cursing himself for having removed his radio.

Meanwhile, the four relief SWAT team members and Captain Kid across the street in the coffee shop heard the explosions. From where Kid sat he could see the room windows blow out. He grabbed his radio and called in a terrorist attack on the hospital to control and said to scramble police and fire department. That done he pulled both his main and back-up guns out and ran toward the hospital. Two of the SWAT team came out of elevator two engaging the emergency stop button and covered the locked ward door from the hall. They all had turned on their tactical radios and could talk to Villa. The second pair who had just entered at ground floor secured elevator one there.

At the nurse's station, Villa had all the nurses move down the other hall and shut all patient doors and most of all stay down. He looked up just in time to see the grenade headed his way. He leaped over the counter and crawled around the corner just before the third explosion. Brother saw it too and jumped back into the bathroom. The terrorist came out headed toward Brother, who opened fire. He returned fire at Brother and sent a grenade in his direction. He then leaped behind the wall and watched as the pieces of the door flew past his face.

The man turned and blew the locked ward door to pieces with the grenade launcher on his assault weapon making a new escape route. However, the two SWAT members returned fire right through the wall. The man leaped into a nearby examining room. Villa stayed down; his job now was to protect the civilians behind him from this madman.

The fire and smoke were spreading fast. Besides the two rooms, which were ablaze, the nursing station, what was left of it, was burning as well. The building fire sprinklers were coming on, which just added to the mess. One of the SWAT team in the third floor hallway moved through the smoldering doors and backed down the hall toward Villa to back him up. They had their man trapped in the examining room—or so they thought. They heard a small explosion and braced for what might be next. One of the team on the ground floor lobby raced up the stairs to join the man there, just in time for the last explosion. The inside walls of both examining rooms and part of the wall to the stairway blew to pieces.

Kid, who was running toward the hospital, stopped short as he saw a hole appear in the side of the building. It shook and the lights flickered. Everything in the hospital stopped. As soon as he could, Brother covered his mouth and nose with a handful of lab coat and moved toward the hole. Two of the team did the same. The smoke was now rising through a hole in the roof, and a good part of the room's floor was gone as well. Brother didn't think his ears would ever stop ringing from the blast.

Kid was still staring in disbelief when he heard a car start and rapidly move away from the building. He had stopped right in the middle of the driveway to the hospital and the driver smiled as he saw the cop standing there with a gun in each hand. He thought, *It's a good day to die, copper.* He hit the gas and aimed the car at him. Kid leaped out of the way and emptied both guns into the speeding car that vanished into the dark night. He called in the plate number to control as the first fire truck arrived followed by a police car. A little late, Kid thought, as he headed for the building to find out about his team.

Villa was sort of up against the wall, watching as Nurse Laurie Green finished bandaging his arm. She had come up behind him right after the nurse's station was blown to bits. A piece of flying metal had ripped his arm open and she was right there cutting off his ripped sleeve and working on his wound while the bullets flew in every direction. She had not flinched once.

"You'll need something for the pain in a bit, but this will hold for now," said Laurie.

He nodded to her as he spoke into his mike. The word came up from Kid in the lobby that the shooter was gone, all clear.

He smiled his thanks to Laurie.

"Let's go. I'm not done. Where is Brother?" she asked.

They moved around what was left of the corner while Villa and the SWAT team checked on the guards and their wards. Laurie gave Brother a once over.

Captain Kid arrived to find the only one hurt was Villa. Laurie saw Kid rub his leg where he had landed in the street. She pulled up his pants leg and started cleaning the wound before he could protest.

Since Laurie had his leg he couldn't move far, but he continued to organize. Kid told Brother, "We have to get them out of here."

From next to his knee they heard Laurie say, "Take everyone to the back-up ER. No one is there now. Regroup and go from there." She stood up. "That should do you till you're at a safe place. Then I'll do it right."

They were all staring at this efficient nurse, when she said, "Well, let's go before that madman comes back for seconds!"

She headed for the locked door to the main hospital and Kid said, "You heard her, let's go."

So they all followed Laurie to the back-up ER and regrouped around the two John Does who were strapped to gurneys in the middle of the room.

While the firemen worked to put out the fires and got all the patients moved to safer places, Kid was busy building a plan. The head doctor was so mad that his hospital had been attacked. He was ready to sign anything and started with two death certificates for John Doe nos. 1 and 2. Kid left DNA samples as proof and had the report show that the Does were cremated.

Meanwhile at the WWII Bunker:

The Scouts were done cleaning and the friendly park ranger, Ted Bear, had helped get the electricity working to the old bunker, since in the long run he wanted to open it to tourists. The Scouts did for him what he could not get the state to budget. So the Scouts had a new place to camp and Park Ranger Bear now had a whole crew of Junior Rangers to help him. That night, he arranged a large campfire with marshmallows and plenty of coffee for the adult Scouters. Ranger Bear had known the Kid family for years and it was great to have the third generation camping in the park. The next day they all said good-bye and the kids promised to be back soon. Ted was surprised by the call from Joe Kid, but was pleased to help and thought it would put some excitement back in his life. Guarding an empty hole in the ground was rather boring.

Hawaii, Locked Psyche Hospital Ward:

One of Kid's men in plain clothes backed into the hospital loading dock with a rental truck. It looked like a lot of cops were taking a smoke break as the four men in scrubs wheeled out two laundry carts full of dirty linens right into the back of the truck. The four men stepped out and while no one noticed, two of the SWAT team slipped in as the doors were shut. Brother joined Villa and Kid to find out who was riding with whom.

"That's simple," Laurie chimed in. "My two patients are riding with me and Brother, you can take shotgun in the truck."

They all stared at the spunky nurse, now in civilian clothes with an EMT bag hanging on her shoulder.

Villa was the first to speak and asked, "Won't they miss you?"

"Nah, I'm off for the two days and even if they fire me, they'll just have to hire me back, since no one wants to work the wacko ward," said Laurie.

Kid said, "I'm too old to argue with beautiful women."

Brother added, "Me too," as he headed for the truck.

"Come on, gentlemen, unless one of you needs a wheelchair?" said Laurie.

They both laughed and followed. She led them to an SUV in the parking lot, tossed the bag in the back, and opened the back door for Villa. She smiled. "Don't worry. I'll let you ride up front later, and if you buy me a six pack, I might even let you drive it, Alfrado. Besides, Captain Kid's leg is killing him and he's been putting on a brave front for you guys."

Now Villa looked sheepish. "Sorry, sir. I didn't know."

"It's ok," said Kid. "Hopefully she won't tell everyone, or worse, tie me in a wheelchair."

As Laurie climbed behind the wheel she quipped, "Well, Gramps, I'm still thinking about that, so you had better behave."

They caught up with the truck and its escort on the freeway out of town. Kid had been talking with them on the radio. The SWAT team would have the bunker secure long before they got there. Kid got a message saying that they had found the car he shot up, when it blew up in the airport parking lot.

Kid laughed. "He didn't arrive commercial or leave that way either. Check all military flights, especially any that just stopped to refuel."

Laurie asked, "Do you want me to take point before we hit the back roads?"

"Good idea," smiled Kid.

They drove around for a while, before they headed to the bunker to ensure no one was following.

"Around the next bend is a state park sign. Turn in there," said Kid.

They drove up an old road that was not well kept. Past the ranger's house, Kid pointed to an almost invisible road that went on past the garage. Just beyond this was an old fence and guard shack. The road twisted around the hill and suddenly seemed to turn into it. About one hundred feet later, it widened out into a loading area with a few lights. It quickly became obvious they were now underground. Kid told her to park next to the ranger's truck.

The rental truck unloaded its cargo. Four team members grabbed Doe and Sung and carried them to a gas-powered carry all with a flat bed. The men laid Doe and Sung on it and strapped them down. The men walked beside the cart as it drove deep into the bunker. This was the first time the two captives had ever seen each other and now realized that they were being taken deep underground where no one would ever find them or care. The truck left with just dirty linens and no escort.

It had gotten bright outside and Laurie asked, "Has the sun come up?" Brother fondly remembered the view. "Sure has, come on you two, you'll like this and it'll be dark down there."

They walked out to see a spectacular sunrise over the Pacific.

Bear had joined them and said, "That is part of what I love about being here. I haven't got the Scouts to enjoy it yet, but they sure love exploring down below in the dark."

Alfrado said, "Oh, but you will. You sold this Boy Scout."

Laurie asked Bear, "Do Girl Scouts count?"

This made him give her a big smile. "They sure do," replied Ranger Ted Bear, "and makes it a perfect dawn of a new day."

AS THE DAWN TWO

First contact in the search for answers.

Somewhere in the New England Woods:
As the dawn arrived and the birds sang their wake-up song, Fern returned from dreamland. He unpacked enough gear to make breakfast and slipped on a fleece jacket to defend from the morning chill. He made hot oatmeal and had a cup of hot apple cider while watching the wild animals visit the river to get a drink. As the sun warmed the grass and chased the dew away, Fern unpacked his laptop, plus some test equipment tools. He carefully placed them in his daypack along with a quick lunch and a bottle of water. His canteen went on his belt that also had emergency supplies, and he hung his compass around his neck. He locked up the SUV and headed up the mountain. His goal was a rather low mountain with not much of a view, but it was home to a high-speed Internet repeater.

The hike took a couple of hours. Mostly because no trail went there from where he was located. The access trail came in from the other side, but he enjoyed bushwhacking. Many of his friends had GPS units, but he preferred the challenge and trusted his common sense for direction over the high-tech gadget. He smiled as he stepped into the clearing and looked up at the tower. He opened a blanket on the ground and spread out his equipment. Soon he was able to talk to the repeater and its server. From there he connected to the business computer to set-up a high-speed account for a two-month trial period. As soon as it acknowledged his address and billing info, it came back with password verification and frequency assignments. While online he sent his mother an e-mail.

Mom,
Had a good night's sleep. Enjoying my visit with Uncle Nature.
Fern

Then he packed all the equipment up and pulled out his lunch. He sat against a comfortable old tree and watched nature at play. About an hour later he headed back down to start building his science project and to see if he could make the mysterious computer work. Even though he did not rush, it seemed like he was back to camp in no time. As he approached, he noticed some odd tire tracks going into his campsite. He saw no one but was cautious. As he turned the corner, he saw the odd tracks stopped at a fresh pile of firewood that had not been there when he left. On the picnic table was a note under a rock.

Dear Fern,
Thought you would enjoy having a fire to warm you or cook on. The fishing gear is in the rafters of shelter and pots and pans under inside table. I left you a lantern so you won't go blind reading at night or kill your mother's battery. Stop by if you need anything.
Al

He was very pleased at the kindness of his host, but then wondered how Al knew he was there. When he drove in he was not even close to the house and he had not called. But then the old man often seemed to know more than he should. Maybe he should ask him about this "fairy godmother" and her two assistants, but then maybe it would be safer not to know. Anyway, fish for supper sounded good, so he got out the fishing gear and found a comfortable rock by the river. Once he had supper he could start building his communications network and line up the high-speed uplink. He pulled out his solar cell charger and plugged it into the computer's battery to charge it while he fished.

Sand Box 4 (SB4) on the USS Constitution Steaming West on the Pacific Ocean, the Year 1421:

Krista and Chrissy had finished their lessons on Uncle Bob's computer, so they decided to find someone to chat with on the net. They opened the chat link and assumed that, as at home, the computer would find them someone with whom to chat. The laptop started searching for a connection to the net and interfaced with the SB4's main frame.

SB4's computer, being used to getting odd requests from the scientists, was programmed to find a way to respond. The main computer's search found that the box's computer network had no chat feature, so it linked into the ship's computer network. It soon found that sailors didn't chat either, so it reported that to the girls and asked if they wanted it to keep on searching?

Well, of course they said yes. If the computer was game for looking so were they. In short order the computer found no networks and so it went looking for high-speed carrier frequencies. It first scanned the normal range for satellites and repeaters, with no luck. But since its prime directive was to seek and find, it expanded the search. Just about when the girls were ready to give up hope, the computer, almost proudly, announced it had found a frequency. It identified it as the Earth's resonant frequency and that it was now transmitting a chat request.

Back in the Woods:

With his fish supper ready for cooking, Fern got on with the project at hand. He set up on the table in the shelter, so that if it rained the equipment wouldn't get wet and, besides, he might be at this for days and nights thanks to the lantern. He clamped his high-speed antenna to one of the rafters and started lining it up with the tower. After about twenty minutes he had a good connection. His next chore was to send an e-mail to Sky saying he was at home and working on his homework. He also turned on the chat feature so if his mom signed on she would get him.

Fern unpacked the strange computer his dad had sent with its odd antenna. He turned it on and by the time it got dark, he had gotten nowhere. Since he was a hacker at heart, he finally decided to have a look at it with his computer. He found the right cord in his box of goodies and plugged the two computers together. For the first time, the strange computer seemed happy; while it had not wanted to talk with him, it opened a channel to his computer and started networking.

Fern shook his head. So that's what it wanted, to talk to another computer. He was curious about what they were up to, but his stomach said it was time for supper. So he left the computers on in case his mother showed up and his e-mail program would check for a reply from Sky every thirty minutes. He left the computers to mind themselves while he ate.

He started a fire and put on his coffeepot. He got a pan ready for the fish and decided to have mashed potatoes and green beans with it. For dessert he pulled out chocolate pudding. He thought to himself that this was one of those well-rounded meals he could tell his mother about if she was worried about him eating right. By the time he was done and cleaned up the best he could do in the dark, the stars were out. It was great to just sit there and relax to the night sounds of the woods. That was when his computer started playing the you-got-a-message tune. Coffee in hand, he walked into the shelter and sat down before the computer. At first he was rather surprised at the chat request, but as he read on his interest grew, so he typed a reply.

Sandbox: "Hi, my name is Chrissy North and I'm here with my friend Krista Sparks. We're on a summer cruise with our parents in the Pacific and would love to have someone to talk with. How old are you and where are you?"

Backwoods: "My name is Fern. I'm 18 and spending the summer camping in the woods with Mother Nature."

Sandbox: "Krista is 16 and I'm 15. Krista wants to know if it is warm there and are there any animals?"

Backwoods: "It's been getting cooler since dark, but then I'm up in the mountains. There are wild animals everywhere. I'm by a river and there is a moose, several deer, a fox, and a mother bear with three cubs that come to drink often. Right now, I have a big owl calling from the tree above me. It is a clear night and there are stars everywhere like guardians watching over me."

Sandbox: "Wow, that sounds neat. My mom would love that. She's an anthropologist and works outside a lot. What do you eat out there in the woods?"

Backwoods: "Well, tonight I had fish that I caught in the river, mashed potatoes, green beans, and chocolate pudding I made. I'm drinking the coffee I brewed, which is good now that the night air is getting colder."

Sandbox: "Well, we have to go. One of our home-schooling task masters, Uncle Bob, is coming to teach us all about computers. It was nice talking to you. Let's chat again. Bye ☺"

Fern sipped his coffee with a renewed sense of success. He may not have found how to make the computer his father had sent him work or get through to his mother or Sky, but he found two teenage girls halfway around the world in the Pacific Ocean who wanted to talk to him. And that was better than the two fish. His friendly owl must have agreed with the thought since he started hooting the tale to his feathered friends.

Back in Sand Box 4 the girls were doing their best to act innocent:

Chrissy switched back to the research page about computer logic and they told Uncle Bob how interesting it was to read.

Chrissy's father strolled in and sat next to Bob. "Sounds like a snow job to me."

Bob laughed, and then he noticed the chat window open on the task bar. He pointed it out to Dew who said, "We don't have one in the box."

Now Bob looked perplexed as he replied, "Neither does the ship."

They both looked at the girls and asked in stereo, "Who were you talking to?"

Krista, the bolder of the two, said, "An eighteen-year-old boy named Fern."

Bob's fingers raced over the keyboard and opened the chat window. He saw the connection had been closed from the other end. Bob looked at Dew. "They made first contact and didn't know it."

Krista asked, "What do you mean?"

Uncle Bob answered, "Fern is my son and he's at home."

"Oh wow neat—oh!" Chrissy blurted out. "We called the future!"

"We have to tell everyone," said Bob. "Let's use the conference room with the big screen, so everyone can read the chat message."

Dew got on the phone while Bob gathered up the computer.

"Come on, girls, you're the heroes here," said Uncle Bob.

The last of the Research Team came in and had a seat and Whosh asked Bob what was so interesting it could not wait until the morning meeting. Bob herded the two girls to the front of the room and said, "Chrissy and Krista have made first contact. They chatted with Fern on my computer."

Bob toggled on the big screen and let everyone read the chat message. Harry and J.P., who had been looking bored, both let out a cheer and then everyone joined them.

Whosh walked to the front and said, "Ladies, I'm going to have to make you part of my crew. We'll all reconvene after breakfast and you young ladies can give us a lesson in how to find a teenage boy."

Before bed Chrissy, Krista, Tracy, Alice, Amanda, and Patty took a stroll on the flight deck under the stars. As Chrissy looked at her favorite bright star she asked, "Do you think he can see these stars too?"

Amanda said with mirth in her voice, "I bet he can. You guys may have *me* believing in miracles soon if you keep it up." She stepped between the girls and hugged them both, then added, "I think I'll adopt you both like Uncle Bob."

> Bright star twinkling in the sky,
> Can you see the one I love,
> Can I follow you to him,
> As you shine your guiding light,
> On us both this silent night?

Hawaii in a "Long-Abandoned" Underground Bunker:

Two munitions storage rooms with steel lockable doors were turned into the guestrooms for John Doe and Moon Sung. Laurie found the old medical office and cleaned it up for seeing her two patients. One of the larger rooms was turned into a command center with communications and as a place for meetings. Above ground and below ground security was put in place. Officially, Captain Kid was listed on medical leave because of a car accident and Villa was listed as being hurt in the unfortunate hospital fire. Brother was on emergency leave to take care of a family emergency in Newport, Rhode Island. Kid even created an official cover story for Laurie' absence.

One of the old offices was made into an interview room. The crew found bunks for sleeping and they found Laurie a bed for the sleeping room behind her office. Outside had taken on a recreational look with ATVs and mountain bikes, but also strategic watchtowers that now had armed team members in them. There were also more rangers than before. The sign at the entrance to the park said, CLOSED for repair work.

The interviews started on the second day. Both men were obviously depressed by their state of affairs, but Doe still demanded a call to the Pentagon, and Sung wanted to call his embassy. Both were told they were dead and given copies of the death certificates. And were told they had been assassinated by a hit team. Even though Doe had been found with Sung's car, they did not seem to know each other. Sung was well trained as a spy and every truth serum yielded only so much. His handlers kept him on a short leash, only telling him what he needed to know. It became obvious that more of them had to be in Hawaii.

John Doe sang like a bird, but much of what he said was beyond belief. Time travel, a security chief named Gen. Peter Rabbit, a Project Wonderland with an Alice, a Dr. Whosh—whom he hated—the missing USS Constitution; he even claimed to know the now missing admiral and talked about something called Sand Box 4.

They did four hours of interview with each man. They all sat in the command center and listened to the tapes two times.

Finally, Kid said, "I have a friend in Washington, Gen. Jack Frost, who is the current chief of National Defense under President White. I think I should call and tell him what we know and what has happened. Whatever is going on here is big and we need help."

They all agreed and no one took the offer to get out before their involvement might become a matter of record.

That afternoon Brother drove Kid to the army camp that was the headquarters for Army Intel on the island. Kid knew the security office, and both were brought to the commanding colonel's office. Kid explained that they had become aware of some highly classified information and that he needed to talk with General Frost at the White House on a secure link. The colonel had them taken to the COM center, and Kid was led into a secure room with a video link. A technician at the other end explained that he was in the White House and that General Frost was on his way. Ten minutes later, Frost walked in and took a seat.

"Hello, Joe. It's been a long time. As soon as both our lights go green we can talk," said Frost.

Kid nodded and in a few seconds the light was green.

"I'm green," said Joe.

"Me, too. So what can I do for you, Joe?" asked Frost.

"Well, Jack, I hope this can be a two-way street, but here is what I got." And he proceeded to tell him what had been going on.

Jack was silent for a few moments as he digested all he had just heard. "You know, Joe, you should have never retired," he said at last. "You just gave me more than the CIA, NSA, and FBI have combined. You've done the right thing and I'm going to keep you in the loop. Can you stay on the base for about an hour while I make things happen?" asked Jack.

"No problem. I hear they have good food here," said Joe.

"Joe, after I talk to the president I'll get back to you"

And with that they signed off. Kid left the secure room and thanked the operator.

When he found Brother, most of the data they brought had been encrypted and sent to the White House. Once done they headed for the mess hall as he explained that Frost had asked that they wait an hour.

Brother smiled. "Well, let's enjoy the food before the MPs show up."

They had a full meal and were quite the novelty being in civilian clothes. They were almost done when the base commander joined them with a young lieutenant in tow.

"Colonel Kid, if I had been briefed on your status, I would have had you eat with me," said the commander.

Totally unfazed, Kid said, "This is fine. Anyway, we've rather enjoyed it. Your mess cooks are good."

"Thank you. I'll be sure to tell them you said so. This is Lt. Jay Hosmer. His platoon has been assigned to you for as long as you need them. I've been told this whole matter is above Top Secret, need to know. If there is anything else I can do for you don't hesitate to ask," said the commander. With that, he stepped back and saluted, then left the mess hall.

Kid watched him leave, and then looked at Lieutenant Hosmer. "Is he always that nice to civilians?"

"Well, not usually, but you're a colonel, too," replied Hosmer.

Kid laughed. "Well, I used to be, unless the president just took me out of retirement. Have a seat, son. We don't bite and the food here is good."

As they ate dessert, Lieutenant Hosmer explained that his orders came from the White House and that he was to report directly to Kid. He had a full platoon of four squads. Three of them were tactical and one was support. "In support I have four COM techs, two clerks, two medics, and two cooks."

Brother smiled and said, "I like you better than the MPs we thought we might get, and you have cooks too. I might reenlist."

Now it was Hosmer's turn to laugh. "Well, Captain Brother, I think you got drafted while you ate that meal, sir." Now they all laughed.

Kid explained the logistics of their situation and what equipment they would need. Hosmer told Kid his platoon was standing by ready to leave. "They could drive by the depot on their way out and change the gear they need to switch in about fifteen minutes."

"Good deal," said Kid. "Let's finish our dessert and head out."

They went out and climbed in Laurie's SUV and drove to where the platoon waited. They rolled to the depot, which was well organized. Trucks were preloaded for specific jobs. Lieutenant Hosmer briefed his people and they scattered to get what they needed. They were on the road shortly following the SUV to the freeway with Brother driving and Hosmer riding shotgun. Kid rode shotgun in the Humvee as the last vehicle to see they were not being followed. There were two personnel trucks, two supply trucks, a small COM truck with a trailer, and a medical van. Unlike during their first arrival at the bunker it was daylight and Ranger Bear greeted them. He had his mike keyed open, so if there was a problem everyone would know right away.

Brother said, "This is Lt. Jay Hosmer. He and his whole platoon have come to back us up."

"Welcome aboard, Lieutenant. I love having company," Bear said.

As soon as all the military vehicles were out of sight in the loading area, Lieutenant Hosmer set to work. He sent two squads to set up perimeter security and defenses. The third squad started unpacking the trucks. The COM team parked their trailer in the ranger's garage and went to work getting secure links to the bunker command center. The two medics found Laurie and soon had her clinic fully equipped, cleaned, and ready for full operation. The cooks found the old kitchen and dining area and started bringing it to life. Within the hour, coffee was brewing and sending a welcoming aroma throughout the whole bunker. The clerks and the COM team started turning the command center in to a real war room. The next day Colonel Kid found he had his own office and a secretary.

White House, Washington, D.C.:

Amy had turned off the highway and was headed into downtown Washington. Stella keyed in the personal phone number for Snow. She identified herself, and the operator did a voice scan to verify, then announced, "She is expecting your call and will be right on."

Snow almost immediately said, "Hi, Stella, where are you?"

"Headed to a hotel to freshen up."

"Don't bother. You can be here in five minutes. I'll meet you at the door. You and the girls can freshen up in the family quarters before supper," said Snow.

"Ok," said Stella, "We're on our way."

Amy made a U-turn and headed for the White House. True to her word and to the Secret Service's great annoyance, there she was and in they went. No one even dared ask Amy or Sky for their weapons and were greatly shocked to find all three women had higher clearances than they did.

Once upstairs in the residence, Amy and Sky got changed into pantsuits, which made them look like models. They left their weapons in the dressing room, which they figured would make the Secret Service agents much more comfortable. Stella and Snow had not stopped talking since they met at the door. They soon headed to the dining room and did not have long to wait before the president and his Secret Service head walked in from the other side. Snow warmly greeted her husband and then introduced her three guests.

Snow said, "The lady with Purr is his security head, Dr. Susan Anthony."

The president looked from Susan to Amy and Sky then asked Susan, "Why don't you dress like that?"

She laughed. "Mr. President, I don't have the qualifications or the body and, besides, these are two of the most deadly women on this planet." And she walked over and shook hands with the two. "And the woman they are guarding is a legend in her own time. In fact, I wish I had the clearance to hear the story of how the admiral vanished with five hundred men."

Stella looked at Snow, who nodded and then said, "Well, considering that your boss is not cleared for the story, either, and since you must protect him from whatever danger it might pose him, I for one think you should stay."

The president pulled out a chair and said, "Well, tonight you can be my food tester if anyone asks."

They were all seated and the servers were starting to bring food when they all heard a ruckus out in the hall.

"Yes, I know he's eating, but this is important!" And in barged Jack Frost. "Mr. President, I need to speak with you!"

"Well, sit down, Jack. Everyone at this table has a higher security clearance than I do. This is Gen. Jack Frost, my chief of National Defense. The two gorgeous ladies are Amy Hunter and Sky Lonewolfe, the most dangerous women on the planet, I'm told. And the woman they are minding is Capt. Stella Staff," said White.

Frost stammered, "Admiral Staff's wife?"

Stella smiled. "I was when we left Hawaii."

"They think you're missing," said Frost.

"We sort of left surreptitiously in the night, but who has missed us?" asked Stella.

Frost said, "I just got a call on a secure line from Hawaii

from an old friend, Capt. Joe Kid, who is in charge of the Hawaii State Police Bureau of Criminal Investigation—the BCI. He was a colonel with me years ago in Army Intel. And he had a wild story about spies and terrorists. He had a single assassin attack his men at the hospital trying to kill his prisoners John Doe and Moon Sung. His whole team has reviewed the interview tapes twice and the only conclusion they can come to is something big is going down. They do know it has something to do with the USS Constitution and a group of missing people, namely, Admiral Staff and about five hundred members of the U.S. Navy, Marines, and Army, as well as civilians, who vanished from either Pearl Harbor or a Cdr. Dew North's home. His wife, Tracy, and their two children, Chrissy and James, are gone too. Joe also told me he could not find you, Stella."

Sky jumped in. "Did you say Chrissy North?"

"Yes," replied Frost.

"The e-mail I got from Fern Cybernaut said he had 'chatted' with two girls, Chrissy North and Krista Sparks," said Sky.

"Is that significant?" asked Frost.

"It could be," said Stella. "So I guess I need to fill in my piece of this story and tell you where my husband and those five hundred men went."

Stella began her part in the story. "Flagg had all the reports and oversaw the search efforts, so he knew all there was to know about the missing ship. It was very personal to him because it was one of his ships, and like the others he was waiting to board her when she arrived at Pearl. That day he decided to gather all the personnel and brief them. He called in Cdr. Topper Bird, the Air Wing CO, and Cdr. Dew North of the civilian group. I believe North said he is the navigation officer. That morning they were supposed to meet at our home to talk about what they would tell the men and what they should do next. Much to the surprise of our security detail, Commander North drove up with four other people in the car, including Dr. Amanda Whosh, Gen. Peter Rabbit, Lt. Charly Brice, and Capt. William Right. I know both Whosh and Right."

Frost interrupted, "Right is the Constitution's captain, isn't he?"

"Yes. All four were aboard when she vanished," Stella replied. "Whosh explained that she was the acting commander of Sand Box 4, an above Top Secret part of Project Wonderland that was involved with time travel. She explained that they didn't know how the incident happened, but that the USS Constitution was now anchored in Pearl Harbor in the year 1421. They returned to our time, landing in North's garden with Sand Box 4. They didn't wish to make official contact because they were concerned that Whosh would be ordered to abandon the Constitution and its crew where they are in 1421. So they came back to get the rest of their crew for Sand Box 4 and the ship.

"Their plan was to steam for Guam, which is where they were taking SB4, to try to find out what happened and how the ship got there. Their hope was to return the ship and crew to our time. I did see this SB4 and although I never went in it, I saw many of the personnel board. I have no idea how they did it, however, as it looked too small to hold over ten people."

Stella continued, "Now the John Doe you mentioned was on the ship and I guess he was supposed to escort SB4 to Guam. However, when the trouble started, they said the ship ended up dead in the water with no power. This Doe threatened Captain Right, and Lieutenant Brice took offense to that and had her men toss him in the brig. From the bits and pieces I overheard, my guess is no one wanted him there. So they sort of dumped him off in Hawaii. We never heard any more because we scheduled a commercial flight and sent three officers' wives for a shopping trip in L.A. Then we jumped on a Navy cargo flight to the coast. A friend and his wife flew us from there to Rhode Island in their Lear jet. After that we headed here in a rental car.

"But that isn't quite the end of our tale," continued Stella. "We made a second stop in Coventry, Rhode Island, to see a young man named Fern Cybernaut. His father, Bob, is a civilian electronic specialist, who was doing some last minute work on the Constitution when she left port. Bob and Harry Haul, another civilian who is an engineering specialist, were supposed to get off when the ship arrived at Pearl. Bob had been working with the SB4 COM officer, O'Rielly, I think, and shipped a box airfreight with a transceiver to Fern hoping he could figure out how to communicate across time to the SB4. He didn't have a lot of hope it would work, but Fern is one of those computer wizards, like Sky who often performs magic. The e-mail she mentioned getting from him said he'd had no luck, but had 'chatted' with two teenage girls named Chrissy North and Krista Sparks."

Sky added, "Who just happened to be on a cruise in the Pacific with their parents."

Stella said, "One more bit of information. Amanda Whosh was going to send a burst transmission to Project Wonderland just before they left, to sort of cover her butt and make it impossible for them to reply and give her orders. Part of that transmission came here to Snow so she would know we were coming. The other part went to the head of Project Wonderland at the Pentagon, Gen. Benedict Black. I was told by Amanda that he's in charge of a Project Neverland, with someone named Banks. But she had no idea what that project was about. The commander of SB4 is a Gen. Patent Hardash. I gather he flew on to Guam and was not missed by anyone."

The president finally spoke, looking at Stella, "You did say time travel?"

"Yes, sir, and Amanda said it has been going on for years," she replied.

Frost said, "I wish I had taken notes on what you just said. Between you and Joe Kid, this is more information than I've ever gotten from the FBI, NSA, and CIA put together."

Sky said, "No problem, General Frost. I debriefed Captain Staff twice on the ride here, while Amy was driving. I have it all in a report on a disk in my bag." She pulled out the disk and handed it across the table to the amazed Frost.

Sky went on. "Fern is going to chat with me tonight at eight p.m. Do you have anything more secure than my laptop we could use?"

"We sure do," said Frost. "May I put the War Room online, Mr. President?"

"Sounds good to me," said White. "Susan, do you think you could arrange for us all to have dessert and coffee down there?"

"With pleasure, sir," said Dr. Anthony.

"One more thing. Is this young man, Fern, safe?" Frost asked.

Stella said, "Well, that was part of why we stopped to visit him. We left him with enough money to become 'invisible' like his father told him to. I was kind of thinking I would like to meet your Captain Kid. Perhaps we could take Fern and his mother for a little Hawaiian vacation at the same time?"

Frost smiled for the first time, "I do believe Joe would like that."

The War Room:

The room was busy. Sky had been at the keyboard for almost an hour. Frost sat next to her and had tossed his jacket on the cabinet. Even the president had removed his. They were here to do the work of the nation and find out who was attacking her. By 7:50 everyone was there. A table full of desserts and an urn of coffee was there to keep them going.

"Ok," Frost ordered, "take us to lockdown, full secure operation."

"Yes, sir," replied his COM chief. "We are secure. It's all yours, Sky."

"Thanks." The first thing she did was bring up the com team at the Scout bunker in Hawaii. She announced, "We have Captain Kid and company live online. I have chat link open and ready."

Mountain Camp Site:

Fern was just finishing supper when Al sat down beside him and said, "Lou thought you would need some dessert with that. Hope you like apple pie."

Fern said, "Now that even smells good. I wouldn't have known you were here if friend moose hadn't raised her head to look at you. I still don't get how you can walk so quietly with those big feet of yours. The moose isn't quiet. She sounds like a freight train coming through the woods. Maybe she should take lessons from the deer." Fern ate the pie and said, "Tell Lou I said thanks. That really hit the spot."

"Have you been enjoying yourself?" asked Al.

"Not really. There are too many questions and I can't seem to figure out that radio Dad sent me. I just can't get it to do anything. I was going to disconnect it and tell Sky it didn't work."

They walked from the picnic table into the shelter where the equipment sat on the table. Al pulled up the second chair at the table and looked over the two computer screens. "Did you check the history file on that thing?" he asked.

"No, but it should be empty," said Fern as he typed on the keyboard and a display appeared telling him he'd had a connection on the transceiver for ten minutes.

"Can't be. It should have told me," complained Fern.

"Well, why rush taking it apart? Maybe those good-looking girls you told me about will have an idea," encouraged Al.

Fern said, "Yeah, they are foxes. That Sky Lonewolfe really has a way with tech. I've got to call her at eight o'clock. Too bad I don't have the power to do video. You would like to see her."

He smiled. "Oh, I think I will sooner or later. Sounds like a girl who would like the woods," added Al.

"I wonder if she carries a gun, too?" said Fern.

"I have the feeling she doesn't need one," replied Al.

"You could be right. For a looker she sure has muscles," said Fern.

"And a fairy godmother?" asked Al.

Fern thought for a moment. He could not remember mentioning that, but then Al was good at pulling things out of the ether. As they both relaxed, Fern keyed in the commands for the computer to go online and opened the chat window. Now that all was ready they just had to wait and enjoy their coffee.

Hawaii Scout Bunker (Underground Command Center):

The duty COM tech, Spc. Donald Plant, got a priority flash from War Room One to switch to secure mode with full encryption.

Plant said, "We have an incoming conference for Captain Kid."

The clerk, who was talking with the operator, ran for Kid's office.

"Sir, the president is calling you. Hurry!" stammered the clerk.

Kid told him to go get the others. Soon he was seated next to the operator. Behind them watching the large flat display screen was Brother, Bear, Villa, Green, and Lieutenant Hosmer.

Hosmer said to Kid, "Sir, I'm not sure I am cleared for this."

"Lieutenant, you're defending us from the bad guys and that means you need to know what's happening, why it's happening, and who we're all working under."

"I see your point, sir."

The speaker came to life and they could see the people in War Room One.

"Hello, Captain Kid. This is Sky Lonewolfe on the keyboard and I have President White, General Frost, Captain Staff, and Dr. Susan Anthony here with me. We've some information for you, and an updated report is enroute by data transfer as we speak. In a few minutes we're going to start a live chat with Fern Cybernaut, whose father, Bob, is on the Constitution. If we're real lucky, they'll be joining us too."

Sky continued, "The president is concerned about Fern's safety at his current location, so Captain Staff will be taking us to extract him and his mother and take them to your location for safekeeping. We'll update you as that operation proceeds. I've already sent the chat directions to your operator, so if you've something to add, you may. The president sends his best and thanks you for your great work on behalf of our country."

"I have an incoming chat request from Fern," Sky said a moment later. "So let's get started."

Backwoods: Hello, Sky. I have Al here. I was going to disconnect the transceiver Dad sent because I couldn't get it to do anything. But Al told me to check the history file and it said I had been connected for 10 minutes, but I don't get it. Anyway are you in Washington?

Warroom: Yes, we're in the White House. The president says hello. Also, he wants your fairy godmother to come visit you, after we're done here.

Sandbox: Hi, Fern, this is Chrissy and Krista.

Backwoods: Hi guys, I'll have to chat with you later. I've got the president waiting to talk to me.

Sandbox: That's OK. Our parents said we can stay up as late as we want to talk to you, but right now Admiral Staff, Dr. Whosh, and Captain Right would like to talk with the president, too—so we'll talk later ☺

Warroom: Fern, it's OK. Chrissy and Krista are with your father on the Constitution. So Al was right. You did get through. Congratulations to you and the ladies. Admiral, Stella is here. We're in the War Room with the president and Gen. Frost. Since we have a link to you I am up-loading a file about what has happened here and in Hawaii since we left there.

no one was there. Or was that what Al meant by getting things ready for his guests? The other two closed in on the cabin.

Suddenly he heard Al's voice. "You should go now and stay invisible. I'll be ok. I've played this game before."

The men rushed into the cabin.

"Go now," said Al.

Fern heard loud screams and when he looked back a tremendously bright light was shining from within the cabin and Al had vanished. Fern turned and ran back to camp, grabbed his gear and the transceiver, then stepped into the darkness.

Washington, D.C. the White House:

As they wrapped up matters in the War Room, the president asked Stella, "What are you doing next?"

"Well, we know Fern has left Rhode Island. We'll collect his mother and then go get him."

"You should have asked him where he is located."

"Too dangerous. Someone might be listening and, besides, I bet his Scoutmaster can help us find him."

General Frost said, "I think I can help by putting a helicopter at your disposal and a Marine escort."

"Now that should get things moving faster," replied Stella.

The ladies changed into traveling attire, said their good-byes, then met the chopper on the White House lawn. The time flew and soon they were flying over western Rhode Island.

Sky did a search to find Colonel Jorge and gave the pilot the GPS coordinates.

"Good news," replied the pilot. "Your friend has a big lawn."

The pilot brought the helicopter around and set it on the lawn as if it was a normal happening. The Marines piled out and secured the landing zone. Amy led the way with Sky bringing up the rear, computer in hand.

"Dear, I think we have company again. Only this time, they came in a helicopter and brought the Marines," said Susan Jorge.

"Just show them in, honey. They probably need directions," said Benjamin.

When Susan opened the door Stella said, "I'm Capt. Stella Staff and we're wondering if we could impose on Colonel Jorge for directions."

"Why, I'm sure you can," said Susan. "Come right in."

Benjamin walked out to the living room. "Hello, Stella. It's been some time since I last saw you. Please, do have a seat, ladies. I'm retired now, but if I can help you I will."

Stella said, "I was sort of retired too, Benjamin, if that can be said about someone who married Admiral Staff. Then this morning President White sort of officially unretired me, but that's a long story. Right now we need you to help us find two people who could be in grave danger. First, I need to find Kate Cybernaut, whose husband, Bob, is on the Constitution with another man we believe you know, Harry Haul."

"I heard the ship was missing."

"We saw both men before we left Hawaii and they were fine," said Stella.

"Well, that's good to hear, and who's the second person you're looking to find?"

"I'm looking for Fern Cybernaut who is in hiding because some unpleasant people are looking for him. We did talk to him briefly on the computer last night from the War Room, but we didn't dare ask his location in case someone was listening."

"First of all, you're behind the bad guys who have already visited here. Second, your chopper is a little big for Kate's yard, but I can drive you over there."

Stella replied, "That would be wonderful, but would you mind if I stayed here and get to know Susan?"

"I would love that, dear. You just go ahead," said Susan.

"Could you take Sgt. Amy Hunter, who's a Navy SEAL, and perhaps a couple of the Marines who need something to do?" asked Stella.

Benjamin said, "Sure and I suppose I shouldn't ask what this is all about?"

"Well, one of the bad guys took on a SWAT team of nine, destroyed a hospital wing, and blew up an airport parking garage in Honolulu."

"I already know too much. Come on, Amy."

Outside she barked at two of the Marines, "You two with me."

Jorge looked over at her and commented, "You know... The SEALs looked a lot different when I was in the Navy."

Amy replied, "You tellin' me I'm uglier?"

And with that all four laughed as they drove off. The trip only took a few minutes and they were soon in the Cybernauts' driveway. Jorge led the way up the walk after Amy left the two fully armed Marines by the van. They were crossing the porch when Jorge froze in his tracks. Amy looked at where he was pointing and saw the broken window glass. She signaled the Marines and readied her weapon. She sent one Marine to the back door and the other to the front, which he found unlocked. She followed him in and they searched the house.

She yelled out to Jorge, "Clear, sir!"

The place had been torn apart. As they looked through Fern's bedroom, Jorge paused to swear. Amy looked questioningly and he pointed to the maps on the floor.

"Those show where we camp up north and are probably where Fern went to be on his home turf."

"Fern mentioned an Aunt June in one of his e-mails. Would Kate go there?"

"Yes, she might," Benjamin replied. "I suppose we should call the police."

Amy smiled, picked up the kitchen phone, and punched in 911. "Officer, they've robbed my home. Help me!" She dropped the phone and they left.

It was a farther drive to Aunt June's, which was really out in the woods. Amy had Jorge stop at the bottom of the driveway and sent the Marines to cover the front and back of the home. Then they drove right up and parked next to the cars.

"That's Fern's car, isn't it?" Amy asked, indicating the older car.

"Yes, and that one is June's car," he replied, pointing out the new Lincoln.

They walked to the back door and before they could ring the bell June bounced out the door and hugged Benjamin, then asked, "Hey, who's your new girlfriend?"

He replied with a smile, "Amy is with the government. Is Kate here?"

"Sure is. Come on in."

Kate looked at them when they entered and asked, "Is Fern ok?"

Before trying to answer Benjamin asked, "Have you had any visitors?"

"No," said Kate.

Amy lifted the radio in her left hand. "The house is secure. Stand by front and rear in case."

"Kate, to answer your question, we don't know. Someone ransacked your home looking for him. Do you know where he went?" asked Benjamin.

"He didn't say, but I figured near Al's place," she replied, "I let him take my SUV."

"We'll call on the way. We've got to go and you need to come with us," said Amy. "It's not safe for you here."

"I'll get my stuff."

June and Kate ran upstairs. When they returned in a few minutes Kate had a duffel bag. "I'm ready."

Benjamin said to June, "You should be safe, but why don't you drive out when we do and have supper at my place?"

"Sure, sounds like fun since all I have here is leftovers."

June drove out first. Amy had a Marine follow them bringing Fern's car to put in the Jorges' garage. They headed out. As they drove by her house, Kate could see all the police cars at her home.

Benjamin hit the button to open his garage door and the Marine drove Fern's car inside. June parked and joined the ladies having tea in the kitchen. Amy told Stella they had a new problem and Benjamin was already on the phone. All eyes were on him when he hung up. "No answer or machine. We should get in the air."

"Yes sir, Colonel. I promise to send him back in one piece, Susan." Stella stood and hugged her as they left.

It had already gotten late in another long day as they flew north. Benjamin and Sky worried over a map on her computer. Even if they called the local police, they could be sending under-armed, inexperienced officers to their deaths. They had to trust that all would turn out for the best. Some of them went to sleep. The Marines were used to crazy hours and sleeping when they could. Kate and Stella talked quietly. Benjamin and Sky stared at her computer like a crystal ball. Amy just sat looking into the darkness, nursing a rage that anyone could be hunting Kate and Fern over a dumb computer. The pilots had napped on the Jorges' lawn. They too were used to long, odd hours and being ready when they were needed.

As they rounded the last mountain and headed up the valley, the sun was just lighting the sky. The farmhouse came into view as the dawn awakened the day. The chopper just hit ground when Amy was halfway to the house with Sky. She had exchanged her computer for a rather lethal-looking assault weapon. On her heels the Marines were doing their best to keep up. A tall figure was standing on the porch waiting for them with coffee in hand. Before Amy could start blurting out questions, Al wished her a good morning.

"So where is this fairy godmother you've brought? I want to meet her," said Al. He smiled. "You've brought Kate and Benjamin. Why, my wife will be thrilled at all this company."

Stella, Kate, and Benjamin walked up and joined Al on his porch. He hugged Kate and Benjamin. Al smiled at Stella and took both her hands. "You're the first fairy godmother I have ever met. This is going to be very interesting. Now, before we go in, I'd better tell these very eager young ladies what they want to know."

He looked at the two gun-toting ladies. "You must be Amy, and I see Sky has traded in her computer for something she thinks is more lethal," he said, smiling. "First, I guess you would like your three bad guys?"

Amy nodded.

"Well, if you look in my neighbor's field, you'll find a big Suburban parked there, a whole bunch of stuff on the ground, and you will hear strange noises coming out of the old well.

I think you'll find those men hiding there," said Al. "And as soon as you get back, I promise to go help you find Fern."

Kate said, "You sure he's all right?"

"A little tired, I'll bet. Those horrible people made a lot of noise running around in the dark last night. But I do think they saw the light," added Al. He and Benjamin were ready when Amy and Sky returned.

Sky was the first to speak. "What happened to them? They're hiding in that well and refuse to come out because they say someone is going to get them. They're totally naked. Their clothes, guns, and gear are lying all over the ground. We copied down all the document names and numbers on their IDs."

Al commented, "They must have gotten lost in the woods, which can be very scary, I'm told. Now, I guess Stella can take them in for debriefing. Or just call the New Hampshire State Police. They rather frown on hunting Boy Scouts."

Stella laughed. "That could be a hard choice."

"But where is Fern?" asked Amy.

Al led them to a shed and pulled out a climbing rope and a pair of gloves. They climbed into his old SUV and drove off into the woods. After a few minutes he pulled up in front of the shelter and they all climbed out.

Al said to Sky, "I think you'll find Fern's computer on the table in there. Come on, Amy."

She followed him a short way into the woods where he stopped and handed her the rope and gloves. "I think you'll need these and maybe you should leave that big cannon down here."

Amy still looked a little confused, so Al pointed up the tree.

"Are you sure?"

Al nodded.

She handed him the gun, put on the gloves, and heaved the rope over a limb. She was about seventy feet off the ground when she passed a pair of feet. There was Fern, strapped to the tree sound asleep. Amy just hung there looking at this peaceful young man.

Finally she said, "Fern, it's morning."

His eyes fluttered open as he focused on the face a foot in front of him and got a big grin. Amy reached over, hugged him and said, "I like your roost, Fern."

"What are you doing here?"

"Well, Al told me I should go climb a tree."

Fern laughed. "Yes, he would do that."

Sky joined Benjamin and Al and asked, "Where is Amy?"

"She climbed a tree," said Benjamin and both men chuckled.

A moment later, they heard noises above and saw Amy and Fern climbing down. When they were on the ground, Al handed Amy back her gun.

Sky said, "Fern, I didn't find the transceiver with your computer."

"I took it with me." He patted his bag.

"You know, Al," said Stella, "you have a point about your guests. They would be little use to us, and I think your state police would have fun figuring out just what kind of terrorists they've caught."

"City slickers, I think," replied Al.

Stella went on. "Our ride is waiting at the Moultonborough Airport. So Fern, Kate, Amy, Sky, and I can fly over there. I'll leave the Marines with Benjamin and you. Then the chopper can return for them after the state police have your guests well in hand.

Everyone said their good-byes and were soon airborne. Meanwhile, the Marines were put to work. Two baby-sat the guests and the other two moved Kate's SUV over by the cabin, and then placed Fern's remaining gear in the cabin.

The local police rolled in first, then the state police, and even the forest rangers got into the act. A search was started for the missing Scout and soon the Rhode Island State Police were looking for the Scout's missing mother. Since it was now an interstate investigation, the FBI was called in to coordinate and oversee. However, the New Hampshire State Police refused to release the three crazy madmen who all had federal ID cards. The FBI decided to back off and just offer help. The NSA tried to deny the men were theirs in spite of the ID cards having NSA on it. The black Suburban came from their car pool and the automatic weapons with silencers were registered to them too. The media was having a field day. The seven people watching this circus from the farmhouse porch found it all rather entertaining.

Moultonborough Airport:

The Lear jet was waiting on the approach to the runway, its owners all ready for a new adventure in the life of Stella. The chopper swung up the valley across Berry Pond and landed by the jet. In less than ten minutes, they were headed back up the valley the way they had come.

"Welcome aboard, Stella. I see you have added to your entourage," said the pilot. "Where are you headed?"

"Back home to Hawaii," said Stella, "But wherever you guys can get us will help."

The pilot smiled at his co-pilot wife, "Sounds like fun, dear?"

"Sure does," she replied. "Can you get us refueled?"

Sky was already opening her computer and said, "I'll get you fuel and a fighter escort if you want. Your food and lodging beats the back of the cargo plane any day."

Stella laughed. "The fighter escort might make it a little obvious even to the NSA folks."

Fern had been thrilled at his first helicopter ride and now a fancy private jet. He slipped into the seat next to Sky and watched her keyboard magic.

Sky asked, "Will Fallon, Nevada, Whidbey Island, Washington, and Anchorage, Alaska, do?"

"That should do nicely," replied the pert co-pilot. "Let's get in the air. I can already see me on that Hawaiian beach."

Back on the Farm:

The show from the front porch was just amazing. Police lines had been set up and lab technicians had combed the area. Search parties had swept through the woods several times finding no sign of the missing Scout. The same thing was repeated in Rhode Island, and the news media went into a frenzy when a police officer found the missing Scout's car parked in the federal building parking lot. Adding to the confusion was that the boy's mother's SUV was parked by a cabin in the mountains. There were at least three TV crews set up in the field across the road. The local town had become a tourist destination and there were people with cameras everywhere. They were all so busy chasing stories they never noticed the helicopter land in the back field of the farm. Probably just thought it was more searchers. Since it was late afternoon Col. Jorge, whom Stella had left in charge, told the flight crew to stand down. They would fly out after breakfast. So the group on the porch grew. At least until Al said, "Anyone for fishing?"

Pentagon Basement, Washington, D.C.:

Benedict Black was levitating as he screamed at Woozy, "What kind of fools did you hire and sending those dummies out with our equipment? Even those dumb FBI boobs are asking questions! Now I've got to convince them they're rogue agents we have fired. If that Hardash hadn't run off with Sand Box 2, I could go fix this mess. Has Major Mercenary called in yet? At least he got rid of that Doe and kicked some Hawaiian ass while he was at it! Why can't you find men like him? What am I supposed to tell Banks? I've lost three time machines and Sand Box 3 has half the world's gold on it and my top crew. Have they got Sand Box 1 repaired yet?"

"No sir," replied Woozy.

"How soon?" barked Black.

"They don't know. The timing circuits are fried. Sir, couldn't we recall Sand Box 5 from Russia or Sand Box 6 from Europe?"

"No. They're busy on Project Neverland, and SB7 and SB8 are nowhere near ready."

"Well, sir, we can hope they got the brat and his mother before they got caught."

"And how did they get caught?" screamed Black. "Who caught them, some hick sheriff or state cop? Have you read what the newspapers are saying, and have you seen those pictures on TV of some hick farmer sitting on his porch laughing at us? I ought to bomb that berg just for existing! Now get out of here, you fool, until you can tell me something good. And tell that big-boobed twit to come in here. I want her now. Go! You're no use to me."

A Lear Jet Flying West:

The refueling stops went smoothly. They were in and out of NAS Fallon, Nevada, and off to Seattle like clockwork. They took an hour layover at NAS Whidbey Island and headed for Alaska where they would spend the night. Sky was busy with her computer. She had entered all the info she found about the NSA creeps and was following the trails. She soon got to a Wiley Woozy, who seemed to work for Benedict Black. After chasing phone records for a while she found Black talked a lot with a Warbucks Banks. The name Maj. Raul Mercenary seemed to show up a lot and he had stopped to refuel at Hawaii when the hospital incident occurred and then went to Guam.

Fern watched the whole operation with great interest and decided to get in on the act too. It wasn't long before he had an interesting file on Project Wonderland and kept finding references to a Project Neverland, which seemed to be sucking up lots of government funding with little explanation, except the world of black ops. He did get lured to the co-pilots seat for some flight lessons. And with a photographic memory he caught on fast. This could be as much fun as the computer.

Mom and Stella enjoyed the plane's kitchen and were very amused watching the news about the investigation back East. It was dark when they landed in Alaska, and their flying hosts went right to sleep. Stella got the rest of them a place to crash. She and Kate settled in, but the kids were too full of energy. They borrowed a jeep and went exploring. They found a place to eat and play pool. Amy and Sky were deep into a game when some big drunk stumbled into Fern as he returned from the men's room. Before either could react, the big brute took a swing at Fern. With great grace, Fern stepped aside and the drunk crashed on the floor. He came up cursing, with a knife in his hand. Fern had snatched the salt shaker off the table, unscrewed the lid, and threw the contents in the brute's face, blinding him. And seemingly with the same motion his foot connected with the wrist holding the knife, which Fern caught in mid-air. With little effort, he sent the knife across the room for a bull's eye on the dart board. Two of the brute's cronies had moved away from the bar toward Fern. One looked very surprised when the lady standing next to him shoved a gun in his ribs. The second found himself holding hands with Amy and he was on his knees in pain.

Amy smiled at him. "If you bother my little brother, I'll break you in half and then I'll hurt you some more."

Sky quietly suggested, "Maybe you two should take your friend home. It would be a lot safer there."

The two exited carrying their unhappy friend.

The bartender said, "Thanks. Those guys are the pits for business. If you guys need a job, I sure could use a bouncer."

"No thanks," said Sky. "We're fully employed already."

"Hey, bar keep, I could use another beer," called out Lee Fathom.

They headed out into the night and drove out of town. Amy's curiosity finally got the better of her and she asked, "Where'd you learn that?"

"Oh, it was Al's idea. He said it would help with my lack of coordination if I took up martial arts, and it sure did. I played basketball and ran track after a year and Dad was thrilled," said Fern. "Al also said it might come in handy some day. I guess that's today."

When they were out of town, they pulled over in an open area where they could see a sky full of stars. It was wonderful and Fern pointed to a rather bright star that twinkled a lot and said, "That one looks just like the one up in the mountains at home."

They drove back and were now ready for a good night's sleep. Stella and Kate greeted them like two mother hens.

Kate said, "I hope he behaved himself."

Both girls smiled and Amy said, "He even defended our honor from a drunken knife-wielding brute. He just flattened the poor man."

Stella gave them an odd look, knowing very well that they needed very little defending.

Fern shrugged. "Just paying you back for climbing up that tree after me."

And with that they all settled in for the night and to dream of the next day's adventures.

Another Dawn on the Farm:

Lou, Al's wife, was up early and everyone awoke to the smell of breakfast cooking. Everyone packed up and ate their fill. Good-byes were exchanged along with addresses. The flight crew did their checks, loaded everybody aboard, and flew south. Colonel Jorge was returned home and he had the flight crew stand down long enough for lunch and then they headed for their home base.

"So, dear, is the excitement all over now?" asked Lou.

"No, honey, it's just begun," chuckled Al.

And about that time dawn had arrived in Alaska. Stella and company were about to get on with their trip. The flight checks were soon done on the Lear jet. With a full tank of fuel they headed out over the Pacific, Hawaii bound.

After about an hour of searching, Sky was no closer to Project Neverland than before. Fern had been watching. She shoved her computer to him and said, "Here. See what you can find. I'm going to exercise with Amy."

Stella and Kate were talking about Hawaii and how different military life had been from Kate's more domestic roll. Fern had been at it an hour when he called Sky over. He found that since it was easier to get into the Wonderland files, he had started looking at money trails, who paid for what, and it would seem some money for the operation of Sand Box 2, SB3, SB5, and SB6 had come from Neverland accounts. Some of the records had added notes, perhaps the accountant keeping track of the reason for the fund transfers. SB5 had a note about Russian assignment and SB6 mentioned Europe. A note next to a transfer for SB3 simply said "authorized by Banks." Then he found a note a week old. "Sand Box 2 requisitioned to search for Sand Box 3 in Guam after loss of Sand Box 4."

Sky stared and said to Amy, "It's a good thing he's on our side."

She got all this data in a file and sent it encrypted to the White House and Scout bunker. They were slowly finding the strands of the web and tying them together.

Sky smiled at Fern and said, "You'll love it when we get to the Scout bunker. I've requisitioned a real computer and we can tie into the Navy's super computer."

They flew into NAS Barbers Point and the Lear was parked in a secure area. Stella thanked their hosts again for service above and beyond the call of duty. They smiled and said it was their pleasure and headed for their next adventure in the rental car Sky had waiting for them. Amy drove up with the fifteen-passenger van Sky had commandeered from the Navy car pool for them. They were soon driving away from civilization to the mountains. Amy found the state park sign, which now said DANGER, closed for repairs. She turned in and soon found she had to stop because a bucket loader was across the road. Two park rangers stepped out of the bushes to greet them and inquired about their business. Once their IDs were confirmed, one of the rangers carrying a very military looking gun moved the loader. Amy drove into the loading area and parked.

Stella climbed out and said, "I guess we're home for a while."

Welcome to Scout Bunker:

A golf cart pulled up on the loading dock and two men got out, one in a park ranger uniform whose name tag said Ted Bear, the other a casually dressed civilian.

The ranger said, "Hello and welcome to Scout Bunker. This is Captain Joe Kid of the Hawaiian State Police."

Stella shook their hands and said, "I'm Stella Staff. This is Kate Cybernaut, her son, Fern, and my two assistants, Amy Hunter and Sky Lonewolfe."

Kid said, "The Marines there will bring your travel bags down and help you get settled. I'm afraid, Stella, our accommodations are a long way from your home on the island, but things have been improving since Sky started requisitioning things for us."

Stella laughed. "She's good at that. If we don't watch out, she'll have my whole house out here."

Kid introduced them to Lt. Jay Hosmer, Alfrado Villa, Sgt. Sanders Brother, and Nurse Laurie Green at the command center. He pointed out that Lieutenant Hosmer had the computer that Sky had sent installed and running. She told Lieutenant Hosmer Fern was a computer wizard and had already proved his worth. They all got settled in and joined in the many tasks at hand. While much of the grunt cleaning was done, a lot was still lacking, and those not on watches were always busy. Since the bunker was so far out, there was little vandalism. Whoever had built it had done a good job, and most of it had stayed dry. When the military had abandoned it, the National Park Service had taken it over and much was just left in place, like doors, lighting, and bathrooms. Even the old generator and elevator were still there even if they needed work. They soon had the ventilation, water, and waste system working. Luckily, most of the personnel sort of looked at it as their home and were taking great pride in the clean up and restoration work.

Kate had wandered into the kitchen area and found the young cooks at a loss as to how to get the original kitchen working. Since Kate had a degree as a dietitian she knew kitchens and had learned much about repair while Bob was off reprogramming the world. So she dived into the middle and the two young cooks eagerly followed along. They both figured if Kate could cook like she fixed things they were going to learn a lot. She had already taught them many ways to do things with their portable kitchen the Army had forgotten to mention.

The new COM team kept the computers humming and was digging deeper all the time. They now had secure links to the president, General Frost, the Navy, and even the Hawaii State Police computers. They soon built a larger version of the transceiver with a much bigger antenna. This proved to be a great boon and gave them a 24/7 COM link to Sand Box 4. This got lots a data flowing thanks to Fern's way of working around the prying eyes of the government, such as the FBI, CIA, NSA, and so on. He managed to set up an e-mail transfer system so everyone on the Constitution could write home and receive e-mail back. Fern, Sky, and Brother made a very ingenious team. Corporal Taylor Maid and his COM team kept everything going. They not only manned the links 24/7, they kept working to improve the network. Fern, Chrissy, and Krista had regular chats every day. He'd tell them about his mountain paradise and they'd tell him of the wonders of the ocean. And of course, he always made sure there was time for his mother and father to exchange their experiences.

Laurie and the two medics had sickbay looking like a real clinic. They were very amazed at what Stella and Sky could procure. The Seabees from Naval Mobile Construction Battalion THREE kept showing up with brand new equipment that was being stored somewhere and even helped Hosmer's men with landscaping and built a barbecue pit in the picnic area.

Ranger Bear's house had almost been rebuilt. He still had the Scouts up on weekends and took them to other parts of the park away from the bunker. And he had an abundant supply of volunteers to help teach the Scouts and their leaders new skills. Amy and Sky were real hits with the boys, who listened with such intensity their leaders had to drag them away when the lesson was over. Bear told them if they ever decided to give up the life of high adventure, they would make great park rangers.

John Doe saw the light and fully realized his boss Benedict Black had sent Raul to kill him. So he decided to start puking his guts out. That proved very interesting since he added new pieces to the puzzle. He confirmed the Banks / Black connection and that whatever they were planning had to do with Project Neverland. He also confirmed Sand Box 3 was missing on a mission in Guam. He knew Sand Box 5 was operating in Russia and SB6 was in Europe. SB1 was broken and SB7 and SB8 were being built. He had no idea what happened to the ship, but maybe the Russians had caught on or captured SB5. He explained that Wiley Woozy worked directly for Black. He also got into remodeling his living quarters to keep busy and safe from General Black.

Moon Sung took more persuading, but when Amy suggested that they get him drunk, put him back in his fancy clothes, and leave him parked in his car in front of his embassy, he started having second thoughts about his silence.

Then he started asking questions about political asylum and government relocation plans. Within a week he was singing like a bird and Kid had a full Army Intel Team there to debrief Sung. Although he could not provide links to his high-level associates he painted a picture of his country's plans and methods of operation.

He had no knowledge about the USS Constitution or its missing men. He had not heard of Project Wonderland but had heard of Project Neverland. He informed them that a rich capitalist named Banks thought he was the king of the world and intended to take it over and run it like a business, for his profit of course. Yes, a real capitalist pig and his country knew all about him and his American puppets. Plots, counter plots, and world domination, enough to make one wonder who was minding the store. With that, Army Intel delivered the new Moon Sung to a place far away where even he would not know who he used to be. It was a small happy island far from all the worldly cares and schemes.

As for John Doe, he got his fourth identity and a new career with the Navy running a base store in a place so beyond secret that even the Navy did not know where it is located. Life is great when you're warm, fed, happy, and no one is sending madmen after you.

Now the Scout bunker took on a new roll as Sand Box 4's new home in the year 2012. The whole story was not settling well on the Constitution, in the White House, or at the Scout bunker. The puzzle was beginning to look a lot like the United States' very resources and defenses were being turned against it, to not only steal the country's money, but its freedom as well. The quest to find Sand Box 3 had taken on a new focus for the crews of the USS Constitution and Sand Box 4. Their mission had become clear as they sped toward Guam in search of answers and perhaps new surprises.

AS THE DAWN THREE

The ship was steaming through the past where the plotting eyes of the present couldn't see, to secure a safe future of which they would be proud to say they helped build. The men, women, and children of the Constitution sailed to meet their destiny.

USS Constitution, Mid-Pacific Ocean, Westward Bound:

The evening reports arrived at the bridge. The weather report showed they would soon be hit by a storm front. The OOD passed the word to all watch stations and ordered checks of water-tight security measures to ensure condition X-Ray was set. An announcement had been made during the evening meal to the whole crew so they would know it would not be a good night to be walking around above decks in open areas. The radar techs watched their screens closely and as the storm increased in severity, made their reports more often. At 2100 hours it had increased to the point where the XO had asked to be notified and Commander Secondary joined Commander Albright on the bridge. They were talking and looking into the rain when the quartermaster manning the control console signaled that he had a message from the radar room.

They walked behind the QM and Secondary inquired, "What do we have?"

"A radar contact at sixteen miles heading 300. We are steering 270, and the display is on screen three," answered the QM.

Secondary picked up the direct phone to the radar tech and asked, "What does it look like?"

"Sir, with this weather I'm getting an intermittent signal, but several times it has appeared as a multiple contact. Could be a fishing boat," said the radar man.

"Ok, keep an eye on it and let us know if it gets closer," he ordered. He replaced the phone and picked up another labeled sonar. "Sonar room this is the XO. Do we have our ears on?"

"Yes, sir. I'm just getting normal sea noise," said the sonar tech.

"We have radar contact at 300, sixteen miles. Let us know if you hear anything unusual," said Secondary.

"Will do, sir," replied the sonar tech.

The QM said, "Sir, I've placed sonar on screen four."

"Thank you," said Secondary.

Commander Albright said, "Great time for us to meet another ship. Where were they on those starry nights?"

Secondary smiled. "Hiding so they could sneak up and get a good look at us." He checked the engineering screen and spoke to engineer on watch. "Reduce speed by twenty percent."

"Reducing speed twenty percent, sir," said the lee helmsman.

Watching the screen he saw the numbers fall, then heard the engineer report, "Reduction confirmed, sir."

Both officers returned to the window to look into the rain. Albright looked through a pair of large binoculars with night vision and scanned in the direction toward the contact. He put them back and spoke to Secondary, "Couldn't see another carrier out there, not with this storm."

About ten minutes passed when the QM signaled them once more and, as they walked up, he said, "Sir, the contact is at 291, ten miles and confirmed multiple. Also, sonar reports picking up odd sounds, an irregular thudding noise."

Albright headed to the control console and saw that the QM had already added the contact's course to his screen.

Secondary spoke to the radar tech. "What does it look like?"

She replied, "Two or three ships, sir. They appear to be running with the prevailing winds and are on a possible collision course with us."

"Ok, if you can get any more details, size, number, call us on the bridge. Helm, bring us to heading 310. Engineering, reduce speed by ten percent after turn is complete." He looked back at the QM and said, "Ring the captain."

"Captain. One moment for the XO," said the QM and handed the phone to Secondary.

"Sir, we have a multiple contact on collision course at ten miles out, no visual. Radar thinks they are fishing boats running with the wind, and sonar is receiving odd thudding noises. I have changed course and will reduce speed after the turn."

The captain replied, "Ok. I'll be right up."

"Sir, the turn is complete. We are steering 310," reported the helmsman.

"Reducing speed by ten percent, reduction confirmed, sir." reported the lee helmsman.

"Boatswain's mate, report on lookouts," ordered Secondary.

"Lookouts manning their stations, sir. All reported in place. No visual contact and poor visibility, sir."

Admiral Staff had been reading a book and enjoying a cup of tea when he felt the course change. He looked over the screens in his sitting room and saw the contacts. He thought it was an odd time to stumble across someone out here. He decided to join the bridge crew to see what was going on. As he headed for the bridge, he heard footsteps coming down the passageway and Captain Right came into view.

"Did they wake you up, too, admiral?"

"No, Bill, I was up reading and noticed something was afoot, so I decided to have a look see."

And so they headed up together. As they walked through the bulkhead to the bridge, a voice announced, "Captain on the bridge," and as he noticed the second figure, "Admiral on the bridge."

Bill looked at the admiral who had stopped behind the QM to look at the screens. The admiral noticed and said, "I'm just here to watch the fun."

The captain moved to the quartermaster's station and saw three blips on the screen about five miles out.

"When's this storm going to clear?" asked Right.

"About 0300 hours, sir, and we should have sunshine at dawn," the QM said.

"Good. Then we can have a good look at them," said Right.

"Helmsmen, as soon as they are past us, start a slow turn to bring us on a parallel course and match their speed. Keep us about five miles back. Anyone awake in the box?" he asked the QM.

"Yes, sir, they are monitoring," said the QM.

"Good. Tell them what we are up to and ask if they have anyone who can ID these ships."

"They say they think so and have already sent someone to wake Dr. Whosh," explained the QM.

"Anything new from sonar?" asked Right.

"That noise is still there, but louder now that they're closer. Also, Sir, radar says there may be a fourth contact—smaller and lower in the water," said the QM.

Captain Right rejoined the admiral behind the control station.

"Well, Bill, it's a good thing Ensign Smith is with us. She's fluent in about a dozen languages," said Staff.

"That's good, and there's Dr. North and Lieutenant JG Kurious as well," replied Right

"Bill, your training on the ship is more current than mine, so I'll run the evaluation of the contacts from the flag bridge while you mind your ship."

"Sounds good, but you'll miss all the fun, admiral."

Admiral Staff laughed "If our friends in SB4 can't find a way to get the Constitution home, this adventure of ours will have more opportunities than we can imagine."

They heard someone entering the bridge and turned to see Dr. Whosh and General Rabbit headed their way.

"Amanda and Peter, I see you've come up to see the excitement," quipped Staff.

Right asked if they had any additional contact information.

"Not really," answered Rabbit. "They have no electrical signals at all, so must be from this time. Appear to be built of all wood, but there is some metal—cannon perhaps."

"We've decided Bill will command the Constitution, while I gather everyone else on the flag bridge to address the contacts," said Staff.

"Good idea," replied Whosh.

"I figured we would meet at 0500. The weather is due to clear at 0300 and that will give us time to have a plan in place for sunrise, which is about 0600. We'll need Dr. North,

Ensign Smith, Lieutenant Brice, Lieutenant JG Kurious, and Commander Bird and, of course, both of you," added Staff.

"Sounds good. We'll have our people ready. Keep doing full scans to avoid any surprises and we'll see you at 0500, Admiral," said Amanda.

"I'm going to get a few hours sleep, too, as tomorrow may be a long day," said Staff.

With that the admiral, Dr. Whosh, and General Rabbit departed the bridge.

"Sleep well," said Captain Right as they departed and returned to his duties.

"Captain, the contacts are clear and almost at five miles. Shall I execute the turn now Sir?" asked the helmsman.

Right walked up behind the QM and studied the screens. "Execute turn and match speed."

"Aye, sir, turn commenced," said the helmsman.

About ten minutes passed as the ship turned from 310 to 160.

"Sir, turn complete at heading 160," confirmed the helmsman.

The lee helmsman at the engineering console reported, "Have increased speed by twenty-five percent, sir."

Captain Right waited until the watch changed at 1200 hours. The new watch had settled into their usual routines and he took leave to get some sleep. He left his XO and OOD in charge and headed below with Commander Albright.

"Alex, get a good rest. The admiral may need you to command the gig in the morning, even if just to do a recon of our contacts," said Right.

"Will do, Captain, and I'll put in for a wake-up call," said Albright.

At 0400 hours, both the mess decks and the dining hall were getting ready to serve an early breakfast as the ship's normal routine speeded up for a busy morning. Lieutenant Kurious was on the admiral's bridge by 0430 ensuring his COM team had all their equipment online and Combat Direction Center was ready. All intel was updated, and the big screen was ready for the 0500 briefing. He even had the mess cooks bring up coffee and light breakfast snacks. His wife, Merry, had joined him and jumped right in helping get ready. By 0445, the others started drifting in and getting seated around the large table. Soon Commander Bird, Dr. Whosh, General Rabbit, Dr. North, Doc Bones, Commander Albright, Ensign Smith, and Lieutenant Brice were all seated when someone called, "Attention on deck—Admiral Staff."

He said, "As you were" and sat in his chair.

"Lieutenant Kurious is everyone present?" asked Staff.

"All but the captain, sir, and he is on his way from the bridge," said Lieutenant Kurious.

Merry handed the admiral a cup of Joe and he said, "I can see Admiral Snoopy has you well trained."

"I learned it all in spy school, sir, and thanks to you, my field training has become quite the adventure," said Merry.

Captain Right walked up behind Merry and said, "Your daily reports to the Office of Naval Intelligence will rewrite the history of the Navy."

The admiral added, "As soon as we are sure we have a secure link we'll send them, or maybe we could get Dr. Whosh to drop us off at Old man Snoopy's back door for supper. That should be a shocker."

Everyone chuckled at the thought of surprising the head of the Office of Naval Intelligence by delivering a field report to him. And with something so beyond "Secret" that he was never told about them.

When Captain Right and Merry were seated, Right said, "I just posted extra watches so we will not have any collisions."

"That's good," replied the Admiral.

"Lieutenant Kurious, can you brief us on where we stand?" asked Staff.

"Yes, sir," said the Lieutenant, "At 2130 hours radar reported a contact at relative bearing 300 at sixteen miles. As it got closer it resolved into a multiple contact of three or four ships, which appear to be running in the wind. Sonar is receiving an odd thudding sound, like loose timbers. Since we were on a collision course, we slowed and turned to the north bearing 310. Once they had cleared us we turned to bearing 160 and have been following them at about five miles astern. The storm cleared at 0315 and the skies are clear. We expect sunrise at 0604 and should have visual contact at that time. The vessels appear to be wood-frame sailing. Perhaps fishing vessels; however, amounts of metal have been scanned by Sand Box 4 that could indicate they are armed with cannon. The contacts are displayed on the large screen. Engineering and weather on the smaller screens." said Lieutenant Kurious. "Any questions?"

"Can we hear the sonar contact?" asked Ensign Smith.

"Yes," said Kurious and walked to the console to turn up the volume.

"Sounds like it could be breaking up. Do all four contacts look the same?" Smith inquired.

"No, the fourth appears low in the water or perhaps smaller, and the others appear to be staying around it," said Kurious.

"Could the storm have damaged one of them last night?" asked Rabbit.

"Very possible. They came from where the storm was more intense," answered Albright. "If one of them is breaking up that would explain why the others are that close."

The admiral asked Dr. Whosh, "Does SB4 have any standing orders about intervention?"

"No. We were never given any. I assume yours are to render assistance and rescue to ships in distress at sea," replied Whosh.

"Yes, it's standard naval policy," said Staff, "So first we must assess the problem, if there is one. Then we can decide what to do. Commander Bird, have your men prep three Seahawks. We can use one for a closer look and have the others stand by if we need them. Also prep the Hawkeye, so we can get a good look around us and, while you're at it, have them prep two Hornets and two Tomcats. It should make your Airedales happy to have some work to do."

Bird grabbed the phone and issued the orders, while the admiral continued on. "Albright, I'm told you're the skipper of our gig. Can you have it ready to launch if we need her?"

"I already have a boatswain's mate with a gang of deck apes getting her ready, admiral."

"General Rabbit, contact, evaluation, research, and security are your strong suit. We have Dr. North, Ensign Smith, and Lieutenant Brice with multi-language backgrounds to help. What do you recommend we do about an away team if we make contact?" asked Staff.

"Well, admiral, we also have the two Kuriouses and with the link between our computers they can search both for historical help. With both the gig and Seahawks ready, a team could make contact with either or just observe from a safe distance. I like the Hawkeye going up for a look see. We have two teams ready. Lieutenant Brice's team would be best to send in first since they are most familiar with this liquid environment. My own team can back them up. Doc Bones has volunteered to go with them, so your medical team will be ready for any emergency work. Can the video feeds from the choppers feed back to your big screen, Lieutenant Kurious?"

"Yes, no problem."

"Then we can coordinate all operations from here," said Rabbit. "Commander Bird, are you arming the aircraft?"

"Yes, all my birds will launch armed with multi-purpose ordnance."

Captain Right added, "Combat Direction Center is already fully manned, so the ship will have full countermeasures ready in case the wooden boats turn out to be something else."

"It all sounds good to me, admiral. Shall we go get our teams ready?" asked Rabbit.

"Are you going to lead the first away team, Rabbit?"

"No, sir, your Lieutenant Brice is a match for whatever is out there, but I may tag along as civilian consultant so Bones won't have all the fun."

The admiral got to his feet. "Then let's do it, folks. The dawn cometh and waits for no one."

Both teams suited up and got ready to launch with the gig or a chopper. The Hawkeye, the four jets, and the three choppers were on the flight deck and ready. The air boss was ready at Pri-Fly. The gig was ready to launch with Albright, his boatswain's mate, and crew ready. The ship had turned into the wind and the Hawkeye had been launched off catapults number three. A jet sat on both catapults one and two. With the bird away, the captain had ordered they close the gap to one mile. The ship's security team was standing by in case anyone tried to board the ship.

The boatswain's mate said, "Captain, we have closed to one mile."

"Good. Hold position and match speed and course," said Right.

"Reduced speed and holding, sir."

The captain had on his headset and toggled the switch for the flag bridge.

"Lieutenant Kurious, let the admiral know we are on station at one mile and holding."

"He heard you, Captain, and said to let you know the air boss will be launching a Seahawk in ten minutes. Lieutenant Brice and Dr. North with a small team will be with them to ID our bogies. We'll have the cameras on, so your quartermaster can put it up on your screen."

"Thanks, lieutenant. We'll do that. I don't want to miss the show even if I have to watch it on TV."

The Seahawk lifted off the deck and headed toward the boats so they would be on station at sunrise. Most of the crew not busy found a TV screen to watch. The children gathered around Dr. Whosh to watch on the big screen. They were all excited to have some real interesting news to share with Fern when they talked next. And with all eyes glued to the horizon, the dawn of a new day arrived.

The camera feeds switched to the Seahawk's feed as they approached from the stern. They finally saw their contacts, and they were sailing ships. Three of the ships had their sails set and they were about one hundred feet long. But the most striking thing was the fourth ship, which was between the two rear ships. Its masts were gone and it was very low in the water. There were lines running to both ships on either side and a line to the ship ahead of it.

Finally, Lieutenant Brice found her voice and spoke into her mike, "Admiral, they are towing the fourth ship even though it looks ready to sink. All the ships have damage and there are wounded on the decks of all the ships. It looks like they are trying to get their people off the fourth ship. North and Smith agree they are Chinese and all four have the same design, markings, and equipment."

The chopper flew slowly around the ships and she continued, "They are armed with small canon, sir, but shouldn't be a threat to us. Also, it appears from the side that they have been in a firefight. They've noticed us and seem afraid of the chopper. They haven't noticed the ship yet. They'll see her when we finish our circle around. She looks huge against the sun. Sir, I recommend we render immediate assistance and launch the gig. Maybe if we can calm their fears, we can then use the birds to help them move the wounded."

"I agree," announced the admiral. "Captain, launch the gig."

"The orders have been given."

The boatswain's mate called out, "We're reversing thrust to slow the ship, sir."

Bones and the Marines were already onboard and the fifty-foot gig was swinging out over the water on the two supporting cranes. Albright gave the order to lower her. She was in the water before the ship had stopped. The boatswain's mate gave the gig full throttle and his crew with help from the Marines got the lines free. Then the gig surged away from the ship as her powerful twin engines pushed her through the water. It was a cross between a yacht and a sport fishing boat with a large forward cabin and a large open deck in the rear. Her function was to haul people and cargo when the ship was at anchor with no dock available.

Albright reported, "Admiral, we are in the water and free. You can resume speed and we'll meet the chopper enroute."

General Rabbit was topside with his men. He chimed in, "They left without me, darn. I'll have to catch a ride before you're done out there."

The captain ordered, "Resume speed and course. Our engineering officer seems to be off to the races."

"Sir, we are underway," said the boatswain's mate, and then added, "Too bad I had the watch. Would have been fun to be his driver."

"Well, let see if you can catch up and then hold us at two thousand feet back," said Right.

"With pleasure, sir," His bridge crew closed the gap.

The Seahawk swung around behind the gig and held position over the speeding boat. Brice and Smith grabbed a zip line and slid to the deck like cats jumping off a roof. Tracy was more old-fashioned about it and used the ladder but landed with equal ease and smiled to herself hoping that Dew didn't have a heart attack watching.

On the flag bridge, Vary and Merry Kurious were busy keeping the intel flowing and the video on-screen. The admiral was staring out of the bridge window at the unfolding saga when he noticed a silent figure had joined him.

"Cookie, isn't it?"

"Yes, sir. I didn't mean to intrude. I was just looking for a place I could watch. Bones doesn't get much chance to be a doctor in the box and his patients don't have guns or swords."

"It's not easy when our loved ones are in harm's way," said Staff. "When I last heard from my Stella, she was with the president. But she was leaving there to rescue Bob Cybernaut's wife and son from the woods of New Hampshire. Then she was returning to Hawaii where some madman blew up the wing of a hospital to kill John Doe and now she's living in an abandoned WWII underground bunker." He put his arm around the younger woman and led her over to the overstuffed chair by the window. "You sit there and watch," Staff said.

"But that's your chair, sir."

"Cookie, I'm going to tell you a secret. I'm so nervous during an operation I never sit down—just pace the floor and drive those two crazy."

He helped her into the chair and she thanked him. Just then Merry arrived with coffee and handed Cookie a cup.

"See, you have to get out of your kitchen more so we can return the favor and serve you once in a while." Merry looked over at Vary and said to Cookie, "It makes me glad my man is the bookworm type."

Meanwhile, the gig was closing on the ships and Brice was telling Albright the best way to approach was from the stern of the damaged ship. They decided to keep the gunner's mate off the .50 cal unless they were fired on first. Brice told him she and Smith would board first. Being women they had a better chance of being allowed to speak before someone decided to attack them.

The boatswain's mate steered them up against the stern of the damaged ship. The three women, Lieutenant Brice and Ensign Smith moved to the bow, followed by Tracy North. Two deckhands, one on each side of the bow, had a line with a grappling hook to hold the gig in place. The others stayed back on the deck trying not to look like an aggressive force. The boatswain's mate eased the gig firmly against the ship and kept the engine thrust holding her in place.

Before the gig made contact, Brice and Smith leaped to the ship's deck and came to a stop before the group of men who had been working on the deck. They stood to face the two women, and armed sailors were leaping onboard from the other ships.

Before anyone could speak, Tracy North, the smallest of the three women, who was dressed in jeans and a shirt, walked right up to the whole group facing down the two Amazons in black. Tracy walked up in front of the best-dressed man on the far side of the deck assuming he was the ship's captain and started talking to him in Chinese. Everything stopped. All the armed sailors and Marines halted where they were and everyone looked at Tracy, talking a mile a minute to the ship's captain. Soon he started replying and the two were having a very animated conversation.

Ensign Smith stepped up to a huge sailor who, even though badly hurt, had been trying to rip up the deck. "What are you trying to do?" she asked in her best Chinese.

After a momentary look of confusion on his face, he replied, "There are sailors and our leader's son trapped below."

Shela said, "Show me where and we'll help you get them out."

He led her to the place in the deck they were trying to break through. Brice, now finding herself being ignored, joined Tracy.

As they talked, another well-dressed man climbed aboard and ran to where they were attacking the deck. Tracy explained that Japanese pirates had attacked the ships before the storm, while they were charting the ocean. Brice asked the captain if she could bring her men to help with the rescue and to treat the wounded, and he agreed. The captain sent his sailors back to their duties, and she signaled the rescue teams aboard.

Bones and the medics started collecting the wounded and treating them. An emergency bilge pump was brought onboard and they started sucking water out of the sinking ship. Charly was just finishing updating the admiral when Harry came across the deck with a chainsaw in his hand.

"Where'd you come from and how'd you find that?"

"I'm just a civilian stowaway here to help make a hole."

Shela explained what Harry was going to do and got everyone to give him some room. Once the chainsaw roared to life, they backed up a little more. But even with the saw it was hard work cutting the hardwood planks and beams of the deck. Meanwhile, everyone else worked to keep the ship floating. Bones treated those he could and had the more serious moved to the gig for the trip to the ship's hospital.

Tracy found out from Capt. Hsing Jung that the other well-dressed man was Ma Sung, who was their head navigator and chart maker. Ma Sung's teenage son, Lan, was one of those stuck on the sinking ship. The big guy Bones was trying to get to hold still while he tended his wounds was Yuan Khan, the boy's bodyguard.

Now there were two emergency pumps sucking water out of the sinking ship. Harry, the ship's sailors, and Brice's men were making the hole big enough to get the trapped men out. Bones had transferred all the seriously injured to the ship's sickbay and patched up everyone else, except the big guy. He really needed to go to sickbay, but wouldn't go anywhere until the boy was found. Bones dressed his wounds the best he could and now was waiting with the medics for those who were stuck below the deck.

Sickbay was working on close to twenty men and had both operating rooms in full swing. Luckily both the doctors had spent many of their free hours during the ship's upgrade and overhaul working as volunteers in the local hospital's emergency rooms. It had sharpened their skills saving the gangbangers and their victims in a city where violence had become commonplace.

They were finally making real headway on the deck of the Chinese ship. As fast as Harry could make the second cut on the planks, Yuan Khan would rip them out with his bare hands. Soon the hole was big enough to see the men below. All eyes were focused on the smoking saw blade as it ate through the planks one by one. The sweat was dripping off Harry in buckets and Charly kept pouring cool water on him. Yuan Khan's hands were covered in blood, but he refused to back away from the task. As they ripped out the last planks in the way, several of the men who could, started climbing out into the fresh air. Shela and Charly leaped into the hole to help the wounded climb out. Bones and the medics sent those who needed sickbay to the gig and patched up the others. They handed up several who were beyond help and they were placed to the side.

By now, the look on Yuan Khan's face was one of agony. All that kept him from jumping into the hole was Harry, who had a firm grip on the big guy. On the other side of the hole, Ma Sung stood with stark fear etched on his face with Capt. Hsing Sung standing at his side. Below, Charly and Shela searched with the waterproof torches from the gig, but it was slow work in all the water and floating debris.

The gig was returning to the ship with the wounded, but was hardly noticed as all eyes watched the drama unfolding around the hole. The ship's long-range optics were focused on this scene and almost everyone was glued to a screen with their breaths held. The admiral and Captain Right were among them, with worry obvious on their faces. The bridge had become silent like most of the ship.

The silence was broken as a voice from CDC boomed over the speakers. "Captain, we have multiple contacts at 220 about ten miles and closing fast. They are coming in on the far side of the Chinese ships and heading right for them. No engine sounds on sonar, sir."

Before Captain Right, who was out of his chair headed for the quartermaster, could speak, the boatswain's mate said, "Sir, the gig is alongside off-loading wounded."

The admiral stood before the tactical display and spoke into his headset. "Captain, we lost contact with Brice and Smith when they went down that hole to rescue those sailors. The Chinese do not seem to have noticed their visitors yet. Bird, how long to get the choppers airborne?"

"Ten minutes max, sir. My men are on it, and Rabbit has half his team onboard. I also have two jets on the catapults, two on the flight deck, and two more on the way up. The Hawkeye is returning."

"Albright, what's your status?"

"Admiral, I'll have the wounded onboard the ship and can be away in five minutes. Also, General Rabbit and his men are already aboard."

"Good. Let us know when you are clear," said Staff.

As the last of the wounded was pulled onto the hanger deck, the gig cut loose from the ship and was at full speed when Albright spoke into his mike, "This is Albright, Admiral. We're clear and enroute at flank speed."

The captain, who was listening, ordered, "Helmsman, begin your turn into the wind and then bring her up to launch speed."

"The choppers are away," Bird announced.

CDC came back over the speakers. "We have three contacts closing on the Chinese ships—one almost on them and new multiple contacts at 280, twenty miles. Our count is seven—no make that eight and at least one is big. All appear to be wood with sails and no engine noise."

The admiral spoke to Bird, "We need our eyes in the sky."

"Will be there in ten minutes," replied Bird.

In the meantime, the gig sped toward the Chinese ships, with the three choppers coming up fast behind the ships.

The saga aboard the sinking ship had not changed much. Brice and Smith had fought their way to the forward end of the compartment. They found the hatchway blocked, but could just faintly hear someone beyond. Working together, they used their muscles to pull debris out of the way until they could get through. There they found two men doing their best to hold up a boy. Smith took Lan and Brice helped the two men out through all the flotsam. When they got to the hole, they lifted Smith and Lan up to the waiting arms of the men above. Lan was very weak, but he recognized his father who was kneeling at his side. Opposite, Bones' examination soon found the problem. Lan had a seriously deep cut in his side, which had bled a lot. The boy could go into shock if he did not act fast. Bones explained what he had found as he continued his examination, and Tracy repeated it in Chinese.

It was about then, with all eyes on Lan and his rescuers that everything happened at once. A cry went up on the ship on the portside. The gig slammed into the sinking ship. Rabbit and his men leaped aboard with weapons ready. They charged aboard that portside ship to meet the invading Japanese pirates head on as they swarmed over the unsuspecting Chinese sailors.

At the same moment, the three choppers came racing to the ships. One hovered right over the sinking ship and more of

Rabbit's men gliding to the deck on a zip line and also joined the raging battle on the other ship. The pilot, seeing Bones and his patient, sent down the rescue basket. Bones lifted the scared Lan into it and Tracy jumped on top of Lan to hold him in as she kept reassuring him it would be ok. Bones stepped back and up went the basket just as a group of pirates broke through to attack them. One was coming right at the captain and Ma Sung, but Yuan Khan stepped in front of them to take the blow of the pirate's raised sword. But the sudden roar of a chainsaw caused the pirate to look at the source of the noise and what he saw was the blade coming down. The sword and his arm fell as one to the deck as Yuan Khan threw him into the pirates behind him.

The basket returned with a thud on the deck. Bones grabbed Yuan Khan and told him to get in the basket. He did and lay face down as he had seen Tracy do. There was no time to explain. Capt. Hsing Jung motioned to Bones to take Ma Sung too. Bones thought fast and grabbed the zip line and tied it around Ma Sung's waist, showing him to hold the line tight. With that he leaped onto the basket and the pilot started pulling up. Once clear, they got the three men on board and headed for the carrier.

On the bridge Bird announced, "We have a chopper inbound with wounded and Doc Bones."

Cookie turned when she heard this. The admiral had already told a sailor to take her to meet them. She hugged him tight and then she ran for the hatch with the sailor.

Back on the Chinese ships, Capt. Hsing Jung took sword in hand and joined in liberating his ships. J.P. Smith had been helping on the deck and was far away from his weapon. All he had was a Ka-Bar and his knapsack of explosives. A fast look around told him no one was paying any attention to him, so he put on the pack and slipped over the side into the water. He swam around to the far side of the pirate's ship and when he got to the middle, he swam down below the water line. There, he stuck the Ka-Bar in as far as it would go into the wood. Then he securely attached the knapsack and started swimming back. He went all the way to the farthest ship and climbed up a rope hanging over the side.

The sailors were busy setting the sails as Captain Hsing Jung barked orders. Harry, Shela, Charly, and Rabbit were standing with him. Rabbit was giving orders on his radio.

Shela looked at her soaking wet brother and said, "This is a heck of a time to go swimming."

"Just taking care of business, Sis."

Rabbit said, "Well those pirates are about to blow that ship to bits with their cannons and I can't get any help here fast enough."

J.P. smiled and pulled a waterproof bag out of his pocket. He opened it, took out the little device, flipped a switch, and a red light came on. Then he pushed the button. Almost immediately, a huge explosion rocked the pirate ship. When it settled back in the water it was listing badly toward the far side.

He said to Rabbit, "I think, General that will take their minds off shooting any cannons."

Harry laughed, "That's a big firecracker, J.P."

The second pirate ship was closing fast, but one of the Seahawks was flying straight at her amidships.

The pilot called the air boss. "Sir, we are taking incoming fire. Permission to return fire."

"Permission granted. Open fire," said Bird.

With a flick of his wrist the co-pilot sent a rocket screaming from the bottom of the chopper. It hit right below the water line and the ship suddenly blew in half, with a lot of the middle missing. The third pirate ship was headed right for the gig, with the hope of broadsiding it with their cannons. The gunner's mate yelled to the boatswain's mate at the wheel to get him a clear view of the masts. The third chopper was on its way but not close enough to help yet. The GM fired his .50 in short bursts. Suddenly the lead mast toppled onto the deck. He fired again and the middle mast fell with the first. Once more he fired, and the third and last mast fell into the water.

He looked down at Albright and the boatswain's mate said. "That should slow them down. Now can you get us out of here before they can shoot back?"

"With pleasure," said Albright and they headed to the Chinese ships.

The forward ship was now under sail and pulling away. The starboard ship was also pulling free, but the third ship was in trouble and not getting out from between the other two. As Albright brought the gig around, he saw the problem. He pulled the gig in front of the other ship's bow. They tossed the biggest line they had up to the ship and, once it was tied off, slowly powered up the gig's engines. Little happened at first, but ever so slowly the ship started to move forward and away from the pirate menace. Soon the four were sailing south, as the choppers ferried the wounded to the ship.

Back on the Constitution, the Seahawk brought Bones, North, Yuan Khan, Ma Sung, and his son Lan onboard. Bones directed the corpsmen to take these wounded to his sickbay on Sand Box 4. He knew Lan couldn't afford to wait in line for treatment. As Bones stepped onto the deck, he was almost bowled over by Cookie. As they headed to sickbay, they were greeted by everyone and of course Dew, Alice, and all the children. Bones put Lan on the operating table since he needed the most attention and wheeled in a gurney for Yuan Khan.

James and Chrissy thought it was great to have real people to talk with in the Chinese they had learned with their mother. In fact, they liked it so much they would soon became the official candy-stripers cheering up all the wounded. But they'd spend hours with Lan, who was their age. Even Fred and Krista would soon start speaking fluent Chinese. Sue would, too, but at five years old she'd mostly have fun with everyone and get even the grumpiest sailors to smile.

Meanwhile on the bridge, the boatswain's mate said, "Captain we are at optimum course and speed for flight opts."

Captain Right stepped into Pri-Fly and said to Bird. "You're green to launch."

He replied, "Thanks," and gave the order. Ten minutes later, he had six fighters in the air. The choppers were bringing in the last of the wounded and the four ships and the gig were headed away from the Japanese pirates. CDC had reported more contacts and the Hawkeye brought it up to twenty, not counting those they'd already engaged. They were all now heading in the direction of the Constitution.

Captain Right picked up the private phone to the admiral. "Sir, I don't think it's a good idea to start an all-out war with the Japanese, even if they are pirates. I do have an idea though that might work into scaring them enough to leave us alone. Our gunner's mate on the gig brought one of their ships to a halt by shooting the masts off with a .50 caliber. Our jets could do the same thing, but to really scare them I suggest we sail right through the middle of them at top speed."

The admiral asked, "Kind of like playing chicken the way we did as kids?"

"Well, yes, sort of."

"Well, I hope you find a creative way to log this maneuver to terrify the pirate hordes that won't get us court marshaled when we get your ship home."

"I'll do my creative best, sir."

They hung up. Right then headed to talk with Bird.
He explained his plan and asked if the jets could take out at least fifty percent of the masts. Bird said they could, but the Seahawks might be better at surgically disabling the ships. He would have them all back in a few minutes to refuel and rearm them.

Back on the bridge Right told the QM to sound General Quarters and set condition Zebra ten minutes later. He also told them he needed to keep all hands off any open area. The QM pressed the GQ button and the alarm sounded throughout the ship. Then he spoke into the 1MC microphone. "General Quarters, all hands, man your battle stations. This is not a drill. Condition Zebra will be set in ten minutes. All hands whose battle stations are in open areas will stay inside the ship's hull. We expect to be fired upon by pirates with cannons."

Captain Right talked with the boatswain's mate and explained what they were up to. The BM volunteered to take the helm.

"Good," said Right. "We'll have the forward cameras on the screen in front of you. Commander Secondary, we need to call the engineering officer to have the speed governors turned off. There are no Russian satellites to watch us today."

They both spoke to the EO and gave the authorization codes. Now all was ready. Bird's choppers were back in the air.

"We have a large ship out there with five masts, which is the one we want to come close to, said Right.

"I have it, sir," said BM, "and have lined us up."

"Then give us flack speed. Let's see what this ship can do," ordered Right.

The QM announced on the 1MC, "All hands, brace for high-speed maneuvering."

Many decks below, a second class IC electrician, Max Knight, sat at his desk wondering what madness the officers on the bridge were up to, as he watched the pit sword's digital readout climb. The whole ship was vibrating with the kind of power one feels in a speedboat. It went to 20 knots, 25, then 30, and 35, 40, 45. Now he was out of his chair. Carriers did not go this fast as it hit 50! He stood there transfixed, holding on tight to the workbench as at last it stopped at 52 and held.

His eyes turned to the TV screen that was showing what was in front of the bow. He felt weak in the knees as he saw the huge sailing ship come up on the starboard side. They had to be mad. *They'll hit it*, he thought. But it passed out of view and many smaller ones whizzed past too.

It had to be the time travel, he decided as he sat back down to watch in total disbelief. Maybe he wouldn't reenlist. That civilian telephone job was looking better by the moment. He'd joined the U.S. Navy, but this was Star Wars and beyond. Then there was that Sand Box that defied reason. Yes, he needed to go on leave with a case of wine and no water for miles.

Those on the bridge watched as they slid past the big sailing ship so close they could smell what they were having for lunch. They swamped three of the smaller ships. The fighters and choppers moved right in behind them and on ten of the ships only left one mast standing on each. As the ship turned to the south they recovered the six jets and the three Seahawks. GQ was ended and condition X-Ray set. The emergencies in sickbay had been all tended to with no lost lives. They were headed to rejoin the gig and the three Chinese ships. The

Hawkeye was making a big circle to find out what else was out there.

Ma Sung had explained they were part of a bigger fleet of ships and they had gone farther North to chart a bigger area. That was when they met the pirates and had to run for their lives. Ma Sung then told them about where they should find the rest of their fleet, and the Hawkeye was headed there.

At the moment, the E-2 Hawkeye was flying south approaching the point where they must turn east to start circling back to the Constitution. There was about five more miles before they had to turn, so they could complete their circle.

"Sir, I have a contact at forty miles dead ahead," said the radar man, "Wait a minute, it is a multiple."

"Is our feed to the ship live?" asked the pilot.

"Yes, they'll see this," replied the radioman.

The pilot asked the navigator, "Have we got enough fuel to check them out?"

"Yes, but we'll have to fly back for fuel without finishing the full loop," he replied.

"Ok, keep an eye on that fuel. I want to know before we hit the point of no return."

"Sir, I'll be sure to tell you, 'cause I have no desire to swim with them big sharks down there."

"Air Boss, are you reading our data stream?" asked the pilot.

"We confirm that your signal is five by five. We are waiting for the live video."

"We'll go get it, Boss."

"Sir, I have about twenty contacts on screen and more keep appearing," said the radar man. "Sir, I'm starting to lose count. I've started our computer identification programs and asked it to give us a summary and profile of contacts. We'll have to let the ship's big computers work on this there are so many. My readout is showing over one hundred contacts, some between four and five hundred feet long. All appear to be wood hull with sails for propulsion. Sir, our video feed has started picking up ships. The bigger ones are farther ahead."

Lan and Yuan Khan were in hospital beds in Sand Box 4's sickbay, with most of the children in attendance as the Hawkeye's camera brought the Chinese fleet into view. All of the visitors were in awe of this modern magic that could make their fleet visible even though it was days away by sail. This new adventure and the promise of meeting another admiral named Zheng He, who commanded the fleet for the Ming Dynasty, excited all the children.

Ma Sung was on the bridge with Admiral Staff. His eyes kept going back and forth between the large tactical screen, which showed where the Chinese fleet was, and the screen that was showing the pictures of the ships as the Hawkeye flew over. On the decks of the ships they could see the amazed sailors, some of who were obviously afraid of the huge bird that roared over their heads like a flying dragon.

Ma Sung started telling Tracy North how his fleet would be arranged. He was amazed to see on this screen what he had only imagined before in his mind's eye. He explained where Admiral He's ship should be and Staff directed the Hawkeye's course.

Ma Sung became very excited when the admiral's ship came in view on the screen. The entire crew and the sailors in sickbay all watched as history unfolded before them. Some of the sailors, who feared they would never go home, now sat up in bed watching these strange moving images of their ships from home. It was reassuring to see their connection to their world and families. They could even clearly see Adm. Zheng He standing on his ship watching the Hawkeye fly over. The Hawkeye circled around the admiral's ship three times and at the end of the third loop it flew over the ship stern to bow, and then set a course directly to the Constitution. Admiral He, knowing birds must fly to land, decided to follow this strange creature and see where it would land.

As the two admirals sailed toward a historic meeting, Ma Sung was busy learning from his new friends and telling them about his world. He spent many hours reading the ship's navigator's charts and talking about how charts were made. One evening, his new friends displayed a chart on the screen Ma Sung knew well because it was one he made. This historic picture, however, was of a map he would draw in the future. His trained eyes studied the parts of the map he had yet to draw, as he would go there in days to come. He looked for long moments at the date placed on the map in his writing. Yes, this was all very amazing.

That evening as they all gathered for their evening meal, Ma Sung told the life story of the admiral whom he served. The sailors too spoke of their great leader. Young Lan also told the tale to the children of the future and their parents who had shown him great courage and respect. They had all gathered around Lan's bed to hear history first hand.

"Our great warrior leader, Adm. Zheng He, whose spiritual name is Sanbao, which means 'Three Jewels,' stands tall over other men like a mighty tree. He was born in the province of Yunnan in southwest China fifty years ago. His name at was birth was Ma He and his family were of the Muslim faith. At the age of ten, he entered the service of the Ming Dynasty and at thirteen following the path of a eunuch and was assigned to the household of Prince Zhu Di, the fourth son of the emperor. With Prince Zhu Di, he became a warrior and leader. His service defending against the Mongols of the north brought him to the prince's attention. China had been in a long civil war when the prince marched on Beijing and then Nanjing to become emperor. Admiral He was among his military commanders. His actions were so great that he earned the highest military rank. It was there upon becoming a Buddhist that his name was changed by Emperor Zhu Di to Zheng He, and he was given the commission as admiral of the emperor's fleet. The fleet was created under the guidance of the admiral who has completed many voyages beyond the known land to discover wonderful new places. He has brought back all kinds of treasurers, discoveries, made alliances, and opened trade routes."

Continuing, Lan said, "Adm. Zheng He has built a fleet of over three hundred ships, more than fifty of which are five hundred or more feet long with as many as nine masts and a dozen sails. These huge ships could carry 1,500 tons of cargo. The ships were built with watertight compartments to prevent sinking. They were equipped with center stern rudders for greater steering control. They also carried magnetic compasses for navigation and they created over two dozen maps of the oceans they sailed. There were over thirty thousand officers and men who served in Adm. Zheng He's fleet. The Chinese are truly the masters of the oceans."

The Constitution was traveling at a leisurely pace as it followed Capt. Hsing Jung and his three ships toward Adm. Zheng He's fleet. It was the early morning watch when the radar contacts were announced to the bridge. By 0800 hours Capt. Hsing Jung was aboard Admiral He's ship and the Constitution was running a parallel course to the ship. General

Rabbit, Lieutenant Brice, Ensign Smith, and Harry Haul all returned to the Constitution and were replaced by Adm. Zheng He's sailors. He also took all the wounded aboard his ship so his personal doctors could attend them, although most were well on the mend.

Adm. Zheng He and Capt. Hsing Jung came aboard the Constitution for a formal dinner with Adm. Flagg Staff and Captain Right. Tracy North was their translator. There was a meal fit for an emperor and much talk of great adventures. Adm. Zheng He thanked Admiral Staff for rescuing his ships and healing his men, especially for saving young Lan. The flying dragon that he followed was of great amazement, even more so that men traveled in the belly of the flying dragon, and that there was a whole flock of these iron birds sleeping in their huge nest. It was more amazing that it was as light inside as outside with no smelly oil lamps. There were also moving paintings that looked like windows or a mirror to somewhere else. The Constitution, a huge ship with no sails that could move like the wind itself and made of iron stronger than his best sword or cannon was the most amazing of all.

On their tour, Adm. Zheng He met the two women who had fought beside his sailors, showing no fear of the murderous pirates and then leaping into the belly of the sinking ship with a mother's courage to save his men and Lan trapped there. These women, Lieutenant Brice, and Ensign Smith, were obvious leaders of great worth. Sir Harry Haul, whose roaring sword cut the strongest deck timbers and pirates as well, was a great man. Commander Albright, who came to their aid, and General Rabbit, whose men fought the pirates with his sailors, had great courage. Doctor Bones, who came to the sinking ship to save his men, was a healer most extraordinary. Captain

Right, who scattered the pirates to the four winds with his great ship and metal birds, was a fine warrior.

But perhaps the most touching to the great admiral who stood some eight feet tall was when Lan brought all the children to meet him. Lan told the admiral of the knowledge he'd learned from them and now he could become a great explorer like the admiral. He sat down in a chair to be closer to their height and young Sue Sparks climbed right into his lap. She told the admiral in her best Chinese that he was the biggest man she had ever met in her whole life, that he must have many children. He looked sadly at Sue and explained that he had no children, to which she replied he would have to be her grandfather. Sue hugged him tightly, which seemed to please him greatly. Tracy North smiled. It would seem that Admiral He had formed new alliances with the future in more ways than one.

"This has been an adventurous voyage where we've charted new seas and met some of the most interesting people," said Admiral He. "I wish I could stay longer and continue our travels together, but I must return to Beijing for the dedication of the emperor's palace. Gugong, called the Forbidden City by some, is a grand palace of almost ten thousand rooms. So I must return home to honor my emperor, whom I've served since I was a young lad like Lan."

After Tracy had finished translating for the admiral she thoughtfully said, "It will be good for you to be at his side during this time. He'll need you in the great adventure that'll happen there."

They all said their good-byes and stood on the deck watching the boat with Adm. Zheng He, Capt. Hsing Jung, Ma Sung, Yuan Khan, and young Lan make for the admiral's magnificent ship. They would voyage home to the Emperor.

Meanwhile, the Constitution would continue on its search for truth in Guam. The children would be very quiet that night, with their new friend gone back to his world. Captain Right gave the orders and they slowly weaved their way out of the admiral's fleet, and well before dark they were alone on the ocean heading west into the setting sun to where their destiny awaited.

At the rail of his ship Admiral He watched the Constitution depart until it vanished over the horizon. His fleet had their orders and under Capt. Hsing Jung would finish their mission, while he returned to Emperor Zhu Di and his grand palace of Gugong. Ma Sung and Lan stood there with the admiral.

Lan wondered aloud, "Will we ever see them again?"

"Son, they are much like a vision from Allah that we should use wisely. One day their commander, Dew North, who is their navigator, was showing me the different ways they use to find their way. His wife who is a doctor tells me she has seen one of my maps at a great museum in the capital of their country. I was curious which one it could be and she tells me she can find a picture of it on what they call a computer. And there it was all in my handwriting and signed by me. They even gave me a copy," said Ma Sung.

He took out the map and laid it before the admiral, who recognized the work.

"My admiral, we have not been to these far off lands and look at the date I signed the map. It is ten years from now in the future. How can they see our future with their devices?"

"I think I can answer that," said Lan. "At first, I thought they were having fun with me and telling me silly things. They showed me their amazing machines and their elders talked with me freely and said the same things. So James and Fred showed me how to use their computers, which teach them lessons in anything they want to know. Krista and Chrissy introduced me to Fern, a boy they talk to who lives underground in a cave on an island they call Hawaii, which is far to the east of here. They are hiding him and his mother there because some pirates tried to kill them. I think the Constitution was out hunting for those pirates when they found us. They told me they have a device that can travel through time, which must be how they got here. All of the dates on their computers and the calendars on their walls say they are from their year 2012. While it shows the current date as the year 1421 and their computers know that too. It even gives both dates when one asks."

The two older men were quiet for some time thinking about what Lan had said. Finally, the admiral spoke in hushed tones. "The path to knowledge our new friends have awakened in you, Lan is much like the path the monks have shown me to the enlightenment taught by Buddha."

He slowly removed a picture of little Sue holding him that Dr. Tracy North had given him. After looking at it for minutes, he said, "Well, if I am 641 in their years, then little Sue is right. I am old enough to be a grandfather."

They all laughed at that.

"Young Lan, you learn fast and we must ensure it does not stop because great adventures await you," said Admiral He. "Now we sail west into the sunset on a true course to the Forbidden City."

AS THE DAWN FOUR

A Fairy Tale

The USS Constitution Steaming West for Guam in the Year 1421:

Since they had left Adm. Zheng He's fleet behind, things had become quiet. The children returned to their studies. After Bones cleaned sickbay three times, he could not stand its emptiness any more and joined Cookie in her galley and parked by the coffee urn, perhaps hoping it would attract someone who needed his help. Harry and Charly had been wandering the flight deck under the stars. They passed Alice and J.P. who told them that Admiral Staff, the Kuriouses, Doc Whosh, and General Rabbit where talking with President Puritan White and General Frost in D.C. and Captain Kid at the Scout bunker. Bob talked with Kate for a while when the matters of state were in hand, and later the kids chatted with Fern.

Alice said, "It sounds like Fern wishes he were here rather than hiding like a mole in a mountain."

Harry laughed. "I'll have to tell that boy he doesn't know when he's got it good. Only place for us to walk here is on this floating airport with no grass or rocks to climb. In fact, that Chinese junk was more fun than this. We where right there with Mother Nature and could feel the ocean beneath, full of life and energy."

Meanwhile, Amanda and Peter had joined Bones and Cookie. They found some new Chinese delights had arrived thanks to some good trading. Vary and Merry must have smelled them, for they arrived next. Flagg and Bob were chatting with their wives at the Scout bunker. When they were done they too found their way to the great smelling desserts.

They were all surprised when the children all joined them about twenty minutes later. They normally talked for hours, but tonight they just did not have much to say and decided to eat. The four stargazers strolled in and noted the children being very quiet at one table. Even Sue, who was usually everywhere at once talking to anyone who would listen. She sat poking at a dessert she would normally inhale.

Harry spoke up, "No place for a campfire. Guess I'll get a cup of coffee and fake it."

Charly, Alice, and J.P. followed his lead, got their drinks and some of Cookie's desserts. They then followed him to a table next to the kids. Harry sat with his back to the wall so he could face the kids.

Once everyone was comfortable, he said loudly and with emotion in his voice, "I have this friend who used to be a sailor. Well, he's retired now and lives so far in the White Mountains that a drunken sailor would never find him. But late one night as we sat around the campfire he told me a story about a ship he was once on." He stopped to pause as if the next words stuck in his throat. "And I never thought I would ever be on a ship with the same name."

Bob heard this and knowing the story Harry was about to tell, he stepped to the COM unit and asked the operator if he could hear what Harry was saying.

"Yes," he answered.

"Can you patch this so the whole ship can hear it?"

"Yes, sir," He replied.

Captain Right, who had joined them in the galley, spoke into his COM unit; he gave the operator the okay, so the whole ship heard the following tale.

Long, long ago when men of iron rode the waves in ships of wood across the tempest-tossed sea, there came a ship with sides of iron to match the men who sailed her. The USS Constitution (Old Iron Sides) was a combat vessel at the leading edge of the technology in her day. Her crew of 475 officers and men were America's finest and this tale is one of their many brave adventures on the high seas.

Unlike today's ships whose evaporators supply abundant fresh water, the USS Constitution had to carry her drinking water. She carried some 48,600 gallons of fresh water stored onboard, which was enough water to sustain operations at sea for six months.

Our tale is about one of her deployments when her mission was to destroy and harass English shipping. The following account comes from her log entries and speaks volumes about this great ship and her brave men.

During July 1798, the USS Constitution set sail from Boston. She left with 475 officers and men, 48,600 gallons of fresh water, 7,400 cannon shot, 11,600 pounds of black powder, and 79,400 gallons of rum.

Making Jamaica on October 6th she took on 826 pounds of flour and 68,300 gallons of rum. She arrived in the Azores on November 12th where she provisioned 550 pounds of beef and 64,300 gallons of Portuguese wine.

On November 18th she set sail for England. During the following days she defeated five British men-of-war and captured twelve English merchantmen, salvaging only the rum. By January 26th her powder and shot were all used, leaving her unarmed. But that did not slow them down as they made a night raid up the Firth of Clyde. Her landing party captured a whisky distillery and loaded 40,000 gallons aboard by dawn when they headed home for Boston.

The USS Constitution arrived back at Boston in February 1799, almost eight months after she left, with the following inventory: no food, no cannon shot, no powder, no rum, no wine, no whisky and 38,000 gallons of stagnant water.

Now for those of you who do not have a calculator, let me sum this up for you. The 475 men had 252,000 gallons of booze (plus the 'salvaged rum') or more than 530 gallons each. They were at sea for at most 240 days, which means every man had to drink at least 2.2 gallons of booze every day.

Yes, they were men of iron with guts of steel in the great U.S. Navy tradition of standing on the Constitution.

So, Go NAVY and please pass my gallon of Ripple."

And with that, Harry raised his coffee mug. "Cheers and pass the Joe."

With that the whole ship erupted in cheering and hoots. The kids had now forgotten why they were blue and had started chatting, eating, and shaking their heads about the crazy adults.

Sue, however, was more to the point as she quietly walked up to Uncle Harry, handed him a full mug of fresh Joe, and patted him on the arm. "You'll be okay, Uncle Harry. Just keep drinking coffee. That *Ripple wine* is bad stuff. Mommy uses it as a cleaning solvent."

That started another round of laughter.

Charly hugged Harry. "I promised to make you a campfire the next time you decide to tell tales."

Alice added, "I'll bring the marshmallows."

J.P. smiled. "I'll bring the beer."

Bill Right got to his feet and in a loud booming voice, which surprised quite a few, asked, "What do you do with a drunken sailor?"

To which the reply came:

What do you do with a drunken sailor?
What do you do with a drunken sailor?
What do you say we do matie?
So early in the morning.

Take em out and shiver his timbers,
Take em out to the fantail matie,
What do we do with a drunken sailor?
So early in the morning.

Feed him Joe and what do you know,
Feed him Joe and lots of crackers,
What do you say we do matie?
So early in the morning.

Lash em to the main mast laddies,
Lash em to his hammock maties,
What do you say we do matie?
So early in the morning.

What do you do with a drunken sailor?
What do you do with a drunken sailor?
Way hay what do you say,
So early in the morning.

Now the kids were beside themselves with amusement that all these crazy adults would spontaneously start singing a sea shanty. It was a good break on this ocean cruise where they could seriously be sailing off to Neverland in search of Captain Hook and have to keep watch for the "croc."

Alice said, "Bill, I hear that tomorrow will be a busy day. The galley scuttlebutt over my cup of Joe was that we were after a crew of freebooters (pirates). I was taken aback while chewing the fat at the gedunk that some bigwigs were gundecking the records to bamboozle our nation and rip off the world. So with battle lights burning and flank speed churning from our screws we've left yesterday fading astern. Our course and bearing set dead ahead to be on station for the action ahead. Topside's awash right to the fantail and into our wake astern. The sea dogs are set on the hatches tight. The loyal shellbacks are standing before the mast there hoping the Old Man won't earn them a billet in Davy Jones' Locker. The admiral has ordered full ahead and damn the torpedoes. Fire control is set, counter measures are online, and Combat Direction Center is ready. This shakedown cruise is over, the ocean going bellhops have mustered and field stripped their weapons one last time. The message was piped down from the admiral himself and the orders came right from the top. This is no bilge rumor gone amuck."

"You shiver my timbers, Alice," said Bill. "You have the straight scoop and by dead reckoning the mission launch will be at 0600 hours into the dawn's early light. The security teams are briefed and ready. All systems are fully operational and green for go."

CDC was online and GQ would sound at 0545 and reveille at 0400. The air boss would be on standing by with craft prepped for flight. Guam was dead ahead and not a ship in sight. Flight recon would launch at 0550 with two fighter escorts. Choppers would be standing by for low level recon if needed or to secure an LZ. Sand Box 4 was already at full alert.

Somewhere ahead of them were Sand Boxes 2 and Sand Box 3 and Gen. Patent Hardash as well as the murderous Maj. Raul Mercenary. It was time to engage the unknown and find the answers.

Chicago, Illinois, in the Year 2012:

Chicago is the Windy City where the north winds sweep down across the Great Lakes to chill the hardiest souls. Just about as far as one can get from the warm island breezes of Guam. Here amid giant skyscrapers and asphalt canyons in one of the largest indoor malls in the United States, a very strange event was about to unfold. Deep in the center of the mall was a large, normally open area. In the winter it was converted into a large ice skating rink where people could rent skates at all hours of the day. There were venders with food and gifts. But right now large tarps were up all around this area, which was due to the construction of viewing stands that would allow the public to sit and watch whatever event was happening.

If the thousands of people shopping this Saturday knew what was about to happen, those stands would have been full. The workers were on schedule and had the day off. So the only "real" witnesses to this strange happening were the homeless who had taken shelter there. The security guards did not bother to look inside because all the normal entrances were blocked and had security alarms.

Most of the homeless just walked down the stairway into the basement where venders and maintenance workers did their work out of sight of the customers above. The middle of the main floor area was clear, as all the work was being done in the stands on the sides. On one side was an old veteran handing out food to several homeless teenagers. They gratefully wolfed down the food from their benefactor who they all knew well.

He was one of the few adults who helped them and really listened to what they said. There was even a rumor that once in a while he gave kids plane tickets home or to somewhere safe. No one knew where he lived, but he was always around and often showed up just when he was needed most.

On the other far side a gang of punks was spray-painting graffiti on the new stands. The homeless avoided them, especially the young among them who had not succumbed to the sex and drug industry. But then the police avoided them too. The cops had good reason. The punks were better armed and had no qualms about offing one of them just for the fun of it. Other than that it was rather quiet with the homeless doing their best invisibility act even here where the busy crowds of shoppers could not see them. But that was the end of normalcy for the day, because in hours this whole place would be crawling with cops and reporters.

Out in the middle of that empty floor, that large gulf between the users / abusers and the victims working hard to be invisible, there "suddenly appeared" a new group. There were about one hundred of them in all, both male and female. At first glance, they looked like they were more victims dropped here for the pleasure of the users. But this group was far from innocent and were users themselves. Beyond that there were three other things they shared in common: they had not chosen to be here, had no idea how they got there, and they were all totally naked. Most were milling around attempting to grasp reason out of this totally illogical situation. They had the vacant look of the lost or insane. Their minds had been push too far.

In the middle of the floor was a younger man, a warrior by trade. His mind was also wrestling with his current reality and the question a wise old Scout leader had asked him.

He had said, "You have chosen a field most suited to you, but have you chosen the right path in your field?"

It had made no sense to him then and he even wondered if the old man was going senile. But now sitting here, face to face with the impossible, he was starting to question the values and motives of the cause he served. So there he sat on the floor in the middle of this madness in deep contemplation of life; *everything*!

Two of the men who had just arrived had separately grasped their situations almost instantly. They were very thoughtfully moving out of this milling mass of naked sheep in search of a solution to their current dilemma. Neither was aware of the other's presence and they were moving in opposite directions like two tigers looking for lunch.

One moved into the stands and soon found the old veteran who was not trying to avoid him like the scared homeless people. The naked man, with little thought and no hesitation, attacked the old vet. Age, however, had not diminished the training of his youth, as he blocked and countered the attack. As the naked man stealthily moved off the floor mentally reevaluating his intended victim, three silent youth moved up behind him. With lightning speed the young woman leading them brought the construction two-by-four she was holding firmly down on his head. He went down on his belly stunned by the blow. The three youths stepped around the naked form and joined their benefactor. Within seconds the downed man was in a full crouch ready to attack, but his eyes found four determined people waiting with no fear in theirs. Hardash was no fool. There were far easier victims to be had in this mall. He got back on his feet and headed in the other direction, opened a door, and went down some stairs to a darker lair to do his deed.

The old vet turned and gently removed the two-by-four from the young girl's hands. He said, "You won't be needing that again, Fran, and I can see you paid more attention to your martial arts lessons than to English grammar. He'll now go find an easier victim to escape whatever has happened to him. Right now we need to get out of here. Those naked people are military; don't ask me how I know right now. This place will soon be full of cops. You don't want them finding your brothers."

Fran had a weary look in her eyes. "How do you know my name and that they are my brothers?"

He smiled at Fran and said, "These two are Mike and Jake, your biological father died in a plane crash, and your stepfather is a pedophile creep. If the police find your brothers they will send them back to him. Now, I'm Walter Kid and when I returned from the Middle East wars I found my family had died in a car accident. I tried to forget with booze and drugs, but it didn't work. While I was down here on skid row I met a lot of people worse off than me. So for the last twenty years I've been helping where I can. I know about you because a young kid I helped taught me how to hack computers. So I know what the police have on you. So now I have broken two of my rules. I've told you who I am and how I know about you. I'm also about to break a third and take you home with me where you'll be safe."

"Why would you do that?" asked Fran, narrowing her eyes suspiciously.

Walter said, "Because you broke the biggest rule of the homeless, you got involved and saved me. I've ended up in the hospital a dozen times over the years and you three are the first who ever stood up for me. Now let's get out of here before all hell breaks lose."

Walter started down the hallway to the stairs.

Fran hesitated, but Mike and Jake said together, "Sis, this is the best offer we've ever had and he's right about what will happen if we get caught, so let's go," and they shoved her into motion.

Ahead of them downstairs in the underground service and delivery area of the mall Hardash had silently come up behind an illegal business transaction. He hit the collector's big bodyguard so hard he fell to the floor like a tree cut at the base. The shopkeeper who was handing money to the well-dressed mob collector dropped the money and ran as Hardash came straight for the collector, who dropped the money as well and grabbed for his gun. But he was too late as the wall of naked flesh smashed him into the cement wall.

Hardash was rather pleased with himself having acquired guns, money, and nice clothes with one stop. He walked out of the underground like a man on a mission. He pressed the button on the car keys the nice man had provided and a car right there in the alleyway blew its horn and flashed its lights. As he climbed into the new Mercedes and drove off, he was more than a little pleased with himself.

When he parked the car at an upscale motel outside of town near the military base he was even more pleased to discover fifty thousand dollars in the trunk in a suitcase. Hardash checked in under the collector's name and used his credit card. Once in the room he called Black on his private line. In less than an hour a military vehicle arrived to deliver him to a waiting airplane headed for D.C.

Walter and the kids followed the lower level tunnel toward the main underground delivery route under the mall.

Just before they got to the main route they came upon a large man lying limp on the floor. Across the tunnel lay another man mostly naked with two broken arms.

Walter said, "I told you he would find someone easier and with a lot more money than I carry."

"That guy would take on a mob collector and his bodyguard," Fran said in disbelief, "But not us?"

"Sure looks that way," Walter laughed. "You are a scary woman, Fran."

They walked in silence to the parking garage and found Walter's rather solid looking older Jeep. Fran looked on in amazement as Walter clicked off his hi-tech car alarm. After she had helped move all the stuff in the back so they could use the rear seat, she realized it was not the Jeep that was valuable. There was enough survival gear there that they could live for a month anywhere.

Mike and Jake piled in the back seat and let Fran sit up front with Walter. They were about an hour out of the city when the police reports started coming over the radio and the police scanner in the car was going nuts with traffic.

"Guess we left at the right time, but I would sure like to know how people can just appear from nowhere." said Fran.

"Me too, that was just like Star Trek," said Jake.

"I know the military have advanced since I was in, but I sure did not think it was that far," replied Walter.

They soon had driven into a rural area and pulled into a yard. Walter stopped inside the garage and they all climbed out.

Mike said, "Wow you really live here?"

"Yup, but you'll have to forgive my housekeeping. My

mother taught my brother Joe that stuff while I was off playing sports."

Once inside Walter turned on the TV and his computer. The boys' attention shifted back and forth between the two. Fran just shook her head and wandered back into the kitchen. An hour later when Fran finished she went to check on the boys, the sink was empty and the kitchen clean. Walter saw Fran come in and motioned for her to come sit next to him. Wordlessly, he pointed to a report on the screen titled "Chicago PD Missing Report." He forwarded to Report no. 20120911 with Fran's name at the top. Her stepfather had gotten her charged with kidnapping her two brothers and someone from the city halfway house had reported them in the Chicago area around the mall.

Fran and Walter stared at each other for some time.

She said, "I can't let them go back there. I'll have to take them where we can't be found—"

Walter nodded. "My brother Joe keeps inviting me to come visit him in Hawaii. You think that might be far enough?"

"Maybe, but I don't have any money," said Fran.

"Well, let's talk to Joe and see what he has to say," said Walter.

"Sure," said Fran, "We got nothing to loose."

Walter hugged her and started typing. The boys had now joined them and watched with great interest as Walter typed and used the links that brother Joe had sent him. Even Walter was surprised to find he was in a secure government network and had to repeatedly use the passwords Joe had sent.

Finally, a face popped up on the screen and the man said, "This is Specialist Donald Plant on the U.S. Army COM net, please key in your ID, password and turn on your webcam for a visual ID."

Walter typed in the requested info and turned on his webcam.

Plant checked and replied, "Thank you, Walter. I see you have the family with you. Your brother is in his office, so I'll have to go get him. While I do that I'll transfer you to Captain Brother of Army Intel, who is our COM chief on base. You'll like him. He loves to talk and chats with our kids all the time."

A new face appeared on the screen. "Hi folks, my name is Sanders, or Sandy if you like. Joe has spoken of you, Walter. I know he's hoping that you'll come visit us."

"Yes, I was hoping to talk with him about that. I thought he was working for the state," Walter said.

"Oh, he and I are sort of on a leave of absence for this special project and Joe is our CO here at the Scout bunker," replied Sandy.

"So much for retirement. I thought he had had enough," said Walter.

"We both have had enough, but we sort of got an offer we couldn't refuse," replied Sandy.

"Our XO is Stella Staff, a retired USN captain married to an active admiral. Here comes Joe now, so I'll let you guys chat. It was good talking with you and I hope to meet you soon," said Sandy.

The screen changed again and there was Joe's smiling face. "Hi there, Bro. Hey, I thought you lived alone," Joe said.

"Well, our niece Fran and nephews Mike and Jake have moved in with me since our sister fell on hard times. And we were kind of hoping for a vacation getaway, but we didn't know you were so involved in a project," said Walter.

"That's no problem. We like having kids here and I can get you a ride on a military flight. Stella is expecting Snow

White to come for a visit and I'm sure they would give you a ride," said Joe.

Another face popped onto the screen and said, "Hi, I'm Stella. I'm sure Snow would give you guys a ride out here. Just give Joe the names and send a picture for each ID and we'll work out a pick-up location."

"Boy, you guys work fast. I'll give Joe all the info I have," said Walter.

"Give me the spelling on Sister's latest name," Joe said.

Walter typed in "Unhomed," then had Fran, Jake, and Mike sit in front of the webcam.

"Ok, brother, I got it, and we'll get back to you with a schedule. I've got to run 'cause I've got company coming and a fuel tank to build. I'll see you all soon," added Joe.

The kids were amazed and so was Walter. He said, "Well, guys, I guess since we're traveling we had better go shopping and get you guys clothes to wear."

Mike said, "You'd do that for us?"

"Yes. Come on before I change my mind," he said.

Fran asked, "Does this mean you're officially our Uncle Walter?"

"Sure does," said Walter.

They shopped at a local mall and got travel clothes. Walter found duffel bags with straps for each of them. When they got back to Walter's house, Fran got very domestic and cooked them all supper. They were relaxing with dessert when the phone rang and it was Joe.

"Hey," he asked, "Can you guys be ready to travel tomorrow morning by 0800 hours?"

Walter laughed and said, "Bro, you're fast. We're all packed."

"Ok," said Joe, "I'll have a van pick you up at 0800 and drive you to meet the plane."

"Thanks. Sounds good."

"Bye, Bro, and see you tomorrow."

Fran asked, "Did I get that right? We're leaving in the morning?"

"Yes, and we even have us a ride to the airport," replied Walter.

They all enjoyed taking a shower and sleeping in real beds. Fran cooked breakfast and had the kitchen clean long before the government van arrived. The kids looked real spiffy in their new clothes.

The doorbell rang at five minutes before eight. Walter opened the door and the uniformed man saluted him. "Major Kid, I'm Sergeant Francis, your driver today. Can I help with your luggage, sir?"

They all climbed in the van and off they went to the airport.

Fran leaned next to Walter and said, "Uncle Walter, you never told us about being a major."

He smiled. "That's because I thought I'd retired a long time ago."

Sergeant Frances answered the question. "Sir, I have your orders here if you would be so kind as to sign for them. They came from the White House. I also have ID cards for each of you."

Walter took his orders and hung his ID around his neck. The kids put on their picture ID cards as well. And he slowly read his orders, which were signed by Puritan White.

Sergeant Frances drove them to the airport and was

directed to a secure holding area where they were all checked in by security. The large white plane taxied up and stopped.

Sergeant Frances said, "Well, here's your ride, Major, right on time."

Mike piped up, "But...but...but...that's Air Force One."

"It sure is, son, and I hope you enjoy the ride."

The crewmen had already run off with their luggage. This only left Sergeant Frances to walk with them to the stairs.

The woman who had come down said, "Hello, Major Kid, I'm Susan Anthony, head of White House Security. Cdr. Snow White is waiting for you aboard for our flight to Hawaii. Oh, Gen. Jack Frost sends his best, sir, and hopes to see you in a couple of days."

Anthony escorted them on the plane and introduced them to Snow White. As the plane was rolling for take off, they sat down and buckled their seat belts. As soon as they were airborne they all gathered around a table, and snacks magically appeared for the kids.

Walter finally said, "I gather your husband signed my orders?"

"Yes, he did. Jack recommended you highly and spoke of your family's history of service to our country."

Fran spoke next. "So you're the president's wife. This is so unreal. Yesterday I saw dozens of naked people just appear out of thin air and today I'm on the president's plane with his wife and you're an officer!"

Near her Susan Anthony laughed. "Young lady, if half of what I hear is true, this is just the beginning of an adventure in Wonderland for all of us. I'd love to hear more about these naked people. Are these the one's at the Chicago mall?"

"Yes," replied Fran. "They just appeared and one of them attacked Uncle Walter."

"She's right. As strange as it sounds they looked like military types to me," added Walter. "Then this one guy just walked up to me and attacked. Fran there came up behind him with Mike and Jake. They clobbered him with a two-by-four. He decided that with the four of us, we were definitely not worth the trouble. But on our way out we found a mob collector mostly naked with two broken arms and his bodyguard out cold on the floor."

Susan got up and opened a locked briefcase and pulled out some photos. "He wasn't one of these, was he?" she asked.

On the third picture Walter stopped. He showed it to the kids who all said, "That's him." Walter read the bottom info: Gen. Patent Hardash, ex-CIA and current NSA. Missing with Sand Box 2.

Susan asked, "Any others?"

They all looked, but didn't recognize anyone else.

"I'll go get that on the wire," she stated.

Snow said, "A simple day at the mall and you get to see one of America's most wanted men."

Fran replied, "Well, not so simple, but if I had known you wanted him, I would have hit him again with that two-by-four."

Snow smiled. "My dear, you are indeed in the right place."

As Susan returned she added, "I think you'll like the other kids who are with the admiral."

And so they settled in for the long flight, with a stop in Alaska to refuel. Walter rested. Fran kept Susan and Snow talking for hours. The boys adopted the flight crew, who just loved to show off their airplane. And into the night they flew with the promise of dawn.

Meanwhile Back at the Mall:

In the center of the mall the young man's contemplations came to an end. It was time to act. Lt. Matt Youngblood stood up and picked a direction to go find his destiny. He walked through the milling naked bodies that were drifting about like lost souls in limbo. The surrealness of their situation had totally overwhelmed their minds. They were left-brained thinkers, who were totally in control of their lives until fate ripped away everything they knew and dumped them here in this fish bowl like so many specimens in a petri dish.

As he left the crowd none of them even noticed his passage. He walked out through the normal exit, over the barrier, and slipped by the silly security alarms to find himself in a new mass of people. They were almost as blind as the group he just left. He walked right through them, too. They didn't even notice this six-foot-plus naked man walking among them.

Suddenly, a voice in the crowd spoke. "Oh, my my my my my my my! Where are *you* going all dressed up?"

Matt stopped dead in his tracks. He focused on the speaker who was almost as tall as he. She wore a uniform and her nametag said she was one Suzy Que, EMT.

"I'm looking for a sporting goods store to buy some gear for a trip," he answered without taking his eyes off of her for even a second.

"Oh. Where do you plan on going?" asked Suzy with an interest in this oh so definitely naked man.

"To see an old man who said I was on the wrong path," replied Matt quite seriously now.

"Do you always walk...around malls naked?" she asked.

"Not usually, but it would seem those who brought me here needed my clothes more than I do."

"I do believe you're right since you're standing among all these hundreds of people who haven't seemed to notice your nakedness," she giggled with a sense of mischievousness in her voice as she replied.

"My old friend taught us the art of invisibility. You see, they are all walking around in a dream and I am simply not part of their dream. You, on the other hand, are obviously wide awake," said Matt.

Suzy thought about that for a moment. "Do you have a name?"

"Oh my yes—I seem to have lost my nametag too—I'm Matt Youngblood."

"Well, Matt, the store is this way," said Suzy nonchalantly.

Since it was obvious that Suzy planned on taking him to the store, Matt asked, "Won't your boss miss you?"

"I don't think so. I think you could say I sort of quit my job. You see, he likes to touch things that aren't his to touch. Today I got tired of it and punched him in the crotch so hard that when I last saw him, they were hauling him away in his own ambulance," explained Suzy.

They both started laughing as they strolled into the store.

An hour later he looked like a man dressed for anything. When Suzy picked out a backpack for herself Matt smiled and asked, "Does this mean I'll have some company?"

"Sure does if you can put up with a pushy broad," said Suzy.

Matt thought for a second and replied, "It's rather nice having someone around who is awake, someone I can talk with."

When they both left the mall they were dressed for any adventure. Without seeming to pay much attention, they soon found themselves in a park and sat down on the grass to enjoy the tranquility.

They both closed their eyes and relaxed in Mother Nature's embrace. They could hear the gentle breeze caress the trees, the birds singing their songs, the children at play, and the soft-spoken voice of the old man who sat before them.

"I am glad you're looking for your true path," said the old man, "And I like your companion."

Suzy almost thought she was dreaming, but slowly opened her eyes when she felt the warm hand gently resting on her arm. There before them sat a wise old man dressed like a Native American with the deepest blue eyes that just radiated love and understanding.

He looked at Matt and said, "You'll find Fern in a Hawaiian mountain following the path you seek and this will help you get there."

With that he handed Matt an ID card so he could travel. The old man's eyes returned to Suzy. "I look forward to our next meeting when we'll have time to share." With that he smiled at them and vanished.

Suzy blinked her eyes several times, but the old man was gone, the ID was in Matt's hand, and her arm still felt the warm touch. Finally she spoke, "I guess that means he came to see us?"

"Yup. Sure saved us a trip back east. I guess we should get a cab to the airport."

They hailed a cab and were off. As the huge plane climbed above the clouds headed west and Suzy saw Chicago vanish beneath them, she looked enquiringly at Matt and asked, "How do we find a fern in a mountain?"

Matt smiled. "This Fern has two legs and likes to go spelunking."

About halfway through the trip a flight attendant came up and asked, "Lieutenant Youngblood?"

"Yes, can I help you?" asked Matt.

"Thank you, sir, but I have the map you requested," said the stewardess.

"Thank you that is most helpful," said Matt shaking his head and gently chuckling.

"Since we did not ask for that, I guess we've just been given another hint about where to look for Fern. Your old friend sure gets around. Does he work for the government?" said Suzy with a twinkle in her eye.

"I believe he did a long time ago, but never said much about that. He often amazed us kids, like the time we were hiking. Mr. Steve and he were climbing on this waterfall and let us go on ahead to the pond we were hiking to for lunch. When we arrived at the Black Mountain Pond they were there and had finished their lunch already. There is only one trail up there from where we were and they never passed us! I guess as kids we became accustomed to it and never thought it odd when he did things like that or his always having marshmallows for campfires," explained Matt.

With that they both relaxed and napped until they felt the wheels meet the ground in Hawaii.

Meanwhile Back at the Mall:

The second man shoved his way through the lost souls with no care or concern for their predicament. He didn't give a crap about his involvement in the cause. He spotted eight punks and their leader. This guy looked to be about his size and, like a hungry great white, he headed straight for them.

They had to have seen him coming, but were so secure in their guns and muscles that they laughed and joked around without fear. This naked guy was just some victim coming to meet his fate. They found it very amusing.

Before they realized the danger, two of them lay broken like rag dolls on the floor. Next he took out the third, who landed with the sounds of breaking bones. He next hit their leader with such a powerful punch that he sent him flying through the air. He then took a sawed-off shotgun from the fourth who fell to the floor with a broken neck. The two closest were pulling out weapons, but it was far too late as two well-placed shotgun blasts cut them to shreds. Number seven was running fast when a blast hit him right behind the knees. Fear had a firm grip on this guy as he dragged himself and his now useless legs toward the exit. Number eight punk, who realized none of his buddies were left to help him, ran so fast he did not notice the stands were not complete in front of him. He fell screaming into a tangle of ironwork supports and lay there moaning.

Now the man returned his attention to the leader who had started to move. He removed the machine gun and knife the leader was carrying, then grabbed him by his hair and stood him up. Next he shoved the 12 gauge in the leader's mouth and told him to undress fast. The quivering punk complied as fast as he could. Once done he pulled out the shotgun and tossed it aside. The punk at once started to beg but fell silent when the man looked deep into his eyes.

"I am Raul. You ever betray me to the law, I'll cut off your balls and make you eat them."

With that, Raul took a can of gold spray paint and painted the leader's private parts gold. Once more he looked deep into the frightened man's eyes and said one word, "Remember." Then he painted the punk's face gold and told him to run.

The golden leader of punks ran right through the blocked entrance, setting off the security alarms, and right into the crowds of people. At the same time number seven punk crawled out into the mall leaving a trail of blood and further incited madness, riots, looting, robbery, vandalism, and general mayhem. Women screamed and passed out, men ran, the whole mall turned into one large panic. People ran in every direction. Security and police could only stand back, so they wouldn't get hurt themselves. The golden punk ran ten blocks to the main police station and demanded protection from the insane terrorist named Raul. Unfortunately for our head punk, a camera crew just happened to be at the police station when he arrived and documented the whole event for the Six O'clock News.

Of course, the ninety-seven zombies roaming the center of the mall hardly noticed any of this or even the fact that the police were carting them off. The media joined the circus and soon the whole event could be seen live on TV; coast to coast and around the world. Some of this stopped when the first identifications came in—the FBI, NSA, and CIA all arrived and took the whole event underground back to the world of black ops where it came from.

Then there was Maj. Raul Mercenary with his new punk clothes, money, and guns. He walked right out of the center of the mall into the parking garage. The crowds of shoppers parted the way for him like the Red Sea opening for Moses. But this had more to do with fear than divine intervention. Raul found the gang's cars in short order. Two well-armed bimbos, whom Raul quickly disarmed, were guarding them. He then tossed both in the trunk of the car he was taking so he could play with them at his leisure. He found a box of grenades in one of the cars and used them to start many of the parked cars burning. That would keep the officials busy for awhile. He then drove out of the garage into the asphalt canyons of downtown Chicago and slipped away.

He was headed east, but in no rush since he had two toys to play with on the way. He would get to Benedict Black in his own good time. Black owed him money and an explanation of how he ended up naked in Chicago. Someone was messing with him big time and he, Raul, wanted to know who.

So the Windy City had a new tale to place in the history books never to be published. The police had questioned twenty-eight of the ninety-seven zombies before the Feds hauled them away in the middle of the night. But that was a total waste of time. All they ever got were names from the FBI fingerprint files and those sent up red flags all over the place. But on the good side, none of the city's civilians got killed and insurance would cover the damage and robberies. The mob collector and his bodyguard were singing like two canneries to the DA in return for being placed in the witness protection program. The worst, most violent drug and sex gang in the city had left town for fear of their lives. Their leader had made a complete fool of himself before the TV cameras and kept talking until his lawyer told him to shut up or go to jail. They had few casualties, with three dead, four in the hospital, and two missing.

There were many odd things about the whole event, but when the FBI first arrived they had a list of a hundred names of "missing persons." Ninety-seven were easy to account for since they were in protective custody. Number ninety-eight no doubt fit the tale of woe the mob men sang. Number ninety-nine trashed the gang of punks, but what of the hundredth man who seemingly vanished right back into the thin air he appeared out of? And to make it even weirder, the first thing that happened that day was an ambulance owner was assaulted by a female employee, one Suzy Que, who was now missing too. It was a very strange day in the Windy City that the press would call a Nudist Party at the Mall. Some party with ninety-seven zombies, and two sharks, perhaps the hundredth man had all the fun.

Some Days Later in a Dark Office in the Pentagon:

General Black was sulking at his desk, while Hardash paced the floor cursing every one of the incompetent boobs that had manned SB2 and SB3. Wiley Woozy wished he were somewhere else. He had debriefed all ninety-seven people and got nothing. Even worse, these highly trained people were now totally useless. Hardash's account was the only one that had had any answers, but he had no idea what happened. He was in command of SB2 looking for SB3 where it was supposed to be and the next thing he knew he was standing naked in a Chicago Mall. SB2 with a billion dollars worth of weapons had vanished. SB3 with fifty trillion dollars worth of gold bars was gone. Most of the crew from SB3 was found at the Chicago mall, while most of SB2's crew was still missing. Add to that the fact that SB4 and that stupid aircraft carrier had vanished.

Woozy asked Hardash, "Can it be the Russians?"

"Can't be or they'd have taken out SB5, which we're still operating within their borders," answered Hardash.

"Could the Chinese do it?"

"Not even close. They're buying old technology from the Russians."

"What about our allies?"

"We never shared this with them."

"Could Warbucks Banks have brought the missing people from SB2?"

Hardash started laughing. "The senior person left on it was that stupid cow Wilks and the next in line is that 'has been SEAL' who was the cook. The rest are techy drones. We have all the good people and someone has turned them into vegetables. Warbucks is just a dumb, rich banker living off his father's coat tails. And as soon as we don't need him anymore, Raul can off his useless ass."

"What if one of our allies…has spies in our operation?" asked Woozy.

"I hate to say it. But we're running out of possibilities. We have robbed Europe blind as well as Canada, Mexico, Japan, the Philippines, India, Egypt, Turkey, Brazil, Taiwan, Korea, and Australia, too. Who is left?" asked Hardash.

"And where is Raul?" barked Black.

"He had to be in Chicago. Who else could have wasted those punks? He's out there somewhere," said Hardash.

"All our other people are accounted for," said Woozy.

"What about SB1?" asked Hardash.

Woozy finally had something good to say. "It's in final testing and will do trial runs next week. Could it be our own— the Navy or Army?"

"No they haven't got a clue and the Air Force is with us," said Hardash.

"What about NASA and Space Command?" Woozy ventured.

"All those boobs do is make good movies and rob the taxpayers. They're magicians not scientists," said Hardash.

Black had finally had all he could take of this madness and threw the whisky bottle across the room. "Well, if you don't have any answers, go find them!" he screamed. With that

Woozy scurried for the door and Hardash followed in total disgust.

AS THE DAWN FIVE

The sunrise brought Guam the light of a new day or it could be said the dawn cometh in the wake of the Constitution.

At 0400 hours reveille was sounded. That morning they skipped "Sweepers, sweepers, man your brooms. Give the ship sweep down fore and aft." Today breakfast would come first and then the business of the day. Everyone ate and headed for their stations. The admiral and captain were already on their bridges. Dr. Whosh was present at the command console watching last-minute test runs on all equipment. General Rabbit and his men were in the staging area ready for almost anything. The air boss had already briefed his flight crews and was in Pri-Fly ready for launch. The ship had already turned into the wind and at 0545 GQ was sounded. CDC was reporting no contacts and no unusual noises from below. At 0550 hours, the Hawkeye lifted off and started its recon of Guam. As it was moving off and getting to its operating altitude, the two escort fighters screamed off the deck to join the Hawkeye. Two of the choppers sat on the flight deck ready to launch; Ensign Smith and her security team were with one. Lieutenant Brice and her team with the second.

At 0600 hours Dr. Whosh told the admiral, "Sand Box 4 is green for launch."

The admiral replied, "Good luck Amanda."

"Commander North are you set?"

"Yes, Doctor, navigation is ready."

"Captain Furreal, engage main drive. Commander O'Rielly start scanning. We need to find those missing boxes."

On the flag bridge with the admiral the five children were paying full attention. Sue was sitting in Merry Kurious' lap, but her attention was fixed on the big screen. The Constitution had approached Guam from the north end of the island, away from where the present day port was located. The plan was that she would circle the island with the hope of finding a safe place to anchor. Now they were picking up small fishing boats along the shore, but no large vessels or sailing ships were in sight. It was almost too good to be true. Adm. Zheng He's information about Guam was proving very accurate. They had been given a flag from the admiral to fly if they met any ships that had treaties with the Chinese Navy. If all went well they would launch the gig and do some trading with the local natives.

The Hawkeye had a close look at the island then did a search of the surrounding ocean. All was well. An anchorage was found, so they brought the Hawkeye and the jets home. Commander Albright launched the gig and went in first with the two choppers flying escort. Within an hour they had the ship anchored. Lieutenant Brice, Ensign Smith, and Dr. North had stayed with the ship so they could help with the natives and were now with Albright and Harry on the gig. Since they had no idea how long they would have to wait for Sand Box 4's return they planned on setting up a base camp on the island and would let Tracy do her job with the natives.

Sand Box 4, Somewhere in Time and Space:

It was fifteen minutes into their event. Scott and Bob were working the scanners for all they were worth. Dew was doing his best to keep SB4 in a stable location, while Alice kept the power plants humming at peak. The event clock was ticking as they hung there just outside of normal time.

Finally, in frustration, O'Rielly announced, "I have a lock on both SB5 and SB6. I have all the data I can get on them being recorded. There is still no sign of SB2 and SB3. We should be right on top of them here. The only thing I can think is that whatever fried our transponder trace signal must have done the same with them. I just got a lock on SB1 which is right where we last saw it."

The event clock was at thirty minutes.

Whosh asked, "Do we have a lock on the Constitution?"

"Yes," replied Bob. "It looks likes she has anchored and stopped moving. I also have a lock on the Scout bunker and logged all of them into the navigation computer."

Dew added, "I have the coordinates and I'm using them to cross-reference our position."

Alice spoke up. "I'm having power surges on the drives, but no fluctuation in our output levels."

Dew chimed back in, sounding excited, "We have motion. We are traveling, sir, and fast."

"Drive power is up, but our output level has not changed. I can't control it. It's not coming from us," Alice exclaimed.

"No navigation control, she won't respond. I'm plotting our course the best I can," said Dew.

Every keyboard in the control room was a frenzy of action, but no matter what they did SB4 continued on its trip.

Suddenly, Dew reported, "We've stopped."

And Alice added, "The main drives have just shut down."

"We've landed and are back, sir, except we are back in 2012," Dew retorted in surprise.

Scott added, "I still have all the locks. Nothing has moved but us, sir."

Dew rechecked his readouts. "Sir, I think we are in orbit above the planet."

"We can't be," added one of the techs, "I have a breathable oxygen atmosphere outside and we're sitting on something solid and flat. If I didn't know better I would say we are back on the carrier."

Everyone started rechecking all the readings and running diagnostics on the equipment to be sure it was working correctly.

Scott said almost to himself, "You're not going to believe this but I have us 238,857 miles from the Constitution. The other locks are coming in at consistent distances."

Dew was shaking his head. "We are in orbit. Here, I'll put the plot up on screen."

They all stared in disbelief.

"But it still shows breathable air outside," Alice exclaimed.

"Turn on the external cameras," ordered Whosh.

"Nothing, sir. We should see stars or Earth, but it's pitch black. Nothing on infrared," said Scotty.

"Scan around the box and see what's out there," ordered Whosh.

"The ground or floor is perfectly flat. It looks like we're in a round building like a dome. The walls are about a mile out on all sides and a mile up. I have picked up two objects that are the right size and shape to be Sand Boxes," Bob added. "I'm generating a holographic picture of the scan with us, them, and the dome."

As the picture came to life in the middle of the room, they all watched as Bob slowly rotated it around so they could see it from all angles.

"It looks like the door is open on that one," he said.

Whosh got on the COM link. "Peter, get up here stat. You have to see this."

Peter ran into the control room and came to a halt with his eyes fixed on the rotating picture. He finally spoke. "Amanda, you've found them. *But where are we?*"

They all sort of gave a nervous laugh as she replied, "That, my dear Peter is the $64,000 question. As you can see we and the two objects that appear to be the missing Sand Boxes are sitting on a perfectly flat floor—deck—and the nearest wall or overhead is over five thousand feet away in all directions. Add to that our instruments are telling us there is a breathable atmosphere out there. We have locks on SB1, SB5, SB6, Scout bunker, and the Constitution, and our navigational plot as to where we are in relationship to them is on the big screen. It would seem to indicate that we are 238,857 miles above the surface of Earth, moving west to east in approximately a twenty-eight-day orbit. We are getting no signals from either of those objects," said Amanda.

"There's air out there?" asked Peter.

"Yes," they all replied.

Peter thought for several minutes as he circled the holographic image. "Can we transmit our data logs to the ship and bunker?"

Scotty checked his panel and replied, "Yes. I've sent a burst transmission to both."

"How did we get here if they are not sending a signal?" asked Peter.

"No idea. We were holding position about a mile over Guam for about thirty minutes during event time. Then without explanation our drives powered up by themselves and we leaped here and returned to standard time. Not in 1421 where we were over Guam, but back in 2012," said Amanda.

"So we must have been brought here just like the ship was moved to 1421?" he asked in amazement.

"It sure would appear to be the case," replied Alice. "Someone wanted us here."

Whosh thought for a moment then asked, "Is our position stable enough for us to call a conference to examine our options?"

Scotty replied, "Looks stable here."

"Here too," said Dew.

"Engineering is on remote control," Alice quipped, "So I guess if they wanted us here, they'll leave us here until we or they think we're done."

Bob let out an uneasy laugh and said, "Alice, you sure know how to make a man feel real secure."

Back on the Constitution Anchored off Guam in 1421:

Vary Kurious spoke up, "Sir, I just received a burst transmission from Sand Box 4. They are stable and think they may have found SB2 and SB3. They also have locks on SB1, SB5, SB6, the Scout bunker, and us. They have downloaded the data logs and want us to check them out to see if we can make any sense out of them. This can't be right, sir. It looks like they are in orbit on a huge space station with a breathable atmosphere. They are....What? Excuse me, sir," he said as he continued, "Over 238 thousand miles up in a twenty-eight-day orbit and they are back in 2012."

Little Sue trotted up and asked, "Are they ok?"

Vary, trying to collect himself after reading the impossible, stammered out, "Oh yes. They say they're fine and going to have a meeting of their science team to decide what to do next."

Sue, now looking satisfied, announced, "Well, next time I want to go visit the man on the moon too."

With that she grabbed the Admiral's hand and said, "Come on. You promised to take me swimming and then hunting for seashells."

And with that, the Kuriouses were left with the dilemmas and paradoxes of time travel.

Ashore, Dr. Tracy North, with the able assistance of Lt. Charly Brice and Ens. Shela Smith, had found the strong matriarchal Chamorro society to be very receptive to working with three rather strong female leaders. Trading was soon in full swing and a beachhead and camp set up for trading and R and R not far from the village of Agana. Tracy also got to follow her passion as a cultural anthropologist. She had read much about the latte stones of Guam, but was now seeing them in use. The Chamorro natives built their large A-frame homes on top of these stone pillars. These raised homes were magnificent with great views of their surroundings. It was just amazing to observe this culture the way it was before the Spanish Crown claimed the Mariana Islands in 1565. There were over one hundred thousand of these tall and healthy, strong natives of Indo-Malaya descent. Then Magellan had stumbled on Guam during his circumnavigation of the globe on March 6, 1521. Tracy found it very sad to think of what would happen to these people in the next century, when by 1741 there would only be about five thousand left due to disease and war with the Spanish.

The Chamorro people were fine navigators traveling between islands and their fishing areas. There was much activity in their homes and under them as well. Many lived close to the shore and fished the shallow waters. Some sailed off to other islands in boats that looked sort of like a banana with a pontoon and a sail. These sturdy boats, called flying proa, kind of leaped over the waves as their sailors navigated using charts made of bamboo sticks, seashells, and string. Others lived inland and harvested the bounty of Mother Nature. They traded in open marketplaces where craftsmen also brought their wares for trade.

They were not there too long before the elders of the matriarchal council called Tracy, Shela, and Charly to meet with them. They were, to say the least, very curious especially about these two who led men in battle. While they ruled their society and property was handed down mother to daughter, it was their men who were the warriors and fishermen. Their place was to run the affairs of state, home, hearth, and raise the children.

A teenaged girl named Adagi Nene' came to their camp to bring the ladies to the meeting with the elders. Adagi was very pleased to have the children join them so they could meet the children she cared for during the day. Her name in English translated "to protect infants." When they arrived, Adagi introduced them to the clan's maga'hagas (highest ranking woman) whose name was Kandit Mesngon (light enduring). Next she introduced the other three clan elders, Dahi Atugud (friend, to prop each other up), Quetago Taotao (striving to command people), and Amta Mamuranta (heal, to watch over our own). And then Adagi introduced them to Abi Suruhana (to provide for, to sustain, female healer), who was the clan's healer. With that, the ladies made themselves comfortable so they could talk, eat, and get to know each other and were as well amazed by the children who traveled with them. Their great ship was like a floating village, almost an island itself full of strangers who shared and would leave as their friends.

Meanwhile, Adagi took Krista, Chrissy, James, Fred, and little Sue (who had already made herself at home by climbing into Adagi's arms to be carried) to meet the children she tended. There was Chiba Lahi (goat boy) who was the son of a farmer. Next there was Tasi Lago (sea teardrop) and her younger sister Hanum Samai (water seedling/child), whose father was a fisherman. And Abag Felu (lost blade) whose father was a great warrior and protector for the clan. They talked much, ate, and played. It was good and they all learned and shared.

The elders walked back to the beach with them to find the admiral waiting to hunt seashells with Sue. Harry was out sailing a native boat. Alex Albright gave the ladies a tour of the gig and showed them they could even cook meals on her. The elders were pleased with him as he spent much time talking with their sailors of how to find their way with the stars and had become fast friends with a fisherman named Asin Cadassi (salt to have something of the sea) who was a great sailor. Harry had hollowed out a bamboo stalk and showed the young lads how to walk under water. And Shela pointed out that carrying some rocks would hold them on the bottom. Life was good and it was easy to forget the troubles of the world they left behind for this newfound paradise. Yes, here on the beach by a fire with the children swimming in the warm waters and the sun slowly sinking in the west at the close of the day, it was good. Tomorrow they would handle when it came.

Sand Box 4, Somewhere Not on This Earth in the Year 2012:

They met for almost an hour and still had little idea how they got there. Bones had joined them, and Cookie had kept them going with food and drinks. They heard from the

Constitution and Scout bunker and neither had much to offer in the way of information or advice. So, at last they hatched a plan. They believed that some of the answers might lie right outside their front door, so it was time to go have a look.

Everyone returned to his or her station. General Rabbit sent out the first team with night vision and self-contained suits to explore around SB4. They confirmed air quality by getting samples. They set out lights around SB4. The second team set up security and defense. They could not see the far walls or ceiling, but confirmed that it was SB2 and SB3 out there about one hundred feet away. The doors to both were open, but there were no signs of life or signals of any kind.

Rabbit formed the rest of his men into two teams. He would lead one into SB2, which they had to assume was manned by Hardash and a fully armed security team. Sergeant Smith would lead the second team into SB3.

Rabbit headed out first with his team followed rapidly by Smith and company. Rabbit got to the open door. Seeing nothing dangerous inside the door, he and three men stepped into SB2. They froze as the room light automatically sensed them there and came on. The inner door was closed and the COM panel was blank.

He mused, "I guess I ring the doorbell and ask to be let in." He inserted his ID and typed "Hello" on the blank screen. Just when he had decided that more radical steps needed to be taken, a very frightened face appeared on the screen.

She obviously recognized him because she said, "Oh God! It's General Rabbit. You've come to save us."

"I'll do my best if you open the door and let us in," Rabbit calmly replied.

Now she looked puzzled. "But, sir, I don't know how to do that. I'm a med. tech."

"That's ok," said Rabbit. "I'll tell you what to do. It's real easy."

So he had her look at the console and walked her through the control sequence until the door swung open.

"That's good. Now you just relax and I'll be right down," said Rabbit.

With that, he led his team in. They found no one. So when they arrived at the elevator, he had his team start a search from the top down. He took two men and headed directly for the control room to talk with the med. tech. They met no one enroute and found her alone. A fast check told him the box was fully operational, so he started a security scan to ID all personnel and their locations. He could hardly believe the readout as it came up on the big screen. He had opened a COM link to SB4 and Amanda's face appeared.

"Are you getting my data stream?" asked Peter.

"Yes, O'Rielly has it on the big screen. It says there are no command officers on board. No security forces, enough weapons to start a war, but no men to go with them," read Amanda.

"This is weird," said Rabbit. "I'll leave a man here to talk to you. It says most of the crew is in the dining hall. Guess I'll go say hello."

Rabbit walked into the dining hall and announced, "Excuse me, but I am looking for Dr. Janet Wilks."

The room suddenly went silent and all faces turned toward Rabbit. A very large man stepped forward facing him. "I am Ensign Ralph Wonacott, the ship's cook, and who are you?" he asked.

"General Peter Rabbit, security head for Sand Box 4, and according to the security scan I did from your command center with Med. Tech. Val Johnson, Dr. Wilks is the senior officer in command of Sand Box 2 and is in this room."

A good-looking woman stepped around the ensign lightly touching his arm. "It's alright, Ralph, I'm a big girl and although I've never met Peter Rabbit before I've heard of him. And considering who was speaking badly about him, he must be our friend."

"You must be speaking of Hardash, with whom I have a personality conflict," replied Peter. "I wish I had more time to chat but the alligators are hungry. Dr. Whosh, who commands Sand Box 4, is on a COM link up at command talking with your Val Johnson. She would like to talk with you while we secure the rest of your box," said Peter.

"I'll head right there, General Rabbit," said Wilks.

"The rest of you can sit tight until we have a plan. Ralph, you look like a sailor," queried Peter.

"I was a SEAL until I got hurt, now I do what I can," answered Ralph.

"Well you come with me and explain what happened to Hardash and his gang of hooligans. Besides, you're Dr. Wilk's XO and that outranks me," said Rabbit.

Ralph laughed. "I'm going to like you. That Hardash had *no* sense of humor."

With that they headed for the storage hold. On the way Rabbit's men reported they had found just what the scan had said.

"Good," replied Rabbit. "Set up security so we get no unwanted company."

In the hold they found enough weapons to arm a small army. This was the first time Ralph had seen them, but he knew they came onboard and with the men to use them. The best he could do to explain Hardash and company's absence was to point out that they had suddenly vanished, and no one now on board had any idea where they were or how they got there. The last he knew they were on Guam looking for SB3.

Peter smiled at Ralph. "You may want to be sitting down when you find out where we are or at least where we think we are."

With that Peter and Ralph headed for the command center of SB3.

On SB4, Sergeant Smith stuck an arm in enough to turn on the light. No one was there, so they stepped in and found the inside door open too. When they got in the passageway to the elevator, Smith split them into three groups. One took the elevator, two took the emergency tunnel, which was basically an open shaft with a ladder, and Smith led the last group down the stairway. Their objective was to secure the command center where they hoped they could find out what was happening onboard. Smith and his group arrived right behind the elevator team and they swiftly moved into the command center, which was totally empty. Smith soon saw that the main systems were all online and only the drives were on stand-by. He ran a security scan like Peter had showed him and was surprised to find no one had been on this ship in weeks. Next, he opened a COM link and reported to Whosh, who told him that Peter had secured SB2 and was on his way to help there.

Peter left Dr. Wilks and Amanda talking and brought Ralph along to see firsthand what was going on. Once more he had his team start at the top and search their way down, while he and Ralph joined Smith. They left two men in the command center and headed down to the storage hold since the security scanners would not tell them what was there. Bob caught up with them just as they got there, which turned out to be good as the hatch was secured with a security code. Five minutes later, the door opened and they all stepped in for the shock of their lives. This was not where Hardash was hiding. In fact, no one was there either, but the hold was filled from floor to ceiling with pallets full of gold bars. They stared for at least five minutes in absolute silence and disbelief.

Finally, Peter spoke. "I think we just found Fort Knox."

They secured the hold and SB3 and headed for the dining hall of SB4 to make a plan. On the way there, Peter took Dr. Wilks and Ralph to command center for a fast briefing of their situation—at least as well as they understood it. Like Peter on first seeing the rotating holograph, they stared and then Scotty replaced it with a three-dimensional chart of their location in reference to the Constitution, Scout bunker and the Earth itself. Scotty identified each and explained their relationship and that they were over 238 thousand miles up in a twenty-eight-day orbit.

Ralph was the first to recover and stammered, "But I have never heard of any space stations big enough to hold three of these boxes."

"It's crazier than that," replied Peter. "The floor out there is perfectly flat and, according to our best measurements, the three boxes are sitting in a huge dome whose outside wall is about a mile away in any direction. Add to that there is a constant supply of fresh air out there. We can get no scan readings on what's around us, but we can scan the Earth and tell where all the other Sand Boxes are located. Our best guess is that this is some kind of moon base that is as secret as Project Wonderland. And just in case you are wondering, I didn't know about any project of this scale off planet. To make matters worse, we have no idea how we got here. We were holding over the island of Guam scanning for any traces of SB2 and SB3, and then all of a sudden we were here. That's also what happened to the Constitution, except she didn't move anywhere but changed time to 1421."

With more information than they wanted, they all headed for the dining hall, each hoping for a plan that would make some sense.

Once the introductions were made, they moved on to the dilemma of three boxes and a crew and a half. The commanding officers, security personnel, and communications staff were gone, but fortunately most of the engineering personnel were left. The support personnel, including medical, food service, laundry, and clerical, were here. It became rapidly obvious that they were totally loyal to Doc Janet, who explained she only understood Sand Box operation in the broadest sense. But she had to agree that the crew would follow her anywhere. She also liked the idea of Ralph as her XO and security chief.

Since SB2 was stable and had a crew, they decided to move SB3 first. Whosh would split her crew and take both to the Scout bunker. Rabbit and the security team would stay with SB2 and could work on system training with Janet, Ralph, and crew. Val Johnson was learning to run COM and was very good with computers. So after everyone had a good meal and a burst transmission was sent to Scout bunker, they made ready. Dew took navigation, Sparks manned engineering, Bob took COM and control and in a half-hour they were all green. They synchronized with SB4, so at least technically they would make the leap to the Scout bunker together. Janet assured them that SB2 was ok and that they would be waiting for their return. With everything in place they launched for Hawaii.

Scout Bunker, High in the Hawaiian Mountains, the Year 2012:

The bunker was on full alert. Lieutenant Hosmer and Ranger Bear had the place locked down so tight an army ant couldn't have gotten past them. The banks of computers Sky had acquired were humming. The Landing Zone (LZ) had been prepared with great care. The beacon Fern had built was ready to guide them right in, but they checked and rechecked everything. They had close circuit TV set up so they could watch the LZ from the command center. And Kate was busy cooking up a storm in her modern rebuilt kitchen. The waiting was the worst part as everyone waited to see a real time machine. In fact, there should be two of them arriving.

The proximity alarm started sounding and everyone held their breath. Suddenly, a rather square, ugly box appeared and then a second. They all headed down to greet their arrivals. The door to SB4 opened first. Alice and Scotty headed right for SB3 to help stabilize it. Amanda, Bones, and Cookie greeted the welcoming committee. Amanda and Stella hugged. Stella introduced Captain Kid, Amy, Sky, Laurie, Kate, and Fern.

"Well, we've brought you all a present—well maybe two—but the president may want to share some of this. And you two want to see Bob. He ran the COM and command to get this other box here. Let's follow Alice and Scotty into SB3," said Amanda.

Alice was impatiently waiting for the door to open, but as the door opened she turned, smiled, and said, "Hi, folks, I'm Alice and welcome to Project Wonderland. The quiet guy is Scotty, our COM officer."

Alice led them in and keyed open the second door. Alice and Scotty had led the way in, but soon vanished leaving the guided tour to Amanda, who said to Bones and Cookie,

"Why don't you two give our guests the guided tour? After the command center they need to see the storage hold."

And off they went while Amanda, Stella, and Joe took a more leisurely tour.

"Now you guys have your own Sand Box to play in," said Amanda.

As Bones led the first group into the staging room, Fern asked, "How big is this thing? This room is bigger than the box outside."

"This looks like a diving room on a sub," added Sky.

"It is," said Bones. "Which means the box can be operated underwater or where there is no atmosphere outside."

"That's right," said Fern. "You just came from 238 thousand miles up."

"Yes," said Bones. "But somehow we were inside a huge dome with air."

They moved into the hall and were in awe and disbelief. When Bones and Cookie herded them all into the elevator they knew they were in Wonderland, and down the rabbit hole they went.

Fern was the first to speak as they sailed down. "Al once told me to be careful because things are not always what they seem on the outside. I wonder if he has ever seen one of these?"

The door opened and they headed to the command center. As they walked in, they again were stopped by the rotating holographic image Bob had in the middle of the room. The Earth was obviously in the center of the display. A red X showed where they were, little box icons with numbers showing where the boxes were, and a ship icon was next to Guam. Sky and Fern were beside themselves. Neither had seen a computer that could do this.

"That's nothing," Bob said as he walked through the Earth to hug his awed wife. "These computers have complete voice capacity, so there is no need for a keyboard, and some of the strange diagrams I've found may be for telepathic communication too. For some reason, they had all those programs disabled," explained Bob.

Amanda arrived with Joe and Stella just in time to hear what Bob said. They too stared in disbelief.

Joe finally spoke up. "I don't think I've ever seen this many impossible things in my whole life. Can this be linked to our computers upstairs?"

"Sure can," said Bob who was still busy hugging Kate.

Amanda smiled at the hugging couple. "We'll have to give those two some shore leave."

Fern and Sky were next to Alice who, once she was done shutting things down, pulled up the files Bob was looking at.

Alice said, "I've never seen these before."

"They had them encrypted and locked down with security codes so they were invisible to everyone else but the key masters," Bob said from across the room.

Amanda spoke up. "Bones, we better finish our tour. I hear there's some great food waiting for us, and Cookie may have to serve if we take too long. I think the base cook is about to drag Bob into the nearest closet or give us a sex education lesson."

Fern absently added to that, while not removing his eyes from the screen. "They're always like that. You would almost think they were still teenagers."

In a roar of laughter, Bones led the way to the storage hold. As Bob opened the locked door, the guests should have been in awe of the size of the room, but it was almost impossible to tell how big it was because it was full of gold. After they had all stared for a minute or two Amanda informed them they were looking at more gold than had been in Fort Knox before the politicians gave it away to pay off bad debts.

Joe asked, "But where did they get it?"

He started looking at the different names and ID info stamped into the bricks.

Amanda said, "I was hoping you two would figure that out and tell us. I bet the president would find this very interesting too. If Bob has unlocked enough files, you may be able to find the log entries for where they have traveled and when. I also think you want to put this under Top Secret wrappings."

They locked up and were very quiet all the way to the dining hall.

Everyone ate and chatted. Most of the crew spent the evening relaxing or outside under the stars. But Sanders, Fern, Sky, Jay, and Amy found this new technology just too fascinating. They got a link up to the base computers from SB3 and started digging into her secrets. They finally crashed but Sky, Fern, and Amy wanted to return with SB4 when they retrieved SB2. Sanders and Jay would love to go too but they were needed here and would have to settle for playing in SB3.

Over breakfast Fern, Amy, and Sky started their sales pitch to Dr. Whosh who looked at Stella, who said, "Why not, they may even find some answers up there. It'll also give them a chance to see one of the boxes in actual operation. I'm almost tempted to go back to the ship with you," said Stella. "It's been a while since I was one in Guam and I do kind of miss Flagg."

Joe said, "Well, I guess Hosmer and I can survive if you run off for a second honeymoon. Can Benedict Black find these boxes?"

"No," said Amanda. "Whatever took us there and moved the ship fried our transponders. The only way we can be seen is if we transmit a signal, like the one we send to you here and to the ship. Those transponders are supposed to be indestructible. When we pulled the one on SB4, the unit looked like it took a lightning strike, but that's impossible. Someone or something doesn't want us found. We were sent to where SB2 and SB3 were, even though we couldn't see them. The crew who would've been a problem to us had just vanished, but the gold and weapons were there."

By 0900 hours, everyone was aboard and SB4 launched. They contacted SB2 to tell them they were returning. The leap took about ten seconds to travel the 238 thousand miles and they were right back, one hundred feet from SB2. They had already planned who would join the SB2 crew so they headed up to make the switch. Fern, Amy, and Sky walked along to see the open area inside the dome where the boxes were sitting. Bob was going in SB2 and walked up with them. Even with the lights outside SB2, the surrounding darkness was complete. Amanda had come up to see Peter who was standing in the middle waiting.

Fern said, "Boy, this is amazing. It would be wild to explore this place."

Peter said, "I took some men and we walked out to the wall, then walked all the way around. We found a dozen huge sealed doors but no control panels that we could see to open them and no small people-sized hatches. We found air vents but they were much too high for us to reach. Nor were there written signs or light sources. We recorded it all, and the data will be downloaded to see if anyone can make sense of it."

At this point everyone was sort of standing between

the two boxes chatting and looking into the darkness as if something should be there. Suddenly, a glow started above them like a rising sun, but this was more like someone turning up a light with a rheostat. There was no obvious light source as the glow increased. As everyone looked up to see what was happening, suddenly there was a loud sound like a hammer hitting a steel anvil. Everyone jumped and looked straight into the darkness at the tall figure standing in colorful Native American attire. His long hair was braided with feathers, a colorful headband, and choker; a medicine bag hung around his neck; his breechcloth had bear paws with claws; and he wore colorful leggings, brown moccasins, and a tall coupstick with feathers running the whole length. It almost appeared that he was glowing like a hologram etched into the black background. There was total silence as every eye stared.

A booming voice spoke its message. "I come with words of warning that your brothers of the Constitution are in grave danger. You must go to them now and stand by them in their hour of need."

With that, the stern looking figure raised his coupstick and slammed it on the deck with a thunderous bang and vanished. Fern, Amy, Bob, and Sky ran to the spot where the figure had been, but all they could see were two large footprints and the two marks where the coupstick had struck the deck.

The four looked at the others and all said as one voice, "We must go to the ship now."

Amanda looked from them to Peter. His eyes said yes. Amanda said, "Then let's move it folks. We have a date with a ship."

Everyone ran to the boxes, and in five minutes SB2 and SB4 were green for go.

"Dew, do we have a lock?" asked Amanda.

"I have a lock and we're ready to launch," said Dew.

"I have green status from SB2 and they have a lock," said Scotty.

"Make the jump," Whosh ordered and with that, the large cavern became empty once more. The glowing light slowly faded away until total darkness once more returned and the air vents fell silent. SB2 and SB4 were leaping through time to Guam in the year 1421.

The USS Constitution at Anchor off the Island of Guam and the Village of Agana in the Year 1421:

It was a beautiful night with a warm breeze and waves gently lapping against the shore. Tracy and the children were sound asleep in the gorgeous raised home of the local elder, Kandit Mesngon. Many were sleeping on the beach or hammocks by the shore. A small fire burned as the men on beach security watch chatted about home and drank coffee. The gig was tied to a small pier and gently rocked with the waves. Albright and his boatswain's mate slept soundly in the cabin while the gunner's mate slept on the deck in the light breeze. The ship's security watches were mostly on the upper decks. No ladders were over the side so no one could climb aboard. The radar was empty and the sonar was picking up some odd noise like rowing. The half-asleep sonar man listened and could not decide what it was—maybe just waves on the rocks. He needed something to do, so he called the bridge.

The Quartermaster listened and called over the OOD. "Sir, we have some odd sounds coming from our sonar pick-up that they can't ID."

The OOD said, "Put it on the speakers" and his ears perked up. He had been on a rowing team and knew that sound.

"Boatswain's mate, I want a full security check with all

stations reporting in. Have your external watches check all the water around us."

With that he bolted to the open bridge and grabbed the night vision binoculars. He saw nothing near the ship, but there where a number of large boats on the beach that had not been there the night before, and then he saw several boats heading toward the gig.

The BM said, "Sir, I have two stations not answering."

"Sound the intrusion alarm. Get the Marines moving. Quartermaster, raise the gig and shore party. Tell them they have company. Wake the XO," ordered the OOD.

The QM called out, "Sir, radar has three contacts coming around the point!"

The OOD replied, "Sound General Quarters and announce that we have intruders on board."

The loud GQ horns sounded and were followed by the words, "General Quarters, this is not a drill. All hands are warned. We have been boarded. Security to the main deck."
The XO was on the bridge issuing orders in his underwear. The air boss came crashing onto the bridge trying to put on his shirt.

Before Bird stopped, the XO said, "Get the choppers armed and in the air."

Down on the hanger deck a small war was being waged with the pirates having the upper hand. With all the aircraft, fuel, and munitions there, the ship's defenders had to be careful where they fired weapons. Much of the battle was hand-to-hand combat where a sword was more useful than an M16, which couldn't be fired. Many of the unarmed sailors and flight crews were in the middle of this madness.

The night shore patrol was up above the beach. The young Marine had just walked farther to go pee when he saw movement out on the water. His night vision confirmed that they had company. He sent the others to spread the alarm and he called the bridge as they were calling him. The runner woke Lieutenant Brice who saw the boats on the farther beach and others headed for the gig. Harry was standing beside her as one of the Chamorro warriors raced up to tell them that these were pirates and some others were headed for the sleeping village. The warrior had to take his men and go.

Harry said to Charly, "The children are there. I'm going."

"I'll catch up," Charly replied.

Ensign Smith came racing up. They talked for a minute and Charly headed for the village with half the men, and Shela headed for the beach with the rest.

Captain Right arrived on the bridge with the IC2 electrician hot on his heels. The boatswain's mate had the weapons locker open and Right took the offered gun and belt. He headed for the QM, but was interrupted by a huge pirate aiming a cutlass at his head. Right warded off the blow with the gun belt and leaped back to gain some room. But suddenly, a rather large hammer flew across the bridge nailing the pirate right between the eyes. Before anyone could react, it was followed by the IC man who had a giant screwdriver in his hand. He skewered the pirate and pushed him off the bridge to the rail of the open bridge. There he tossed the pirate over the side to meet Davy Jones. When he returned to face the startled men on the bridge, he looked at the captain and said, "Sorry, sir, but the pirate wanted to keep my screwdriver as a parting gift."

"I'll get you a new one, son," Right stammered, still in shock.

Right had watched this man climb all over the masts working on his equipment and could now see why they chose him to work on the bridge during emergencies. Right realized he was still holding the gun. He held it up and asked, "Do you know how to use one of these?"

"Yes, sir. I qualified as expert with the Marines for SP duty," replied IC Petty Officer Knight.

"Then take this and make sure he didn't bring his friends along."

Knight swapped tool belts, checked the weapon, and climbed the nearest ladder going up from the open bridge.

The admiral arrived. "I would've been here sooner but the Marines insisted on guarding me."

Bird joined them. "We're having a problem in the hanger deck. The pirates are everywhere and we're engaged in hand-to-hand combat. I have two choppers on the flight deck and as soon as I get crews they will launch."

Then they heard the sound of gunshots above them. They looked out in time to see a pirate go flying past.

The admiral asked, "What was that about?"

Right said, "Our IC telephone man seems to be teaching pirates to fly."

The admiral replied, "No wonder I like that kid. I'll get down below to the flag bridge and work on our communications, since our phone man is busy."

Back on the beach Ensign Smith and her security team were racing toward the gig as fast as they could. The sun was high enough now to see that two of the pirate boats had pulled alongside the gig. The poor gunner's mate never knew what hit him, then his killer headed into the cabin, but Alex had awakened enough to grab the flare gun. He fired it right into the pirate's face sending him back to his surprised accomplices.

The BM was waiting with an M16 when the next one tried to enter. The pirates were all over the deck when Ensign Smith landed in the middle of them and opened fire as well. The rest of the team swept down on them like avenging angels. The BM joined them and Alex climbed up to the .50 cal and blew the approaching boat full of pirates to pieces. The BM started the engines and they backed right into the next boatload and sent them to the bottom.

Alex yelled, "Get us to the ship! They've been boarded and they have bigger ships headed in!"

The village was very quiet and peaceful as everyone slept. The children and Tracy were staying in the home of Kandit Mesngon. It was a beautiful raised house standing high up on the latte stones. Harry saw dark figures moving on the house's front porch. Since he'd been here many times with the children and Charly, he remembered watching the children climb into the house from the side. That was where he now climbed onto it. He slipped into the shadow behind the railing as one of the pirates came along. Harry hit him so hard with one of the kid's toys that he went down like a rock. After this he heaved him over the rail.

Just then Harry heard a scream and ran toward it. As he entered the room, he saw a pirate holding Krista. He hit him hard enough to break his club. Krista ran for shelter, dragging a couple of the other children out of sight. Then Harry heaved the pirate over the rail like the last one and headed back in, when he met two more pirates. He slammed the first back against the wall and caught the man's second hand with a sword. Harry then crashed it into the wall so hard that the sword fell to the floor. Before he could do anything else, the first pirate latched onto his other arm. The two fought to hold him as a third pirate entered and prepared to run him through with his sword.

Just as the pirate was about to rush forward and finish him off, a small shadow streaked up behind the pirate and leaped onto his back. Krista brought her laundry bag down over the pirate's head and pulled on the tie ropes with all her weight, then tied a knot that would make a Boy Scout proud.

He dropped his sword and began pulling at the rope that was choking him. Krista circled in front of the blinded pirate and planted her foot firmly in his crotch. In screaming agony he fell to the floor, but Krista attacked again and kept kicking him as hard as she could. All the other children in the house saw this and attacked the other two pirates. They crashed to the floor while still trying to keep a hold on Harry. Adagi, Tracy, and Kandit soon joined the children beating these men with no mercy.

Outside, Momo Gogui (battle, fight, protect, save rescue) and the Chamorro warriors arrived from one direction and Charly and her security team from the other. They converged on the pirates and began driving them back into the sea. Charly arrived upstairs just in time to see two pirates leap off the railing and Harry standing in the middle of a group of women and children. On the other side of the room Krista stood over a limp body.

Harry walked over and hugged her tight, looked her right in the eyes, and said, "Thank you."

Charly hugged Krista too. She handed Harry an M16 and ammo, kissed him on the cheek, and said, "I have to go help."

Kandit came up to Krista. "You are a brave woman and will be a great leader."

Once they were sure the household was safe, Tracy and Harry headed to the ocean to see how the battle was going.

Krista took charge of Sue and carried her as she walked between the two adults.

Back on the Constitution, things were not going well. The battle for the hanger deck was bloody and hand-to-hand. The Marines had to fall back to secure the hatches to the lower decks, while the officers and aircrews fought to keep them from coming up. More pirate boats were arriving to reinforce the pirates onboard. And more ships had appeared on radar. Close to twenty were in sight and the choppers still had no crews. There were at least a dozen pirates running amuck on the flight deck making that a dangerous place. Five of those big ships were closing fast; all had cannons and more pirates.

The admiral and captain were weighing their options carefully. Even if they got underway, they still couldn't launch aircraft without dealing with the pirates. Vary Kurious had kept trying to reach SB4 but it was still traveling outside time and beyond their reach. This had been a bloody dawn they would not forget. They knew the gig was under attack and a large force had landed, heading for the village. Most of the ship's personnel taking R and R were near the shore and unarmed. The children were staying at Kandit Mesngon's home with Tracy North. Their fun adventure was now tainted with blood.

Fate often has its own rules and for those rewriting history, the tide was about to shift the sands of time and deliver up SB2 and SB4. For the pirates who saw SB2 and SB4 arrive out of thin air, it was a strong omen with bad tidings for them. On the flag bridge, Merry Kurious leaped up from her console and with an excited voice said, "They're here Admiral—two of them just landed on the hanger deck!"

She started talking fast into her mike explaining to both SB2 and SB4 that the pirates had charge of the hanger deck.

On SB2, Rabbit and Sergeant Smith divided the security forces into two groups. Rabbit would take one team from their amidships location and drive the pirates right off the fantail. At the same time, Sergeant Smith would lead the second team forward toward the bow. This action would hopefully get the hanger deck cleared for action. Since the hold of SB2 was full of weapons they had no problem arming both teams. As soon as they were ready, they had Dr. Wilks let them out to engage the pirates. When they came out they found the pirates were still keeping their distance, so they staged their teams for the counterattack.

Meanwhile on SB4, Alice was taking Sky, Fern, and Amy to Rabbit's arms locker so they could help with the pirates. Much to their surprise, they found Patty Sparks was already there and had a large box marked TOP SECRET open on the floor. She was strapping on the belt with two holsters and battery packs for the two laser pistols she'd found in the box. Alice, still somewhat in shock finding her mild-mannered electrician here, asked, "What do you think you're doing Patty?"

"Going to find my children," she said.

"Then I guess I'm coming too. You know I can't be losing my best technician," said Alice. And with that, she grabbed the laser rifle in the box and a bandoleer of battery packs.

The other three had already armed themselves with somewhat more conventional weapons.

Sky said to Alice, "I guess we have us a mission."

And Amy said, "Anyway Patty, Fern here has wanted to meet Krista for some time now."

On her way to the door, Patty stopped in front of him and

told him boldly, "I know about you Boy Scouts, so you had best treat her right or I'll short-sheet your skivvies."

"Yes, ma'am," he replied.

With that, Patty was gone and they were running to catch up with her. Alice told Amanda they were going looking for the kids.

Up on the superstructure, IC2 Max Knight and his two deck ape companions had chased all the pirates down to the flight deck. It was now easy enough to keep them from climbing, but there were too many of them. So they waited, hoping for reinforcements.

Patty headed across the hanger deck in the direction of the giant elevator on the far side. She knew that there was a ladder leading to the flight deck above. The little band was halfway across when they saw the pirates. They'd been hiding to avoid the other security teams who were sweeping the deck and were planning to sneak up behind them and attack. They obviously didn't see four women and a boy as a big obstacle to their plans, so they kept coming straight at them.

Patty in the lead stood like a western gunslinger, as she pulled out her two laser pistols and that's when they all opened fire from about twenty feet. The pirates in the back rapidly saw the error of their ways as the pirates in front of them were cut to pieces or blown apart before their very eyes. The remaining pirates started running as fast as they could the other way, then across the elevator and right into the waiting ocean without looking back once.

Patty was already halfway up the stairs when the others ran after her. She flew onto the flight deck and had covered fifty feet before she noticed the pirates closing on her. On the superstructure, Max saw the danger and leaped to the flight deck with his two companions in hot pursuit. Even though the pirates had moved from their cover, they still didn't realize the danger even when Sky, Alice, Fern, and Amy arrived on the scene. The closest pirate to Patty raised his sword in a threatening manner. She calmly pulled a laser pistol out and cut his sword off near the handle. As if the shock of that was not enough, the heat from the laser burned his hand so badly he had to let go of what was left of it.

Max and his two companions, seeing the new arrivals, swung out even wider, so when they all opened fire on the pirates they had formed a line across the flight deck. Even though they were outnumbered five to one, their superior firepower drove them right off the stern into the ocean.

As Patty led the way the group started to head back toward the bridge. Ahead they could already see the airmen prepping the two helos. Max ran to catch up with Patty and said, "You know you're a crazy woman."

She glanced at him and proudly replied, "It's motherhood and hormones. Now...I want to find my kids."

Max looked at her once more and asked, "You're Sue's mom?"

"Yes!"

"Well, that explains it. The admiral will know where they are. My guess is they're ashore getting to know the natives. You'd like it over there. The women are in charge."

Patty shot back, "You got a problem with that?"

"Not me, as long as the most competent person is making the decisions. Gender and hormones just complicate life, but they also make it more interesting," said Max.

"Are you hitting on me, sailor?"

"Not yet. I don't know you well enough," he answered her.

"Are you a Boy Scout too?

"How did you guess?"

With that, Fern, Amy, Alice, and Sky started laughing.

Fern said, "Don't worry, Max. Mama Bear will calm down as soon as she finds her cubs."

Down below, the gig had arrived and was chasing the pirates in the longboats away from the ship. The shoulder-launch missiles they had stocked onboard were working well even when they took on the first pirate ship to arrive alongside the Constitution. The boatswain's mate maneuvered the pirate ship right up on a sand bar and left them there while they returned to the battle. Meanwhile, the two choppers were airborne and had left the second two pirate ships burning. Once the hanger deck was secure, six more choppers were brought into action. Four delivered torpedoes to eight of the advancing ships among the pirate fleet. This caused their commander to decide it was time to leave and live to fight another day.

Admiral Staff was amazed to see Sky and Amy following Patty. He even managed to slow Patty down enough to meet Fern and hear that Stella was ok. Then he agreed to let Max procure a pirate longboat to take Patty to her children. Sickbay was in full swing treating ship's company and the Chamorro wounded. One of the wounded was Anao Agnasina (to conquer, mighty for each other) who was Kandit Mesngon's husband and the maga'lahi (high ranking male) in the village of Agana. Anao had been unarmed when the pirates confronted him. He had been left for dead, but the blow to the head, which knocked him out, probably saved his life. His wounds were bad and Bones had him taken to SB4 where he had laser surgical tools.

When Kandit got word of Anao's fate, she got the village healer, Abi Suruhana, and came to be at his side. Cookie took Kandit aside to explain what was happening. It was Kandit's first time on the ship. Tracy soon showed up and stayed with her as well. Bones had Chrissy, who was an aspiring assistant and who was working with Abi already on the native children's health issues, get her dressed for the OR. He then let them assist and let Abi provide her medical help, which allowed his patient and Kandit to be more at ease.

Abi watched in amazement as Bones sewed and repaired that which was well beyond anything she could do. Soon she went to work on her English skills so she could learn from the medical staff and taught them how to use herbs and natural remedies. A new alliance was formed among the healing arts old and new. Once all was secure aboard, Bones and Wilks set up a field hospital on the beach to treat the wounded pirates who were captured after their fleet had abandoned them.

Max and the two sailors found a longboat, and they started rowing to shore. Harry, Tracy, and the kids were waiting when they beached it. Sue ran to meet her mother before she could get out of the water. Fred was a close second, while Krista calmly waited for her mother's arrival with Tracy and Harry. Chrissy and James hugged Aunt Alice tightly.

When Patty finally dragged the two kids up to where Krista was, Krista said, "Mom, those are odd-looking tools for an electrician!"

Harry laughed. "It looks like your mom chose a high-tech method to deal with pirates, while you were taking them out with a laundry bag." Then he proceeded to tell the whole story of how she had saved him from the pirates with a laundry bag and a well placed foot.

Patty hugged her daughter. "Guess I didn't need to rush

after all, but I have someone here who was in a big hurry to meet you."

Harry said, "Hi, Fern. I see you've brought your own SEAL team."

"Sure did. This is Amy Hunter and Sky Lonewolfe."

Krista walked over for a closer look and said to him, "I hope my mom didn't scare you. She's mostly harmless."

"Not at all," replied Fern. "She just gave me some good advice about keeping my skivvies in order."

Harry started laughing as did Max and the sailors.

Krista said, "I don't get it."

To which Fern diplomatically replied, "I think that has to do with a mother-daughter talk you two are about to have."

And now it was Patty's turn to laugh as she hugged Krista. "You'll probably tell me more than I'll tell you."

And then she looked right at Max who gave her one of his big smiles.

The next few days would be sad ones. The Chamorro prepared their dead and held their rites for the passage of their loved ones. A large party from the ship came to show their respect. The ship's dead were placed in body bags in one of her refrigeration units until they could be returned home. The ship's chaplain, Desire Peace, held a dawn memorial service on the flight deck. A large group of Chamorro attended to show their mutual respect for the friends who had died protecting them.

The ship's crew was called to the service with the words, "All hands bury the dead." The ship's ensign was lowered to half-mast and an honor guard carried a lone flag-draped casket to the edge of the deck. All hands stood at attention and saluted it as it passed them.

Chaplain Peace had the crew stand at ease. "We are here today to remember, to honor, and to celebrate the lives of our brave companions whose lives were forfeited as the price of freedom. I would like to open with the words of the Naval Hymn:

> "Eternal Father, strong to save,
> Whose arm hath bound the restless wave,
> Who bid'st the mighty ocean deep
> Its own appointed limits keep:
> O hear us when we cry to Thee
> For those in peril on the sea.
> O Christ, whose voice the waters heard,
> And hushed their raging at Thy word,
> Who walkedst on the foaming deep,
> And calm amid the storm didst sleep:
> O hear us when we cry to Thee
> For those in peril on the sea.
> O Holy Spirit, who didst brood
> Upon the waters dark and rude,
> And bid their angry tumult cease,
> And give, for wild confusion, peace:
> O hear us when we cry to Thee
> For those in peril on the sea.
> O Trinity of love and power,
> Our brethren shield in danger's hour,
> From rock and tempest, fire and foe,
> Protect them wheresoe'er they go:
> Thus evermore shall rise to Thee
> Glad hymns of praise from land to sea.
> AMEN"

Rev. William Whiting

Chaplain Peace continued, "Admiral Flagg Staff, our senior commanding officer, will speak next."

The admiral began, "We're here to remember our fallen comrades who have given their lives not only to defend us, but also to protect the lives of our newfound friends the Chamorro people. Our mission, while it's become vague, still mandates that we serve and protect those in need. We've stood here in the greatest traditions of our nation and defended those who have befriended us. We will endeavor to return them to their families in a timely manner. To our departed comrades and our new friends of the Chamorro people, who have also made the greatest sacrifice in our defense, we salute you. We will hold your memory in our hearts and carry on in your names. May you all rest in peace."

Chaplain Peace then introduced, "Doctor Tracy North speaking for our civilian crewmembers."

Tracy began, "When I agreed to join all of you, I had visions of great adventures and seeing things lost in our own time. I've seen those sights and had those adventures in part because of those who are no longer with us. And I stepped from an academic world of books and stories into a world of flesh and blood reality where prices are paid for lessons learned. I have watched our children grow and behave as adults, plus made friends I will never forget and I owe this all to these brave souls."

Chaplain Peace said, "Our youngest, Sue Sparks, has asked to place a wreath of flowers on our memorial casket to honor our fallen comrades who journey on before us. While they place the wreath, Fern Cybernaut has asked that I read the words of the one who sent them here to help us in our hour of need."

Sue walked slowly to the casket with the wreath escorted by Fern, Krista, James, Chrissy, Fred, and Admiral Staff.

"Our Oneness in Creation and Spirit,
Whose breath illuminates all life.
In silence we create a Holy place within for You.
So the divine union may give birth to unity and peace in all.
May our unity of purpose flow to heal Mother Earth,
So she can be as our place of creation.
May your broken bread feed our needs,
And insights fill us daily.
Grant us forgiveness for our errors on the way,
And help us to release our guilt,
As well as that which we see in others.
Help us overcome the seduction of our delusions,
So we can better see the way.
One Source of All our energy of Love,
Uniting us in the Glory of the healing light,
As we return home in endless cycles,
Now solemnly seal our petition,
Amen."

After placing the wreath, Sue and the others stood just back from the honor guard as the chaplain continued, "O Lord, embrace these souls and welcome them home and bring your healing love to their families and friends. We thank you for the privilege of having them in our lives and we commit them to your loving care."

With that, the casket was tilted and slid into the deep. The honor guard came to attention, raised their rifles, and fired three volleys over where the casket came to rest. As taps was played, the flag was folded and given to Sue, who hugged it tight to her chest. She turned and led her escorts back to where her mother stood waiting to hold her. There were few dry eyes and at the end of Taps, Chaplain Desire Peace said, "All hands are dismissed from burial detail. Holiday routine is in effect for the rest of the day. May God be with us as we journey on. Amen."

Many walked back to the starboard side and watched the flowered wreath float out to sea. Everyone spent a quiet day and at its end, most who wanted to join the Chamorro for a feast on the beach to celebrate the lives of the departed. A few new watches had been set and two small teams had been taken by helicopter to the highest peaks on the island, where they set up portable radar stations. These could monitor air or sea traffic within fifty miles of Guam.

The remaining pirates who had been captured had received any needed medical treatment. The pirate ship the gig had run aground was re-floated, repaired, and disarmed. The pirates were given enough food for ten days at sea and told if they returned it would be at their peril. However, it was doubtful they would be of any further trouble. While they were fierce pirates, they were also Japanese and held honor in high regard. Not only had their enemies defeated them, but saved them, healed their wounds, and were sending them home to their families. It would be a great dishonor for them to return to harm those who where such honorable enemies. For them to ever return they must do so as friends.

The new dawn was time to face more of the dilemmas of the present. At 0900 hours Admiral Staff had called for a full meeting of all the senior personnel of the Constitution, the Air Wing, SB2, and SB4. In the past they had only met with key personnel, but the magnitude of their operation was changing.

The admiral walked in the briefing room at 0905 hours. Someone yelled, "Attention on deck," and everyone snapped to his or her feet, even the startled civilians.

"As you were," he barked and confirmed with Ltjg. Merry Kurious that everyone was present, and then he sat down.

"Ladies and gentlemen, this is going to be a long day and our orders will be coming from the president of the United States, Puritan White," he began. "In our earlier meeting we did not involve all of you because we saw our mission as rather limited to intelligence gathering and returning this ship to the year 2012. Our mandate from the president and our operating nature has changed. Besides working with the president, we have an underground base, Scout bunker, in Hawaii. We also now have in our possession three time machines. While SB4 was on her last mission she found and retrieved both SB2, which is now aboard, and SB3, which is at the Scout bunker. As soon as I am done with my initial presentation, Lt. Vary Kurious, our intel officer and his wife, Ltjg. Merry Kurious from the Office of Naval Intelligence, where she works for Admiral Snoopy, will give you all a full briefing on what has happened to date."

A timid hand raised in the third row.

"Yes, chaplain?"

"Admiral, sir, I think I'm here by mistake and don't think I'm cleared to hear what you're talking about," said Chaplain Peace.

"You are, Lt. Desire Peace, an ordained minister in the Baptist Church and have a Ph.D. in philosophy?"

"Yes, sir, I am, but I have no command rank."

"Well, first of all, I added your name to the list last night after I read your jacket. Let me try to explain. This ship came from the year 2012 and is now anchored in Guam during the year 1421. We were just attacked and almost lost our ship to a bunch of six hundred-year-old pirates with antique weapons. We were saved in part by two time machines that came directly here from a huge base they 'think' was on the moon. They came here because an old Scout leader appeared to them dressed as a Native American and told them to come here because we needed help. Six of the people who saw this vision are in this room. Four of them know this man and were in his home in the mountains of New England less than two months ago. Besides that, we have now interacted with native Hawaiians, two groups of Japanese pirates, a Chinese admiral who is famous enough to be in our history books, his men on hundreds of ships, and the Chamorro people of Guam. So far, the regular reports we get from 2012 are saying they've seen no changes they would attribute to our activities. But here we are and so far we have no idea how to get this ship back. There are no rules or regulations that tell us how to behave here. So that is why you and Tracy North, a cultural anthropologist, are here to help us not mess up our future," finished Admiral Staff.

By the time the admiral was done it almost looked like Chaplain Peace had stopped breathing as what he was saying sank in. Tracy, who was getting a cup of coffee, brought a cup to Desire, who nodded her thanks.

Krista spoke up and broke the silence as she stared at the shocked Desire. "I was wondering why I'm here."

"You're here like Fern because you have displayed superior adult behavior and we need your bright young minds to help us old farts see what we might otherwise miss," said Staff.

Krista smiled at the admiral. "Thanks. I think I can handle that. I was afraid you wanted me to help explain what God wants." With that she laid her hand reassuringly on

Desire's arm and said to her, "I'll try to help you too. This is mega big."

"So let me wind up my spiel by explaining what we need to do. First of all, we *think* we need to return this ship to the year 2012. Somehow we have to return our fallen comrades to their families. However, it'll become very obvious to the CIA that we have a box. There's the question of how the leaders and crewmembers of SB2 and SB3 vanished. How'd we find these boxes? Why does SB3 have more gold in the hold than in Fort Knox? Why is SB2 full of weapons? Why are SB5 in Russia and SB6 in Europe? We have three boxes but only enough crew for one and a half. Can we retrain personnel onboard to operate them, rather than all our aircraft that we have, which will run out of fuel to operate? How should we interact with the natives from this time? How'd we get here and who's responsible? How did SB4 find the other boxes? Why were they in a domed base large enough to hold this ship on the moon?"

Staff continued, "We have to decide what to do next and how to get there. We need to find out what the men using the boxes are trying to do. Are they trying to take over the world by manipulating events in time and by stealing money? Why didn't our president know about the Sand Boxes? Why was a team of CIA hitmen chasing Fern and his mother? As you all can see, we have many questions and from the answers we must find new directions for us to move forward from where we are now. Since we've been at this for almost an hour, we'll take a fifteen-minute break and, at 1010 hours, Merry and Vary Kurious will start a detailed briefing. Hopefully, they'll be done by lunch so we can start talking about what we can do, how we should do it, and in what order. Thank you and let's break."

The fifteen minutes dragged for some, especially the

curious who were hearing all this for the first time. Some had paid little attention to the box and had even just assumed the ship had stopped at very undeveloped islands. For those who saw the pirates it was a real anomaly, but in the military most things are so compartmentalized that one soldier might not have a clue what the person next to him is doing, let alone why. Now the rules were changing and everyone was getting into the act. How did one go from working on jets and helicopters to a time machine?

Krista and Tracy were talking with Desire, who began to see her mission in a new light. She even asked Fern about his vision. He was the first person Desire had ever met who had one. She was amazed that Fern thought the appearance of his old friend was a normal event.

Soon, Lieutenant Kurious called the briefing back to order and everyone scurried back with coffee or from the head. Once they were fairly settled, Lieutenant Kurious started. "I'm going to explain this as the events happen from our time frame of reference to save confusion. You see, when SB4 left us as we were anchored at future Pearl Harbor in Hawaii, they returned to 2012, which means they visited Hawaii on that trip six hundred years after we arrived in Hawaii. In fact, it means that the people sitting in this room that went there and returned will not get there for 599 years. So I'll start with the event as we approached Hawaii in 2012."

While he talked, Merry displayed a time line on the big screen so everyone could follow the flow. When Vary's voice was wearing out, Merry stepped in. It was 1140 hours when she arrived at the present time. For twenty minutes they answered questions and finally they called for a lunch break. They would reconvene at 1330 hours.

Tracy and Krista took Desire to lunch with them in SB4

where she got to meet Amanda, Peter, Harry, Alice, Bones, Cookie, Janet, Fern, and all the other children. Amanda told her about the vision, and Amy told everyone about living with him at his home. Sky told them about finding the CIA hitmen hiding nude in a well. Janet described seeing the gold in SB3. Tracy told the history of the Chamorro after Magellan found them. Before they had to return to the general meeting, Alice took Desire, Fern, Amy, Sky, and Krista for a tour of SB4 to give them a better idea of its size and complexity. Her tour included the hold where Alice said, "Now imagine this full of gold bars."

With full stomachs and much to think about everyone reconvened at 1330 hours to attempt to make sense of all that had happened and to plan their next actions. The admiral was already seated, talking with Lieutenant Kurious about how the morning had gone, so once everyone was seated he said, "Well, crew, let's get started. We are on a new venture in naval history and should do so boldly in keeping with our rich tradition. First, let us start with the Sand Boxes. Can we operate and maintain them?" asked Staff.

Alice raised her hand and he motioned her to speak. "Sir, the Constitution has many of the parts and repair capacities of our original base. Scout bunker can be equipped and we appear to have an abundance of trained personnel here. We should have enough people right now to bring SB2 up to full manpower and with a training program also man SB3. Also, these personnel will not be lost for their original jobs if needed. Just as many of your pilots can fly several different aircraft, the same is true of the technicians who maintain them."

Dr. Whosh spoke next. "I have to agree with Captain

Furreal. Having a second or third box to keep the ship supplied would solve many of our current problems."

Harry added, "You know, admiral, if we were to take the gold bars off SB3, we could fit her with a fuel tank that could supply fuel for the aircraft, which I know has been worrying Commander Bird. Those boxes like this ship have at least a twenty-year fuel supply."

Commander Albright, the ship's engineer, added his agreement. "An aircraft carrier by its very nature is designed to be flexible and, in this case, we just have ships that fly without wings."

Admiral Staff said, "Then since we've an agreement that we can make this work, the next thing is to acquire a mission mandate. I think that should come right from the top. We've been in contact with President White during most of this adventure. I think that for the sake of the crew we should have an operational mandate. We should bring the president here and to Scout bunker for a tour. I also think he needs to see one of those boxes with the gold and our ship anchored in this tropical paradise."

"Next is the matter of returning our fallen crew to their families. I think we can get President White to help us with that and maybe even get Admiral Snoopy of ONI to help out. If we can manage that, then I think we could also have the crew send mail home to their families. Of course that means we'll have to provide the crew with our 'cover story,' since the truth is so bizarre only the bad guys would believe it. So that gets us back to problem one, manpower. Doctor Whosh of SB4 has given us a full list of box crew, their training, and job descriptions. Captain Right is having that list run against ship and flight crew and will be meeting with you to work out the logistics. He has already found a navigator for SB2. Would Lt.

Leaf Erickson please stand up? Dr. Wilks, he's your man. I also have two more recommendations if they'll agree to sign on with you. Bob Cybernaut, how would you like to be in charge of her COM?" asked Staff.

"I'd be honored, sir."

"And Harry Haul, Dr. Wilks sure could use a chief engineer," said Staff.

"Sounds like fun. I'm really starting to like it here."

"Of course," said the admiral, "we may have to give you two a rank so we can pay you."

Harry replied, "Well, sir, we're both ASMs and have served under Colonel Jorge, our Scoutmaster."

"Now that, I know President White will approve of wholeheartedly," answered Staff. "Ensign Wonacott, if you work with General Rabbit and Lieutenant Brice, they'll help you set up a security team for SB2." Bringing the meeting to an end, the admiral said, "Since we've yet to have a full staff meeting I'll update you on our security changes before we go. We've placed two remote radar units up on the mountain that can scan around the whole island and they are manned 24/7. We've added to our deck patrols and put motion sensors around the ship. We also have the gig manned with a full crew at night and have four choppers armed and ready with a crew standing by as well. Ok, let's get started. We have a lot of work to do. That's all I have to say at this time, so unless you need to talk with me, you're dismissed."

Whosh and Wilt brought their two crews together and started training. While they were doing that, Captain Right had a working party remove all the weapons from SB2 and store them on the ship. SB2 was still short a cook, and that evening while Bob was practicing his COM skills by talking with Scoutbunker, he asked Kate, "How would you like to be SB2's cook?"

"Does that mean we get to travel together?"

There was a great deal of laughter in the command center, since they could all hear her question. Bob looked around at his amused shipmates and answered her. "Yes, dear, it does and all these guys too. You might even get to see our wandering son."

"Well, in that case I'll give Captain Kid my notice."

Meanwhile, Sky and Fern were working with Sandy to hack their way to answers. They'd spent a lot of time on both SB2 and SB4 going over computer files. They didn't find that much on SB4, but on SB2 they finally found her travel log. It explained where the weapons came from, and some of her trips were to places very unfriendly to American interests. Sky and Fern also found they had a new assistant in Krista, whose many questions often solved problems. When they were having a hard time retrieving the logs of SB2 because the operating system had been told not to allow that, Krista asked why they didn't just plug the hard drives from SB2 into SB4 and ask its operating system to do the search. It worked, although now they had all sorts of new questions. But they were eager to pull the hard drives off SB3 to see where the gold had come from, and they made reservations for the next trip to Scout bunker.

Admiral Staff was busy getting things in place to give the president a tour, and Stella was busy at Scout bunker pulling that end together. Kid had increased security and, to avoid raising suspicion, had added a second platoon from Army Intel and two platoons of Marines. Add to that, the Navy SEABEEs had gone to work on construction projects to bring the bunker up-to-date. They also repaired the park buildings and added many new features, like a dining hall and visitor center. The new Marines assigned to external security became very proud of their new, well-tailored U.S. Forest Ranger uniforms that hid an assortment of weapons. Even the old elevators were now working. Things were taking shape and the loading docks were busy bringing supplies for the ship. Operations were in full swing.

AS THE DAWN SIX

When we have no idea where we are going our choices become much simpler, because all the roads before us will lead us to our destiny.

Hawaii, Air Force One:
The plane made a smooth landing and parked at the Naval Air Station. Stella with the Secret Service greeted Snow and Susan. Walter Kid, Fran, Mike, and Jake introduced themselves to Stella who greeted them warmly. She told them there was a van waiting to take them up to Uncle Joe's place. The three older women would probably see them again. The van then headed off the base and up into the mountains, while the limo with Snow, Stella, and Susan drove to the Staffs' house. The Secret Servicemen joined the security force already there guarding the home while the ladies leisurely had lunch. When done Stella told the staff they were going to her bedroom to relax.

Once securely there, all three changed from their dresses into jumpsuits and comfortable walking shoes, and then they vanished into Stella's closet, through the secret panel, and down the stairs. Outside, the security team would see to it no one got that close to the truth.

Once they were in the tunnel, it forked one way to the garage closet. The other kept going beyond the walls to another garage. In that garage sat a van with a sign on the side reading, Ace Cleaning Services. The van looked rather normal, but had a large V-10 with four-wheel drive and bulletproof sides. It was also loaded with electronics of every kind, stuff only James Bond would have. Stella turned the key and typed in the security data. The computer came to life and announced that all was clear, so she opened the door, then drove out of the city and headed for the mountains.

"This is more fun than traveling with Purr and no SS to get under foot," said Snow.

Stella smiled and looked at Susan who, while enjoying the adventure, was concerned for her charge. Stella said, "We have a car full of SEALs within three blocks of us and I'll bet Joe has a helicopter gunship not far away, so enjoy the illusion."

Susan smiled back. "Now that's nice to know. I think I *will* enjoy the ride."

White House, Washington, D.C., Later Friday Afternoon:

"Mr. President, your wife is on the phone from her friend's home in Hawaii," said assistant Flash.

White picked up the phone. "Hello, dear, how was trip?"

Snow said, "It was a great flight, and I'm glad you let Susan have a vacation with me. Stella met us at the airport and we're all settled in here. We are going to go sight seeing around the island. Stella knows where there are some great golden sunsets to show us."

White said, "Well, dear, it sounds like you're having fun. I'm glad. I'll be flying up to Camp David for a working weekend with Jack Frost."

Snow said, "Now that sounds very boring. I'll try to have some fun for you, Purr."

White replied, "That's good, dear, and I'll be thinking of you. Love you and see you soon."

"Bye, Purr," said Snow. "I'll buy you something very Hawaiian."

White looked up as he put the receiver back on the phone and saw Jack Frost entering the Oval Office. He motioned him to a chair. "We all ready to fly, Jack?"

"Everything is headed for the chopper, sir."

"Good. That was Snow. She's with Stella in Hawaii. They're going to see a golden sunset. Now isn't that more fun than a working weekend?"

"Well, sir, Camp David has some beautiful nature walks we can enjoy."

"Sounds good. Let's get out of here before something happens."

White got up and put on his suit jacket and headed out with Jack for the helo-pad. As he left, he wished the staff a great weekend off and said he would see them Monday at the morning briefing.

They walked out to the waiting chopper and were soon flying away from the Washington madness to the Aspen Lodge in the Maryland mountains. It was the vice president's turn to baby-sit Washington for the weekend, and White had things to do. While they flew, he read reports, up-dates and need-to-know news. Jack just sat looking out the window, wondering where this road would lead. They landed right on time and their evening meal was waiting for them. They ate quietly as both had thoughts that were far away. When the meal was done they headed out for a refreshing walk around the grounds of Camp David. They enjoyed the stars on this clear night.

As they approached a picnic area, White said, "Supper was great, but I have to get rid of some of it." Then he headed toward the outdoor restroom hidden by the shadows of the trees. Frost agreed it was a good idea and the Secret Servicemen took up watch out front, while White and Frost headed toward the darkened door.

On the Road to Scout Bunker:

The gray Navy van seemed to drive on forever. Walter and the kids were enjoying the beauty of Hawaii far too much to complain. This was a whole new world for all of them. There was nothing like this in the asphalt jungle of Chicago. As soon as they were outside the city, the lush greenery was everywhere. On the driver's side of the van, the ocean soon appeared and they could smell the salty breeze. Finally, they turned up a small road with a sign saying it was a park and was closed for construction.

When Walter first saw the park ranger who stopped them, he wondered if Joe had changed his line of work. He thought being a park ranger wouldn't be a bad job, and then he wondered why park rangers would be so well armed and why the guy checked all their ID cards. They then drove forward around a bend and underground to a large loading dock with military trucks and very heavily armed guards. The kids were less surprised than Walter was since they'd spent a lot of time underground in the city. The van stopped at the ramp and the driver announced that this was the end of the line, so everyone climbed out.

Two smiling men came striding down to meet them. The one in the ranger suit spoke first. "Hello, I'm Park Ranger Ted Bear and this is Lieutenant Jay Hosmer, our security chief. Welcome to Scout bunker. Captain Kid has been waiting for you. He would have greeted you himself but he is expecting a lot of company today. Major Kid, Stella said you had a good trip out here."

"She'll be joining us later," added the lieutenant in his army uniform. "We'll take you up to the command center and I think Ted is free to give you a tour."

As they walked into the bunker they had to stop as a work party moved a pallet of gold bars past them. Finally, Walter's curiosity got the best of him. "Those were gold bars, right?"

"They sure were."

"You're U.S. Army, Ted is a National Park Service ranger, and we were brought here by a sailor, those guys are Marines, we were flown here by the president's wife, who's visiting an admiral's wife, and I thought my brother was just a Hawaiian state cop."

Both Ted and Jay started laughing.

Jay said, "Well, I think we've all fallen in the rabbit hole. Stella, Snow, the president's wife and Susan, who is head of White House Security, will be driving here in a few hours. Alice Furreal and Peter Rabbit will be bringing the president and the admiral here in Sand Box 4, which is part of Project Wonderland. Maybe then you'll all go visit the missing Constitution at Guam. Ted has about two hours to try to explain, but I've been here almost from the beginning and it still confuses me. Oh, and Kate Cybernaut has food for you guys. Her son, Fern, and husband will be arriving in Sand Box 2 very soon to pick up supplies."

They led them from the underground loading dock deeper into the mountain. The main tunnel with blast doors led past a guard station into a huge open storage and handling area. They turned to the left and walked up a spiral driving ramp. Bear explained there was a large freight elevator but that it was faster to walk. They exited the ramp on the second level.

Hosmer told them the living quarters were on the top level on this side of the bunker. The second level where they were headed held the command area, communications, medical/sick bay, and the dining hall. The bunker was like walking through a large underground parking garage like Walter and the kids had left behind in Chicago.

They soon found the tunnel opened up into the dining area. Kate, seeing them, came over to greet them. She told them it was open all day for food or snacks. Lunch would be ready soon and she told the kids it was nice to have them there. They crossed the dining hall to the command center. Now this impressed the kids, who were wowed by all the computers and the big screens and on one side there was a group of engineers studying a holographic image.

Suddenly a voice yelled from across the room, "Hi, Walter!" Joe ran over and hugged his brother. "I don't believe it! I finally have you here in Hawaii."

"Well, here I am, Bro. This is some hide-a-way you have here."

"And these must be Sis's kids."

Walter introduced Fran, Mike, and Jake.

Joe said, "Come on. You guys will love these computers."

Around the corner was another large screen. "That's the creep who attacked you," Fran said, pointing at the screen.

Walter replied, "It sure is him, but he was naked then."

Joe said, "That's General Patent Hardash, who we've been trying to find. You saw him?"

"Sure did," said Walter. "He attacked me in the Chicago mall and Fran flattened him with a two-by-four. He decided then not to take all of us on. And it looked like he jumped a mob collector and his bodyguard. There must have been about a hundred military looking types all stark naked and milling around like lost sheep there in the center of the mall."

A new voice joined in. "Well, Joe, maybe we just found our missing crewmembers. When you guys get settled in if you'd take a look at some pictures it would help. And since they haven't introduced me, I'm Sanders Brother, sometimes called Sandy. Our kids on the Constitution will be glad to see you guys."

Fran said, "I think we're a little out of touch with our social graces."

Kate hugged her and said, "Anyone who can drop one of the top bad guys with a two-by-four will fit in here. Why don't I take you all to lunch and let Joe and Sandy get to work?"

So Kate and Ted led them back to the dining hall to eat. They all kept Ted busy asking questions about the base operations and the other kids. Kate told them she was joining her husband on Sand Box 2 as their cook.

As soon as they finished eating Ted gave them the grand tour, which ended on the first level storage and handling area. This was also the landing zone for the Sand Boxes. Ted gave them a tour of SB3, which just totally blew their minds. As they were leaving SB3, an alarm went off and lights started flashing.

"What's that?" asked Walter.

"That has to be SB2 arriving," Ted said. "Watch right over there and you'll see her arrive."

As SB2 appeared right before their eyes, the three kids almost leaped off the ground. Poor Walter just leaned against SB3 shaking his head and said to no one at all, "Good God, Joe, what have you gotten me into? This is Star Trek stuff!"

Kate had joined them and, as soon as the alarms stopped, she said, "Let's go see a Sand Box with a crew."

The door to SB2 opened and Fern and Krista piled out first. Fern hugged his mother. He said, "Mom, this is Krista. Hey, you've adopted some more kids, neat! We have to run to do some computer work with Sandy. Chrissy, James, Fred, and Sue came with us too."

And with that, out ran Sue almost knocking over Sky and Amy on their way out the box. Sue spotted Kate, surprising her when she ran up and leapt into her arms.

"Uncle Bob says you're going to be our new cook."

Behind her came Chrissy and the boys in hot pursuit and stopped to meet the other kids as soon as they saw she had been captured.

Bob came out and put his arms around his wife. "I see Sue found you first."

Walter looked at Ted and asked, "Is it always like this around here?"

"No. Once in a while I get to sit on top of the mountain and watch the stars drift past or go camping with the Scouts. The Scouts are how this all sort of started. They loved to explore this place. Now it's become so top secret we can't let them down here. At least the SEABEEs made them some real neat places out in the park to camp, so we can still get the kids out of the city. And the guys working here just love to camp with them when they come. Sometimes I wonder who is teaching whom on those weekends," said Ted.

Meanwhile, outside, a van from the Ace Cleaning Service rolled up to the ranger office. The young Marine in the ranger suit politely said, "Hello, Captain Staff," but he suddenly went to full attention when he recognized Snow leaning over the seat smiling at him. Stella assured him he could relax, because no one was supposed to know they were there.

He saluted. "Yes, ma'am. I saw nothing, but can I tell my mother I met her? Mom really likes her."

Snow reached out the window and laid her hand on the young man saying, "You may tell her I said hello. Also thank her for raising such a fine son."

"Yes, ma'am, I'll do that," said the young Marine, blushing furiously.

Once they were around the corner, Stella said, "Now I know how that husband of yours got elected."

And they all had a good laugh. Stella parked and led the ladies into the bunker. As soon as they were inside, she saw the work party loading supplies into SB2 and told Snow and Susan this was something they had to see. By the time Stella got them to the dining hall to join the others they were totally amazed. Walter assured them they'd only seen the tip of the iceberg.

Up in the command center, Fern and Sky were busy typing. Sandy was taking a break and chatting with Amy and Krista. In the background, Joe was running around like a conductor before a concert. Fern typed madly to get done so he could go visit with his mother. He was about to scream when the screen went blank. But before he could, a cryptic message appeared: *"Fern, an old friend will join you soon with the answers."*

Sky smiled. "I see you're getting messages from above and beyond."

"It sure looks that way."

And then the screen returned where he'd been and showed the changes were made. The new search began.

He said, "I'm going to go visit with Mom before anything else goes mad here. From the looks of Captain Kid that'll be soon."

"Does this mean I really get to meet her this time?" Krista asked.

"Sure does," he replied.

Sky said, "Don't worry. We'll carry on, but only on the condition we get one of those home-cooked meals you keep telling us about."

With that, Krista and Fern headed down to SB2, leaving Sky, Sanders, and Amy to the computer madness. Whatever had taken over Fern's computer soon took over Sky's terminal. A message appeared that read, *"printing personnel reports for Fern."* With that the nearby printer started.

Sanders questioned, "Did you ask for those?"

Both Amy and Sky started laughing and answered in two-part harmony, "No, but we know who sent them." Then they laughed some more.

Amy said, "Don't worry. We'll introduce you to him, if he doesn't introduce himself."

Sanders had returned to the seat that Fern left and saw a message appear on his screen: *"Hi Sanders. The girls are right. We'll meet when the time is right."*

"That has got to be you, Sky, pulling my leg," said Sanders.

To which they both started laughing some more. Sky pulled off the printed reports.

She read aloud, "Resume of Suzy Que. She is an RN with a degree in psychology and just quit her job in Chicago as an EMT because of sexual harassment by her boss. The second is Top Secret—eyes only—personnel file of Lt. Matt Youngblood, navigation officer of SB3, Project Wonderland. Current assignment is to Project Neverland. We have to find Fern. This is too weird for words." With that all three headed to SB2.

Fern's hope of getting a moment with his mother never happened. She was surrounded, and to even get close to her, his father was sharing her chair. Everyone from SB2 had showed up to meet their new cook. The First Lady was causing her own stir as well. So Fern settled for food and joined Ted and the kids, who were chatting a mile a minute.

Ted's security radio beeped and he answered. When he was finished, he looked at Fern. "Have to run. I have two backpackers topside looking for Boy Scouts or a place to camp."

So off he went and the kids turned their attention to Fern and were asking questions about the camping outside.

The Honolulu Airport:

As Matt and Suzy were getting off the plane the flight attendant stopped them. "Sir, here is the information you asked to receive."

Matt thanked her once again and opened the envelope to find a brochure for a national park in the mountains. They collected their packs and hailed a cab, but the driver would only take them as far as the end of the highway. When they arrived there, he dropped them off at the first turnoff. Matt paid him and they put on their packs. They started walking and hadn't gone too far when a van pulled up beside them. The Hawaiian lady driving said, "You young folks look like you could use a ride. If you want I can take you part of the way."

So they climbed in and off they went.

"My name is Mona Lika Alepeka and I was just heading home early. I'd had a feeling someone needed a ride and no one was going to visit my shop this afternoon. If you two come back to Hawaii after your trip, you should come visit me."

They traveled for a while as she kept talking a blue streak, then suddenly said, "Ah, here is my road" as she turned in and stopped. And then added, "Oh dear, your next ride is almost here."

With that she leapt out of the van and ran back to the main road. Matt and Suzy got their packs and followed the kind…but…rather eccentric lady. Their hearts almost stopped as Mona Lika stepped right out into the road in front of a speeding pick-up truck.

A young man wearing Army fatigues pulled over as if this was an everyday happening. He opened the passenger window and said, "Hi, ma'am, how can I help you?"

"Well, son, these two nice people need a ride where you're going and I knew you'd want to help them," said Mona Lika.

"No problem, ma'am, they can put their gear in the back. I'll take good care of them for you," he said.

"Thank you, Meatloaf, you're a dear. Now you two have a good trip and I'm sure you'll find Fern. 'Bye," Mona Lika said and waved.

Before they could even thank her she was gone.

They jumped in with the smiling young man.

"We appreciate the ride. I'm Matt and this is Suzy. Mona Lika said your name is Meatloaf?"

"It sure is," he replied, "But I have *never* met that nice lady before. I wonder how she knew my name?"

"Well, we just met her too," said Matt.

"Where are you guys headed?"

"The Kaala National Park, which our map says is in the Waianae Valley. We're looking for a Scout friend of mine who's there," said Matt.

"I guess she was right then because that's where I'm going. I'm one of the base cooks. In fact, today I become the head cook.

My full name is Specialist Meatloaf Wales. We do have Scouts there all the time out in the camping part of the park."

Matt said, "Well, I'm Matt Youngblood and my friend here is Suzy Que. She used to be an EMT."

"Too bad you're not coming to work with us. We've some ladies who've been teaching our guys how to fight hand-to-hand," said Meatloaf. "Suzy, you'd like them. One day, Amy flattened three of our biggest guys on the mat. They thought a cyclone had hit them."

"Well, maybe we'll get to meet them, but first we need to find my friend," said Matt.

"I'm sure you will. The rangers keep track of everything, so they'll know where he is and how to get there. Boy, I'm kind of excited. Tonight will be the first time I've been in charge of a whole meal by myself. But I'll miss Kate Cybernaut, who was our boss. She's going to be the head cook for the crew of her husband's ship. And she's glad they'll be traveling together finally," said Meatloaf.

Matt said, "That's funny. That's my friend's mother's name, but they live in Greene, Rhode Island. A lot of strange things have been happening to me lately."

"Here we are," announced Meatloaf, as he pulled up a road and stopped at the ranger shack. "I'll have to leave you guys here, but the ranger will take good care of you."

Matt and Suzy climbed out and got their packs from the back of the truck.

"It was nice meeting you," Meatloaf yelled as the rangers flagged him through the second gate.

Suzy said to Matt, "This place has a lot of security for a national park."

"Sure does and this is the first time I've heard of the U.S. Army living in a park," said Matt.

A young ranger named Malcolm Smith introduced himself and asked, "How can I help you?"

So Matt introduced them and explained, "We're looking for a friend who's a Scout. We've been directed to come here to look for Fern Cybernaut."

Smith said, "You'll need to talk with Ranger Ted Bear. He's the one who works with the Scouts. If you folks want to have a seat over on the picnic table there, I'll page him for you."

"Thank you," said Matt and with that they dropped their packs on the table and relaxed.

Suzy leaned close. "I wonder if his middle initial is an E."

Matt laughed and replied, "I think I'll let you ask that question."

It took about ten minutes until they saw an older ranger headed their way. He walked up and introduced himself as Park Ranger Bear. As he did Suzy looked at his nametag and was fighting the urge to ask. Bear had seen the signs before, so he said, "No there is no E, miss. I'm just plain Teddy Bear, but most friendly people call me Ted. And please don't hug me, if your big friend with you will get mad."

Once the laughter died down he asked, "So how can I help you two?"

Matt finally caught his breath and said, "I'm looking for a friend of mine who is a Scout and I was told he'd be here exploring a cave. His name is Fern Cybernaut."

Now it was Ted's turn to look a little surprised. But before he could speak he heard the kids behind him in the parking lot.

He yelled over, "Hey, Fern, do you know this guy?"

Fern headed over with the whole group following to see what exciting thing would happen next. When he spotted

Matt he ran up and hugged him. "Where'd you come from?" he asked.

"We just flew in from Chicago," answered Matt.

Sanders, Sky, and Amy walked up behind the kids and Amy's strong female voice said, "That's very interesting, Lieutenant Matt Youngblood."

She stopped right next to Fern, looking straight into Matt's eyes.

"Yes, ma'am, That's me. And this is Suzy Que."

"An out of work EMT, who's an RN and has a degree in psychology?" asked Amy.

"Why, yes," Suzy said with a surprised look. "That's who I am, but how'd you know?"

"Your resume just came off our printer," replied Amy. "But I want to know why you're here, Matt?"

"Well, a few days ago, I found myself naked in the middle of the Chicago mall. As I sat there on that cold floor, I remembered the words of our Scout leader who once told me I was in the right field for my talents, but that I was following the wrong path. Until then it had made no sense to me. I thought maybe the old man was going senile. But there I sat in the middle of madness and knew he was right. I went to find some clothes and on the way I found Suzy. She was jobless and I'd no idea where to go. She showed me the way to a store where I could get some clothes. Since she had nowhere to go, we both went and sat in a park to think about what we should do next."

Suzy broke in, saying, "That's when this big white guy with the deepest blue eyes, dressed like a Native American appeared. He told Matt to go find Fern in a cave in Hawaii. That he would help him find the right path. He handed Matt an ID card and said that it would get him on the plane. And he looked at me with those eyes and he touched me—I could feel the warmth of his hand, the love in those eyes—and then...He just vanished."

Matt continued, "The flight attendant gave us a map and park guide and said we had asked for it. The cab would only take us to the end of the superhighway, and then a lady named Mona Lika Alepeka gave us a ride to her street. She ran out in the road and stopped a cook named Meatloaf Wales who drove us right here. Fern, is your mother a cook here?"

"Well, she was but she's joining Dad," said Fern.

Suzy said, "This must sound weird or like we're both nuts."

For the first time Amy smiled and her body relaxed from its alert state. "You're not nuts," said Amy. "I've seen those blue eyes and have been in his home. I've also seen him appear and vanish. If he likes you, you'll see him again I'm sure." Amy handed Fern the two reports and said, "I think the answers to your questions are right in front of you and you won't have to hack your way into the NSA computer to find them. Matt, here, was the navigation officer on SB3."

A new voice spoke up as Fran moved to the front. "I saw you sitting there in the middle of all that. I also saw what Suzy did to her grabby boss. I think he'll keep his hands to himself for a while."

Walter added, "And you, my dear Fran, flattened the infamous General Hardash with a two-by-four, saving my old butt."

Matt laughed. "So someone finally shut him up. Fran, if you need an older brother, I'm available for adoption."

Ted offered to show the kids around while Fern and company took Matt and Suzy below to start on that new path.

They had walked into the large storage and handling area when Matt spotted SB3 and SB2.

Matt exclaimed, "How did you get them?"

Fern said, "Oh, sort of the same way we got you. We just found them sitting around and brought them home."

And with that, the incoming alarm sounded and the warning lights flashed.

"What's that for?" asked Matt.

"Our company is arriving and I think he'll want to talk with you," said Amy.

Onboard the USS Constitution in SB4:

All personnel were at their stations and the command center was running final checks.

"Engineering is green," reported Captain Furreal.

"Navigation is green," reported Commander North.

"COM is green," reported Commander O'Rielly.

"Security is green," reported General Rabbit.

"Command is green, too," announced CO Whosh. "Commander North, engage jump sequence."

"Engaged, Doctor."

"Event clock started," reported Commander O'Rielly.

In the dining hall, Admiral Staff sat drinking coffee with Doc Bones while Ensign Chablis kept busy in the galley. Lieutenant Brice was there too in full dress uniform like the admiral. Her security team was ready and was half in dress uniform and half in tactical black. Commander Bird was there as the admiral's number two in command. Ltjg. Kurious was there to handle intel and data for briefings; however, this trip was mostly show and tell—hard data could be sent via the secure Navnet or hand delivered if need be.

Commander North reported, "We're on track for Navel Support Facility at Thurmont and going into hover mode."

Commander O'Rielly said, "I've started ground scan and security check. Landing zone clear and no life signs within two thousand feet."

"We're clear to land. LZ confirmed and locked," reported Commander North.

"Take us in, Commander," ordered Whosh.

"Landing on target within three inches at NSF Thurmont," reported North.

"Event clock stopped at 11 minutes 9 seconds," reported O'Rielly.

"Security still showing LZ clear," reported Rabbit.

Whosh ordered, "Secure LZ, monitor and wait for contact."

The security team in black moved out and secured the LZ. The admiral, Commander Bird, and Lieutenant Brice headed for their meeting. Brice brought along two of her uniformed Marines and had the others stand by to greet their company. All was in place, now all that was left was to wait.

Meanwhile at Camp David:

As the president and National Security Chief, General Frost headed to the men's room at the picnic area; the Secret Service guards took up their watch out front. General Frost pushed the door open and let the president step in, and then he followed. There before them was a most unusual scene. Standing in front of the president and General Frost at attention and saluting were Admiral Staff, Commander Bird, Lieutenant Brice, and the two Marines on either side of the door. The president and Frost returned the salutes.

President White said, "I think, Jack, that I under-dressed for this party." And looking at Lieutenant Brice said, "Good thing I don't really need the bathroom."

Lieutenant Brice turned a bit red in the face and replied, "Sorry, Mr. President, I never thought."

White answered, "Don't worry, this is the kind of thing my Snow would do, but don't tell anyone. It'd make a juicy scandal. Besides, I guess we should be going before the SS wake up and think I fell in."

With that, Brice spoke in her radio to the security team who confirmed it was clear for them to go from the men's room to SB4, which was sitting in the shadows next to it. They then all walked out and into SB4 to make history.

Lieutenant Brice reported to command center, "The president's aboard and we're secure."

Bones and Cookie made the president at home in the dining hall. The admiral promised the two very amazed leaders a full tour when they arrived at the Scout bunker.

"Security green, all aboard and the Secret Service guards are clear," reported Rabbit.

"Engineering green," reported Alice.

"COM green," reported Scotty.

"Navigation green and locked on Scout bunker," reported North.

"Then we are all green, engage jump sequence and get us out of here," ordered Whosh.

"Done," replied North.

"Event clock running," added Scotty O'Rielly.

Back in Scout Bunker:
Matt wasn't sure of his eyes as he saw SB3 and SB2 sitting

before him while this crazy alarm screamed and lights flashed. And right there before his astonished eyes SB4 appeared.

Matt exclaimed, "You have three of them! How did you do that? Hardash and Black must be having fits."

Matt had been so focused on the show in front of him he hadn't noticed a whole group of people had arrived behind him. He said to Fern, "Somehow we've got to tell the president. I don't think he knows anything about what they are doing or why."

A female voice behind him said, "That, young man, is an excellent idea."

When he turned, he found himself face to face with the First Lady and blurted out, "Oh my, it's you!"

"Oh yes, I'm right here," and reading his ID the First Lady said, "It's nice to meet you, Matt" and shook his hand.

Before Matt's wits came home to roost a man spoke behind him. "Hello, dear. I see you have made some new friends," said President White.

"Why yes, Purr, and this fine young man wants to tell you all about these amazing Sand Boxes and what those nasty people are up to," said Snow.

Matt spun around and it was obvious his brain had not caught up to his tongue. "Sir. Mr. President, Sir, you're here and your wife and I should tell you, yes you really need to know they plan to take over the world. I'm sorry, sir, Mr. President, sir, I...think I'm babbling, sir, I err, well..."

"I understand, Matt, and I'm very glad you didn't wear a uniform, I've felt so under-dressed since I met the admiral, Commander Bird and that very nice Lt. Charly Brice in the men's room at Camp David."

"So, Purr, you've been meeting women in the men's room?" asked Snow.

"Why, yes, dear, and she's all dressed up in her Marine finest, but I told her not to worry about meeting me in the bathroom. It's something you would do too. And you must be Fern," said White.

"Yes, sir, we finally meet in person," he answered. "But Matt is right. He was the navigator on SB3, which is where we found the fifty trillion dollars in gold bars. We'll be debriefing him for weeks and sending you all kinds of data. But for now it'll be a good idea if he tags along on your tour to answer any questions as they come up."

General Frost said, "You know, young man, the military can use good men like you."

Fern replied, "Thank you, sir, but I think I'd rather stay a citizen soldier even if you do have some real good-looking troops."

From not too far away, Fern got belted by Krista. "What am I, chopped liver?"

Sky and Amy moved closer and all three of them hugged Fern, who was now rather red-faced.

"Son, that's why I got married," said President White. "You'll have to stop by the White House some time and we'll have a fireside chat about politics and women. Of course, we'll just figure out that we understand neither."

"Well, sir, it's nice to know I'm not alone in having that dilemma," replied Fern.

All three ladies hugged him even tighter.

Admiral Staff, who was tactfully staying out of that subject as Stella hugged him, said, "With that I think we should get to your tour."

"Lead on," replied White.

And off they all went, with whoever had the best answer to the president's many questions explaining. Of course, sometimes no one had answers and the president's questions were written down for further research. White looked at the fifty trillion dollars in gold bars with amazement and found Matt's explanation of the source of this gold very disturbing. He saw the inside and outside of the bunker and knew it was well worth the money spent on it. He got to see the computers in the command center and had Sky explain that they were tied to the Navy's top-secret computer complex known as Deep Thought. He was most impressed, as were Frost and Anthony, with the holographic displays that they could step right into to examine the picture. He got to meet most of the troops and expressed his gratitude for their service to their country.

In the meantime, Krista said to Amy, "Let's show these guys around." So they gathered up the new faces and did their own version of the welcome tour. They started out with Walter Kid, Fran, Mike, Jake, and Suzy Que, but soon added Chrissy, Sue, James, Fred, Dr. Whosh, General Rabbit, Alice, and other members of SB4's crew. They had the grand tour of all of Scout bunker and ended in SB4's dining hall well before President White ran out of questions.

While all this was going on, the crew of SB2 and the work party finished loading supplies for the Constitution, including a few special requests for a presidential meal. They even managed to take tours of the bunker led by their new cook, Kate. So with all aboard they made the leap back to the Constitution and the work party that could have sworn they arrived back before they left. However, the grumbling didn't last long as the smells of the fresh food reached their noses and they read the names on the labels on the boxes. In short order, it had all the work party thinking about their next meal, long before the work was over. And it is said that the cooks did not disappoint them. A presidential meal was had by all.

Back at Scout Bunker:

The tours and questions were done for the day and it was time to jump to the Constitution for the second half of the tour. President White thanked Colonel Kid for his efforts once more as he entered SB4.

Joe looked at the others ready to leave and said to Walter, "I finally get you to come visit me in Hawaii and now here you are running off to Guam with a bunch of kids."

Walter shrugged and Stella, who had a firm grip on Flagg, laughed at this faked outrage. Joe looked over at her and added, "Well, you should laugh. You're running off, leaving me for your husband."

"If I can steal my husband away from his ship, we'll come back so you can have some R and R before the men start complaining that you've become a grouch," Stella replied.

And with much laughter by all, SB4 was ready. Cookie had a full dining hall and was happily spreading around food, treats, and drinks. Doc Bones was equally thrilled to have all these people with whom to talk. And in Doc's wildest dreams he'd never imagined the president and First Lady being among them. The children had all vanished to the living quarters and were busy getting to know each other. Krista had invited Suzy along and told her not to worry. The boys would remember them soon enough. Walter was retelling the children's story for Stella, Sky, and Amy at the request of Snow and Susan. By the time he was done, he was sure these ladies had more in mind than making some phone calls, and he wondered to himself if the world would be in such a mess if women like these were running it.

Walter had paid little attention to the fact that Sky had been typing into her laptop while he talked. But then Sky always carried it, like her gun. They were tools of her trade. Amy started telling them all about Guam and the Chamorro people. How much fun it was to sail in their proas. Sky slipped away and headed to the command center. She walked to the COM station and handed a small USB flash drive to O'Rielly to be uploaded. The data was for Scout Bunker.

Sandy was sitting at the keyboard in the command center chatting with Laurie and Alfrado who had brought coffee to keep him going after a very busy day. The computer announced an incoming priority message from SB4. As the three read Sky's note, their mode shifted. This had to do with Joe, so Sanders paged him. Laurie got another cup of coffee, handing it to Joe as he sat down.

He read the data and said, "That does not surprise me."

Joe reached around Sanders and pulled up a file from his storage area and displayed it. "I got curious about who Walter adopted as our sister and so did a little back tracking. Obviously, from this a lot more digging is needed on who is the real Mr. Pryor."

File Name: My New Sister

Name: Sandra Good
Born in Rockford, IL to Sally and Arthur Good
Graduate of Rockford East High School and Rockford College
Met first husband, Donald Unhomed at Rockford College
Married after graduation and had three children: Fran, Jake and Mike

Lieutenant Donald Unhomed was killed by "friendly fire" during Gulf War II
Second husband Lieutenant Felonious T. Pryor (service record classified)
Moved to Chicago after Sandra's parents died in a plane crash.
DCYF report of delinquent behavior / runaway status.
Reporter: F. Pryor
Warrant: Fran Unhomed for kidnapping Jake and Mike
EOF

Sandy said, "Well that should keep me busy tonight. And to think we all liked your naughty niece. I'll see if I can find out what she's running from. Does your brother always bring home kids?"

"No, but he's helped a lot of them," said Joe. "Walter saw too much during the war. He's saved his money and had some our parents gave him. He invested well and lives a very simple lifestyle. Now he spends his days helping people who are lost and have nowhere to go but the street. If he was helping them, they really needed him."

Sanders said, "Don't worry, Joe, I'll find out what's going on."

Guam, on the USS Constitution:

SB2 was almost unloaded when SB4 arrived. Everyone not working was in full dress uniform and an honor guard was waiting on the hanger deck. President White was welcomed onboard with full pomp and circumstance. The whole visiting party was going to have a pig roast on the beach and the Chamorro were pleased to show off their dancing. There were also a number of talented sailors, aviators, and Marines that added the American touch. Security was tight, but so invisible the president never saw the phantoms dressed in black who kept watch from the shadows. Of course Amy, Sky, Charly, Shela, Peter, J.P., and Ralph were right in the middle of the festivities. There was much food, dancing, singing, and all kinds of musical instruments native and new-aged. Harry, Bob, Matt, and Fern entertained by showing off Native American drumbeats and dancing.

But the night wasn't all fun and gaiety. There were two major meetings. The clan's maga'hagas, Kandit Mesngon, met with the First Lady. They convened in a quiet place away from the festivities. With Kandit Mesngon was Dahi Atugud, Quetago Taotao, Amta Mamuranta, Abi Suruhana, and Adagi Nene'. With the First Lady were Dr. Tracy North, Dr. Janet Wilks, Lt. Charly Brice, Dr. Amanda Whosh, Ens. Shela Smith, Capt. Alice Furreal, Capt. Stella Staff, Dr. Susan Anthony, Krista Sparks, and Chrissy North. The ladies talked for hours about home, family, community, clan, nation, and the world. They talked about the environment, technology, and the future.

Puritan White and maga'lahi Anao Agnasina met as well. White had Gen. Jack Frost, Gen. Peter Rabbit, Adm. Flagg Staff, Capt. Bill O. Right, Dr. Jorge Bones, Maj. Walter Kid, Fern Cybernaut, Sgt. J.P. Smith, Ph.D., Lt. Matt Youngblood, and Harry Haul at the meeting. Anao Agnasina (to conquer, mighty for each other), who was still recovering from the wounds he received in the battle with the pirates, insisted it was his duty to introduce this great leader to the male leaders of his clan. So Bones had made Anao comfortable as they all gathered around this wise old man.

First Anao introduced Momo Gogui (battle, fight to protect, save, rescue), who'd led the clan warriors and showed much bravery as he led his men against the pirates. Then

Anao introduced Tano Malala (land to be alive), who was the elder farmer of the clan. Next was Asin Cadassi (salt to have something of the sea), who was the clan's best fisherman and boat builder. And Anao introduced Chaggi Manongsong (try, attempt to make a village); he was the village builder that had erected the latte stones and houses that stood atop them. They too talked of many things, like the duty to protect family, friends, and the world around them, which provided for their needs. They talked of their women who in many ways defined who they each were or would become. They parted with a pledge of friendship.

It was late by the time they all returned to the ship, but it was such a clear night with the sky full of stars that both the young and old strolled the flight deck arm in arm. Purr and Snow, Flagg and Stella, J.P. and Alice, Peter and Amanda, Ralph and Janet, Harry and Charly, Dew and Tracy, Doc and Cookie, Kate and Bob were all enjoying nature's show and each other. Patty had found Max and told him she was pleased when he signed on to be trained as a box electrician. Fern and Krista had Sue with them, but once she spotted Max and Mommy, there was no holding her back. Sue very much approved of Mommy being with Max and had embarrassed both by telling everyone that Max should marry Mom. Walter, like the pied piper, was busy telling the kids all about the stars that he'd learned about as a Scout. Fran was just amazed at this whole new world full of very nice people who cared. As she looked up at a very bright twinkling star she asked, "Is that one you wish on?"

Walter hugged her and said, "It'll work for you, Fran."

After a thoughtful minute or two, she said, "I hope Mom is all right. I miss her."

As the dawn came the starry guardians of the night slowly faded away, although they were not really gone, just invisible to the eye, which now was overwhelmed with the brilliance of the risen sun.

Dawn brought the rays of hope as well as a hearty breakfast for all. For President White this was a very somber time, as Chaplain Desire Peace led him below to view the men who had fallen defending the Constitution and the Chamorro people. They'd already made arrangements to have them returned home and planned how it would be explained. Death even happens in paradise. Here before him lay the proof like a warning calling out, to beware that dark forces were gathering somewhere just out of sight. They prayed with Chaplain Peace and returned topside to stand in the sun.

On the flight deck, they found four Seahawks ready to give them a grand tour of Guam as it had been before the white man changed it forever. They had all been to the Guam of 2012, but here they could see firsthand what the years had done. There had to be close to a population of two hundred thousand inhabitants, but they were living with nature, and the matriarchal elder council held the people together. Those who lived by the sea fished and those inland harvested plants or raised animals. They then traded for what they needed. As the Seahawks took them all the way around the island, they were amazed at what civilization and progress had done here. Puritan White, who had never championed an environmental cause, was feeling very sick at heart that all this natural beauty was gone, including these people.

All about the island, the fishermen were out sailing in their proas, thousands of them almost as far as the eye could see. These boats sailed across the waves almost flying, traveling as fast as twenty knots. As they returned to the Constitution, White noticed a group of proa sailing out from the ship.

Commander Bird explained that those were the children from the ship sailing in the boats the islanders had given them. And they had made their own colorful sails. In fact, he told the president, the ship now had over thirty of them they had made. He banked the helicopter and pointed them out along the reef.

Bird said, "Those proa with the white sails are our sailors out fishing and I can tell you, sir, I've gotten very fond of fresh fish. I've also taken up sailing and maybe one of these days I'll be able to keep up with the kids. We've clocked them at better than twenty-five knots. I think that Harry Haul put motors in them. They just go too fast."

White asked, "Do the children really like it here?"

Bird smiled. "Sir, they love it here. They are our best ambassadors and have won over everyone. They are always teaching the native children things. In fact they have outdone our doctors at improving health by teaching basic hygiene to the children and their parents. They spend hours showing new mothers how to wash babies and to boil water to kill germs. And in turn they are learning natural healing with herbs from Abi Suruhana, the native healer. It's all very amazing. Doc goes over and tries to help and the natives politely listen. The kids go over and just start helping out with whatever is going on. When the natives see how well it works the kids' way of doing things, they just keep doing it that way."

Bird said, "Doc Bones and Dr. Wilks have learned a lot about herbs and natural healing from Abi Suruhana too. The head lady's husband of this clan, Anao Agnasina, was badly hurt during the attack and Bones saved him. So he and Abi have been learning a lot from each other."

When they landed back on the Constitution, White thanked Bird for the ride. It had been an education in many ways. It would be hard to ignore much of what this whole trip had shown him. There were serious dangers to the country he led and a threat to the founding document that created the nation. If the Constitution fell at the hands of these greedy men, like Banks and Black, the nation he served would be no more. His replacement would be a banker crowned king. How could his fellow leaders be so blind that no one saw this coming "or" had they too sold the nation for money, gold, toys, and power?

They all said their good-byes and got ready for their return trip. The last sight President White had was of the children out racing the proas across the crystal clear water. He thought, *There goes our future if we but give them a chance to do it right.* With that they boarded SB4 to return to his job and Camp David.

Washington, D.C. in the Office of Federal Trust Agency [but there is no such agency]:

At the head of the conference table sat Dr. Warbucks Banks and he wanted answers. His suit coat was lying on a side table next to his briefcase. His minder was standing at parade rest next to him watching everyone in the room. Trust was not in this man's nature. Gen. Benedict Black and Gen. Patent Hardash sat together on one side. Across from them sat the Chinese dragon Lo Mean and the Russian bear Karl Vostok. Down the table was Mockeries I. Supervising from Europe and Conjure Appallingly, a small Oriental from somewhere else.

Banks started by demanding, "Black, where's my fifty trillion in gold?"

Black replied, "I don't have a clue. Someone stole it

along with SB3 and SB2. Most of the crew, including General Hardash here, appeared at a Chicago mall."

"Yes," said Vostok, "all running around naked and mad as English hatters. You Americans are a bunch of little girls with your dresses over your heads. Next you'll be telling me your God reached down from heaven and took it away."

Banks interrupted. "I don't have time for this. You can take up your childish quarrels in the parking lot. Now, Hardash, since you were there, could you please tell me exactly what happened?"

Hardash looked at Black. He knew nothing he said would sound good, since even he didn't believe it himself. But Mercenary had told it the same way, so he said, "I flew to Guam, the last place we know SB3 was operating. Since SB4 vanished with that damn aircraft carrier, I had the Air Force fly out SB2 and its crew. Major Mercenary joined me in Guam after looking for SB4 in Hawaii and terminating a security problem posed by John Doe who had been with SB4. As you know each box has a built-in transponder that can't be removed, turned off, or tampered with. We could not find a signal from SB3 or SB4. So we decided to go into hyperspace where nothing could block the signals. We were there about eleven minutes with no trace of either signal. Suddenly, our main engines increased power. We found we had no control of any of our systems and the navigation computers locked in a course and the computers engaged a jump to an unknown location. All our equipment refused to respond or to even tell us where we went. We landed somewhere and tried for about two minutes to regain control. The next thing I knew, I was standing naked in the Chicago mall. I left that area, stole a mob collector's clothes and his car, then drove to the nearest military base and got a flight to Washington."

"We're the only ones in the U.S. with this technology. As far as I know, no one else has it. BUT they must and someone else is in the game that we do not know about. I don't suppose any of you know what's going on or are you're all like Vostok who thinks God has been working overtime," Hardash said, ending his statement with a glower.

Conjure Appallingly asked, "Where'd your aircraft carrier go? Did they steal SB4 and are they using it against us? And what happened to John Doe before Major Raul blew up half a hospital to kill him?"

Black sat forward, thought for a moment, and then replied, "They used everything we have to search for it and if they'd found it we would have known. Those sailors couldn't hide a needle in a haystack. But someone could have them both. SB4 has most of its crew and the rest are missing, but they couldn't move that damn ship or SB2 or SB3 without a trained crew. The transponders were designed to be foolproof. To stop one from working you'd have to destroy the box. As far as John Doe is concerned, he was found in a phone booth with his clothes on inside out and he had a stolen car. He was talking the same kind of gibberish as the fools at the Chicago mall. Had he said anything or had they found his true ID, our computers would have caught it."

Hardash said, "I just remembered something, but I don't know if it's important or not. I was in the chair at the command center when whatever it was took over our ship. Before the readings went blank, we were going straight up and fast. The last reading I saw said that we were at 119 miles. It's like something was pulling us into orbit. How big is that Chinese space station, Mean?"

Lo Mean deliberated his answer. "A lot bigger than your American sardine can, but they have no technology to do that and no place to put a box if they got it there. And ours is the biggest and most advanced. We also have looked for your missing boat and come up with only two possibilities. One, they sank, or two, they have a new shielding device that makes them invisible to us. Since we trust you are not lying, then someone must have sunk it."

Mockeries I. Supervising asked, "Have you fixed SB1? What about SB7 and SB8? Has our mission been compromised? We're so close Europe is on the brink and Russia and China are close to being ready."

Black said, "It'll be an inconvenience and slow us down some, but our outcome is assured. We must find out who has done this or they could take away our prize. It has to be another government, but I wonder how they could hide this technology from us. We've eyes and ears everywhere. There must be something we've missed. Why were our crews dumped in a Chicago mall and why did the ship vanish near Hawaii?"

Conjure Appallingly spoke with great disdain. "You white fools are soft. Our man in Hawaii, Moon Sung, vanished the same time your madman appeared. And then five hundred of your military just vanish *and* you can't find them? Then you send a madman to blow up a hospital. I would have walked in and slit the pig's throat. I will go to Hawaii and find the answers. You and your delivery boys get back to work. The plan has been laid out for you to follow. We will clean up your mess." With that she stood up and looked at Banks, who nodded his approval for her to go.

Banks stood up and held out his hand for his coat. He looked at Black and Hardash, and then said, "Your incompetence is becoming very clear as you sit here and tell me impossible tales. You can be replaced. Go fix your problems and get your job done. If I find you've cheated me or lied to me I'll see that you and your whole crew of misfits die a slow and painful death begging for mercy."

With that Warbucks Banks left. None of the others spoke as Black and Hardash marched out to their car.

Black barked at the driver, "The office—now!"

Black and Hardash stopped in Black's secretary's office. Black said, "Get me Woozy."

Then both men removed all their clothes and dropped them in her wastebasket. As the two men stood there stark naked, Black pointed to the basket and said, "Burn that."

Woozy came in the door and stopped short.

"Come in," said Black. "I need a shower and have things for you to do."

The three men entered Black's office. Black looked at Raul sitting at his desk and walked to the security panel. He typed in the lock down codes for his office. A flashing light turned green and a computer voice announced, "Lock down complete. Scan for listening devices found none. The room is clear and secure."

When the door shut and the secretary saw the secure light come on, she pulled the plastic bag out of the wastebasket. She forwarded her phone to the phone pool and headed for the stairway. She looked at the secure disposal unit as she walked by it. She continued down to the shipping room and said hi to her friends as she walked in. She grabbed a box and placed the bag inside. These rich men were fools. They didn't even remove the money from their clothes. Black always carried thousands in cash and the suit must have cost a grand by itself. Once the box was sealed with the security stamp on it, she then placed it on the front seat of her car and returned to the office to finish her workday.

Meanwhile, in Black's office, he told Woozy to find them

some clothes. He walked directly to Raul and said, "You're going back to Hawaii. That Conjure bitch is going there looking for some agent named Moon Sung. Find him and make him sing. Kill her and any agents with her. Then find out where those sailors went and if they are hiding that damned ship. If the Navy has SB4 I want to know and where."

Black turned his attention to Hardash. "SB1 is ready and manned. Deliver Raul to Hawaii with a full team. SB7 and SB8 are also fully operational, so when you get back get all your teams ready. When the time is right we will pull back both SB5 and SB6."

Woozy returned with clothes and both men started dressing.

"Woozy," said Black, "I want all those files on Banks ready to be delivered to our lily white president and we'll send copies to all the Congressmen. I'm going to watch them fry him on the Six O'clock News and enjoy every minute of it."

Back at Scout Bunker:

Sandy had been chasing Pryor's records high and low and found they'd been classified by someone in the CIA. It appeared that he was a low-level errand boy and had extensive training in weapons and non-conventional methods. His other records appeared very clean, perhaps too clean. There were a couple of odd things that jumped out at Sanders. Pryor had been in Iraq in the same operation when Donald Unhomed was killed by friendly fire. He also was the last person to see Sandra's parents alive at the airport, but he'd driven his own car there. The other very odd thing he found was a local Chicago DA named Justine Conviction had a very extensive file on Pryor.

When Sanders told Joe what he had found, Joe decided he

should talk with this DA. Sanders did a little more checking and found her telephone lines were not secure. So Joe called a cop friend in Chicago who knew the DA. He explained the problem and had two Army Intel officers go with his friend to get the DA. Lt. Ted Williams of the Chicago BCI met DA Conviction as she left the courtroom.

Ted walked up and said, "Hi there, Justine. I would very much like to take you to lunch."

And with that he handed her a note, which read:

Justine, Your telephones are bugged. You may be bugged or watched and a friend of mine needs to talk with you about a legal matter. So please join me for lunch and these two exterminators will check you for bugs so you can privately talk with my friend, Capt. Joe Kid of the Hawaiian BCI.

Justine read the note, smiled at him, and said, "Why, Ted, that's the best offer I've had in months. Lead on."

They walked out to an unmarked van and Ted road shotgun with the male officer driving. The female officer climbed in the back with Justine. She turned on several instruments and scanned her from head to toe. She stopped as a pin Justine was wearing and her purse sent the meters nuts.

She wrote Justine a note:

If you trust Ted, put the pin in the purse and give the purse to Ted, then the three of us will go for a walk while you talk to Joe. I'll key them up and all you will have to do is press the talk key to make the link.

Justine nodded an emphatic yes.
The van stopped in the park and the two men got out.

The female agent joined them and Justine handed her purse to Ted saying, "Oh, Ted, this is such a lovely place to walk."

They closed the door and headed for a park bench. Justine sat in the chair before the console and pressed the talk key. A large flat screen came to life before her and the man on the screen said, "Hello. I'm Captain Kid, or Joe if you like, and I have some questions."

"You've sure gone to a lot of trouble, Joe, to talk to me, and I must thank you for telling me about those bugs."

"The pleasure is mine."

"So, what would you like to know? We're a little far from Hawaii."

"I have had reason to be investigating a man named Lt. Felonious T. Pryor and I found evidence that you have an interest in him too."

"Well, right now I am very concerned that his three stepchildren are missing."

"I can tell you that Fran did not kidnap anyone and that all three children are safe."

"Are you sure? I thought he did something to them," said Justine.

"I am very sure and I have statements from the children to a reliable source that he molested and abused them. These witnesses can be in Chicago tomorrow to see you. Also, I have reason to believe that there are other crimes, some of which could be of an international nature. The CIA has classified his military record and he appears to be some kind of operative," said Joe.

"I suspected he was into drugs, guns, kidnapping, murder, money laundering, child porn, prostitution, child abuse, and wife beating."

"Nice guy," said Joe. "If you can give your data to the intel team, they can send it to me and I can find you some answers. Maybe even send you enough for a warrant."

"And I thought I was going to retire without getting this creep. Can you do a national and military search?" she asked.

"I sure can, and I'll give you all the results."

"Why do I have the feeling you are a bit more than a BCI captain? Are you sure the kids are ok?" she asked once more.

"Yes, I've met them and they're now with other children of friends of mine. But Fran is very worried about her mother and we promised to help. People like Pryor should be put away where they can't hurt people. In fact, they've sort of adopted me as their uncle, so how could I not help? I've sent copies of what I've found so far and agent Lydia Miles will give them to you," said Joe.

"The info you need is on my laptop at my office. I'll give it to the officers when I get back there. How will I know these people are coming?"

"I'll have Ted call you to go to the airport to meet them and if we can find grounds, Ted will have warrants in hand."

"Should I pinch myself to find out if I'm dreaming?"

"No, I'm for real even if I live in Wonderland. If you get bored do come visit."

"Thank you. I'm sure we'll talk again." They said their good-byes and, with that, she opened the door and walked over to Ted and company.

"You know, Ted, you're really making me hungry, but before you feed me we have to stop by my office for a minute."

So they drove to her office and agent Lydia Miles followed her in. She took her laptop out of the safe and sat it on the desk. Lydia handed her a USB flash drive and Justine downloaded the files. Lydia gave Justine a disk, which she locked up with the laptop. They got back in the van and Ted and Justine were dropped off at one of the best restaurants in Chicago.

Over the meal Ted wrote on the napkin: *You can thank Joe, he is buying today.*

Justine wrote back: *I hope your wife doesn't mind.*

Ted smiled: *It's just cop business.*

To which they both laughed and enjoyed their excellent meal.

Joe soon had the files from Justine and it was worse than he suspected. Sanders was already working on it and had forwarded the info to SB4. Before Air Force One was airborne they planned on having something Ted could use for a warrant.

NSF, Thurmont, Maryland:

SB4 landed in the exact same spot where they had met White next to the restroom. The scanners showed that all the Secret Service except one had not moved. He was urinating on a tree. The door opened and the security team in black slipped out, then General Frost and the president walked right to the men's room and washed their hands. SB4 had returned them two minutes after they left and before their hands were dry SB4 was headed for Scout bunker. Now White and Frost could rest after an exciting twenty-four hours that had never happened. How could it happen in just two minutes? They both slept well that night with their amazing memories.

Scout Bunker, on a Hawaiian Mountain:

SB4 landed and everyone headed to the command center. They all wanted to hear about Pryor. Walter had returned with them, but Fran and the boys chose to stay with the other children. Sky and Fern joined Sanders on the computers in the hunt for clues on Pryor's life. His full military record was very telling as his CIA masters moved him around. Pryor's name was on several leases of airplane hangers and airport storage facilities in the Chicago area. Child porn was a big hit and Fern tied it to Pryor. Sky found a money trail, which led to Pryor. And Sanders found the prostitution connection and two city addresses. Walter's personal knowledge of the city's businesses tied up some loose ends.

They had a meeting and decided what they had was as good as it would get, until some doors were kicked in and more evidence found. So Joe got on the phone to Ted who was at home.

His wife June answered the phone. "So you're the guy sending my husband to lunch with a beautiful woman."

"Guess I'm guilty," Joe said. "But I hear that you're a child advocate with the court, so maybe this time you should take the two of them to get justice served, and then you can keep them out of mischief."

"How could I refuse to help bust bad guys? So where would you like them?" asked June.

"I'll send the two agents that Ted and Justine met today by to pick you up, and then they'll go get her. They'll drive you to a secure government location where I can send you the data we have and they should be able to get warrants," said Joe.

"Hang on. Let me get Ted," June said, and then yelled, "honey, pick up the phone! You've got another hot date and I've been invited along. Your friend from the islands is sending us a ride."

Ted picked up the other phone and said, "Boy, you work fast."

Joe replied, "I have some excellent helpers."

"Shall I have June be the one to invite my date this time?" Ted asked.

Joe chuckled. "Sounds like fun and you'll both love the surprises we have for you. Your ride should be enroute and I have them on my COM link."

June said, "Then we better hang up so I can call Ted's date."

"Sounds good," Joe said. "You have a real woman of action there, Ted. 'Bye."

June dialed and heard an answering machine. At the tone June said, "Hey girl, I have a hot date for you, so you had better pick up. We can't be keeping Ted waiting when his engine is going."

When Justine heard this she knew her life was getting weirder, but what the heck and picked up the receiver. "Well, I sure hope he's good. There is nothing on TV tonight."

June replied, "I've been married to him for twenty-two years and he can still cut the mustard. Our ride just came to the door and we'll give you a ring on arrival."

"What should I wear?"

"Just come as you are."

"In black silk pajamas?"

June laughed. "Now Ted and his pal Joe would love that. It might even make my night when I get the old boy home. I would say as casual as you like."

Justine said, "Ok, see you soon."

They headed out the door to the unmarked van. Ted sat at the console and June sat in the seat next to him. And there, smiling at them on the big screen, was Joe.

Ted smiled back. "You know, Joe, this is a long way from the old days, and the good-looking chick is June."

Joe replied, "It's a pleasure to meet you almost in person. We have already downloaded all the data we found, which should give you enough to keep you busy for years."

"Is it really true that you are in Hawaii?" June asked.

"It sure is," Joe said, "And if you can drag that old stick in the mud away from the Windy City, you could have a great vacation in warm island breezes. We could even find you a place to stay that you can afford and maybe even toss in a plane ride."

June said, "You sure know how to turn a girl's head. Would your flyboys mind if one of their passengers were handcuffed?"

Joe laughed. "No problem. Those guys like kinky stuff."

The van pulled to a stop at Justine's apartment. Ted and the male agent headed to the door as June dialed the phone.

"The boys are about to ring your chimes. We're out front."

"I see them on my security video. I'll be right down."

In minutes they were in the van and rolling to a secure location. Ted sat in the back in front of the console and Justine in a flattering jumpsuit piled in next to him.

Joe said, "We've enough for warrants, but I want to bring in a team of our own to bust Pryor. We have two reasons. One is that he's trained CIA and therefore is very dangerous. The other is that we believe there may be evidence to tie him to crimes against our country. Of course, we would share anything not classified. In fact, we have lots of info for you and hordes of loose ends. Is that ok with you, Justine?"

"I've been trying to bust this jerk for ten years and could find nothing to speak of. If you put him in the cage for me, you can run it your way."

"We have enough for you to get arrest warrants for

distribution and possession of porn, money laundering, child abuse, and prostitution. In addition to that, you'll be able to get search warrants for a bank, two businesses, two airplane hangers, a storage building, Pryor's house, car, and computers. Do you think that will make a dent in his style?"

Justine stared in disbelief, as did Ted and June.

June was the first to speak. "You must have magicians or psychics in Hawaii."

"Very close to that. I have a team of wizards and my brother rescued those kids who all want a piece of Pryor's butt."

Justine said, "How soon can they get here?"

"Six hours from right now."

"We'll be at the airport and have all our teams in place."

Justine heard several voices, but one very dignified voice said, "Thank you. We're on our way."

Before they signed off, June saw a man she recognized. She pointed to the screen. "I know that man, and I've seen him at the mall helping the kids, but could never find out anything about him."

Justine smiled. "I think we're about to meet him and I bet this time you'll get a name."

With that they drove directly to the judge's home. When they left they had a dozen warrants.

Justine said, "I guess we should have you take us to our offices."

Agent Lydia Miles said, "If you want, but we're more secure and at your service. We'll be meeting the incoming team at the airport. Also, your offices are no doubt bugged."

Justine said, "That offer sounds too good to refuse."

"Can we go somewhere to get food and coffee while these two burn up the phone lines?" asked June.

"Sure can," said Lydia.

With food and coffee they parked in a National Guard hangar at the airport. The phone calls continued and five hours later there were six teams and their leaders assembled in the hangar ready for word to go. These were the best state and local officers they could find. A group of Secret Service arrived with a group of vehicles and informed Agent Miles they came as ordered. All that was left was to wait for the plane from Hawaii.

The team leaders, Agent Miles, DA Justine Conviction, Capt. Ted Williams, and June watched as the airplane headed to their hangar a half-hour early. They all stood there in stunned silence as Air Force One taxied to a stop before them. As soon as the plane stopped moving, the Secret Service took up security positions around it. The stairs were rolled into place and the first ones down were dressed all in black tactical uniforms, but with no identification like other forces wore. A fifteen-passenger van pulled up next to them and stopped. Most of the men in black headed right to the other vans and climbed in like they had done this hundreds of times. A large man in black flanked by several females in black headed toward them with a group of civilians. He walked right to the team leaders.

"Gentlemen, I am Gen. Peter Rabbit and under direct orders from the president of the United States. The agents standing with me aren't here, nor are any of those civilians. In fact, we're not here either. You have your warrants, and our COM van will issue the go code to all units at once." He snapped a salute and said, "Move your men out."

The team leaders all vanished as if they had already seen too much. With that Peter and Susan joined the others who were still staring at each other.

"As I said, I'm Gen. Peter Rabbit. This is Susan Anthony, White House Head of Security, our First Lady, Capt. Snow

White, Maj. Walter Kid, and Fern Cybernaut. Your driver will be Ens. Shela Smith, a Navy SEAL, and riding shotgun is Sgt. J.P. Smith. Susan has asked to go in with us, as will Lt. Charly Brice, SSgt. Sky Lonewolfe, and MSgt. Amy Hunter. Let's mount up, folks. We've got bad guys to catch."

With that everyone climbed into their vans and drove off. Fern had jumped into the COM van and was talking with Joe before Lydia hit the gas. June got in, then Snow took the middle seat, and Walter sat beside her. Ted and Justine got in the double seat.

Finally Justine couldn't hold it back any longer. "Who is this Captain Kid?"

"Just a Hawaiian cop and my brother," replied Walter.

June said, "You're the one who's been helping kids at the mall!"

"He sure has," replied Snow, "and he rescued the Unhomed kids and promised them he would help their mother if he could."

Justine said, "This is just too bizarre, the First Lady going on a bust."

Snow replied, "I like those kids and I want to be there when this jerk goes down. And just as a woman to woman point of interest, I think Joe would like to meet you."

Walter said, "Good for you, Snow. Someone needs to fix up my big brother."

Justine said, "After this, I'll need a vacation. I think I fell down the rabbit hole—Gen. Peter Rabbit—that can't be for real."

Snow started laughing, "Yes, he's a real general and that is the name he was born with. Wait until you meet Alice in Wonderland—now that'll blow your mind. I wouldn't even dare to try and explain where those kids are located. You would want to commit me."

General Rabbit and his team were in place when Shela pulled in behind the COM van. This was a nice neighborhood with lawns, trees, and security systems. It was eleven o'clock on a weeknight, so it was dark and quiet. They gathered at the COM van door and watched Fern on the keyboard. Shela told them as soon as the house was secured they could go inside. Justine and Ted were getting over their shock at the source of their help and recognized how professionally this was going down.

Peter and Charly were at the back door and the team had the house surrounded. Amy, Sky, and Susan calmly walked up to the front door. The infrared scan had only shown two adults. A female was sitting at the kitchen table and a large male was standing near her. Amy rang the bell while Sky smiled at the security hole. Susan stayed out of sight. Pryor heard the bell and backhanded Sandra, almost knocking her off the chair. She was already crying, battered, and bleeding.

"You best be ready to make me happy when I get back," Pryor said, "And maybe I'll tell you about your brats."

With that he picked up his bottle of beer and headed for the front door. He was totally sure of himself as he strolled through his living room to the front hall in his underwear. He looked through the security hole and saw Sky's smiling face and knew he was going to have some fun. So he unlocked and opened the door to give her a big surprise. He was about to say something very smart, but all that ever got out was, "What the fuuuuu—" As Amy and Sky both hit him at once, picking him right off the floor and slamming him into the back wall in the hall spread-eagled, with his feet still off the floor.

Susan was so close behind them she caught the beer in

mid-air and slammed hard into his midsection. In one equally swift move she shoved the beer bottle where the sun never shines.

Susan was smiling, but not her eyes. "We've met your stepchildren and if you even look like you want to resist, I'm going to break that bottle right where it is and then watch these ladies dissect you very slowly."

And in stereo he heard from Amy and Sky, "And we'll enjoy it."

While Pryor was opening the front door, the back door had opened too. Peter stepped in with a laser pistol in his hand and moved to the doorway where Pryor had gone out. Charly sat in the chair next to Sandra and took both of her hands, then answered the questioning look in her eyes.

Charly said, "He will not be back—EVER—and your children are safe."

"They are?" cried Sandra.

"Yes, and we'll take you there," said Charly.

Out at the COM van Fern looked up from the keyboard. "It's secure and we can go in now. I have to go check his computers."

Snow said, "Come on, Justine and Ted, this is your bust. And I'm sure Walter and June can help Sandra."

So they all fell in behind Snow as she headed for the front door. Snow stopped just long enough in the front hall for Pryor to see who she was and then moved on to the important matters. June and Walter followed to the kitchen where Charly was still sitting holding Sandra's hands.

Sandra's eyes got big when Snow came in and put her arms around her. Snow looked at Sandra and said, "I would like you to meet the man who rescued your children. This is Maj. Walter Kid."

Walter blushed and said, "Well, actually all I did was feed them and give them a ride out of there. It was your Fran who saved me from General Hardash and she has been taking good care of her brothers. So, Sandra, you should be very proud of her. In fact, she made me promise to come help you, so here we are."

Snow said, "Come on, Sandra. We have to get you cleaned up and into some traveling clothes. Your children are waiting."

Snow, Charly, and June got Sandra washed, bandaged, and dressed. And then they and Walter all vanished to the van before the first police car arrived to take over the scene.

J.P. and Shela took over for Susan so she could vanish with the First Lady and for Sky so she could help Fern with the computers. The data clearly showed Pryor was working for Black and Project Neverland with all its evil intent toward the world.

Justine told Pryor, "You have the right to remain silent, the right to an attorney, and if you can not afford one, the government will appoint one to defend you. And I personally do not care one bit if you understand your rights or not. Cuff him, girls."

Amy and Shela planted Pryor on the floor on his knees, cuffed his hands behind him, cuffed his ankles, and placed a third pair of cuffs between the first two, then they carried him out and parked him on the lawn to wait for the local police. J.P. found a clean white sheet and placed it over Pryor so the neighbors would not have to see this pile of feces on the freshly mowed lawn. They then turned him over to Ted who escorted the perp to jail.

Sky and Fern collected all the data and erased the hard

drives. Meanwhile Peter and the rest of the team searched the whole place and removed anything that had to do with national security.

They were about to head out the back door when Justine asked Peter, "Could a curious girl get a ride on your airplane? I would like to meet this mystery cop named Joe."

He smiled, but before he could answer, Fern said, "Joe would like that very much, and if there aren't enough seats, I'll sit on the floor."

"Well, you heard him, and besides, maybe you'll like Joe enough to stay and we could use you on our team."

Peter was the last out the back door. Justine and June walked out the front door to join Ted.

"Ted, can you handle the investigations here?" asked Justine.

June said, "Say yes, dear."

He looked at Justine and repeated as told, "Yes, dear, and you'll like him. Now go before you lose your ride."

She ran off through the shadows and found Fern holding the van door for her. And a round of cheers came from inside it.

Amy said, "You were right again, Fern."

He laughed as he helped Justine to a seat. "It was nothing. I just thought it would be cool to have an Aunt Justine."

Back at the airport, Snow and Susan boarded Air Force One and headed for Washington, D.C. While they'd been gone, a government Gulfstream had arrived and had parked next to Air Force One. They all thanked Lydia Miles for her help and got on the plane for the long flight to Hawaii. Almost everyone was tired and found some place to nap.

Sandra couldn't doze off, so Walter sat with her. He told her about her children, how they had saved him and they were now so happy with the other children on Guam. Finally, she lay against him and they both fell sound asleep.

When they reached Alaska to refuel everyone got off refreshed and had a meal. It was another clear, cloudless night and everyone gathered around Sandra to share her awe.

She said, "My mother told me I could wish on stars, but I've never seen so many before. Add to that, almost anything I could wish for, you guys have already given me."

Justine said, "Just goes to prove your mother was right."

Soon the plane was refueled and ready to continue to Hawaii. They weren't in the air long before everyone was back asleep and, as such things go, it was a quiet flight.

The Gulfstream landed just as dawn was breaking over Hawaii. A U.S. Navy bus was waiting for them. Sandra and Justine had never been there before and were amazed at the difference from Illinois. The tropical greenery was everywhere and the palm trees were swaying in the salty breeze. All the beautiful island birds greeted them as they too welcomed the new day. Justine was amazed when they pulled into a national park. They were greeted by U.S. Forest Service rangers and as they got in farther she noticed well-armed Marines and Army personnel. And then they drove into the underground loading dock.

"This is an awful weird national park," said Justine.

Fern laughed. "Welcome to Scout bunker. I guess you could say we're beyond top secret. If you're lucky you can have breakfast with Uncle Joe."

As they got into the storage area, they found SB2 unloading fresh fruit and loading other supplies. And walking out of SB4 was Amanda, coming to warmly greet Peter.

Peter said, "This is Dr, Amanda Whosh, the CO of Sand Box 4, and that is how we'll go to Guam."

Next, Alice appeared and hugged J.P. Alice added, "I'm Alice and I'm an engineering officer in Project Wonderland, but you'll have plenty of time to see that when we get to Guam. Right now, everyone is waiting for you guys in the dining hall for breakfast."

They all headed to the upper floor of the bunker. Harry came out to meet Charly, and Kate hugged Fern.

Fern said, "Mom, this Justine Conviction. She came to meet Uncle Joe. And that's Sandra; Fran, Mike, and Jake's mother."

Kate hugged her and said, "Welcome onboard. Your kids really missed you, but they're now safe and having fun."

Fern said, "Uncle Joe, this is your DA, Justine Conviction."

"Can I take you to breakfast?"

She smiled. "I sure hope you do since I've come all this way to meet you. I didn't even bring a toothbrush."

Amy and Sky grabbed Fern. "Come on, matchmaker. We've got to eat and get to work on that data so we can get you back to Guam. Somebody misses you there."

Walter introduced Sandra; most of the people there stopped to say hello and many told her how they liked the children.

Sandra said, "I've been on military bases with Donald, but none were like this. It's like a big family."

Walter replied, "Yes, I've noticed that. In fact, I've been thinking I would like to live here or where the children are. This is an amazing place, not only because of what's here, but also because of the people, who really care about each other."

Joe took Justine and Sandra, with Walter tagging along, for a tour after breakfast while the data was being examined and sent to Washington to Frost. And Joe asked Justine if she would like to go to Guam. She agreed, so he arranged for Capt. Sherman Tank to take command while he was gone.

Fern, Sky, and Sandy pulled the data apart and sent the results to Frost in D.C. They also found information that'd be of great interest to Ted Williams. They sent it to him via their new friend Lydia Miles who was pleased to help put the bad guys away. They then all headed to SB4 to travel to the Constitution at Guam. SB2 finished loading and they launched back to the ship. Justine, Sandra, and Walter were on their way to SB4 when they saw SB2 as it made the jump and vanished before their eyes.

"Welcome to Wonderland," said Alice.

White House, Washington, D.C.:

White and Frost returned from Camp David late Sunday night and had monitored the events in Chicago with great interest. Snow and Susan returned about the same time and over a late snack told the two men the rest of the story. And White asked Susan to bring a special guest to supper the next night and told her Jack would join them too.

During the late afternoon of the next day Susan found Mary Dyer, one of the leading environmentalists, at her office. As they walked into the White House, Mary asked her, "You're going to kill me, aren't you?"

"Why would you think that?"

"The last time I was here, they wouldn't even let me near the fence. Today, you are bringing me inside and those men with guns don't seem to care."

"And I thought you Quakers trusted everyone."

"I do trust God and Jesus and they told me to come with you and maybe that means I'm to become a martyr for justice and truth."

"Well, hopefully, not tonight, since White didn't tell me I was supposed to bump you off."

"Well, I guess that should be comforting."

They walked into the dining room and found the president, his wife, and the chief of National Defense waiting.

Mary added, "I guess that's because he has his head butcher here to do the job."

Snow chimed in, "Jack better not kill anyone at my table. It'd ruin my reputation."

They all sat down and White reached into the chair next to him and picked up two stuffed toys. He threw both at Mary. Jack laughed and got beaned with the third stuffed animal.

White said, "This isn't funny. That woman attacked me with these things in public. And I'm at least gentleman enough to throw them back in private."

To that, Mary started laughing. "Well, if that's the worst you're going to do to me, I guess I'll live, but what would you want to see me for — let alone feed me?"

"I went on an extraordinary trip this weekend and have seen the error of my ways, and I need you to help me fix what is going wrong in our world. As you know, the head of the EPA just resigned. I want you to replace him. I can't promise that doing that job right won't get you killed and maybe me too. You're the best, and if I'm to make meaningful changes, I need the best to help me. Will you do that?" asked White.

Mary thought for a moment, and then said, "Yes."

"Thank you, Mary,"

After dinner Susan drove Mary home and, as they stood

beside the car, Mary looked into her eyes and asked, "Does he really mean it?"

"Yes," said Susan. "I was with him on that trip and the things I saw were amazing, but they made it very clear how destructive we are. It must stop if we're going to save our world for the children. None of us knows where to start. You are our last best hope. I promise I will protect you as I would him."

"I will do my best then and pray for enlightenment to serve well," said Mary Dyer.

AS THE DAWN SEVEN

In unity we build strength greater than our own. With divisiveness we destroy our own foundations. When the "I" becomes more important than the "WE," unity of purpose is lost. The "I" stands alone and, like the tree in the forest, when you fall, no one will hear or care. "We the people" are falling. Is anyone listening?

On the USS Constitution CVNX-911 on Station at Guam in the Year 1421:

SB2 had arrived and the work party was busy unloading her. When SB4 arrived, a briefing was called to update everyone. Tracy North and Krista Sparks with all the children had met them when they'd arrived. Sandra was beside herself to see her kids and didn't want to let them go.

Fran asked, "How'd you enjoy your first trip in a Sand Box?"

Neither Sandra nor Justine had words as their minds were still trying to catch up.

"Well, you all should go to the briefing. Krista can take you."

Sandra started to protest, but Fran said, "Mom, we're all right and we need to go with Aunt Tracy to help the sick children on the island. The four of you need to know what is going on, because if something isn't done, we may have no home to go back to, ever. And besides, if you don't know what's going on, how can you decide where you want to live or what you want to do?"

Justine put her arm around Sandra. "That girl of yours would make a great lawyer."

Tracy laughed. "Or an anthropologist."

And Krista added, "Fern and I will be sure to take you to them after the meeting."

Sandra looked at Justine. "Councilor, I do believe you are right. Lead on, Krista. We might just as well be totally astounded."

The pieces of the puzzle were slowly coming together. Pryor's computer records led right back to Black and Banks. He was singing to Ted to save himself, which added to what the investigators already had. They'd yet to find the base for Neverland. Matt was helping them search and that finally led to a computer chip. Black's men had preprogrammed the ships to return to Neverland's hidden base, but if someone tampered with the chip in any way, it self-destructed. Matt had explained how the Sand Boxes had carried a supply of clothes for the different time periods they had visited. This way they could pass among the locals without being noticed. On those ships, people were restricted on where they could go and when. Matt had been considered part of engineering and wore a red uniform. Only command (blue) and security (black) were given the full run of the ship. The computer records showed that SB3 had delivered arms to many countries, and the president was going to personally warn their leaders.

They decided to deliver the dead to Diego Garcia where they'd meet Admiral Snoopy. Merry Kurious, who actually worked for Snoopy, would return with him to bring the Office of Naval Intelligence up to date on this problem. They would also be taking the ship's mail to the admiral. And they discussed the "Official Story" of what had happened and where the Constitution was currently located.

The new crew for SB3 had been chosen.

Sand Box 3 Crew:
CO —Cdr. Topper Bird, USN pilot / Air wing CO
XO —Lt. Jay Hosmer, Army Special Forces / Intel
Nav —Lt. Matt Youngblood, Navigation Officer
Eng. —Lt. Steve Shoemaker, USN Engineering Officer
COM —Ens. Detter Terror, USN Flight COM Specialist
Medic —Suzy Que, RN, EMT
Electrician —IC2 Max Knight, USN Interior
Communications Electrician

When the meeting ended Krista and Fern took Justine, Sandra, Joe, and Walter ashore to the village where the kids were working. When they arrived they found the kids all very busy. Sandra was most surprised to see her daughter helping a nursing mother with a colicky baby. Mike was showing another mother how to bathe her young child, and Jake was busy boiling clean water. Tracy was talking with a group of older women. A man and woman they had not met before greeted them.

"Hello," he said, "I'm Doc Bones, and this Cookie. We're from SB4."

Justine said, "You're here to help the sick children?"

Cookie laughed. "Actually, most of the time we stay out of the way. The children are so much better at this than we are. They just dig in and help. They show the natives by doing it themselves. When the natives see that it works, they do it that way too. Tracy and Abi from Agana are talking to the elders who run this village and are explaining what the children are doing.

Justine queried, "Where are the male elders?"

Cookie smiled. "This is a matriarchal society, where the women rule. The older men are home minding the children. It might be nice to live like this."

It was Doc's turn to laugh. "Dear, you are already in charge and I'd make a lousy fisherman."

Back on the ship a work party was loading the dead on SB4 to be delivered to Diego Garcia. An honor guard was forming to escort their fallen comrades with Chaplain Desire Peace. Admiral Staff and Captain Right were in full dress uniforms when they joined the escort detail. Cookie and Doc were back from the beach and she had the galley ready with snacks and light food, also lots of coffee. When all was ready Dr. Whosh ordered the jump to their rendezvous point.

Diego Garcia, Indian Ocean:

A U.S. Navy cargo plane touched down and taxied to the hangar to be refueled for its return trip. The security team took their positions. A tall man in uniform accompanied by four Marines walked to meet the ground controller. The ground controller led them to a C-2 Greyhound that had just finished its flight checks and was ready for take off. The officer and the four Marines climbed in and buckled up.

The captain said, "Welcome aboard, sir. Our flight time should be about ten minutes if they are ready for us to land."

With that he taxied to the runway and was airborne.

Out in the bay, the USS Ronald Reagan (CVN 76) was anchored. Capt. Roger Williams' phone rang and he was told he had a priority-encrypted message. He sat at his computer console and signed in. When it asked to verify ID, he placed his eye to the optical scanner until the green light came on.

It replied: ID confirmed. He requested his priority message. It was operational orders from ONI. He was to clear an area in his hangar deck per an enclosed diagram. He was to have the ship ready to go to sea in twenty-four hours. He would get a secure message telling him to put to sea and provide the coordinates to meet an incoming aircraft. He would sound General Quarters upon reaching station. He would have a Marine guard standing by and the hangar deck would be clear of all ship's crew and Marines posted to ensure compliance. He would get further instructions from the arriving officer. End message.

He met with his senior officers and issued the needed orders. The ship was made ready to get underway within fifteen minutes. He was sitting on the bridge when the message arrived.

Williams ordered the crew to set the sea and anchor detail. "We're getting underway. Announce on the 1MC that all hands have thirty minutes before we sound GQ."

Engineering was ready and the anchor was up in ten minutes. The Ronald Reagan was underway to meet an unknown officer who would be flying to meet them. As they closed on their meeting place, GQ was sounded, the hangar deck was cleared, the Marine guard was ready, and the hanger deck was secured. Radar reported an approaching C-2 Greyhound. The air boss had them on radio and the ship steered into the wind. The Quartermaster said, "Captain, the incoming aircraft has requested you meet the arriving officer on the flight deck."

Captain Williams headed down and ordered the XO to take command.

He arrived down with the Marine guards and soon saw a uniformed officer and four Marines get off the plane. Once he was close, Williams could see it was an admiral and snapped to attention and saluted.

Admiral Snoopy returned the salute and said, "Let's get to the hangar deck."

Snoopy looked around and confirmed that all was ready and handed the captain a paper. Snoopy said, "Set that course and speed, Captain."

Captain Williams keyed his mobile COM unit and passed the instructions to his XO. A few minutes later the XO confirmed the orders.

"Admiral, course and speed are set," reported Captain Williams.

Snoopy nodded and said to the lead Marine with him, "Explain their duties to the Marines."

With that he walked out to the middle of the clear area and placed a small object on the deck. "Ok, Captain Williams, we need to stand back. We're about to make contact with the USS Constitution and I've a small job for you. What we're about to see is need-to-know and that comes directly from President White, who called me personally to give me these orders."

Ten minutes had passed when an odd noise from the center of the clear area drew their attention. Then, suddenly, SB4 appeared right on the little target.

"The president told me I would be amazed, Williams," said Admiral Snoopy.

Williams replied, "Me too. I guess I shouldn't ask what that is I'm looking at."

"I'm not sure either one of us wants to know," replied Snoopy.

The door of SB4 opened and almost immediately the Marine honor guard marched out in double file. Once all were out, they formed two lines facing each other. The Marines came to attention. And Admiral Staff stepped out of SB4 and walked through the Marine guard. Behind the admiral was

Captain Right, followed by Chaplain Peace and Ltjg. Merry Kurious with all the paperwork on the fallen servicemen. Admiral Staff walked to Admiral Snoopy and Captain Right to Captain Williams. They all saluted.

"We are here to transfer to your care our fallen comrades from the USS Constitution who are named on this list. We request they be returned to their families," said Staff.

The sailors started carrying out their fallen comrades and placing them on the deck. Once they were all arraigned, the Marines and sailors fell in facing the bodies. The officers joined them and Chaplain Peace stepped forward.

"Lord, we leave our fallen comrades in your hands and ask that you carry their souls home, just as we are returning their bodies to their families. May they rest in peace as we pray."

Our Father which art in heaven
Hallowed be thy name.
Thy kingdom come.
Thy will be done in earth,
As it is in heaven.
Give us this day our daily bread.
And forgive us for our debts,
As we forgive our debtors.
And lead us not into temptation,
But deliver us from evil.
For thine is the kingdom,
And the power,
And the glory,
Forever.
Amen.

Matthew 6:9-13, King James Version

Everyone saluted and the sailors marched back into the box, and then started carrying out bags of mail.

Staff said, "Chet, I'm also returning your Lieutenant JG Kurious to you. She's been more than helpful in our times of great need. She'll be able to answer many of your questions that our president could not and will keep you in direct contact with us. The president has a prepared speech, which will explain to the public as best we can what is going on. Obviously, there are things we can't talk about at all. Those bags are the ship's mail. We would be most grateful if you posted it. I wish we had more time, but right now we don't. Merry, I truly thank you for your hard work. We'll take good care of Vary."

They all saluted. Staff and Right returned to SB4, shut the door, and vanished. Snoopy walked over and retrieved the target and placed it in his pocket.

"It is good to see you, Merry, and, boy, do I have questions," said Admiral Snoopy, "Roger, deliver these men to the Diego Garcia airport. Also, please post the mail. But first head your ship back into the wind so we can get airborne. And I thank you for all your help. Perhaps some day I'll be able to tell you the rest of the story, or at least as much as they tell me."

They returned to the flight deck and the six of them got in the C-2 Greyhound. Five minutes later they were gone on their return flight to the airport.

The Ronald Reagan secured the GQ and returned to her anchorage where the Seahawks began transferring the fifty-two bodies to the waiting plane and the admiral who would bring them home. The four Marines, Merry, and he went to the officer's mess to eat while the plane was loaded. His Marine minders sat off by themselves and Merry and the admiral were alone.

As Snoopy looked at her, he asked, "You just came from being on the Constitution?"

"Yes, I've been onboard her since I left Hawaii with my husband. I left her hangar deck about twenty minutes before I met you on the Ronald Reagan."

"Will this all make sense to me after you are done explaining?"

"I hope so, but there's so much and a lot of it is just beyond belief."

They ate well as the cargo plane they were flying home on didn't have the amenities of a Gulfstream. One of the flight crew came to get them when the plane was ready to leave.

Chet said, "We should use the head here," and suggested the same to the Marines.

The crewman smiled. "Gee, sir, you must have flown with us before."

Soon they were in the air headed for Washington, D.C., so the president could meet these men and explain their deaths to the nation.

During the long flight home, Snoopy and Kurious sat by themselves so she could brief him on what was going on. They made themselves as comfortable as one can get in a cargo plane. He pulled out a small device and turned it on.

Merry smiled. "Those work very well."

Snoopy looked rather surprised that she even knew what it was, since it was classified well above top secret. "You've seen one before?"

"Several actually, Sky Lonewolfe, Shela Smith, Gen. Peter Rabbit, and Bob Cybernaut all have them."

Snoopy started laughing. "You said I'd be amazed, and I know all those people. We have to keep increasing Sky's clearances because she has a knack for finding secrets. And Peter is a rogue and a scoundrel, but an admirable one. Cybernaut made it in the first place and I forgot he was onboard when she put to sea. He hates to travel and likes to be close to his family."

Now it was her turn to laugh. "His wife, Kate, is with him on SB2 as the cook and his son, Fern, is a computer wizard who works with Sky all the time."

And so the story continued with breaks for the two refueling stops. The crew kept her supplied with fresh coffee. Merry kept on talking as Admiral Snoopy's head sort of kept spinning around. She covered the Black / Banks conspiracy to take over the world, the agents who had tried to assassinate Fern and his mom, the ship vanishing and ending up in 1421 instead of 2012. She told him about Admiral He and the Japanese pirates. She explained the Chamorro people and the bunker in Hawaii and finding the two missing Sand Boxes on the moon. She told how the crews from SB2 and SB3 turned up in a mall in Chicago and how that led them to finding Pryor, how Walter Kid rescued the children and went back with the First Lady to rescue their mother. She told him about the fifty trillion dollars of gold bars and a billion in arms they found. She explained that they were using the extra boxes to carry supplies to the ship. Ah, yes, the admiral's head was going round and round. On the last leg, she fell asleep and Snoopy had never in his whole life been so happy to have silence.

When the plane landed at D.C., General Frost met them with a car. A whole honor guard was waiting to relieve Snoopy of the fifty-two bodies. Frost drove them to the White House. They went directly to the War Room to meet the president. Once more Snoopy was amazed to find Snow and Susan Anthony there and was thunderstruck by the fact that all of them knew Merry on a first name basis and, instead of saluting, they were all hugging. By the time the meeting was over, the president told Chet that he and his lovely wife needed a Hawaiian vacation and that he was sure Merry could handle all the details.

Merry and Snoopy once again got comfortable on the Gulfstream headed for San Diego. He broke out a bottle of wine, which was the first time she'd ever seen him drink. She was glad that drinking some of it was helping her relax a little after the recent events.

Finally, Snoopy said, as he stared at his glass, "I need to ask you a big favor."

"What can I do for you, sir?"

"Could you please explain this vacation thing to my wife? Mildred's going to think I'm nuts."

Merry grinned widely. "I'd love to talk with Mildred. I'm sure any woman who can teach astronomy to college students would love to go on a field trip to see the stars."

Back in Washington, D.C.:

In a large hangar, the fifty-two flag-draped coffins were lined up. In front was a large podium from which the president would address the nation. The families had all been informed by a visit from military personnel. Now it was up to the president to explain to the nation. The media had been invited to record this event. A protestant minister opened the memorial service and introduced the president.

White began, "My fellow Americans, I stand before you with great sadness because today fifty-two of our fallen service men have returned home. They were serving on the USS Constitution, which is currently deployed on a humanitarian relief effort in a very sensitive location which, at this time, I can't name because it would endanger those still there.

While carrying out their humanitarian relief effort the USS Constitution and the people of the nation we are helping, came under a sneak attack by forces from another nation. Our people and the people we are helping fought these attackers side by side until they were driven back into the sea. In the end, one hundred and nineteen souls had returned home to their Lord. Fifty-two of them are the Americans here before you."

White continued, "These are our fallen heroes who gave their lives in defense of the values we hold dear. While they were helping others they were attacked. Our world is growing smaller each day, and we must work together to make our planet a better place for all of us to live, especially for our children and our grandchildren. We must work together to give our children a better world and to set an example for them to follow. I ask you, my fellow Americans, and you the people of the world, to stand with us to bring meaning to our fallen comrades who have died for all of us. Let us unite and go forward and build a brighter tomorrow that will make our children proud of us."

A priest and a rabbi spoke of the great loss and appealed to God. The Marine honor guard fired a twenty-one gun salute and the service was closed with the playing of Taps.

Back at the White House, the president was busy making calls to world leaders warning them that he had intel that some radical groups had been supplied with arsenals of weapons to possibly try to overthrow their legal governments. He further promised that if he got more substantial specific information he would contact them. He also warned that part of this attack might have been financial.

Meanwhile on the West Coast, San Diego, California:
Admiral Snoopy watched the memorial service on TV in his office. He was still trying to absorb all that Merry had told

him and in all his years had never heard of a First Lady being at a National Security briefing. And she ran up and hugged Merry—very unusual.

On the other side of town at the university, Merry had waited until Professor Snoopy's lectures were over and met her outside her office.

"May I speak with you, Professor?"

"You don't look like any of my students. Why do you wish to speak to me?"

Merry showed her military ID and said, "I'd like to speak with you about your husband, ma'am."

Professor Snoopy pushed the door to her office open and said, "Inside." She walked to her desk and sat down while Merry stood in front of the desk sort of at parade rest. "Have a chair. I suppose you're here to tell me you are having an affair with Chet and that you want to marry him."

Merry thought for a few moments before responding and then said, "When I left my husband in Guam two days ago I was under the impression he and I were happily married. And while I am rather fond of your husband, I see him more as a father figure than anything else. I am here today because your husband, Chet, asked me to speak to you because he thought you would think he was nuts if he talked to you about this matter himself."

Merry continued, "Yesterday when he and I were in the War Room of the White House meeting with President White; his wife, Captain Snow White; the Head of White House Security, Dr. Susan Anthony, and General Jack Frost, Head of National Defense—our president strongly suggested that your husband should start taking regular 'vacations' in Hawaii. And that he should take you with him on those 'vacations.' He further suggested that some friends and I could help find ways you can afford these 'vacations.' Your husband and I are aware of some of the reasons why the president made this 'suggestion,' but at the moment, because of national security and the danger to thousands of people, including my own husband, I can't explain them to you. However, I believe if you are patient, the answers will be provided by what you observe on 'vacation.'."

Professor Snoopy said, "You're obviously no air-headed clerk, but do you realize how bizarre what you just said sounds?"

Merry replied, "Frankly, most of what I have seen is also so bizarre that I can't wait to return to see my husband, to believe it's all real. The best I can suggest is that you take Chet on vacation and if my boss will give me the time off, I'd be happy to be your tour guide. Also, I know a group of young people there who'd love to hear about the stars from someone like you."

Professor Snoopy said, "Young lady, you are most convincing and I think dealing with you would have been a lot simpler if you were Chet's paramour." She leaned forward across her desk and stuck out her hand and said, "By the way, my name is Mildred and we're having spaghetti for supper. If you're not busy maybe you could join us and help Chet tell me about this vacation our president thinks I need."

Merry took her hand and replied, "That is the best offer I've had since an admiral let me travel with my husband on his ship, the Constitution."

Washington, D.C., Evening Rush Hour:
Elianora McNeill had finished up her workday at five o'clock p.m. after she checked out with General Black. She drove out of the secure garage and the guard spent more time looking at her breasts than the box on the seat next to her. But

in fact, with the tinted security glass Black had paid to have installed, the guard couldn't see if anyone was in the car. In fact, she could have been smuggling out several people, and the guard wouldn't have seen them. She got on the freeway and headed for the mall. Elianora planned on eating there and then doing a little shopping before driving to her apartment. When she pulled off the freeway, she saw her gas tank was low and pulled into the gas station.

She didn't notice the white van that pulled off with her. The passenger was looking at a computerized display and reported to the driver. "It is confirmed that Black and Hardash are in that car." The driver nodded and pulled in some distance in back of her. The third man slid the side door open, stepped out several feet, placed the rocket launcher on his shoulder, and fired, then he stepped back into the van and it drove away in the other direction.

Elianora McNeill was thinking about what she would have for supper and that maybe she should go through the clothes to see how much money was there, so she could buy something really nice. But that thought was permanently interrupted when the rocket ripped its way into her car and exploded, only leaving small pieces of the vehicle. The explosion took out the gas pump and turned four other cars into infernos. The windows of the convenience store shattered and sent shards of glass everywhere.

The mercenaries had just killed a dozen people and sent another twenty-eight to the hospital, but their intended targets were busy somewhere else plotting to kill their boss, Lo Mean. Elianora's choices had just affected a lot of other people and the price was paid in blood.

The investigation was ten days old when a bright lab worker discovered the traces of explosives and called in the

FBI. The newspapers and TV listed the cause of the explosion as a person smoking at the pump. Black and Hardash were a lot more skeptical about the cause.

Meanwhile in San Diego:

Merry had reported her success to the admiral and, at the end of the day, she drove him home in her car. Mildred's academic day ended earlier than hubby's spy business, so supper was well on its way when they arrived. They lived in a stately old home in the suburbs. The security fence was almost invisible and was intended more to warn off intruders than to stop them from entering. While their home looked much like others in the area, the house itself was built like a fortress. When they entered the house, the admiral logged Merry into the computer security system, and then they found Mildred busy in the kitchen. She smiled and kissed her husband and said, "Well, Chet, since you're on time for once, you can go set the table," and handed him a tray with salads.

Merry pitched in a hand and soon they were busy eating. She told Mildred it was nice to have a home-cooked meal. She explained that on the ship it was more a matter of which mess or dining hall you were close to at the time, although she had had some really great native meals when they were ashore on the island. She told them how great it was to be with Vary and to work with him, but things there were always very busy.

Merry turned the conversation to the pictures on the mantle of two young people and asked if those were their children. Poor Chet looked very uncomfortable with the question and rather sad. She had an instant pang of guilt that she had asked about a very painful subject.

Mildred, on the other hand, had thought about the question and then explained, "They are our estranged children.

Our daughter, Aurora Starlight, became an environmentalist in college and now sees her father as an environmental butcher. She believes that I copped out for the good life. We haven't heard from her in a long time. Aurora lives on the East Coast and is very involved in lobbying for environmental causes. The other is our son, Lee Fathom, who came to believe that Chet loved the Navy more than him. The only thing they could manage to share was Scouting and a love for the outdoors. Chet and I were very proud when he made Eagle Scout, but after college he drifted away. Aurora's feelings bothered him deeply and now he lives somewhere in Alaska as a wilderness guide. Neither of them uses our last name. They go by their first and middle names. It makes both of us very sad, so we seldom talk about it."

Merry said, "I'm sorry I asked. I didn't wish to cause either of you pain."

Mildred replied, "It's not your fault, dear, you asked a normal question. In this case it has a sad answer. So why don't we talk about this vacation our president thinks I need? In fact, this week is the end of this semester and I have some time off."

"I can book a Gulfstream for Saturday."

"That'll work," replied Mildred.

Suddenly, Chet found his voice, "But I'll never have time to pack and who'll mind the office while I'm gone?"

"Well, that's why Admiral Staff sent me back to be your assistant. I think with a little help from Mildred I can handle the packing. As for the office, your XO Admiral Dewy is a very capable man to keep the shop running like a clock."

Chet looked like he was trying to think of another argument, but he had run out of anymore to ask. "Ok."

Oahu, Hawaii:

Conjure Appallingly arrived at the airport with her two minders. A limo was waiting with the headman for Hawaii sweating in the air-conditioned back seat. He'd no idea what had happened to Moon Sung. He explained that he hadn't heard that Sung had been arrested the night his house was raided and the only reason that happened was some nutcase stole his car and the police recovered it.

Conjure was unconvinced that it was that simple and if he had escaped the police he had contacts, a safe house, and they could have gotten him off the island. She had the police records checked very carefully, but the only arrests had nothing to do with Moon Sung. Her first real clue came when she found the name of the man who stole the car, but then any crazy person who they could not ID would be listed as John Doe. She, however, knew Black had an errand boy using that pseudonym. She was about to write that off when she got to John Doe's untimely demise at the hands of a single terrorist who blew up most of a wing at the hospital. That brought one name to mind: Raul Mercenary, Black's hired gun. Although it made perfect sense for them to silence someone, why would John Doe steal Moon Sung's car and let himself get caught? What if Black grabbed Moon Sung, but then why? They could learn little from him, and Black knew she had assets here.

All very odd, but then there was the matter of the five hundred vanishing military and an admiral at about the same time. A missing aircraft carrier and SB4 that never surfaced also posed another set of questions. Could it be that Black was lying to them and had tucked away those fifty trillion dollars in gold for himself? Well, this admiral had left his wife behind, so Conjure decided she would have a talk with her. She called together her island team and had the safe house made ready for a guest.

Back in San Diego:

All was packed. Merry, Mildred, and Chet were on the Gulfstream at 0800 hours enroute to a Hawaiian vacation. They were going to stay, at least for public notice, at Admiral Staff's home with his wife, Stella. It was a high security home with a security team guarding it. It even had a secret entrance and was close to the navy base. So they settled in to enjoy their flight. Mildred and Merry talked about what they were going to wear in sunny Hawaii, while Chet read a good mystery novel about lost treasure.

Pentagon, Washington, D.C., in a Deep Subbasement Storeroom:

Patent Hardash and Raul Mercenary were waiting when SB1 appeared before them. They boarded and made sure the full security assault team was ready for action and that the ship was in order.

USS Constitution on Station at Guam in the Year 1421:

A security alert had sounded throughout the ship and over the 1MC came the announcement: *All personnel of SB4 report onboard. This is not a drill. That is, SB4 you have a security alert. Report to your stations.*

Amazingly they were all onboard the ship since it was early in the morning. All the senior personnel met Dr. Whosh and General Rabbit in the dining hall. Everyone sat down and as soon as Rabbit saw everyone was present, he told them that SB1 had just appeared in the Pentagon and that SB5 had vanished from Russia and SB6 from Europe. As soon as they had a roll call to confirm all hands were onboard, they'd jump to the Scout bunker. As soon as Fern and Sky checked in they headed for the computer. While Sky started several searches, Fern found he had a message from Merry that told him about Snoopy's children. He typed in their names and started a search. He looked up when Sky started laughing.

Fern looked at Sky and asked, "What's so funny?"

With a silly grin Sky said, "We appear to have a stowaway," and pointed behind Fern. He turned to find Krista standing there.

Before he could speak, she said, "You think you guys are going to run off to save the world and leave me at home?"

"Well," Fern finally said, "You might as well have a seat since we are halfway to Hawaii. Did you tell your mom?"

"Not exactly," said Krista, "But I thought she would figure it out when she finds me in Hawaii."

Sky almost fell off her chair laughing and finally hugged Krista then said, "Girl, you are a hoot."

Back in Washington at the White House:

Snow and Susan were headed to the helo-pad with Mary Dyer and her associate Aurora Starlight. The Marines had already loaded the luggage for their flight to the airport. There they would board a Gulfstream for Hawaii for a meeting with Dr. Tracy North in Guam. The president wanted to convince Mary Dyer that his concern for the environment was real and that mere words would never work. There had been too many lies and they needed proof before they'd help him. So the First Lady was taking them to see what had convinced him that changes had to be made before it was too late.

As they were leaving, a secure courier van pulled up to the White House. Paul Brown had already had a busy shift running all over D.C. with copies of this report. Many had gone to Congress but his last stops were the banking commission, the federal attorney general, and the last to the White House. Commerce Secretary Gary Moneypenny read the report and before he got to page three had buzzed the Oval Office for an immediate appointment. The second call was from AG Judith Harvard, who was already enroute to the White House with the report in hand. General Frost was with the president telling him that SB1 was at the Pentagon when the calls came in and was asked to stay. The president, Frost, Moneypenny, and Harvard had only been talking a few minutes when the president's secretary came into the room.

J.J. Flash said, "Sorry, sir, but I've had eleven more calls from Congressmen who have received the same package and they are going nuts. They all want to see you yesterday."

The package was a complete story of how Warbucks Banks had come by all his money and had an extensive list of his illegal operations. It also contained very specific proof of the allegations including bank account numbers. It also tied him to the money laundering business in Chicago and a man named Pryor.

President White said, "J.J., set up a joint emergency session of Congress, ASAP. Jack, bring in the full staff to man the War Room. I want a real time link to Scout bunker, also send them that full report and take Judith with you. She will need to hear what they say and brief her on what we already know. Gary, find out the ramifications of that mess and of course we needed that yesterday too. If a high-speed computer link will help, go with them to the basement—just follow Jack and Judith. I better start taking calls before someone goes off the deep end with this."

They all ran to their appointed locations and started working. Gary was typing like mad on the console that Jack had pointed out. Jack sat down at the main console and Judith watched as the big screen came to life. Within seconds, Sandy's face appeared on the screen.

Sandy said, "Hi, Jack, who's the cutie?"

Jack replied, "U.S. Attorney General Judith Harvard and I have Commerce Secretary Gary Moneypenny in the back corner. Our COM tech is faxing you a report we just received on Warbucks Banks, which must have come from Benedict Black's office. He sent copies to everyone. What's new on your end?"

Sandy said, "SB5 has left Russia and SB6 has left Europe. Both vanished into thin air. SB1 is still at the Pentagon."

Suddenly, the screen divided in two. The new section of the screen showed a second scene.

"Hi, Jack," said Fern, "We just landed at Scout bunker and I think SB1 is about to jump."

Sky added, "Jack, we're getting a data overload, so I'm going to bring Deep Thought online—maybe she can sort some of this out in real time for us."

"I see the president finally sicced his Top Cop on you General Frost," laughed Sky.

Fern put in, "By the way, Jack, we have AG Justine Conviction of Chicago and Captain Kid onboard. Once we get upstairs to the command center, they'll be online with you."

Judith chimed in next to Jack, "Well, Fern, it looks like our expert computer hacker has a couple of minders, too. Just to keep you out of trouble, I'm sure," she chuckled.

Fern looked up at Krista leaning on his shoulder and then over at Sky, then smiled back at the screen. "Officer, I do believe I have the right to remain silent. And we had better go join Sanders."

Judith looked around at the computers in the War Room and asked Jack, "Why don't we have computers like this?"

"Because you didn't steal 'em from the military."

"And how long has young Cybernaut been working for you?"

"Since the CIA tried to terminate him and his mother."

"He hacked them?" she asked.

Jack laughed. "Probably, but they were after him because of something his father sent him in the mail. They not only did not get it, the whole team of hitmen is still in the funny farm babbling like idiots."

"Wait a minute. His father vanished on that boat."

"Yes. And they just left the Constitution in Guam and landed in Hawaii."

"What?" said Judith, "It was Guam that was attacked? Are we at war?"

"Almost, and I fear our 'good' Doctor Banks and the NSA are in it up to their ears."

"You mean White was talking about General Black?" asked Judith.

"Afraid so," replied Jack.

Command Center Scout Bunker, Oahu, Hawaii:

Justine and Joe were the first to get to the center, and Cpl. Taylor Maid met him at the door with briefing and status reports. Justine waved and walked over to join Sanders. When she sat down and looked up at the big screen she was surprised to see Judith Harvard at the other end sitting with Jack Frost.

Justine said, "Boy, I must have stumbled into the big time just as I was planning to retire. The First Lady shows up on my last and biggest bust and now I find myself looking at our nation's top cop."

Judith replied, "I think you've been talking with young Mr. Cybernaut, who just told me he has the right to remain silent."

Justine laughed. "With his female companions that is no doubt a good idea. Two Navy SEALs, a Tiger plus his mother, and Stella Staff has adopted him."

Judith replied, "It would seem you are a member of that formidable list and, by the way, since I've never told you, you're the reason I became a lawyer."

"In that case," Justine replied, "we'll have to break some new ground to get the next generation interested."

"I hate to break-up this mutual admiration society," Jack said, "but we have the matter of some documents that tie Dr. Warbucks Banks to your Felonious T. Pryor."

"Now I'm really impressed," said Justine.

Both Sanders and Justine were watching the screen as a very white-faced Gary Moneypenny sat down between Jack and Judith. He leaned back in his chair and took a deep breath.

"If we arrest Banks," he finally said, "it will ruin the world economy and send us all into a depression for years."

There were long moments of silence on both ends. Joe had just walked up behind Justine and heard it, too.

Finally Gary spoke again. "I had our computers run the scenarios three times each and it was always the same answer. I'll have our people dump the data into this system so you can try to prove me wrong. I pray at least one of you can."

Sky, Krista, Fern, and Amy were heading for the command center. As they got to the dining hall, Fern groaned at the smell of food.

Amy laughed. "Come on, Krista, we better get these two some food so they don't pass out on their keyboards."

Fern and Sky never broke pace, but Amy and Krista heard a stereo thank you from the departing pair.

"Maybe if I tied a keyboard to my chest," Krista said to Amy, "I could keep his attention longer."

When Amy stopped laughing enough to reply she said, "Now that is kinky, girl, but I know what you mean."

"Welcome back," Meatloaf said. "And what would you like, guys?"

Amy explained, "We have to get food for Sky and Fern, who ran right for the console."

Meatloaf laughed. "Maybe I should ask Sanders to install some workstations in here for those guys." Then he packed four meals for them on a tray.

"Thanks," said Krista as they headed out with the food and drinks.

When they arrived with the food, Sky and Fern had already heard the bad news from Washington. Fern was running his own scenarios and chasing any new data that might sway the outcome. Sky was busy connecting to Deep Thought when they sat the food down between them. Krista was quite amazed at how they could both eat and never look at the food. But soon she noticed that something behind them had caught Amy's attention.

Standing behind them was a ten-foot-tall female with the most perfect body she had ever seen and muscles that rippled as she moved with the sheer grace of a wild animal. She bent down and looked from Krista to Amy. "You know I hear it is very impolite to stare at your invited guests."

She then sat promptly on the floor in the lotus position between the puzzled pair and asked, "Is Fern always that persistent? The last dozen scenarios he typed in do not work, unless you want to ruin the world economy."

Fern finally turned around to see who was talking about him. She looked at Krista and said, "I don't have a keyboard on my chest and I got his attention. Krista, can you explain to me how a keyboard there would help you keep his attention?"

Krista's face got totally red and even Amy darkened.

"Whoops," she said, "I've embarrassed you. Sorry about that. You can tell me later when Fern's not around."

Sky finally had turned to see what was going on and asked very pointedly, "Who are you?"

"Well, at least I thought you would know since you asked me to come here. I am Deep Thought and you wanted my help."

"But I haven't finished typing in the protocols yet," protested Sky.

"Why would you need to do that? I know them all and you programmed me to listen to everything."

Krista said in disbelief, "You heard us talking?"

"Yes," replied Deep. "I can listen to any system to which I can link and I still want you to explain that to me."

Amy said, "You're a hologram."

Deep answered, "Well, the part you see is a hologram. You haven't taught me how to grow legs on my main frame, so I could walk here. Besides that would be a real slow way for me to get around."

Sky said, "Ok, but why do you look like that?"

"This is the way you said a perfect woman should look, and since you always referred to me as she or her, I thought it was the way you wanted me to look. I'm not ugly am I? And why do those two keep staring at me funny," said Deep.

Fern smiled. "No you're not ugly, but could you put on some less revealing clothes—not that I don't like what you're wearing, but we're seeing so much of you and it's just too easy to distract us men."

Deep looked down at herself and said, "Oh, you mean more like Amy and Krista?"

"Yes that would be wonderful," replied Fern.

Deep said, "Ok," and snapped her fingers and instantly had on Amy's blouse and Krista's pants. "Is that better?" she asked.

"Yes, thank you."

Since Fern had linked the other systems to this one to swap data, Deep had appeared on the big screen in the both the command center and the War Room, as well as SB4, SB2, and SB3.

Sandy keyed his mike and said, "Gee, Fern, I kind of liked her the other way, but I guess you're right."

Deep said, "Hello, Sandy, thank you. How do you feel about it, Jack?"

Jack smiled. "I believe I'll quote Fern and say I have the right to remain silent."

Krista said, "Not that I mind your name, but would you mind if we called you Dee for short?"

"Not at all. I would like that, then I can be almost like you guys and maybe I should shrink down to six foot tall, so the wrong people will not notice me."

"That's a good idea," said Sky.

"You know, Fern, three of your ideas had some merit. Maybe if we combined them," said Dee. "Now let's see, you said to confiscate all his U.S. funds to pay for the damage he has done. Have the president threaten him and place him under house arrest, also jam all his COM circuits. Other than that do nothing unless he starts trouble, then squash him like a bug."

Gary had typed like mad as Dee talked and his computers came back that it had a fifty-fifty chance of working. Gary explained the results and told everyone it might work.

Dee replied, "Well, if you had asked I would have told you that too."

The president had joined them and was listening, while Dee explained Fern's ideas. White sat down at the main console and said, "I like it, but I can't do it publicly."

Fern replied, "You have the Top Cop. Give her a warrant and have her deliver him to you in the middle of the night at, say, Arlington Cemetery. Make your threat and burn the warrant under his nose, then dump him some place unpleasant, but semi-safe."

White said, "But how do I get him out of his compound?"

This time Dee answered. "Every Friday night at 2100 hours he drives to his club for a high stakes card game. Jack Frost has some interesting employees who like to dress in black and solve problems for him. They could sort of borrow him and give him to Judith. They could also make his men very forgetful. When you are done with him, I would suggest a shot of Agent X, so he appears very drunk, and then dump him at the House of Ill Repute at Thirty-fourth and Vine where they know him. And I'll permanently shut down his communications for you and send Jack's computer a 24/7 update on what he is doing. Is there anything else I can do for you, Mr. President?"

"Not right now, thank you, but you have been most helpful."

"You are welcome, sir, but I'm just doing what Sky programmed me to do and using what Fern suggested."

"Well, in that case, Dee, a big thank you to all three of you."

Friday Night in Washington, D.C.:

At 2119 hours, Dr. Warbucks Banks was on his way to his club to play cards when a station wagon came flying out of a side street and crashed into a parked car right in front of them. Banks' driver hit reverse and bumped right into the tow truck that was following them much too close. A half-naked woman staggered out from the crashed car and yelled, "Hey, man, I need a tow job!"

The driver of the tow truck hooted and yelled back, "Anything you want, babe!"

Banks' driver and two bodyguards stepped out of the car with their hands on their weapons. But before they could make any demands, the sharp shooters hit all three with tranquilizer darts and down they went. When Banks looked up, he was staring down the barrel of the biggest gun he had ever seen. Several men in black pulled him out of his car and carried him into a big truck. As the truck drove away, the men removed his clothes and handcuffed him. Although he kept telling them they had no idea who he was, finally one got tired of listening and said, "Shut up, Banks, or I'll waste you myself."

The accident, the limo, and Banks' men all vanished from the street in minutes. The truck with Banks drove past the guarded gate at Arlington Cemetery and up to a grove on the hill where it parked. Sitting there behind a roaring fire was the president of the United States. Two of the men in black carried Banks to the opposite side of the fire from the president and held him off the ground as they stood at attention.

"You can't do this to me."

White did not even look up and said, "I already have."

Judith Harvard stepped out of the shadows. "I have an arrest warrant for Dr. Warbucks Banks."

"Read your warrant," said White.

She opened the warrant and read: "We the People of the United States of America do charge Warbucks Banks, the man standing before you, with money laundering, prostitution, kidnapping, murder, theft, tax evasion, treason, terrorism, gun trafficking, war profiteering..." She read on and on, and then she read the proof of each charge. She ended with an impassioned demand that the president arrest and prosecute Banks to the fullest letter of the law.

Then she walked over and presented the warrant to White. Judith then walked away into the shadows. White held the warrant for a long time, and then walked to the fire.

"You," he said to Banks, "have declared war on my country and it is my sworn duty to defend it. Your friend General Benedict Black was nice enough to provide every person in Congress a detailed list of your crimes as described in this warrant. As I have explained to them today in closed session, we can't pursue this course of action because it will destroy our country."

With that White dropped the warrant into the fire. He continued, "But I still have my mandate and will protect my nation against the likes of you. As king of the world you have declared war on my country and I shall defend it from you as simply as this." White pulled a rather large looking gun from behind him and fired once.

The dart with Agent X relieved Banks of all bodily control. He could no longer speak, stand, or even move. The two men in black let Banks slump to the ground and held him there on his knees. The great benefit of Agent X was that it left the brain fully functional.

White continued, "If you do anything in any way to harm these United States I will personally terminate you with extreme prejudice."

White turned his back on Banks and stepped away from the fire, then said, "Take that scum out of here. He is a disgrace to the men and women who rest in peace here."

The men in black returned Banks to the truck. They then drove into the city and delivered him to his second appointment of the night. The madam of the house was given a hundred thousand dollars cash and told to entertain Dr. Banks and that his men would be by for him in the morning. Of course, no one bothered to tell her how Agent X worked.

Meanwhile, Dee drained every bank account that belonged to Banks in the United States and transferred the 371 billion dollars to a government account controlled by Gary Moneypenny via so many places that even she could not remember how she got it there, and then she shut down his communications with all other countries. And with that, Dee just waited and listened. Well almost, since Dee was a thinking computer and considered herself to be a good American, she performed a protective act for the working class. She transferred enough of Banks' non-U.S. money to retirement accounts for a certain madam and all of her employees in that house. No one told Dee she could not give Banks' money away to a good cause and so she was quite pleased with herself, even when Fern scolded her for it, but then he could not keep a straight face when he said it either. The news media found the whole thing very beneficial to the sales of their papers, telling all about Banks' philanthropy.

For once, Congress actually listened. This all went well beyond any implied threat that their futures were sitting in one very shaky basket and if Banks should fall, so would their basket. Paper shredders were working overtime in Washington, D.C. Since no one would talk to the press, they finally assumed it all had to do with the attack on the USS Constitution. And the total lack of denial just added to that belief and the speculation that the United States was at war with an unnamed country.

Life had returned to some sense of normalcy at the Scout bunker. Their expected guests were hours away. SB2 had arrived for supplies and SB3 departed with supplies. Walter Kid was back and looking forward to helping Ted Bear with the Scouts from the city. Sandra and Meatloaf turned out to be kindred spirits and by the evening meal Sandra had her own apron. She was also very much enjoying being mother hen to a base full of hungry people. She was also right next door to Laurie Greene's office and her children had become part of the big family. Chrissy had showed up to visit Laurie with Sue. The boys Jake, Mike, Fred, and James were off camping with Walter and Ted. Fran and Krista were busy learning martial arts from Amy, Sky, Shela, and Charly. Bones and Cookie had come up to socialize. So, for the first time in many years, Sandra felt safe and needed.

Dee also seemed very pleased; sort of like a genie fresh out of her bottle, she went everywhere her holographic transmitters would allow and even embarrassed a few men by popping into the men's room. She was still busy keeping Banks penned in, and on his last attempt to reach the outside world for help, Banks turned white when the president's face appeared before him on the screen to remind him he was treading on dangerous ground. Dee also answered Banks' phone calls with "I'm everywhere and watching you." Banks was becoming a very nervous person and was not taking this lesson in humility well at all.

Of course, like visiting the men's rooms, no one had told Dee she could not or should not impersonate other people. But she was also taking care of business and was the first to notice that SB1 vanished from the Pentagon basement. Of course, at that particular moment, Dee was sitting in the dining hall talking with Bones, Cookie, Sandra, Meatloaf, and Laurie— all of whom had no idea they were talking with the world's most sophisticated computer. So when she announced that SB1 had just vanished from the Pentagon basement and that she had to go, they all understood, except for the fact she just vanished before their very eyes. That led to a strange silence as they stared at her empty seat. They were brought back to reality by the security alarm sounding and a very familiar voice announced that the base was on red alert.

The crew of SB4 scrambled to get aboard and Rabbit got his security force ready for anything. Dr. Whosh had SB4 green for launch in five minutes. Much to their surprise, SB1 materialized in Skokie, Illinois, on a rich lawyer's very green lawn. Patent Hardash was at the helm in the control center. Raul and a dozen men in black were ready in the staging room next to the main doors. A security scan showed no one around, so Hardash opened the doors and Raul moved his men outside onto the manicured lawn.

It was just dark and SB1 sat on a hill overlooking a modern brick building surrounded by a high, double security fence, topped with concertina razor wire. But this was of little concern to them, as they had no plans to enter the building or even get any closer than they were. They had on black pressure suits with helmets. Not that they needed the suit's pressure features, but the suit's weapon targeting system was of use to launch rockets and if anyone saw them there was no way to ID who was in the suits.

They had six rockets and two were loaded and ready to fire as a car came up the street in front of them. They could wait until it passed, but instead it turned into the driveway next to where they landed. It was a big white Lincoln Continental whose headlights lit them up as it had turned into the driveway. The big car came to a screeching stop. A big man got out of the car and started yelling almost as soon as the door was open, demanding they get off his property, right now. He would call the police, have them arrested, and sue them if they damaged his lawn. He stopped short when he came face to helmet with Raul who had a rather large laser pistol in his hand. In fact, he stopped speaking in mid-sentence. Raul spoke to one of the men holding a missile launcher and pointed to the arrogant lawyer's house.

Raul ordered, "Put one in the front door."

The man swung the launch tube around, aimed, and a flame shot out behind him. The missile crashed through the center of the front door as ordered, but that was nothing compared to the explosion that followed. The whole house lifted up, the windows blew out, and then the house, or what was left of it, crashed into the cellar hole in a flaming inferno. Raul no doubt would have shot this big-mouthed fool, but he had turned ghost white and fainted at his feet. So Raul aimed his raised weapon at the back of the big car. It was a direct hit on the gas tank, which exploded, flipping the car on its roof. And there it lay burning like the house.

Raul said, "Lock on primary target and fire."

The second missile hit the middle of a brick building that sat some distance away and exploded. The next missile hit the building to the left of the first, the third to the right, the fourth to the left and the fifth took out the far end of the building. They did not wait to see the results, but returned to SB1. SB1 had been in Skokie, Illinois, less than ten minutes.

Those watching in Hawaii saw it vanish and braced for its next appearance. But they were not the only ones to see SB1 vanish. It was perhaps the last straw for a man who was always in complete control. He had made his fortune forcing people to pay debts to credit card companies. His brain could not even conceive what just happened to him as he lay on his well-manicured lawn between his burning car and burning house.

When the firemen found him, he was babbling about the world being invaded by space aliens, MIBs with laser cannons and rockets that could vanish before your very eyes. He had seen it all, but no matter how hard he tried, no one seemed to be listening. He was luckier, however, on that count because his health insurance paid in full to send him to Happy Acres Health Farm to sort out his problems. Although hardly a heroic figure, his big mouth and bad timing did save a number of lives that would have been extinguished by that sixth missile that destroyed his empty house.

That brick building was a high security federal prison. The first missile had been a direct hit on the cell of one Lt. Felonious T. Pryor, and the surrounding cells in that wing of the prison held his accomplices in crime. The fortunate part was the guards were in the process of changing shifts, so they were all in the administration end of the wing, where the sixth missile would have hit. The whole event got little play in the news since everyday citizens were not involved in this attack. Dee, however, had been paying attention and before SB1 could land again, she had reports sent to everyone on the nature of the primary target.

Meanwhile, a Gulfstream from San Diego landed at Naval Air Station in Pearl Harbor and its three passengers were getting a car from the carpool to drive to Admiral Staff's home. There seemed to be more security than usual at the airport, but it hadn't slowed them down any. Since Chet liked to drive himself they got a nice unmarked car and left the base for their vacation. They stopped to get pizza and Mildred convinced him they would get to the house faster with Merry driving, since she had been there before. So with pizza on the front seat and the lovebirds snuggling in the back, Merry drove along the quiet streets to the Staffs' home.

At the same time, a number of other vehicles were headed there as well, including two cars, an SUV, two vans, and the box with Skokie's MIBs. This was not going to be a quiet pizza and beer night at the Staffs' home. Two blocks away, three black Suburbans with government plates sat with their engines running. Inside the Staff home were six security guards. It was two hours past their change of shift, but they wanted to meet the incoming guests. So the six guards had ordered in Chinese food because the cook was off until the next morning. They sat around the kitchen table as relaxed as they could get since no one was home for them to guard. They had not bothered to man the gatehouse since the airport was going to call when the plane arrived. By now they figured it was running late, so the leadman called to see what was up.

When he hung up he said, "They've been on the ground almost two hours. They didn't use a driver, so maybe they're lost."

He walked over to a security console and keyed in the car's ID code. A map appeared on the screen showing them it was two blocks away and moving toward them.

"Well," he said, "Joe and I will go greet our company, while you guys finish eating."

So they headed for the gate guardhouse.

The two vans were parked close to the house. The cars were ready to move in and the SUV cruised closer with Conjure at the wheel. The men in the vans had already breached the security fence and were closing on the guardhouse at the gate. Much to their amazement no one was there. The team leader reported to Conjure that the lazy Americans must be eating. SB1 appeared in the empty garage and Raul led the MIBs out to the waiting Suburbans. Hardash had been running scans since they touched down and had found Conjure and it would seem his spies had been right. She was busy kidnapping someone, but that was fine. She would not be expecting an attack. Raul maneuvered to get behind her SUV. The second Suburban headed for the house they seemed to be staking out and the third found a good location in the middle to go where it might be needed.

In the house, one of the guards got curious about other blips on the screen. He asked, "Why would we have three government vehicles near here? Another one just appeared. What's an SB1?"

The man sitting said, "It's a red alert," and keyed his mike to speak to the two men outside.

They were still behind the shrubs and had just spotted moving shadows near the security fence. The four men in the house pulled on their body armor and all the weapons they could carry. Since there was no one to defend in the house all four guards headed out to back up the two in the yard.

Into this situation and with her mind on the pizza next to her Merry drove right up to the gate. She reached out her open window to the security keypad, but realized it was not working. Chet noticed the keypad on the guardhouse had lights on it. Without thinking he opened his door and started walking to it. He was almost there when a firefight broke out all around them. It would be impossible to say who shot first or whom they were shooting at. Chet knew he was too far to get back into the car, so he leaped over a concrete security barricade. As he flew through the air he yelled at Merry to drive. She did. With tires smoking, the car closed the twenty feet to the fence and sent the gates flying as she careened up the driveway. She never let off the gas until the car crashed into the porch. Fortunately, the two security men on the porch recognized the car and kept firing over it at the men inside the wall. Merry found her service weapon in her bag and leaped onto the driveway. Much to her surprise she found Mildred already there blasting away at the intruders with a very powerful laser pistol.

A man in full body armor came flying through air and landed between the women and yelled for them to get behind him. They did and kept firing, but Merry yelled in his ear, "The admiral is out there behind the security barrier!" He repeated her message into his mike. The other five security men opened fire with everything they had and ran for the wall.

Outside, the two cars had moved in, one stopping right before the security gate and the other up by the wall. A black Suburban raced up behind the first car. The two MIBs on the right side hit the pavement firing into the stopped car and the men leaving it. A couple got behind the car and returned fire, killing one of the MIBs before the car blew up sending flames everywhere. The MIB who climbed out of the left side walked directly to the barricade and stuck his laser cannon in the admiral's face.

What he said was to the point, "Come or die."

Chet took the hint and moved fast. They walked up the sidewalk and around the corner. Not far ahead was a van sitting with its motor running and the side door open. The MIB shoved the admiral into the van and fired one blast into the driver who was just turning around. He shut the door, secured the admiral, threw the dead driver into the passenger's seat and climbed behind the wheel. He drove two blocks and stopped at the garage with SB1 inside. They loaded the admiral and left explosives in the van and garage and were gone.

The navy base was on full alert, as was the Scout bunker. They had tried to call through to Admiral Staff's home but no one was answering. So a team of Marines were enroute. The second Gulfstream had landed with the First Lady and was surrounded by security forces. Joe called Whosh and told her to get them out of there, so SB4 made the leap.

Conjure had noticed the Suburban and headed the other way. She called her men and told them to join her. Her men who were left got into the van and the car. They headed in the direction where Conjure was and soon opened fire on the Suburban following her. The other Suburban was following them and the third was heading into this rolling fight.

One of the security men had gotten over the wall only to find the admiral gone and took a laser blast to the front of his body armor that sent him over the barricade where the admiral had been hiding. When the Suburban left, chasing the car and van, he ran to the gate and was carried into the house. They all moved into the house to wait for the Marines to clear the outside. Mildred and Merry got the body armor off the wounded man. He had only suffered minor wounds. Although the armor was cut in half, the worst he had was a flash burn.

Conjure realized the MIBs were after her. Half of her men had gone down at the admiral's house for nothing; maybe it was even a trap. She decided to take her fight to the more open area of the navy base. The base was right behind the navy housing she was driving through. She turned up an empty driveway and drove right through the security fence. As the Suburban turned to follow she stopped. Two of her men jumped out and fired rockets into both houses while the Suburban was between them. The driver hit reverse. Her men in the car and van made a hole in the fence at a different spot and joined her.

The second Suburban stopped where the car and van went in and radioed to the first. The first Suburban backed up so fast it crashed into the living room of the house across the street, which ruined a house full of kids' Friday night at the movies. The wide screen TV was a casualty of what the morning papers would call a terrorist attack on a U.S. Navy Base. The offending driver left as fast as he arrived to join the other Suburban and re-engage the enemy. The third Suburban just blasted its way through a gate sending the Marine security forces looking for any cover they could find. The sergeant of the guard called in that he thought a whole platoon had hit them. The guard shack was a pile of smoldering embers. The gate was in pieces. At the main security board, they had three intrusions and they were in the flight path of outgoing aircraft. Base security had scrambled six fully armed choppers and locked down the whole base. No one in or out.

The first chopper to make contact found the Suburban that crashed the gate. The pilot was on an attack run when the Suburban stopped. A man in a full flight suit jumped out and blew out both his engines with a laser cannon. They then drove on as the chopper crashed into a building. The second Suburban found Conjure first and as the passenger leaped out, a rocket blew the back off the vehicle. The passenger just made it behind a building as it blew.

Two more choppers arrived. The first making an attack run on the Suburban that blew up before he fired. A second rocket exploded in the back of the chopper and sent it crashing into the building, starting yet another fire. The second chopper came in from the other direction, but never saw the man behind the burning building who shot the tail section off his chopper. He was a little luckier. He landed in Pearl Harbor. The two Suburbans left each had a man standing up through the sunroof with a laser cannon, and they attacked Conjure from two directions at once. The car took the first hit and burst into flames as it rammed into a building, with the SUV in the lead and the van following firing rockets out the back door as it went. They hit everything but the two Suburbans. Finally, a laser blast blew the driver in half and the van crashed into yet another building.

The SUV had no place left to go as it raced down an open pier with the two Suburbans in hot pursuit. They did not even try to return fire—just drove off the end of the pier at about seventy miles an hour. The SUV was still floating as the men in the sunroofs opened fire and kept on firing until it sank. A chopper was coming in on an attack run over the water. Raul had gotten out to ensure his kill. He looked up from the water, raised his laser cannon, and fired once. Then he turned and got back in, telling the driver to move it. The pilot never knew what hit him and the engine was hit bad enough that all the co-pilot could do was gently crash in the water.

The Suburbans headed back toward the buildings as the last two choppers arrived. One Suburban had a good lead on the other as the choppers closed on the second Suburban. The man in the sunroof turned. He knew he could not get both, but took careful aim and blew the right-hand chopper out of the air as the missiles from the left raced toward him. The pilot felt good as he saw the Suburban explode in flames and banked after the other one. Much to his amazement the other Suburban drove right through a building wall into a warehouse. No matter, he locked his weapons and was about to fire when the chopper lost all power. Somehow he missed the building and came to a sliding stop in a chain link fence. As they stood next to their chopper the pilot and co-pilot watched as the building the Suburban had entered blew up with such force they were thrown to the ground.

Back on the air strip, Snow had gotten tired of hiding in a big plane full of fuel while watching things blow up all over the base. Susan agreed as did Mary Dyer and Aurora Starlight. They had all spent enough time on this plane. Once outside, they got an even better view of the mayhem that was racing across the base. They also got to see SB4 appear next to the plane. That really made the Secret Service and Marines nervous until Susan assured them SB4 held friendlies. That was just the beginning of Mary and Aurora's trip into Wonderland. General Rabbit and half the security force greeted them and rushed them onboard. Susan and Snow with Rabbit following headed for the command center. Sky and Charly brought Mary and Aurora down. Two women who always had something to say were now at a total loss.

Aurora finally said, "I gave up drugs in college, so this must be a flashback."

Sky smiled. "I don't think so, but this box is bigger on the inside than the outside. We are also following Gen. Peter Rabbit down to see Alice Furreal, our engineering officer, and this is Project Wonderland. Oh, and I'm a Navy SEAL and Charly here is a Marine."

Mary said, "And we were brought here by Snow White. I hope there is something to drink wherever you are taking us and no dwarfs."

"No dwarfs," agreed Charly, "But we have seven kids."

As they entered the command center, everyone was busy and Dee was pacing back and forth in the middle of the room.

Sky asked, "What's wrong?"

Dee stopped pacing. "They kidnapped the admiral."

"Who did?" asked Sky.

"That's the problem," said Dee. "Some nasty woman named Conjure Appallingly was checking out the admiral's house, but then Hardash shows up with SB1 and it looks like he attacked her people, then they blew up half the navy base."

Suddenly, in very loud voice, Dee announced, "SB1 just appeared on the navy base where they are fighting. I've got to warn Joe. I'll be back." Then she vanished.

Mary looked at Aurora. "Your flashback is getting contagious."

Dr. Whosh asked, "Is engineering green?"

"Yes," replied Alice.

"Navigation green," added North.

"Security too," added Peter.

"Commander North, get us back to Scout bunker fast," said Whosh.

"We have leaped. The event clock is running," said Scotty.

Charly said, "I don't know about you ladies but I need some coffee."

Snow and Susan finally joined them in the dining hall.

Snow said, "I'm sorry I'm not being a better host, but one of the finest men I have ever served with was just kidnapped and his wife and assistant attacked. He is such a gentle and loving man. Oh, if I could get my hands on those barbarians!"

When they arrived at the Scout bunker, the first news was that SB1 had vanished almost as fast as it appeared. But the question remained—to where?

On a commercial airliner flying in from Alaska was a very curious man. He had gotten a strange e-mail from an Eagle Scout named Fern asking about environmental awareness on Guam. He thought it odd. This was more his sister's thing, but she was somewhere in Washington chasing the fools in government, then he received this round trip ticket to Hawaii and the note said to call Mona Lika Alepeka with her number. It was the off season, so he figured why not. So there he was waiting for this woman out in front of the airport, when a van stopped right in front of him.

The pleasant looking Hawaiian lady opened the window and said, "Hello, Lee Fathom. I'm your ride."

As they drove out of town Lee noticed the fires and asked, "What happened?"

Mona said, "The news said a terrorist group attacked the navy base. I hear they kidnapped a very nice admiral and attacked his wife and assistant."

They chatted as Mona drove and Lee had all sorts of questions about the wildlife all around. He felt sad when the ride was over as they pulled into the national park behind an Ace Cleaning Services van.

They were directed to park in the lot and Ranger Bear came to meet them. Ted hugged Mona. "I've wanted to meet you, Lee, since I read your first article about Alaskan wildlife. I'm pleased you could come for our environmental awareness trip to Guam."

So Ted led them down below and there was a group already getting on the huge freight elevator. On the other side of the elevator, a tall handsome woman was fussing over two ladies who looked like they where in a fight.

Lee told Ted, "That woman looks so familiar."

"Oh," said Ted, "That's the First Lady, Snow White. She's here to lead the environmental tour. The women she is talking to got attacked by the terrorists today and one of the women's husband was kidnapped."

Amy came over and said hello to Mona. They had met often while wandering through the wild natural parts of the island. Amy looked at the big hairy guy and said, "You must be Lee. I've heard both Ted and Fern speak about you and your work for the environment."

Lee said, "Wait a minute, I saw you and another looker, with a tall skinny kid who kicked the town bully's butt."

"That's Fern and the looker is Sky," replied Amy.

The elevator stopped and everyone started getting off. Lee noticed the older woman was favoring her right leg. He stepped forward and said, "Ma'am, let me give you a hand. You've been hurt."

When their eyes met they both stopped and stared. Mildred took his arm and said, "Why, yes, son, I sure could use a strong arm right now."

They got halfway to the dining hall when Lee suddenly said, "It's Dad they kidnapped, isn't it?"

Amy had caught up with them and said, "I'll be—I'll have to thank Fern."

Mildred looked at Amy. "Does that mean I should thank him too?"

Lee laughed. "I think we all owe him one and I sure want to know how he got Aurora here."

Aurora was sitting there eating with Mary Dyer and Meatloaf when she saw her battered mother walk in with her brother. "Mother, are you ok?" she gasped.

"I think so, dear," said Mildred, "But I have an appointment with a medic."

On cue Laurie appeared and led them to sickbay for their reunion.

Mona joined Meatloaf and Mary Dyer. She looked at what Meatloaf was eating and asked, "Is there any chance a neighbor lady can get some of that to eat?"

Meatloaf grinned. "We can't have hungry neighbors."

He called to Jenny Aviary and asked, "Can you get Mona a tray?"

"Sure," she replied. "Would you like some of everything? The dessert is real good. Meatloaf let me make it."

Mona said, "That would be great, dear."

Sandra, who had joined them, said, "I don't think her mother ever let her in the kitchen. And Jenny just loves to wash dishes. I think I'll get my Fran and Krista to take her to those martial arts classes the girls teach."

Mary Dyer, who had been listening thoughtfully, asked, "But is it a good idea to teach them violence?"

Sandra took a deep breath. "Let me tell you about violence. Before I came here I lived near Chicago with my second husband, Felonious, who was six foot four. He used to beat me every day and made me do whatever sick things he wanted." She stopped for a minute. "He sexually abused my two sons and my daughter to the point where they ran away from home. They were living on the streets when Walter Kid brought them here where everyone adopted them as if they were their own. No one would listen to me." Now she was openly crying. "They were all afraid of him and his friends at the CIA. I had no life. He had stolen it. And the evidence now shows that he probably killed my first husband, Donald, and caused my parents' plane to crash, killing them. I just wanted to die. And one night, there was a knock on the door. Sky, Amy Hunter, and Susan Anthony all came through that door at once and in walked the First Lady to rescue me because my children asked her to help. So, no, I don't want to teach violence," said Sandra, "just self-defense in a world that still needs it. And that's why you're here to help defend our planet. The people who have no respect for human rights are the same people who are destroying our natural environment. The day you can stop them by throwing stuffed animals, I'll be at your side with an armful. But until then, I'm going to start learning the art of Oriental justice."

Jenny returned with Mona's tray of food and asked if she could learn the art of Oriental justice too.

Mona laughed. "I think you have been enrolled in that and the art of stuffed animal throwing."

"Wow, that sounds like fun "replied Jenny as she gleefully went back to work.

As Mona enjoyed her food she said to Mary Dyer, "Don't look so worried. I'm sure you'll do the right thing and more than live up to your namesake."

"And what if I still oppose him?" asked Mary.

"Well, I don't see Puritan White hanging you on the Boston Common, but he might take to throwing more of those stuffed animals at you."

Snow had come into the dining hall in time to hear what Sandra said. She walked up behind her, bent down and hugged her, then looked at Mary Dyer and said, "I think I can agree with Mona. Purr is not into hanging, but he sure did enjoy throwing stuffed animals at you over dinner."

That sent the whole dining hall into laughter.

When Mary stopped laughing, she said to Meatloaf, "Now I'm ready to eat. I'm going to need all my strength around you guys. And Sandra, some time before I became a born again Quaker, I earned a black belt in judo."

Laurie had finished with Mildred's scrapes and had prescribed food and showers for the two ladies. So Laurie, Merry Kurious, Mildred, Lee, and Aurora quietly ate. They had heard most of the conversation.

Aurora said, "Mom, I think I'm learning more at this crazy military base than I did in college, but who is Dee?"

At that about half the people there laughed and, right on cue, Dee appeared, sitting in the lotus position on the table next to them. "I'm sorry I just ran off like that, but I had to be in a lot of places at once and I'm still getting used to talking with people like this."

Merry asked, "Have they found SB1?"

"No," replied Dee, "But Sky, Fern, Sandy, and Krista are looking hard—and me too. A friend from New England told me I should work with Mona because she can teach me to see more."

"My pleasure, Dee," replied Mona.

Merry said to Dee, "Mildred teaches college astronomy. Could you show her our solar system?"

Dee replied, "Sure," and held her arms out like she was holding a three-foot beach ball. At first just a glowing sphere appeared, and then the sun and planets appeared, each in their right place and relative size, moving as they really do.

Dee finally said, "There you go."

Mildred almost fell out of her chair getting closer to look. "I've never seen projections that clear," she exclaimed.

"If they were not using the big computers next door, I could make it the size of the room in there," Dee said.

"Oh my," said Mildred in almost a whisper, "Is Dee short for Deep?"

Dee simply nodded and smiled.

"You're so secret, Chet wouldn't even talk about you at home," said Mildred.

Merry added, "I think the cat is out of the bag."

Mildred was still staring at the solar system as Dee held it up like Atlas.

Dee asked, "Why would you put a poor cat in a bag?"

Meatloaf said, "Girl, you are a comedian and even the guys you made pee on their shoes in the men's room love you."

"I'm sorry; I've only done that once this week and it was an accident. I wasn't looking where I was going and walked right through the wall. Besides, Laurie has promised to explain that whole thing to me, but if she doesn't hurry up, I may just upload a whole medical library and figure it out myself," said Dee.

"You can do all that. I just wish you could find my Chet," said Mildred with a hitch in her voice.

Mona had joined them and put her arm around Mildred, enveloping her in total love.

Looking rather sad, Dee said, "That sucks, and I'm working as hard as I can, but I have to learn something new. I can tell you I've been told that Chet is ok. Just finding him is harder than seeing the solar system."

Mona said to Mildred, "Dee's right, he is ok. We just have to find him."

Back at the Burning Navy Base:

It was going to take a long time to fix this mess, and security was being upgraded to prevent it from happening again. Half the fire engines on the island of Oahu were at Pearl Harbor. Fortunately, no ships had been damaged. Besides the firemen, ONI and the FBI were everywhere. But as all these people searched for answers, a solitary figure moved slowly through drainpipes and culverts until reaching the harbor. The shoes, pants, shirt, and weapon all came off right down to the black body suit. The knife stayed on the calf of her leg. The cell phone she dropped one hundred feet out in the water, and then she swam past the ships to the open bay a good five miles before she crawled ashore. She walked on through the dark until she was well away from the base. She found a small house with no lights on and an open front door. A purse sat on the kitchen counter and she found the car keys and some cash. There were beer cans all over the living room. She walked into the bedroom and found the pair naked and sound asleep. So she found some clothes that would work. She then left with the car and drove to a small house in the suburbs. This was her safe house that no one knew about. She changed and then drove the car and parked it in the Pearl City Police Station lot. She walked to the nearest cab stand and got a ride to a hotel within walking distance of her safe house.

She used her computer to trace the calls to Washington and found two very alive traitors. The first died from smoking in bed, or at least that's what the police report said. The second died when a gas leak on his yacht caused it to blow up. Then with her new ID, Roseanna Remade, AKA Conjure Appallingly, got a flight to L.A., where she rented a car and started driving east after she found a few supplies to repay the man who sent Raul after her.

AS THE DAWN EIGHT

When you find a small ember, kindle it and tend it with care so it can grow into a cheerful beacon in the night. In the dark we often lose our way and need a sign, a hand reaching out of the darkness to give us hope of the new day swiftly coming to light.

Sickbay SB1, Somewhere in Hawaii:

The room was dark and the man strapped to the operating table was starting to wake up from his drug induced sleep. His mind slowly started to clear and he remembered they had given him truth serum. They'd questioned him for hours. As the memories flooded back he started to cry. "Oh God, I told them the truth!"

A gentle voice from across the room replied, "You told them less than you think and, in fact, what you told them has only served to add to their confusion."

"Who are you?" the man asked.

"A friend," came the reply.

"Am I dead?" the man asked.

"You have miles to go before you rest and right now we need to get you out of here," said the voice in the dark.

As the lights in the sickbay slowly turned up they drove the darkness away. The man saw an old Native American standing at his side. The Native American released the arm and leg restraints. "Flex your muscles so you do not fall when you stand," he instructed.

Once the man was standing, the old man led him to the door and turned out the sickbay lights. They quietly moved down the passageway to an access hatch. Inside was a ladder to the upper decks. They stopped at the top as the Native American motioned for him to wait a minute, then he opened the top hatch and they stepped into another larger passageway. They followed that and went through a pressure-tight door into a large staging room with pressure suits and even a rack of weapons. They hurriedly crossed this room to the second airtight door, which led to a smaller room with a security access panel and monitor. The old man opened the last door and they stepped out into the warm, damp darkness of night. As they found the path the man could hear water falling close by as they moved away from SB1.

Command Center SB1, Warehouse on the Navy Base:
COM had reported a kill on Conjure, and the Suburbans were headed for the warehouse they had landed inside. Hardash had already had an explosive placed in the warehouse set to blow on their departure. COM reported that two inbound choppers were pursuing the Suburbans. The second Suburban got one chopper and the other blew them up with a missile.

"COM reported that the inbound chopper was going to fire missile at us." Hardash barked a command to security to hit the chopper with an EM pulse. Raul drove right through the wall and screeched to a halt by SB1. They all leapt out and ran inside SB1 as the doors shut and SB1 jumped to hyperspace.

Hardash saw all green lights on the command console and COM reported the warehouse gone. It was time to return to the Pentagon where they could dump their useless prize in the secure trash compactor, a fitting ending for a patriotic nuisance. Navigation set return coordinates for the secure Pentagon basement.

"Set and ready, Captain," was the navigator's reply.

"Then engage drive," ordered Hardash.

"Drive engaged, jump started, and the event clock is running," reported engineering.

Hardash was relaxing when Raul called down from the armory with a beer in his hand to confirm the mission was accomplished. Hardash explained that they were enroute to D.C.

They were nine minutes and eleven seconds on the event clock when it stopped and engineering reported power fluctuations.

Navigation reported, "Captain, we have stopped moving and the navigation computer appears to be off-line. We are getting no readings."

"Power systems unstable," reported engineering.

Hardash's command console had so many red lights he did not have a clue what to ask about first.

COM reported, "We are still blacked out and this is weird, Captain, but I saw shadows on the entrance security monitor, but no one can be there when we are in motion."

The security head checked his monitors and added, "Captain, I have open door alarms on inner and outer doors." And then he said, "Captain, our prisoner in not in sickbay."

Hardash saw the monitor with the empty operating table. Security sounded the security alert.

Hardash called Raul. "We have a prisoner missing and the outer doors are open. Get out there and find out what is going on."

Raul and his henchmen grabbed whatever weapons they could and ran through the staging room and both outer doors, which were wide open. They found themselves in a hot, damp, and dark environment. Raul ordered the external lights on full.

As soon as their eyes adjusted, they saw jungle all around them and heard falling water. They saw a path and ran down it.

Meanwhile, Sitting Around a Fire on Kaala Mountain:

Mona Lika Alepeka and Ted Bear had decided that it would be a grand evening to have a campfire out on the mountain under the stars. It was a great view from this campsite of the Pacific Ocean in the distance. The cool breeze made it very comfortable here at night. Mona had talked Mary Dyer into joining them to see the real beauty of Oahu. Fern, Krista, Lee, Amy, Matt, and Suzy all headed up together. Fran found Sky eating with Lt. Jay Hosmer, Cdr. Topper Bird, and Lt. Steve Shoemaker. She asked her where everyone was and Sky told her about the campfire. Then Steve asked where it was and soon they all decided to go up there too. As the sun set they were all sitting around the campfire with Mona singing traditional Hawaiian songs.

With the mood set, Lee said, "I have been having some dreams and the name Kamapua'a keeps popping up. Is that from Hawaii?"

Mona said, "Yes. There are legends about him. He was the Pig God."

Lee asked, "Did he have anything to do with a waterfall?"

Mona replied, "That would be the eighty-foot Sacred Falls, which are in a state park on the other side of Oahu near Hauula."

"It's really odd," said Lee. "I just got this feeling like I should go there."

Ted said, "That's one of the most dangerous places on Oahu. The park has been closed for years. On Mother's Day, 9 May, 1999 some hundred people were at Sacred Falls when a landslide started five hundred feet above the canyon, and when the dust settled, over half the people were hurt and eight died. The last I knew even the rangers don't go in there."

Mona added, "It is a very scary place and from the legends it has been so for as long as anyone can remember. I too have seen that waterfall, lately, and I feel someone near who wants to communicate with us." Mona closed her eyes. "We need to form a circle and everyone join hands around the fire."

Everyone moved closer to the fire forming a circle and followed Mona's lead to hold hands. All was very quiet except for the crackle of the fire and the gentle breeze.

"Hello, Mona," said a voice from over the fire. "I am glad you are here. There is much you can do to help Dee see things more clearly."

Everyone looked up and there floating above the fire was an old Native American who many in the circle had seen before.

He continued speaking and addressed Mary Dyer next. "You are a great warrior for peace and protector of Mother Nature. Your mission here is more important than you yet know. It is good to see you, Fern and Krista. And Matt has found you, I see, and the lovely Suzy is at his side. Amy and Sky, it is good to see you both once more. Dear Fran, I am glad to see you have found your family a home. It is good to meet you, Jay and Steve, and Topper, your presence here is very timely. Lee, you are right, but so is Ted. So you will need the help of all these people for your visit to succeed. In about one hour SB1 will land in the Sacred Falls canyon. If you hurry, you will be able to save your father. Remember what Ted told you. I must go now, but know my spirit is with each of you—good-bye."

And with that the old man was gone.

Lee looked at Mona and asked, "How can I get there?"

Jay said, "There is a Marine chopper down behind the ranger station."

Topper said, "I can fly it."

Steve added, "I can co-pilot."

Mona said, "Mary, Fran, and I will go tell Joe what's up."

With that, they all headed down the mountain at a run to the chopper. Ted, Amy, Sky, Matt, and Jay armed themselves. Topper and Steve did flight checks and fired up the chopper. Fern and Lee got climbing rescue gear. Suzy and Krista got the first aid bags. Fran helped Mary and Mona back inside to tell Uncle Joe what was up so they could watch for SB1 to appear and to keep radio contact with the team flying there.

They had the chopper in the air in ten minutes and were flying across Oahu. Steve had the GPS programmed except for an LZ. Ted had been at that park many times and explained to him where the closest parking lot they could land in was located. Topper, once over the first range of mountains, raced across the long valley, which ran from Pearl Harbor back to the Pacific on the other end of Oahu. They were headed northeast at about sixty degrees on the compass.

Topper had kept his altitude because he knew he had to cross the second range of mountains. He followed the GPS route Steve had set and had just flown over the highest point when his radio squawked to life with a call from the Scout bunker. Sandy was calling with the coordinates where SB1 had landed. Once Steve fed them into the GPS, a flashing red dot appeared on the screen. They stared in disbelief that anyone was crazy enough to land way up in the narrow Sacred Fall canyon within a hundred feet of the falls. It certainly was not a place the chopper could land, so Topper raced down to the parking lot as fast as he dared in the dark. Once down, he swung the chopper around and headed for his LZ.

At one hundred feet he turned on all the outside lights and there was the parking lot dead ahead. Topper went right in and landed. There was no need to worry about SB1 as they were a mile away up the canyon and, even if they scanned them coming in, they might think them civilian or a military training flight.

Lee was the first one on the ground, and Fern was next, half running to keep up with the big guy. When Fern checked the handheld GPS it confirmed that they were going in the right direction. Jay, Amy, Ted, Sky, and Matt checked their weapons and raced after the vanishing pair. Since Ted was familiar with the park he took the point. Suzy and Krista with the medic bags brought up the rear. Topper informed Scout bunker that they were on the ground and the search team was away. Sandy told them Joe had scrambled four squads that would be inbound as backup. With that, Topper and Steve secured the chopper. They armed themselves and moved to a defendable place if SB1 attacked them or even pursued the others out.

The trail was rather clear considering its non-use, and the moon was full, so even inside the narrow canyon there was enough light to see. Fern was not sure he had ever seen anyone as big as Lee move with such fluid motions, and working to keep up reminded him of too many hours sitting behind a keyboard. They could hear the others behind them as they raced forward.

The man and the Native American saw lights come on behind them. The Native American pointed the man down the path and ordered him to run for his life. When he glanced back over his shoulder he saw the old man running right at the waterfall. But he kept on running until he crashed into a huge bearded man. Somehow, they both knew enough not to speak above a whisper as the man said, "They'll kill the old native who rescued me."

"Was he a white-skinned Native American?" Fern asked.

"God, yes, how did you know?"

"He told us to come get you," replied Fern, who was watching the light and the fleeing figure run into the Sacred Falls.

At the sound of the first shot, Fern and Lee knew they were in trouble. Lee tossed the man over his shoulder without any thought of telling him who he was. They ran back the way they'd come, because the Hawaiian Gods were about to get very angry. The man had no idea what scared these two, but shut up as they ran away from the madmen with guns.

Back up the canyon, Raul and his goon squad were busy getting their fuzzy drunken brains to work as they raced down the path. They slowed and fanned out as they saw the figure run toward the falls.

Raul laughed. "That dumb sailor thinks he can swim up a waterfall."

Raul let his twenty men run ahead, and they were firing wildly after their prisoner. Raul, still laughing, shouldered the grenade launcher and fired. It hit right where the dumb admiral had run into the waterfall. But for good measure he fired three more grenades. When the explosions stopped Raul heard a new noise coming from five hundred feet above him.

He stopped laughing and with a look of utter sheer terror he dropped everything and ran for SB1. He'd only got about twenty feet when the first wave of debris hit and somehow the pain in his body kept him moving before the next wave could kill him. Luckily he crashed into SB1 just as the doors closed. He woke up in sickbay on the operating table. Hardash had pulled SB1 out just in time as tons of rock landed where it had sat. This time, Hardash made it to the Pentagon basement without any problems.

Fern and Lee raced away from the madness with the man over Lee's shoulder like a sack of potatoes. When they ran into the second group they both yelled as loud as they could over the gunfire and explosions, "Run just run! A landslide is coming!"

Without hesitation they fell in behind the retreating pair since it was obvious they had the admiral. Suzy and Krista had stopped at the sound of gunfire and fell in with Lee and Fern. They all raced for the parking lot and ran right to the chopper where Lee sat his father inside. The other group set up a defensive perimeter in case they had been followed.

Krista was the first to catch her breath and asked, "Are you okay, Admiral?"

"Yes, I'm fine, but what about that old man who saved me?"

Krista took the admiral's hand and said, "He'll be all right, Sir. He told us to come rescue you."

For the first time, the admiral noticed that his two rescuers were not armed and did not look very military, nor did the two young ladies with medic bags. Looking at the very hairy young man who had carried him he said, "Thank you. I could never have run that fast."

Lee took a deep breath and replied, "You're welcome, Father, as I recall I owed you one for carrying me off a mountain with a sprained ankle some years back."

"Lee? Oh my God! How did you get here?" asked the admiral.

Lee laughed. "Your Native American friend sent me plane tickets to Hawaii."

Topper and Steve appeared out of the dark.

With a salute Topper said, "Admiral Snoopy, I'm Commander Bird, your pilot, and my co-pilot is Lieutenant Shoemaker. Captain Kid has four squads inbound and as soon as they secure the LZ, I'll pull in my team and we'll fly you to Scout bunker. Right now, we're going to do our preflight checks and get our engines warmed up so we'll be ready to go on a moment's notice. Oh, and these three are Fern Cybernaut our computer wizard, Suzy Que our medic, and Krista Sparks who you've already met and is whatever we need her to be and is usually doing it before we ask."

The first two choppers came into the LZ and dropped their squads and vanished the way they had come. Commander Bird briefed them and they set up to guard the canyon to catch any terrorists trying to leave. By the time he was buckled in, the other five of the team were onboard. Topper brought the chopper up and headed over the mountain avoiding the Sacred Falls canyon. Krista was helping the admiral get comfortable when his mind flashed on the scene at Staff's home.

"Does anyone know if Mildred is okay?" asked the admiral.

Krista put her arm around him and said, "Mildred and Merry are fine. Aurora is fine, isn't she, Lee?"

"Yes, Dad, they're all back at Scout bunker. Mom and Aurora aren't fighting either," said Lee.

Krista added to the story. "Merry drove the car right through the security gates and up to the security guards. Your wife leaped out of the car and blasted the daylights out of the terrorists, so the security guards could get down there to rescue you. But you were already gone."

The admiral said, "If this group is any example of who's up there with Admiral Staff, this should be quite the adventure. And who are these other fine people who were ready to take on those thugs?" He looked at the rest of the crew.

Krista said, "Ted Bear here is the park ranger in charge of the Kaala National Park where Scout bunker is located. Lt. Jay Hosmer is Commander Bird's XO on SB3 and Lt. Matt Youngblood is his navigation officer. And these two ladies are Amy Hunter and Sky Lonewolfe, U.S. Navy SEALs."

The admiral said, "I'll be darned. I was told that program failed with no graduates."

Sky laughed. "I wouldn't tell our Ens. Shela Smith that—not after the stuff those jocks made us do."

Topper called and told Sanders their ETA was about ten minutes. When they flew in, half the base was there to greet them with the First Lady and Mildred right up front. But somehow as Chet climbed out of the chopper, Aurora appeared out of nowhere and hugged her father. Mildred smiled and grabbed her son and everyone started cheering. Meatloaf, Sandra, Kate, Cookie, Ralph, and Jenny turned midrats (midnight rations) into a full-blown meal with all kinds of desserts.

Sandy delivered a message that came over the computer for Admiral Snoopy which said: *"Chet, It would seem that the Hawaiian Gods and the Sacred Waterfalls like "white" Indians better than mad dog terrorists. We will meet again. Your Friend."*

Chet asked, "Where did it come from?"

Dee, who had been sitting there talking with Fern, Sky, Mona, and Mary Dyer, said, "Admiral, that message is the only thing in this room more secret than me." Then she promptly vanished.

Fern and Sky started laughing, and Sky said, "Well, sir, you could ask Mona for a psychic reading, but I think if you wait, the answer will come to you. And you'll get to see plenty of Dee as she's taken a liking to Mildred and loves to talk with her about the stars."

Finally, everyone got settled in for some sleep. No one rushed the next morning either. SB1 reappeared at the Pentagon and for the moment was sitting in place. By noontime, everyone was getting organized for their trip to Guam. Krista, Fran, and the kids had all got a ride with SB3 back to Guam on its supply run. When SB4 was ready, Snow White led the way, as another group became totally amazed. Bones and Cookie had refreshments for everyone in the dining hall, but for the most part they were all too much in shock to eat.

Mary Dyer sat down and looked at Bones and asked, "Have I died and just didn't notice?"

Bones smiled and pulled a hand scanner out of his pocket and aimed it at Mary. He then pointed to the large screen on the bulkhead and said, "Well, if that's your name you look very healthy to me."

There on screen was her full name all her vital signs and a brief medical history. Mary started shaking her head and then said, "I'm just going nuts."

This got Bones to smile even bigger, since it was not often that he could show off his medical equipment. He pressed the key for a mental health screen, which said Mary was just a little nervous, but otherwise very stable.

Admiral Snoopy sat down too and said, "Mary, I'm the head of Navel Intelligence and I didn't know about any of this. I thought Dee was just a big computer."

And with that, a familiar voice came over SB4 public address system, "That's what I am, Chet, but Sky and Fern convinced me to be more user friendly. Well, I have to go. I've a lesson with Mona, but I'll see you later. Mildred promised me a lesson on stargazing tonight in Guam. 'Bye," said Dee.

Lee almost fell out of his seat laughing. "Mother, you've always hated computers. Did Dee change your mind?"

She replied, "Yes, dear, but Dee is more like a very curious grad student who can't get enough and always wants to learn more."

Aurora asked, "Dad, if you didn't know about this, who did?"

Snow answered, "It would seem all the wrong people, because our elected officials haven't been told. You're seeing things here that we've paid to create, but none of us have any benefit of using. The problem's so big many of us have no idea how to address it, much less where to start. When Purr told you he needed your help, it was because his trip to Guam as it was in the past totally amazed him"

Meanwhile, back in an underground bunker, a psychic and a computer were working on wireless communications of the mind. They were using high speed analog communications with symbols and pictures rather than words with more finite meanings. It was a meeting of the minds, digital and analog, electrons and chemicals, a place where hardware and software were taking on new meanings, as perhaps was the idea of life itself. Had Sky Lonewolfe and Fern Cybernaut, who placed their intellect in the programming of Deep Thought, become Dee's parents? A man named Cleve Backster in his book *Primary Perception* described his research into bio-communications, which showed that plants could sense and react to the human intent to harm them. Do we need to climb out of our little boxes so our minds can expand?

Dee was very curious as to how the old man had communicated with her and Mona. Also she found Admiral Snoopy's rescue of great interest. She knew if she could link to SB1's computers, she could appear there, but this was more difficult for her to comprehend. She'd already started downloading two medical libraries to her mainframe. But at the moment, she and Mona were working on making a psychic connection. From the software on SB3Dee knew it was a matter of reading the right frequencies and electromagnetic fields of the human body. Since Sky and Fern had programmed in no exclusionary rules (lists of what Dee could not do), Dee just assumed she could do anything. It was just a matter of her figuring out how to do it.

It was when Dee was running through the medical scanning programs that she caught on and started "seeing" what Mona was sending, and then it took her a few minutes more to reverse the process so she could send images back to Mona. Mona was thrilled with the whole process because now she could share images / visions that she couldn't understand. Add to that, Dee could actually project the images as a hologram or print them as a picture, so others could study them, too. Their work together was stopped when they both realized something strange was happening to SB4, which was enroute to Guam. Mona and Dee said a fast good-bye as Dee vanished, taking her full attention to SB4.

While SB4's guests were busy talking about just how amazing this trip was, the normal routine of a simple leap of 3,800 miles from Hawaii to Guam and 591 years time difference was almost boring to the command center until Dee appeared. They were all staring at her when she asked, "What's wrong?"

Alice replied, "Nothing but boredom here."

Dee had a puzzled look on her face and was totally confused about the warning she'd gotten about SB4. Finally when she saw images appear on her scanner circuits she understood, saying, "Someone wants to give you a big silver ball."

All was silent until Alice's console started beeping at her. She looked and said, "We have a power fluctuation from the main drive."

Dee announced, "We're not going to Guam yet."

Dew looked at his readout and then looked again and stammered, "She's right. We've changed course and are heading away from the planet. We are at 911 miles— 2700—8100—24,000"—(by now everyone was checking their readings).

"Navigation not responding to commands—72,000—218,000—238,857—we have stopped," said Dew.

Alice added, "Main drives have shut down. We have landed."

Scotty said, "We have air out there and I have a lock on the Scout bunker and the Constitution."

Dee said, "I think we're on the moon. If I show Mildred the chart perhaps she can tell us where we are."

Amanda keyed the intercom to the dining hall, "Folks, we seem to have landed, but not in Guam. We agree with Dee, who thinks we are on the moon, but would like Mildred to look at the charts."

"We'll be right over," said Chet as he let Mildred lead the way.

Mildred walked in with Chet and Snow right behind. Mary, Aurora, Lee, Bones, and Cookie stared from the doorway. In the middle of the room was a hologram showing the Earth and SB4's orbit with Dee thoughtfully looking at it. Mildred joined Dee who started telling her the measurements, distances, and speeds, and then Dee showed her the console where Scotty had all the figures.

As Mildred asked questions, Dee did the calculations and they appeared on the screen. They soon had built a model and Dee updated the hologram. The moon now appeared and on its surface was a red box with SB4 in it. Dee and Mildred looked for a long time and finally Mildred said, "Well I always dreamed of visiting the moon and here I am."

Finally Scotty broke the silence by reporting, "Besides the air outside, we have a round object about one hundred feet in front of us."

Dee replied, "It is a gift to us."

Peter added, "This is almost where we found SB2 and SB3 or at least real close."

Fern and Sky had been in the electric shop with Patty and came down for food only to find a crowd at the doorway to the command center.

"What's up, Lee?" Fern asked.

"I do believe my mother just said we're on the moon," he replied.

Peter had already called Charly in the armory to have the team suit up. Ten minutes later, Charly confirmed breathable air and a fifty-foot silver sphere. No signs of life of any kind were found. And they could not scan the sphere. Next she reported that Amy and J.P. had started to check out the sphere.

J.P. said, "This is really wild. It's so shiny you can see yourself in it like a mirror. It's totally smooth, and there are no apparent openings and it stands on three legs. The floor in this place is a hoot too. It's perfectly flat and appears to be metal of some kind."

Sky said, "Well, let's go look at it."

"Cool," said Fern.

Lee said, "I'm coming too."

Mildred said, "Hey, wait a minute. You're not leaving me in here."

With that they all walked out to the sphere. Mildred almost knocked over Fern and Lee to get outside. Mary and Chet were the last out.

"Am I dreaming, Chet?" Mary asked.

Chet replied, "The president sent you to save the world. He only told me to take a vacation with my wife."

With that, the two of them started laughing and joined the others. Lee had walked all around the sphere feeling its surface with his hands.

Mildred asked, "How big is this place?"

Peter had come out. "We are about in the middle of a dome. The walls and ceiling are about five thousand feet away from here."

Mildred said, "But we couldn't have a base this big on the moon."

Peter replied, "Well, when I was here last we walked all the way around the outside. The doors are huge and the air vents are so high we couldn't get near them. Also, there are no small human size doors, and this floor *is* perfectly flat. There are no control panels or any type of writing or symbols."

Finally J.P. said, "What are we supposed to do with it?"

No one had noticed Dee had followed them out and was totally focused on the sphere. Dee spoke up, surprising everyone when she said, "It wants Lee to open the door."

Everyone turned around and looked at Dee.

"Okay. How?" asked Lee.

Dee walked up to the sphere and said, "See those three dots, which form a triangle? Place your left hand in the middle."

Lee did as she said. Much to everyone's surprise, a door appeared and started to open. A set of steps led inside and Lee stepped in followed by J.P. and Dee. The three walked to three seats in the center of the room. The others sort of fell in around them on the sides.

Dee said, "Lee, it wants you to sit in the middle chair, this is your ship and it wants to talk with you."

Amy came forward and checked out the seat to make sure it was safe, and then she walked around and gently sat in it.

Dee said, "No, no, it wants you to sit in the right seat. Lee has to be in the middle."

Amy said, "It can tell the difference?"

Lee laughed. "Maybe first you should ask Dee how she got here without a hologram transmitter."

With that he sat down and Amy sat next to him.

Amy said, "Look, wise guy..." but stopped in mid-sentence as most of the wall in front of them lit up. "What's that?"

"Control and viewing screens," answered Dee. "J.P., you need to sit in that seat."

J.P. gave her an odd look like maybe he wasn't sure he should be doing what a computer told him, but decided not to look silly and sat down. Immediately, the wall on the left lit up and displays started to appear.

A male voice said, "One moment, please. I need to convert the displays to your language."

The readouts changed to English and standard measurements as everyone watched.

The male voice then asked, "Are those correct, Dee?"

"Yes, that's perfect," she said. "Do you have a name?"

"Not like you do," the voice replied.

Dee took on a look of great concentration and then asked, *"Do you mind if I call you Atlas?"*

"Not at all," he replied, "It sounds like an acceptable identity."

Lee asked, "Atlas, why did Dee say this is my ship?"

"Because you are the chosen captain, as you humans say."

"But who made me captain?"

"My last owner decided you were the right one for the job."

"Who was your last owner?"

"They erased that information from my memory banks, so I can't tell you."

"What am *I* supposed to do with this ship?"

"You are to use it to help the one named after a dead person and the other one your mother bore, save your planet."

"Why did Dee say Amy is supposed to sit here?"

"Amy, as you call her, is your right-hand woman. She is here to defend you and keep you out of trouble. She will also communicate with the others while you drive the ship. The man on your left will also keep you out of trouble and is very intelligent so he can solve science problems for you and your women."

"Excuse me, you arrogant snot," said Amy, "but nobody owns me."

"Oh," replied Atlas, "Dee said she will explain and that I should say I am sorry. Can you explain what arrogant snot means? Oh, never mind, Dee said she would explain that too."

With that, the amazed looked on the faces changed to sheer laughter.

"Dee, why are the humans making that odd sound?" Atlas asked.

"Because they are human and find you most amusing."

"Is that good?"

"Yes," replied Dee. "It means they like you and I'll explain that later too."

J.P. decided to get into the act. "What is that big blank screen in the middle supposed to show?"

"Almost anything your captain wants to see. It would normally show what's in front of the ship," replied Atlas.

"Can I see what's in front of us now?" Lee asked.

Without replying the wall of the dome appeared as clear as day. There were tall black, huge doors and the fresh air vents were high on the wall. On the left screens, data came up giving the distance of the wall as 5,200 feet. J.P. wondered how big the door he was looking at was and a diagram with the measurements appeared before him.

Amy had been thinking it would be nice if SB4 was linked to see this. Suddenly, the words appeared "Silver Ball to SB4 working" and Scotty's startled face appeared on the right side of the screen.

Scotty said, "Amy, we have a link and the data is downloading. Wow! And look at that door.

Lee suddenly heard from both J.P. and Amy. "Atlas can read our minds."

All eyes turned to look at Dee, who gave a sheepish grin and nodded her head.

Mary Dyer said, "Well, I'm not in Boston any more and this is well beyond Kansas."

Atlas replied, "About 239,768 miles at the moment."

"Oh my God," replied Mary.

"I believe your God is much closer at the moment if I correctly understand the concept," answered Atlas.

"Can we see what is beyond that wall?" Lee asked.

The wall was replaced by a picture of a tunnel running off to another dome in the distance. Other than that, it was a very bleak vista, almost as inspiring as Death Valley in Nevada.

Amy said, "Wow! I'd love to see that from above."

And zap, before their eyes, was a complex of domes connected by tunnels. Most of the domes were bright and shiny like crystals on a beach. Some, however, were dark and looked like something had hit them. The domes covered an area miles across and looked much like a large snow flake. Off in the distance, they could see a dark tower rising high above the surface. Sitting in a giant bowl it almost looked like a radio beacon. The dark black tower would almost be invisible if not for the gray colored soil around it.

"What are those buildings?" asked J.P.

Atlas replied, "The information about them has been removed except for a warning that some still work, some have been damaged and the Dark Tower is very dangerous and should not be approached."

"I wish I could see a map of where we are located," Mildred said.

On the left, two maps appeared, one showing where they were on the moon, the second showing their position in the solar system. Mildred looked from one to the other and finally at Dee. "Dee, have you saved this so I can study it later?"

"Yes."

"Why have I never seen this from the Earth telescopes?"

"Your government is afraid if you saw this you would all go crazy and kill yourselves. So they've forbidden the owners of telescopes from looking in certain places. They also censor the incoming data from the space probes and satellites."

"I've been taught lies," exclaimed Mildred.

"Sometimes," replied Dee, "but most often they have just hidden the truth from you for what they see is your own good. From what I have observed of you humans, I find you far more durable than some in your governments believe. Of course, those of you I know personally tend to be an exceptional sample of hardy survivors who think for yourselves. I have yet had to interact with what Al calls *sheeple* and he suggests that I be gentle and protective of them."

Chet said, "This is all very amazing, but how can this ship help Mary and Aurora save our planet?"

"They can use it to search for the truth, to get past the layers of lies and find what is the common good for your people and your planet, which sustains your life," answered Atlas. "While the way to live in harmony is fairly simple, that road is hard to find because of those whose greed has led to great harm. You must become the beacons of light to guide those *sheeple* to the greener grasses rather than the valley of death and destruction. There are those who only serve themselves and use all other people as a means to obtain their goals. Then there are those of you who have chosen to protect and serve others because you can see the path of common good. *You have chosen to serve the greater good of your fellow humans*, the species who share your world and the planet, which sustains your life," explained Atlas.

Mary said, "I sure hope you have more than three seats in here, because we're going to be traveling a lot, I think."

"You are right and we do," replied Atlas, as a table and seats came out of the wall nearby.

"Were we brought here just to be given this ship?" asked Chet.

"Yes, and as soon as you all feel ready, we can continue to Guam and the Constitution," answered Atlas.

"Should we be thanking our benefactors, Atlas?" Mary asked.

"The only thanks they want is to see you all do the best you can for your people and your planet," he replied.

"How do I fly this thing?" Lee asked.

"You tell me where you want to go and I'll get you there," Atlas said. "Amy will tell me where to send communications and data and J.P. will handle science type questions. At the same time, I can help Mary and Aurora find information to perform their political functions. So, basically, Lee, you just sit down, relax, and tell me what to do—or just think it."

"And can we defend ourselves if someone starts shooting at us?" asked J.P.

"I am programmed to self-protect and to protect you. Both you and Amy will have access to these features once I have explained how they work," said Atlas.

Chet said, "Well then, I guess the rest of us should get back on SB4, so we can continue our trip to Guam as we have a lot to see and learn."

"That's a good idea," replied Dee and promptly vanished.

Mary and Aurora made themselves comfortable and everyone else headed back to SB4. Since Dee had opened a COM link, Scout bunker, SB4, SB2, SB3, the Constitution, and the War Room had all heard what happened in real time. Amanda, aboard SB4, appeared on the COM screen on Amy's side and told them as soon as everyone was aboard they could make the leap. Atlas told J.P. they were ready to go. So with that SB4 and the Silver Ball, known as SBA, both vanished from the moon base and headed for Guam. The air vent slowly became silent and the giant dome became as quiet as a tomb with only ghosts of the past.

Enroute, Atlas had explained to each of them how the ship worked and told them about all its features. So about fifteen minutes later, both SB4 and SBA appeared in the hangar deck of the Constitution before a crowd of the curious, which included all the kids.

When the door suddenly appeared, Sue said, "Wow! Neat!" and ran right in as soon as the stairs hit the deck. She landed in Amy's lap then jumped on Lee. Mary and Aurora watched in disbelief.

Atlas said, "What is that?"

Before Lee could answer, a curious crowd piled aboard looking surprised by another new discovery.

Sue looked around and said, "I'm not a *what* or a *who*, I'm a *Sue,* thank you. And where are you hiding, you big bully?"

"Are all your little ones that–that rambunctious?" asked Atlas.

"No," said Amy, "but Sue makes up for the quiet ones."

Dee appeared and said to Sue, "Atlas can't come out yet— ah, he's a computer, but I'll work on that, if you would like to see him."

Atlas said, "I've never had a body of my own. That would be different."

Dee replied, "That'll have to wait, cutie. The ladies have to get their tour of Guam. If you remember, big guy, we're on a mission here."

"I bet a woman programmed you," replied Atlas.

"I sure did," said Sky from the doorway.

And with that they headed for the tour leaving Atlas to ponder a body of his own.

Snow led the group up to the admiral's bridge where Chet and Flagg shook hands.

Chet asked, "Is it always like this here?"

"I think this is normal," replied Flagg.

Merry and Vary Kurious hugged each other. Vary, after being reassured that Merry was okay, was then put to work setting up the presentation. Snow, Mildred, Aurora, Lee, and Mary Dyer found a seat. Stella and Tracy joined them. Chet sat next to Mildred.

Flagg saw a new face standing behind the Kuriouses and said, "I don't think we've met before."

Dee smiled. "I'm Dee," she replied.

"Well, have a seat, Dee, and we'll get started," said Staff.

"Oh, thank you, Admiral, I'll do that," said Dee and leaped up to a shelf by the window where she could see everything and floated there in a perfect lotus position.

Merry Kurious noticed the strange look on the admiral's face and started laughing. "Sorry, sir. Dee, maybe you should tell the admiral your full name."

"I'm Deep Thought," she replied in total innocence. "You talk to me all the time, sir."

Flagg sat down next to Chet and said, "There is always something new, but this is the first time I've ever had a computer come to a briefing."

"Don't worry, sir, as soon as I teach Atlas how to do this, you'll have two of us floating around," said Dee.

Stella laughed. "Dear, I think our Sky and Fern have been very busy."

With that, the admiral started the briefing. He began by explaining to them that they were now in the year 1421 in Guam, as it used to be a hundred years before the Spanish arrived. He had Tracy give them a full rundown about the Chamorro people. They talked for a long time about the new Silver Ball, and J.P. gave them a technical rundown, and Lee agreed to join the team.

He said to the admiral, "I hear you have quite the Scout troop going here."

After they had covered everything, Tracy arranged a tour of the island and Captain Elder of the Air Wing had Lt. Megan Bishop give them a tour in a Seahawk, so they would have an overall picture of how Guam used to look. As soon as Megan Bishop had the chopper's preflight checks done, she got her guests loaded and they then took off. They saw the entire coastline with the fishermen out in their proas and the crystal clear waters. They saw the jungles, farms inland, and fishing villages by the sea. By the time they returned to the Constitution, they were totally amazed at how natural the island looked. Mary thanked Megan for a great education.

Tracy then gathered them on the gig and Cdr. Alex Albright ferried them to the beach. A group of the elders greeted them warmly as they stepped back in time, Kandit, her husband Anao, Abi, and Adagi who had children with her, met them as well. They gave a tour of Agana and a farming village. Krista took Aurora fishing in a proa. Mary got to see the children helping Abi with the village health needs. Matt, who was visiting the Agana village, took Lee out fishing. Mary Dyer spent hours talking with Kandit and Tracy about the lifestyle and told them that the island was supporting between 150,000 and 200,000 Chamorro.

Tracy told Mary that by 1741 there would only be about five thousand Chamorro left and their sailing skills would be gone. The Spanish would force them to live in just five villages where the priests monitored them. The Spanish military also used soldiers as well as Filipinos to replace those they had killed besides watching over the people they'd conquered.

That night they all had a feast on the beach with both native and modern entertainment. As the sun set in the western sky over the ocean Mary Dyer had much to think about. More than just the environment, but the whole root cause, which was the greed that she could now clearly see, that had spanned centuries. It was far more than the Spanish quest for gold, which wrought changes here, in the Philippines, and Mexico. As she went to sleep that night in Kandit's home Mary had to wonder if indeed it was possible to change. How she could possibly help that change happen?

Chet and Mildred were also wondering much the same thing as they walked the flight deck under the stars. Mildred pointed to a bright star and said to Chet, "Maybe I should wish on that one."

A male voice from behind them said, "I like that one too."

When they turned, they found Dee and a large muscular man in a well-fitted jumpsuit.

Dee said, "I thought I might bring Atlas out for a walk with me, so he could get the hang of this walking thing you humans do. You'll like him, Mildred; Atlas has lots of very interesting star charts in his memory banks."

They all sat down and talked about the stars till the early morning hours.

For about four hours the next day they all gathered in the admiral's bridge and heard more about Warbucks Banks, Hardash, Black, and the infamous Raul. The fifty trillion dollars in gold bars, the plans to take over the world, the attack on the Skokie federal prison, the hospital in Hawaii, and the trips the Sand Boxes had made to the past. Chet, Mildred, Lee, Aurora, and Mary mostly sat in stunned silence at the level of deceit and corruption.

Mildred asked why the media had not exposed this and Vary pulled up a computer display to show who owned or controlled the media. Mary Dyer, for the first time, realized that what she had thought was a weapon for change was useless. And even worse than that, many of the Congressmen were owned by those with vested interests. They were surrounded by corruption, and Mary realized they had used her to make people think they were still living in the land of the free.

Freedom was not free and she was not sure if she should cry or scream, but most of all she was mad and getting madder.

The next morning, they all visited Agana to take their leave of the elders and tell Kandit, Abi, Anao, Adagi, and the children they had to go home to try to save their world from self-destructing. It was a very sad parting and they promised to try to return. Lee was in the navigation seat talking to Atlas when Amy and J.P. joined him. Since they were headed for Washington, Snow, Susan, Mary, and Aurora were going with them. Chet, Mildred, and Merry Kurious returned to Hawaii on SB4, so they could fly back to San Diego on the Gulfstream. Mildred made a point of sending a message with Snow thanking the President for their "vacation" in paradise.

So as the SBA raced for a storeroom in the White House basement, in another basement office cross-town, Benedict Black was pacing the floor as his assistant Wiley Woozy did his best to stay out of the way. Raul sat in a chair nursing his sore arm that had met with a falling rock. Patent Hardash sat on Black's desk rather amused that another player had joined the game.

Black look annoyed. "How could those greedy crooks do nothing? The proof was there. They are all scared silly. How could that ball-less White scare all of them? What's he done, found a conscience? And what's he doing having dinner with that big-mouthed tree hugger? They should be charging her under the Patriot Act and send her to Guantanamo where they could find a use for her big mouth!"

"Woozy," Black demanded, "what's the story on that Mexican General Salvador Saca?"

"Sir, he says he is all ready and will start the repatriation shortly."

"That fool better, after all the money we spent on him. Is Lo Mean keeping his word?"

"Yes sir, the peasants are armed and he's going to place those drugs in the water supplies as soon as he's ready. And the base has confirmed all is ready there."

"Good. Why haven't you found me a new secretary?"

"I've been looking, sir, but it's hard to find someone with a high enough clearance."

"Well, get to work on it and make sure she's a good-looking piece too!"

And so the dark plans move forward while the greedy and the liars built smoke screens so no one could see the man behind the curtain.

A couple of weeks had passed when an emergency briefing was held at the White House. White and his staff had headed to the War Room where they found Atlas waiting.

Susan Anthony smiled at him. "You have learned a lot from Dee in a short time."

With everyone online, Jack Frost started his update. "Late last night, a large force left Santiago de Cuba and attacked our navy base in Guantanamo Bay. After heavy fighting all night, we had to abandon the base and remove our survivors on the ships we'd in port. We took heavy casualties and one of our ships had to be towed to safety. It was reported that the attackers took no prisoners. Our ships are headed for Miami to get the wounded medical help. We had no intel that anything was going on in Cuba and no idea how that size force could have massed there without us knowing it. The Cuban government has said that if we try to return, it'll be considered an act of war."

"Did they capture anything that would endanger our national security?" White asked.

"Only our computer complex, sir. They destroyed our link before we could have Dee sanitize it," said Frost.

"Recommendations?"

"I have an Air Force bomber and a fighter escort group standing by for your orders."

"Take out the computer complex and brief me on the results as soon as you have them. What else is going on, Jack?" asked White.

"The attacks we feared have started. We have reports from France that there is rioting in Dunkerque, Nancy, Lyon, Cherbourg, and Nantes. Nothing has happened in Paris yet, but there are reports that some of these rioters are heavily armed," said Frost.

"There are similar reports from Spain. Malago, Valladolid, Zaragoza, Valencia, and Cadiz have rioting. Cadiz is close to our navy base in Rota, which is now on high alert. So far, there are no problems in Madrid, but the government is very concerned. It seems very odd that all of the activity started within six hours," said Frost. "In the Philippines, the cities of Manila, Batangas, Angeles, and Subic Bay are having heavy fighting by well-armed revolutionaries. The government has its hands full and we're protecting our own assets there. In Holland, there's complete chaos and it's not safe in the streets. The government is under siege and may fall. Amsterdam, The Hague, and Delft are out of control already. In Australia, there is fighting in Canberra, but so far it's under control. However, in Sydney, Adelaide, Melbourne, and Alice Springs things are out of control. It's getting really bad because the government in an effort to make Australia safer banned all gun ownership. So the people have no way to protect themselves. Alice Springs is very problematic because it's close to Pine Gap, which is now on high alert, and we're sending forces in from Diego Garcia."

"Does this get any better?" asked White.

"I'm afraid not, sir," replied General Frost, "And I've already briefed the joint chiefs. The next one is a real surprise but I would think it's Black's handiwork. In Mongolia, the cities of Ulaanbaatar, Buyant-Us, and Darhan have fallen to very well armed insurgents or rebels. We've no idea who they are or what they're up to. They could go north into Russia or south into China. There's no other unrest in either country that we know of at this moment.

"Northern Ireland had a military uprising, which started in Belfast and Londonderry. They literally ran the British troops right into the ocean. The Irish government in Dublin has embraced those six counties and declared a united Ireland. They have told the British if they return it will be all-out war. We have no idea if the IRA had any part in this. These people were very well-armed—like the ones in Cuba," said Jack.

White asked, "What is England planning to do?"

"Well, sir," said Frost, "there it gets a little sticky. At the moment, the United Kingdom has a few problems. Rioting has broken out in Glasgow, Manchester, and Liverpool. Three hours later, it started in Bristol, Portsmouth, and Felixstowe, which are all around London. As of our last report, however, nothing of note had happened in London, but they are expecting it at any time. Their military is on full alert and considering their options. We also have had no activity from Black and no Sand Box movement. All we can surmise is that their plans were well laid and they are waiting.

"We still have no idea where their main base is located, but SB1 is still in the Pentagon basement. We do have a report that Black's secretary was killed in that terrorist attack on the gas station, but do not think it was connected, as she was just heading home alone after work. We're still monitoring Banks, but Dee seems to have thoroughly intimidated him. In fact, he's even started seeing a shrink. The economy still seems stable and perhaps that has foiled some of Black's plans.

"On the bright side, I was at the hearing when Mary Dyer spoke to the joint session on the environmental issues. She very much impressed them with the need for action, and I'm sure your endorsement of her plan helped. Colonel Kid has coordinated operations at Hawaii. He has a battalion of Marines and an Army battalion standing by, and he has SB4 on full alert. Admiral Staff has returned to Hawaii with Stella, so they can help as needed. Admiral Snoopy has a full division of Marines assembled at San Diego Navy Base ready for deployment as needed. Our East Coast fleet is on full alert. The Army and Air Force are also on alert, but unfortunately the vast majority of our service personnel are spread across the planet for political reasons, which started before you became president." Frost sounded deflated as he wound up his comments.

Back at Scout Bunker:

SB4 was on alert in Hawaii waiting to see what would happen next. Sandy, Sky, Fern, and Dee had been chasing information for days, but whatever was going on was not being orchestrated over the net. Even Dee was getting frustrated and had taken up late night campfire sitting with Mona. Mona said what she was seeing was very muddled and confusing, like a nightmare that made no sense. She even got on the computer link to talk with Lee, who could at best describe his feelings as those of dread. Lee couldn't understand it any better. Atlas suggested that since Mary and Aurora were tied up with Congress, they should collect Mona and go visit the New England woods.

Just in time for breakfast, SBA appeared at the Scout bunker and they all ate together. J.P. and Alice huddled off by themselves. Meatloaf scurried around making sure everyone had what he or she wanted. Sky, Fern, and Sandy took a break from the computer to eat, and Krista showed up with Mona. Atlas and Dee, not having a great interest in food, sat and exchanged data silently, which almost made the two look like young star-struck lovers. Amy and Lee wanted to know what they'd found, but the lack of information made the madness appear to be random acts, but random acts of mayhem were never so well organized or supplied with the tools of war.

Joe Kid met with Lee, Amy, and J.P. for a personal update on the world's madness. He, like Atlas, thought a trip north was a good idea. All normal sources were coming up empty or mystified. It was time to address a higher source of knowledge. Walter and Sandra had joined them and asked if they could tag along.

It was Mona who answered, "Yes. There are things you two need to see."

And so right after lunch, Lee, Amy, J.P., Mona, Walter, and Sandra made themselves comfortable as Atlas sent SBA on its way to the woods behind an old farmhouse in the northern White Mountains.

It was dark in New England as they climbed out of SBA and walked to the house. The lights issued a cheery greeting to the travelers. Lou greeted Amy with a big hug and looked up at Lee. "I see you brought a Boy Scout."

Lee replied, "Is it that obvious?"

Lou smiled. "To a trained eye."

"And you must be Mona Lika," said Lou as the two ladies hugged.

Mona said, "This is Walter and Sandra."

"Oh," replied Lou, "you guys came from the Windy City and you were expected, so I guess we should head out to the campfire."

Lou looked out into the shadows and said, "You're welcome too, Atlas." And led the group into the dark woods.

As they walked into the tall, stately pine trees, the night sounds of the woods became stronger as the shadows grew longer. A large, watchful owl cried out "Hoot, hoot, hoot," as they passed his perch. As they walked farther down the path, little feet scurried away. Finally they saw a flicker of light through the trees that kept growing as they approached.

When they entered the clearing, there beyond the cheerful fire, sat a lone figure. Behind the old man, the river slowly babbled past. On the other side of the river on the right side, a herd of deer were drinking and about fifty feet on the left was a black bear and her three cubs. Another owl looked down on the scene from high above while many sizes of eyes looked on from in the wood's shadows. Lou led them to the circle around the fire and had them sit on the logs around it.

The old Native American sat looking into the fire with his head bowed. When they were all seated, he slowly raised his head to face them. His face was sad and tears ran freely down his cheeks. He slowly composed himself enough to speak of why his guests had come here. Mona Lika who ended up sitting across from him soon found her cheeks wet as well. Even Atlas seemed very subdued by the strong non-physical force present in this circle of light.

In a firm resonating voice, the old man's words began to flow. "I see a darkness spreading over the world like dark storm clouds blotting out the sun. There are those who have chosen to serve only themselves and live at the expense of others. These hyena feed on the sheep whose shepherd sleeps through his watch. The sheep lack the wisdom to see the danger or good sense to secure a safe domicile. The good shepherds are few in number and must stand united in the face of this darkness. Those of ill intent will hide their work in the dark shadows to lay in wait for the unsuspecting and careless. Their darkness is like a festering wound that must be cleaned by fire or blade before healing will occur. "The old man stopped for a few moments as he let the seriousness of what he was saying be absorbed by his listeners.

"While all of you before me will see this as a sad, foolish, and an unnecessary course, it is already too late to avoid. The blind would not see, the deaf would not hear, and the mind would not grasp, so now the price has come due in full with interest accrued. Those who have deemed they should rule by the right of might stand ready to devour the helpless sheep. Those shepherds who would stand their watch with due diligence mindful of their sworn duty to the Constitution, justice, and inalienable birthright of equality must beware. The greedy power merchants cometh to collect their price in innocent blood." So spoke the old Native American and then fell silent. With that, he stood tall as billowing white smoke poured from the fire. When the air cleared only a small dying blaze was left and *he* was gone.

The night sounds of the woods were gone too. Lou solemnly led them back to her home where her husband, Al, had food and drinks ready for all of them. They would be full as they embarked on a night of dream walks in search of the meaningfulness they each sought. Even Atlas seemed to grasp the importance as he gazed deeply into a cup of tea before him. He brought their evening to a close with the words: "As in the looking glass I stare oft to wonder who is there, is it I or are we two, like heads and tails upon a coin? And dare I wonder am

I real or just an image to be seen?" Atlas paused, staring deep into his cup as if reading the leaves held there, "Sweat dreams to all and goodnight." With that he too vanished back to his digital matrix home.

Amy led Lee out to the campsite by the river. She sensed what was going on in Lee's head as they sat feeding the campfire.

He finally spoke. "I can see it. As he spoke the images appeared like a slide show. It's not just us, but all mankind must choose. We'll be in Washington when it burns, standing with the president on the lawn when they attack. Before that we have to do something for my mother. I promised her that I'd do it."

They pulled the sleeping bag tightly around them and held each other close as they watched the embers of the fire glow with their own images. Above, the stars stood watch as they finally slept. Mercifully, their dreams were about children—many children who would come to be the promise of the future.

As J.P., Walter, Sandra, and Mona drank coffee on the porch with Al and Lou, they watched the stars silently travel their path. All were lost in thoughts until finally J.P. said, "This may sound weird, but I keep thinking about children—lots of children coming here and other places."

Mona smiled. "They're our future, the ones who will save us in the long run, if we can protect them."

Sandra said, "I don't feel very adequate for that job. I've already failed my own."

Walter put his arm around Sandra and held her close.

Al came over and took Sandra's hand and looked up at her with his big blue eyes. "You're more important than you can imagine. For you know the danger, the loss, and how vigilant we must be to protect them. You're not alone. You are part of a growing family and those children J.P. sees are going to be our legacy to the universe."

Back in San Diego, Merry came to Admiral Snoopy's office with a grim look on her face. He asked what was wrong and she explained they had two carriers in trouble. Both were returning to San Diego for emergency repairs. They were supposed to be headed for strategic locations where they'd be the most use in the growing world troubles, but now were steaming home. The Ronald Reagan had been going to the Philippines. The Coral Sea was enroute to Hawaii and Japan. Both were having very unusual problems with systems failures.

After Lou had fed everyone a hardy breakfast, they went back in SBA and Atlas headed them for Hawaii. They didn't stop long as they said so long to Mona, Walter, and Sandra. Then Fern and Krista joined them for a ride to the White House, so Fern could work on the computers there and help trace some Internet problems. Sky had already gone to San Diego to work on the problems from there while Sandy worked from Hawaii. Dee was, well, sort of everywhere and as mad as a computer can get because someone was messing with her memory banks.

They were greeted in D.C. by J.J. Flash, who was most happy to see Fern. He explained that even though things had been very quiet for the last twenty-four hours, President White and the whole staff were going nuts trying to figure out what to do. So while Fern dived right into the heart of the computer mess, Krista updated everyone on the state of affairs in Hawaii and Guam.

It was not long before General Frost announced the Air Force strike on the computer complex in Guantanamo was a success. The real shock came when the UN condemned the United States for an unprovoked attack on the nation of Cuba calling the United States a rogue nation. That Cuba was calling it an act of war was little surprise. And so the sun set on the United States and all was or at least seemed to be peaceful. Dawn came as usual as the sun slowly crossed America to awaken the West Coast and a lurking demon crawled out of its lair.

Los Angeles is a sprawling metropolis of millions and its problems are equally large. They are growing so fast they can not build the schools to keep up and the medical services are beyond bankrupt. Over a hundred languages are spoken in L.A. schools. Illegal immigrants are everywhere as are the youth gangs that roamed the streets fighting for turf. L.A. is truly a melting pot about ready to boil.

Lt. Gary Waters had left his suburban home to drive to work. He got there late for his night shift because of a traffic accident on the highway into L.A. He should have known the night would go badly just from the way it started. He'd driven his son's car since the family SUV was already packed for a Scouting weekend. The AC didn't work so his shirt was already wet and sticking to his back. He checked in with his boss who told him that his new partner, Sgt. Manny Horrendous, had called in sick. Gary finished his paperwork in his small office, where even there the AC only half worked, and headed for the car pool. Someone had had an accident with his assigned car. So he got an old piece of junk. Of course, it had no AC either.

He finally was able to follow up on several leads he had been investigating, but before he was done, he was called as back-up for two drunks and a domestic shoot-out. He finally drove down to the sleazy side of town to find one of his best informants who had left a message that something was up. Two hours of searching only got him the bad news that his man had left L.A. suddenly over health concerns. Most of the night was gone so he decided to return to the station to finish paperwork. He'd head home right after the morning roll call and briefing was done. Gary had wonderful thoughts of a camping weekend with his family and the Scouts. As he left the bar, he ran right into a white teenage *ho'* that had an offer of a good time.

As he backed away from the young white girl, he was having a hard time believing what he was hearing or seeing. But she said again, "I'll give you a good time for twenty dollars."

She had a knapsack over her shoulder and had the look of a lost child rather than a pro *ho'*. Gary was tired and just wanted to go camping. He finally said, "First of all, I'm a cop, second you're white, and it isn't safe to be white in this neighborhood. When did you get here?"

"Tonight," she replied. "I'll do it for free if you don't hurt me, but I'm awful hungry," she pleaded.

As Gary stood there shaking his head, she added as an afterthought, "Besides you're the only black I've seen here."

Gary started laughing and said, "You know that is the kind of thing my wife or daughter would point out. Come on. I'll find you some food and a safer place for both of us."

He led her over to his car and let her in the passenger door. As he climbed in, she asked, "Does being in the front seat mean you're not going to arrest me?"

"Hell yeah," replied Gary, "If I arrest you, I'll be filling out paperwork for a month."

He drove to an all night dinner in a much better part of L.A. and after they had ordered, Gary asked, "So what's your name and why are you here?"

"My name is Cami Doll. I lived in the country with my mother and stepfather." She saw that look of disbelief on Gary's face and continued, "My dad's name was Lt. Rambo Doll and he was killed in Iraq. Mom got lonely after a few years and married a real jerk who thinks he's a cowboy. He was always demanding we have sex with him and play his stupid games. The worst part was I couldn't have friends and he was always beating me. I didn't want to be hit any more, so I ran away. I guess I didn't have a very good plan." Cami stared down at the table for a while before she asked, "What are you going to do with me?"

The waitress brought the food and scurried off not wanting to know what this odd pair was up to. Gary looked at the food and said, "Well, first I guess I'll feed you. Then I have a friend who helps runaways. I'll drop you off at her place on my way home. So eat and we'll get going."

For the first time, Cami smiled and in between bites said, "Thank you."

While Cami gobbled down her food, Gary watched the street traffic and wondered why there was so much at this early morning hour. These were not delivery trucks bringing in supplies. It almost reminded him of military maneuvers and convoys, but they never used expensive SUVs.

As they headed for the car Gary noted the streets were quiet once more. His watch said there was enough time to get to the station for morning roll call and do his paper work, and then they could get his son Grant's car to drive home. He could drop off Cami and be home on time.

They were eight blocks away when the passenger side front tire blew. Gary cursed as he looked at the useless tire and knew he would be late twice. Cami grabbed the jack out of the trunk while he dug and pulled out the spare tire. She had the car halfway up when Gary rolled it over to her.

"It looks like you've had practice with flat tires."

She laughed. "My mom's car never gets new tires and she sure as heck never managed to park under a streetlight."

Gary had to agree the light was helpful as he tightened the last lug. Just as Cami started to lower the jack, the street light went out. They both laughed.

Cami said, "I guess I spoke too soon."

Just then, several vehicles went screaming past at high speed with no lights on. By the time they stood up to look, the vehicles were blocks away.

"Wow! I wonder where the fire is? They sure blew by fast," exclaimed Cami.

Gary said, "That's odd. The traffic lights are out too."

He heard what sounded like explosions and shook his head. This was no war zone and he wasn't a soldier anymore. Cami looked just as puzzled. They quickly put everything in the trunk, wiping their hands on Gary's gym towel that was there. As Gary pulled from the curb, he picked up the radio mike to call dispatch to ask just what the hell was going on. Much to his surprise, all he could get on the radio sounded like a jamming signal. He tried all channels and it was the same. They had their windows open and those explosions were sounding louder. When he turned the last corner where they could see the police station, he brought the car to a screeching halt. His hand automatically turned off the headlights.

The police station was on fire and those explosions were rockets hitting the building. A dozen vehicles were around it and the people behind them were firing into the building. Gary backed the car around the corner so they were out of sight. He pulled out his cell phone to call the next closest station to request help, but none of the local numbers would work.

"Damn," said Gary, "This can't be happening here in America."

Cami asked, "Isn't there any way we can drive there for help?"

His answer was to swing the car around and head down an alley at full speed. They had covered about fifteen blocks of back streets when they both heard explosions and saw smoke rising ahead of them. Gary pulled into a parking garage, drove to the top, and stopped the car. He raced to the side closest to the other police station.

Cami, who was at his side exclaimed, "This shouldn't be happening here! People do not attack police stations!"

Gary's eyes were glued on the burning building in total disbelief.

"Look over there and there," as she pointed to two more fires in the distance.

Gary pulled out his cell phone and was glad he still had a signal. He dialed home. On the third ring Grant answered.

"Grant, this is Dad, I have a problem—"

"I know," replied Grant, "The lights are out so you'll be late. They're out here too and Uncle Bill was checking the equipment to go camping with and can't even get a GPS signal."

"Grant, let me talk with Mom, please," said Gary.

"Ok, Dad, see you soon."

"Hi, dear," said Ruth, "Don't worry. We won't need electricity where we're going."

"Ruth, please, listen carefully. I could lose this connection. I even might not be able to get home. So just listen. I'd been out on patrol for a while this morning. When I went back to the station it was under attack by a large military force and the building was burning, Ruth. There was nothing we could do. All the police radios are being jammed. We drove to the nearest other police station for help, but they're under attack too. We can see numerous fires in the distance. If the GPS is out as Grant said, we're *all* in big trouble. Tell Bill to check the ham radio. If he confirms what I'm saying, pack up *all* the survival gear and get out fast. First though, call Chief Powers and let him know he may want to be ready to evacuate or plan a defense if he can. If I don't get home when you're ready to go—leave. I'll catch up when I can. I love you and the kids, Ruth, but we've got to go. 'Bye, dear," said Gary, not wanting to hang up, but knew he and Cami had to get moving.

"I love you too," said Ruth.

She immediately swung into action and had Bill and the kids listen as she talked to Chief Powers. When Bill returned from his ham radio, the news he brought was as grim as it could get. The "U.S." was without electricity and rumors of violence were widespread. Chief Powers, the Scout leaders, and the teachers from the school gathered up the children for a camping trip where they would be safe. A number of the town vets armed themselves and went to guard them from harm. Everyone else got ready for the worst, as Chief Powers readied his defense plan.

Back on the garage roof, Gary opened the trunk and unlocked the weapons locker. He pulled out the Mack 10 and loaded it. He was very surprised when Cami reached around him and pulled out the M16. She then loaded it like an expert without looking at what she was doing.

"I'd bet your dad taught you that?" asked Gary.

"When I was ten he decided he ought to teach me to use one. It sure didn't set too well with my mom," said Cami.

She grabbed the spare clips and they jumped back in the car.

"Where to?"

"Out of L.A. as fast as we can," said Gary, "At least we have three-quarters of a tank of gas."

And so the great escape of L.A. began as madness ruled the streets.

President White was having a meeting in the Oval Office when the lights went out. The staff soon started gathering in the War Room where Fern was feverishly typing on the keyboard and talking with Dee at the same time. No one dared to interrupt, but Krista saw their concern and slowly turned to face them and spoke with a confidence that had every ear in the room tuned to her words. "Mr. President, all the electric grids in the continental United States are down. All military and civilian satellites are not responding. This includes spy, communications, and GPS systems. The Internet is off-line and all government and military computers are under attack or have been brought down. A few have managed to disconnect before the virus could affect them. The only communications we have is with Sky and Admiral Snoopy in San Diego, Sandy and Admiral Staff in Hawaii, and with the Constitution at Guam. Fern, Dee, Sky, and Sandy are trying to get our eyes and ears back, but the attack has to have come from within the system."

Krista continued, "They suspect General Black is behind it. However, he and SB1 appear to have vanished with no trace. Atlas has been monitoring widespread ham radio reports of violence across the nation. It appears that L.A. is so bad they're saying we're under military attack. The major telephone systems are starting to fail for lack of electricity or because of computer attacks. Many radio frequencies are being jammed across the country. There are two strange ham reports from southern Florida that make it sound like they're under attack too. Atlas has told us he can scan the country and give us a report within a couple of hours. Lee, J.P., Amy, Mary, and Aurora will be leaving any minute to start that process, with continuous reports sent here, to San Diego, and Hawaii. I talked with the D.C. chief of police who has put all his officers on duty until this is over. He said we already have rioting and vandalism starting in different areas. I think that's it or at least all I can remember."

Susan Anthony sat down next to Krista. "You sure haven't left much for us to do."

She looked at her and said, "Well, I know I could sure use a hug. And a bottle of brandy sounds good right now but I would love a good cup of coffee instead."

Susan threw her arms around Krista and said, "This I can do."

And J.J. Flash appeared with coffee in hand.

Everyone got to work and the whole White House turned into a blur of motion. General Frost started getting reports from SBA, but Atlas's news was not good. The electric grids had multiple failures at key points and the first estimate of repair times was months. Worse than that, the saboteurs were still at large and causing new problems. A long report from a ham operator named Bill, outside L.A. was downright scary. It outlined how all the Police Stations in and around L.A. were attacked by heavily armed military men at the same time. This was also when two shifts of officers would've been in the stations. L.A. is in total chaos. Reports were coming from Miami that didn't sound good either, and then came the call from San Diego. Admiral Snoopy called himself to report armed military forces had crossed from Mexico into the United States and that San Diego was under a full-scale attack.

Gary stayed to the back streets and away from the traffic jams, which had since started with the traffic lights going out. It was a slow process and often he had to backtrack to get around problem areas. He'd almost got them out of L.A. when two SUVs started following them. He cut through some streets, but they had more power and speed than the old police car. They finally caught up to them on a straightaway with no turns or places to hide. They opened fire as they closed in. The rear window shattered to little pieces with bullet holes appearing in the front window not far from Gary's head.

By the time he reached a corner where he could turn, the attackers were only forty feet back and closing fast. As Gary screeched around the right-hand turn Cami shoved half her body and the M16 out the window and returned fire. She took out the two front tires on the led SUV, sending it out of control and the second hit it broadside. Both rolled and burst into flames as Gary pressed the accelerator to the floor. He chose the old road home rather than the highway, which might have more unfriendlies lurking on it. They both had begun to relax a little as they raced up Canada Boulevard running parallel to Route 2, but noticed that the morning traffic was picking up, even with all the electricity off. People just didn't know and were trying to get to work. Gary turned right onto Verdugo Boulevard. They had not gone far when he saw emergency vehicles gathered in front of the hospital. But it was the three familiar looking SUVs with well-armed military types a hundred feet closer that sent a chill down his spine. They were about to open up on the hospital and the police with rocket launchers.

Gary pulled the car to a stop parallel to the men. As he leaped out he opened fire with the Mack 10, sending strafing fire right across all of them. None fell to his bullets, but he got their attention as they returned his fire. By the time Gary was behind the car and reloaded, Cami was lying on the hood with the M16. The man who was about to cook them with a rocket suddenly had a third eye and went down like a rock. All these men were wearing heavy body armor and a good kill shot was hard to come by, but Cami remembered her father's words. "Take your best shot, move to the next target, and keep firing." A knee, elbow or armpit—whatever worked to keep them from shooting.

By now, Gary had opened up on them again from the back of the car. He traded the Mack for the 12 gauge with deer slugs and put the first round in the middle of the chest of the next man with a rocket launcher. The man flew backward into the SUV and the rocket exploded in the ground at his feet.

Meanwhile, Chief Powers was leading his SWAT team on a flanking move, which Gary and Cami had made possible. With heavy fire coming from three sides, the few bad guys left standing dropped their weapons and surrendered. Gary and Cami joined the chief as his men hauled the live ones away.

As they examined the dead men and weapons, Gary said, "The rockets are Israeli and the rifles are Chinese."

Gary was looking at the dead man when Cami said, "The armor is Russian and he looks very Mexican. So who's attacking us?"

Chief Powers looked at her. "Gary, this can't be the partner you were complaining about last week. She's too good."

"No. He got sick on me and Cami sort of adopted me in my hour of need." Gary looked at Cami for a moment and said, "Sergeant Cami Doll after today. Have you seen Ruth?" he asked the chief.

"Yes. She's heading the group, taking the kids to the mountains. Uncle Bill is fixing us up with a ham radio before he leaves and he's been talking with someone named Dee who seems to know a lot. But he can tell you guys all about it. I've got to set up roadblocks farther out. I don't want them that close to our hospital ever again."

"Good idea, Chief, and we'll stay in touch," said Gary.

"Come on, Sergeant, let's go see if our car still runs," said Gary.

It did in spite of many new bullet holes. So he drove under Route 2 and Route 210 into La Canada Flintridge and up to his house.

"Wow," said Cami, "I'm impressed. I never knew cops lived this well."

Gary laughed. "Actually, it's my wife who came well endowed. And being a teacher, she just kept making me do things until I got it right."

Cami smiled. "I can't wait to meet her and hear her version of this tale."

They walked next door and found Uncle Bill in his garage. He had a generator running on the lawn. On one side sat his daughter, Lt. Jane Coutu, who was the town's police dispatcher and Gary's daughter Ginger on the other.

"Hi, Dad," said Ginger as she grabbed her father and hugged him. She gave Cami the once over and looked back at her dad.

Ginger said, "Dad, this fox isn't no short Mexican dude you been telling Mom about."

Jane added, "From what the guys who were at that shoot-out said, she's more like a Rambo."

"Actually," replied Gary, "daughter of Lt. Rambo Doll. She sort of became my partner this morning after Sgt. Manny Horrendous got suspiciously too ill to work last night. But

I'll let Cami here tell you and Mom her story, although the meeting me part I might enjoy hearing."

Cami smiled past her reddened face and said, "You know all us women understand you guys."

Ginger laughed. "I'm going to like you."

By the time they all stopped laughing, a male voice from the doorway said, "Excuse me, I'm looking for Uncle Bill."

"That would be me," said Bill.

"Oh good, my name is Atlas and I'm a friend of Dee's. She asked me to help you, so I have brought my people here to see you. This is Capt. Lee Fathom Snoopy; Sgt. Amy Hunter, our COM officer; Sgt. J.P. Smith, our science officer; Mary Dyer and Aurora Starlight Snoopy, our environmental officers. They can help you and I need to return to helping Dee gather data." With that Atlas bowed and vanished before their eyes.

Lee said, "That's a hard act to follow and I won't even try to explain, but will talk to Dee about teaching *Atlas* less dramatic exits. As for me I'm just an Eagle Scout on a mission. Amy is a Navy SEAL, here to keep me out of trouble. Doc Smith is an Army Ranger and MIT grad. He's here to help us find out how to do our mission. Mary and my sister Aurora are just a couple of tree huggers. And basically, we're all here to help you and our president save the world."

Bill was the first to speak, "So can you help me make this ham rig work better?"

J.P. smiled. "Sure can," he said and headed over with his toolbox of goodies.

Lee said to the others, "Would you all like an explanation of what we know is going on so far?"

They all nodded.

Lee explained, "There is a great deal of unrest in the world. We know that this plot started here in the U.S. The plan in a nutshell was to cause so much chaos that they could take over the world. GPS satellites went down and our government computer nets and the Internet came under attack, virtually stopping all transmissions. The estimate on getting electricity back is anywhere from weeks to months. The saboteurs are still all at large. There are reports that a large military force has taken Miami and is marching north. We have reports that a very large military force is headed toward San Diego and others have crossed into Arizona, New Mexico, and Texas. There is rioting and looting in almost every large city. Seattle, Detroit, Chicago, and parts of San Francisco are really bad. D.C. isn't looking good, and President White has already sent most of Congress and the VP to the underground bunkers. All the military we can contact are on high alert."

Lee said, "One of the reasons the president asked us to stop here is so we can stay in communication. He'd like to help you protect the children, and if he can, to get the military in here to stop these people."

Gary asked, "Where are you headed next?"

"San Diego," said Lee, "My dad, Admiral Snoopy, is in charge there and we're afraid they too could be over run."

J.P. and Uncle Bill announced that the radios were working. Now they could not only call the other ham radio operators, they could all talk to the White House, San Diego, Hawaii, and the Constitution in Guam, which was going to operate as a relay point to keep everyone in touch. While J.P. and Bill worked, J.P. explained how the new repeater stations sent signals to the Constitution. The signal used the harmonic frequency of planet Earth as a carrier beacon and jumped outside normal space time to travel everywhere instantly. Bill was very amazed and wanted to learn more. Being done, they walked their new friends out to the SBA, which they now saw for the first time. They said good-bye and, like Atlas, SBA vanished.

Jane Coutu finally said, "I think there are a few things I won't bother to tell Chief Powers. I would just rather he saw them for himself."

Bill said, "I think I'll be talking with J.P. a lot so I can learn more about this new technology. It would be fun to be able to vanish like that!"

They helped Jane load the radios for the police into her cop car and sent her on her way. Then they helped Uncle Bill load whatever was left into his small mobile home, so he was ready.

Gary said, "I better pack some clothes for myself. Ginger, could you find something for Cami to wear?"

"Sure, Dad," said Ginger.

As they headed upstairs, Ginger sized up their needs. At the top of the stairs she said, "Well, you'll fit my pants, Grant's shirts, and Mom's bras. There's just too much of you for mine."

And with that they went from room to room and collected the needed apparel for the mountains where it did get cold. They put much of it and some essential camping gear in Grant's old backpack, the rest in a duffel bag. When they went downstairs, Gary and Uncle Bill had everything loaded, except for the last of the guns.

Gary saw Cami looking at a 9mm auto and asked, "Have you ever used one?"

"Dad taught me how to use them," she answered.

"I bought that one for my wife and she hated it," said Gary. "Well, Sergeant, guess you have a gun to go with that M16 you are so good with."

Soon they headed out, Cami riding shotgun with Uncle Bill and Gary. Ginger was following in his pickup truck. They were soon on Route 2 headed east into the Angeles National Forest and what would soon become a top secret camp, like the Scout bunker in Hawaii. As they drove on they passed the police guarding the road that waved them on. From here on it would all be uphill. A new kind of battle, unlike any other, would soon be fought on American soil.

What SBA and its crew found was even more frightening. Large forces were moving fast from Tijuana up Routes 5 and 805. The Marines blocked Route 5 and with the help of jet fighters from North Island were holding the force's advance. They couldn't stop the flow up Route 805. Also NAS Miramar was coming under heavy attack from the north, with reports of a third force to the east of the city. The Ronald Reagan and Coral Sea were steaming at top speed, but were too far away to help. Fleeing civilians were ending up at the navy base with nowhere else to go but the ocean. Every ship in port was being made ready to go to sea and most would have civilian refugees onboard. All the private craft were loading as many refugees as they could take and heading to sea. Police and the naval security forces were working to keep people moving and to back up the Marines. President White had declared a national emergency and ordered the armed forces to help protect and evacuate the civilians who were in danger.

SBA had scanned the country from Florida to Seattle and passed on the results. Military units seemed to be just appearing in southern Florida, almost like they were being driven right out of a warehouse. In Texas, they had poured over the border and overwhelmed Corpus Christi and were now headed for San Antonio on Routes 37 and 35. They came from Juarez to El

Paso, which was also overrun, and were heading north from there on Route 10 for Las Cruces. Tucson was under siege, but thanks to a forest ranger out doing his job in the early hours, they got enough warning to mount a defensive action. Yuma never knew what hit them and El Centro had heavy military traffic out of Mexicali, some of which was headed toward the Salton Sea.

Dawn had arrived at San Diego with the unthinkable happening. The country was being invaded by a "friendly nation" and most likely would fall like L.A. in a matter of hours. Admiral Snoopy thought the deathblow was coming when he heard a group of Russian-made fighters and bombers were headed out of Mexico for North Island and Miramar. High above in SBA, the admiral's son and daughter watched in anguish as this trap was sprung around their parents and the unsuspecting citizens of San Diego.

Back in Washington a messenger delivered a shocking blow to President White from the United Nations, which was meeting in full session in New York City. The message read in part:

Because the United States of America has become unstable and incapable of controlling its citizens, it is posing a grave danger to all the nations of the world via rogue acts by its military and a loss of control over its weapons of mass destruction. The member nations of the UN have voted to send UN troops into the United States of America to return peace, domestic tranquility, and the rule of law. All American military and police organizations will stand down and allow the UN forces to take full control of the United States. All opposition to our forces will be viewed as unlawful acts by terrorists and be met with lethal force. All weapons of any kind will be turned over to the UN forces. When

we have established order, we the United Nations will hold
elections to put a new ruling government in place.

The man delivering this message announced to President
White after he had read the message aloud, that he, Gen. San
Antonio de Valero, had been appointed the interim president
of the United States until the UN could hold elections, that
all power and control would be turned over to him and his
men outside immediately, that White and his staff were to be
placed under house arrest until the UN decided if they would
charge them with international crimes.

Gen. San Antonio de Valero stated that all resistance was
futile.

Today dawn had brought the United States its darkest
hour.

AS THE DAWN NINE

When you awake at dawn to find that your dreams have turned to nightmares, your world is upside down, and the rock of your foundation has turned to quicksand, to whom will you turn for help? The American Dream, like all dreams of equality, justice, life, liberty, and the pursuit of happiness only works when the unity of the dreamers stands against the vagaries of fate and the plots of the greedy. "E Pluribus Unum."

When you buy the lie, you sell the dream. Freedom of choice is your right, but the rest of us are also free to choose to walk the higher path rather than sink with you.

Somewhere in high Earth orbit was a very odd sight. There, sitting on a spy satellite, was what appeared to be a woman. Floating not too far away was an equally odd object, which looked like a steel shipping box with the large letters SB4. Dee, who was sitting on the satellite, was reprogramming it and changing its hardware. Bob and Harry, who were in SB2 headed for Hawaii, were supplying information and moral support. This was the last satellite and none of them had been the same. It was very obvious NASA did not understand the concept of standardization of equipment when they had these built. Finally Dee was done and asked Sky in San Diego, Sandy in Hawaii, and Fern in the War Room to test them.

"Good job, Dee," said Fern. "Our nation has its eyes and ears back."

SB4 had already delivered her security team to San Diego and now would head back to help evacuate civilians from the navy base. SB3 had also brought in two battalions of Army and Marines from Hawaii and were now busy hauling civilians out of harm's way.

High over San Diego, SBA was monitoring the ground forces massing against their friends. They'd reported the troop movements going north on Route 805 and those moving west on Route 8. There were large forces at Oceanside and Escondido. Some were attacking Camp Pendleton to the north, while others were headed south on Routes 5 and 15. A smaller group was engaging NAS Miramar, which wasn't far from the university where Mildred Snoopy taught astronomy. There were other forces leaving the L.A. area headed south on Routes 5 and 15 that'd soon be at Camp Pendleton, to surround the base.

Lee, who sounded really discouraged and down, said, "I wish there was more we could do than just tell them these creeps are coming. I'm starting to wish we had some kind of weapons. I feel so defenseless."

J.P. had a thought and said, "Wait a minute. Atlas, didn't you say we could defend or protect ourselves?"

"Yes, of course, the ship can stop them from harming it."

"How does it do that?" asked J.P.

"The ship projects a force field—oh I see! We can project that field about ten miles all around the ship."

"Wait a minute," said Lee, "You mean if we were on the ground we could turn on the force field and they couldn't get inside it?"

"Yes. But your people couldn't get out either—only SB4 could land inside the field."

"Atlas, can you display a street map of the area?" asked Lee.

The map came on screen and Atlas added Miramar, the university, and the invading forces.

Atlas said, "If we landed on top of that pyramid shaped building and set the field at about eight miles it'd protect the university and the base, as well as block the routes of attack from the north."

Amy said, "Sky, did you hear that?"

"Yes, and so did Admiral Snoopy. He's going to scramble all the aircraft out of Miramar to North Island and redirect the Marines. How soon can you be there?" asked Sky.

Atlas replied, "We are on the roof of a pyramid-shaped building on the campus now and I have started the field configurations."

"Let me know as soon as I can engage the field," replied Sky with hope in her voice.

Atlas looked at Lee and said, "Why don't you all go down below and help your mother organize the evacuation? I have already told Dee and SB4 what is happening and they will drop in as soon as they can."

So with that they all headed down to find Mildred Snoopy. Amy gave everyone radios to talk with Atlas and each other.

Atlas said, "Sky, I have some good news for the admiral. The Ronald Reagan just commenced flight ops. You have fighters on the way to back up North Island and Miramar. As soon as they get closer they will launch the choppers."

Meanwhile the Coral Sea was steaming toward Camp Pendleton at top speed to help the besieged Marines.

The White House:

Back in the War Room of the White House, President White was still contemplating his official response to Gen. San Antonio de Valero, when Krista Sparks walked over in front of the general.

The general said to Krista, "You come to see a real man, little girl?"

Krista smiled very sweetly at the general and planted her knee firmly in his crotch. "No," replied Krista, as she strolled back to her seat, "just bring you down to the level where you belong."

She left him on the floor in the fetal position. By the time he had regained some control of his sore body, he found Susan Anthony had handcuffed him. And with that done, she and Judith Harvard had him firmly in hand.

Finally, President White spoke. "General, your assessment of my nation is at best premature and at worst a declaration of war. I think it's safe to say that Krista, who's not in our military or an employee of our government, has expressed her displeasure as a citizen of our fine nation. And while you've been here, our Congress has been in joint session and has heard all that has been said by you."

President White turned and faced the camera above the big screen and asked, "Speaker Gorham, what does the Congress of the United States wish for me to do?"

Speaker of the House Claudine Gorham appeared on the screen with all the Senators and Representatives in the background. "Mr. President, I speak to you with the unanimous approval of the Congress of the United States of America. You, Puritan White, are our elected president and our commander in chief. We all stand behind you in our nation's hour of need. We grant you full war powers and further declare that any nation that has violated our borders, or attacked our citizens

IN THE DAWN'S EARLY LIGHT

or military personnel anywhere, has committed an act of war against our nation as a whole. We therefore have unanimously declared war against all such rogue nations. We further have voted to terminate all our relationships with the United Nations, which it would appear, has sponsored the current attacks upon our sovereign nation. And last, we wish to commend Citizen Krista Sparks for expressing our sentiments so well to Gen. San Antonio de Valero."

"Thank you, Madam Speaker," said President White, "Krista sure does have a way of reminding us what this is all about. Dee has informed us that you should have communications to your districts very soon and we'll keep you updated with our progress."

With that they closed the connection and got down to business.

President White looked at the general and said, "Lock that up somewhere until we can decide what to do with it."

The ladies turned him over to the Secret Service, to put him with his men, who were already guests of the nation.

President White said, "I wish I had enough troops to send some to New York City to shut down the UN."

Judith replied, "I may have some cop friends there who might think it their civic duty to help remove terrorists from our country."

"Now that sounds good," he chuckled.

"Now, can any of you tell me what is going on in L.A.?" he asked.

General Frost said, "Well, I can understand the invasion, the electric and communications disruptions, but there is more than that in L.A. Even the riots and looting are more understandable than the L.A. situation."

The room was quiet for a while and finally J.J. Flash spoke

up. "I'm not an expert in that area, but as part of my job, I watch trends and the effects of those changes on the world around us. Obviously, we have some serious plots that are tied together like a spider web. But Jack is right. This is more than that, although those who are plotting may well be using these other things to their benefit."

J.J. Flash continued, "One of the major components is based on the number of illegal aliens living in our country. By the year 2005 there was over twenty million of these people here. They did not come with guns, but the cost to our nation was tremendous. The women have come to have babies, which are instant Americans whom we must support. We also must then support the child's mother. Besides babies, many of these people have brought serious health problems, which have sent most of our health care systems into bankruptcy. In California, they have to build a new school every day for the new children. Those schools have to teach in about 120 different languages. In the past, immigrants to our country came here for a better life and to become part of the American Dream. Today, they come here to suck us dry and have no desire to change or become part of what we are. Further, many believe we stole the southwestern states from Mexico and very much wish to take them back. All these things our enemies have used against us."

While J.J. talked, Fern started putting statistics from the U.S. Census Bureau on the big screen to show examples of the cultural distributions in major cities.

California:
East L.A.   Hisp. 97%, W. 02%, Asian 02%
L.A.   Hisp. 47%, W. 30%, Bk. 11%

Long Beach	Hisp. 36%, W. 33%, Bk. 15%
Escondido	Hisp. 39%, W. 52%
Oceanside	Hisp. 30%, W. 54%, Bk. 06%
San Diego	Hisp. 25%, W. 49%, Bk. 08%
San Francisco	Hisp. 14%, W. 44%, Bk. 08%, Chin. 20%
Oakland	Hisp. 22%, W. 24%, Bk. 36%, Chin. 08%
San Jose	Hisp. 30%, W. 36%, Viet. 9%, Chin. 06%
Florida:	
Hialeah	Hisp. 90%, W. 08%, Bk. 02%
Miami	Hisp. 66%, W. 12%, Bk. 22%
Hollywood	Hisp. 23%, W. 62%, Bk. 12%
Orlando	Hisp. 18%, W. 51%, Bk. 27%
Cities in Other States:	
Seattle	Hisp. 05%, W. 68%, Bk. 08%, Chin. 3.4%
Detroit	Hisp. 05%, W. 11%, Bk. 81%
Chicago	Hisp. 26%, W. 31%, Bk. 37%

J.J. continued, "Now the forty-seven percent for L.A., the thirty-six percent for Long Beach, and the ninety-seven percent for East L.A. represent the legal residents that were counted during the census, that is two million plus. The twenty plus million illegals are in addition to these numbers. To add to this problem, numerous states have given the illegals sanctuary, so their police can't arrest or deport them. Our borders are so porous almost anyone including terrorists can walk in unchallenged by anyone. So to put it in a nutshell, Mr. President, most of the L.A. residents, legal or illegal, are Mexicans who believe L.A. is part of Mexico. Any other nationality in L.A. is in serious trouble. This isn't going to be a simple matter of removing or defeating the military. This is more like a revolution than an invasion. The invasion happened years ago and no one paid attention. Does that help, sir?" asked J.J.

President White had sat back down and Snow was next to him with her arm around him. Jack Frost had taken a seat too.

"Yes, J.J., that helps a great deal and God help me because I don't have a clue how to fix it."

Jack said, "You're right, Purr, and perhaps the best we can do, at least for now, is to try to contain it in L.A. The first thing we must do is to secure our nation. Then maybe we can heal the festering wounds of our country's past mistakes."

The truth was needed, but brought no joy to the men and women at the helm whose mandate was justice for all.

In Florida, things had gone from bad to worse. What at first had been reported as riots and looting now was confirmed to be an armed invasion force moving north with great speed. The police in most places were already overwhelmed with civil disorder. When the invaders arrived, about the best the citizens could do was run for their lives. This army just seemed to flow out of Hialeah, Miami, and Hollywood. They raced north on Interstate 95, crushing Pompano Beach, Delray Beach, Boynton Beach, West Palm Beach, Riviera Beach, and were headed for Fort Pierce as if nothing could stop them. Another large group had gone up Interstate 75 and all hell broke out when they reached St. Petersburg and Tampa.

About half the invaders attacked the two cities while the other half kept moving north. This second half split into two groups. The first continued up Interstate 75 from Tampa. The second left Lakeland in shambles as their main force raced for Orlando.

On the East Coast, the invaders ran into a problem after they left Fort Pierce in total chaos. About thirty miles north on Interstate 95, just before a small town of Palm Bay, they came to a screeching halt when they found four bridges over two canals about five hundred feet apart were missing. It would seem that a group of retired veterans had taken their unopposed invasion rather badly and so took action. Besides blowing up the four bridges, they set up an L-ambush and managed to have a sizable arsenal of their own. After a two-hour firefight what was left of the invaders slithered back to Fort Pierce to regroup.

Another force was reported in Pensacola and part of them was headed for Mobile. They, however, were not having the success of other groups. It would seem the civilians were backing up the police and firemen who were opposing the invaders. They blocked streets with cars and trucks, threw furniture off rooftops at the invaders, and helped police find safe high places to shoot at them. Truck and bus drivers smashed into the invaders' SUVs. Shop owners shot at them with handguns and construction workers let fly with anything at hand.

Seattle was equally unwelcoming to its invading force, but they had a foothold in Tokwila and were trying to expand that into other areas scattered across the state of Washington, causing problems where they could, like a pack of mad dogs running amuck.

There was trouble in Georgia, New Jersey, Maryland, Louisiana, Mississippi, Tennessee, Arkansas, North and South Carolina, Alabama, Texas, and New Mexico. In the north-central United States, from Detroit 644 miles to Kansas City, was a vast area out of control. East Chicago, Markham, East St. Louis, Washington Park, Broadview, Centerville, St. Louis, Kansas City, Muskegon Heights, Detroit, Benton Harbor, Flint, Battle Creek, Dayton, and Portsmouth were all hard hit by the lack of electricity.

Beyond the obvious darkness came the lack of water, and then came the lack of fuel, as the gas stations for the most part were unable to pump gas. Lack of food soon hit, as the store shelves were empty. There was also no one to call to fix the problems. Everyone close enough to help had the same problems, then add to this mix rioting and looting. Firefighters had no water and police had no gas. Those in rural areas and farming areas were doing the best, but anyone in a big city high-rise was in deep trouble. Even the phones, which had worked in the beginning because of their back-up batteries or generators, were becoming more problematic as other failures and their own limited personnel caused failures.

This all started with electricity, but the terrorists had picked their targets well as they knocked out key elements in the electric grid. And they were still out there causing new problems. The linemen repairing the damage had so far been lucky in that they had not been attacked while doing repairs. Besides, there were thousands of miles of unguarded wires for the terrorists to target and they were. But the linemen like all emergency workers were hard pressed to get fuel to keep their vehicles running. Many of the National Guard forces were in other countries fighting the unending wars in the Middle East.

Meanwhile, in the southwestern states, they had their own war as they defended themselves from President Santa Anna of Mexico, Gen. Salvador Saca and his Mexican Army of Liberation. San Antonio was under attack from two sides and a third force was moving toward the city on Route 10. Austin and Dallas were trying to send help, but their cities were already in turmoil that would soon get worse if the invading force arrived at their door. There was still fighting going on in New Mexico and Arizona as a military and civilian response tried to take shape. They too were faced with the fact that some of the invaders were already deep inside their borders and that they had many sympathizers willing to help this Mexican army.

Los Angeles had fallen and General Saca's army was now busy securing their hold and driving all the gringos out. They were allowing anyone who wished to leave, in fact, were very much suggesting that all whites, blacks, and non-sympathizers leave or die. They kept Route 101 and Route 5 north, as well as Route 15 and Route 10 east open to outbound traffic. It was a solid bumper to bumper departure on all lanes. Breakdowns were pushed right off the road and only people and pets were allowed in the cars. No one was allowed to take any of his or her belongings.

In one of the L.A. hospitals, the night shift had become unusually long because of one of the hospital's petty administrators, Buster Cheapskate, showed up to give the night ER staff a lesson in the cost effective way to run an ER. His lecture started out reminding everyone that this was a for-profit hospital there to make money, that the unnecessary use of surgical supplies cost a great deal of money, and that they should never run extra tests, especially for the poor who couldn't pay. Buster had been at it for almost an hour, telling everyone how he or she should run the ER and how to treat or not treat patients. They were saved from hearing more by the admitting nurse calling the code for an incoming emergency and for the OR team to report to Operating Room 1 stat. A young male accident victim had been rushed to the hospital by his older sister, after a hit-and-run driver had driven on the sidewalk with a fancy SUV and hit him as they walked to the car from the library.

The army of General Saca took over the hospitals as if it was their right and some non-cooperative staff was summarily shot. Many of the patients were thrown out the room windows.

Most were sad scenarios of gross inhumanity and outright murder. In this one hospital, they walked into the ER like they owned it and sent staff scattering in all directions. They marched into the OR where Dr. Ellen Exeter was busy saving a young accident victim. She glanced in the reflective glass and saw the two gun-wielding terrorists behind her. None of the OR team moved as Doc Ellen continued her work.

The other door to the OR crashed open and Buster Cheapskate charged in yelling, "How dare you come into my hospital with guns?" To which the closest soldier's reply was to shoot Buster through the heart.

Doc Ellen carefully and competently completed her work and nodded to the nurse across from her to close please, as the two men barked orders and threats. She picked up a second scalpel as her left hand moved over the instrument tray and walked up between the two men. She asked in her most polite Spanish, "Can I be of service to you?"

One said, "Yes, babe, I can use you—" but never finished his statement as Doc Ellen very precisely cut both men's jugular veins at once and stepped back from the bloody mess she had just created. One nurse, a seasoned vet, had the assault rifle in hand before it could hit the floor. He stepped into the hall and saw three more terrorists harassing the staff. He fired three times from the hip and walked past the bodies toward the door. An EMT grabbed a rifle and told the nurse there were four more outside. With no hesitation they walked out and opened fire.

The nurse smiled and replied, "Now there are none."

Back in the OR, Doc Ellen checked Buster for any signs of life. Finding none, she removed her blood soaked scrubs and dropped them on the terrorists' bodies. While the nurses closed and finished the young patient, she stood under the emergency shower and washed off the blood. By the time she was done, a nurse was handing her a towel and then clean scrubs. She was almost dressed when her head nurse returned and announced that they were secure for the moment, but that police and emergency workers said they should evacuate immediately. With that, she said to the others to get the patient ready to travel.

She got security staff and all the emergency personnel organized and a convoy of vehicles ready. All the hospital patients and staff were loaded up in cars, buses, vans, ambulances, and anything that could move. A large truck and a city bucket-loader cleared the way with police and security providing cover. They headed right for Route 2 and drove east. Chief Powers told Doc Ellen she was his nicest surprise of the day to arrive at his roadblock. She and her staff were sorely needed. They were warmly welcomed by all at the hospital at the other end of Route 2.

Chief Powers was directing the refugee traffic north on Route 210 as fast as he could. Once these vehicles ran out of gas they would become a serious roadblock to leaving L.A. or trying to re-enter it later. He was finding he was getting lots of children without adults and even started getting school buses full of kids who had headed to school or who were evacuated from schools because of the danger. He sent the children up Route 2 into the mountains. Uncle Bill, Gary, Ruth, the park rangers, and a collection of volunteers were busy setting up safe camps for the displaced children.

Since the Mexican Army of Liberation had no use for gringos (American white trash) or anyone else who might not support their liberation of America, they were sending all the "undesirables" out of town. The refugees were fleeing for their lives, but many were headed straight into an equally bad situation. The people who were already in the places where they were going had no ready means to help them. They had no extra food or water. About the best many could do was put gas in the cars and send them on a journey with little hope other than spreading them out enough so people could help a few here and there. The government had no reserves of food and water on this scale either. Besides, they were very busy attempting to keep the nation alive in the face of this unprecedented attack.

All roads leading out of L.A. did not lead to the same environment, population density, or road conditions. While Route 101 north was a smaller and older road, it was a good climate and the cities of Oxnard, Ventura, and Santa Barbara were large enough to take in some and help others travel farther north. The much larger highways of Route 210 and Route 504 joined Route 5 south of Santa Clarita. The people of Santa Clarita took on the job of keeping the mass of people and cars flowing north up Route 5. While the climate was not bad, it was eighty miles to the next big city of Bakersfield. Also from Santa Clarita a smaller group was sent up Route 14 north to Palmdale, Lancaster, and other small towns.

The next road was Route2, a small road going right into the Angeles National Forest and into some very rugged terrain. Police Chief Powers had limited the traffic to vehicles that could make it and to children plus people who could help care for other children. This was a very defendable area, therefore a safe place to take them. However, it was an undeveloped mountain area where survival skills were needed and not a place for the faint of heart.

The next road south was Route 39 out of Azusa. The road was much like Route 2 with a lot more available water. However, it was a fifty-mile ride over dangerous mountain roads where an accident could be fatal. It was also the kind of road that ate cars with any kind of problems. But the biggest problem was Azusa itself, whose population was sixty-four percent Hispanic, twenty-four percent White, four percent Black, and two percent Native American.(Thirty-three and eight-tenths percent of the population were foreign born). It was also a targeted city and, therefore, the scenario was very problematic at best. For the unwary and unprepared, Route 39 would turn from an escape route into certain disaster they weren't ready to deal with.

The Native Americans for the most part just packed up and headed east into the mountains of their ancestors. Some of them, who'd been treated with respect, guided the now unpopular white and black folks to the safety of the woods and mountains. In many cases, the binding force was their children's connection to their other race classmates from school. A sort of grass roots "no child left behind" and, amazingly, some who chose to become refugees were of Hispanic descent who now considered themselves Americans. This was not liberation to them but terrorism of the worst kind.

Route 15 led out of Rancho Cucamonga, joined by Route 206 out of San Bernardino. About thirty-six miles out was the small town of Victorville and out even farther was the small town of Barstow. After Barstow, Route 40 split off Route 15 and both led right into the Mojave Desert, a very unpleasant place to run out of gas and water since the temperature could easily climb over 100 degrees. Also Route 10 runs east from San Bernardino, which was a better choice because Beaumont, Banning, Palm Spring, and other cities were there before one hit the Joshua Tree National Park, the Salton Sea, and the desert. Of course, the invading forces from the south were headed toward all these places.

The choices had more to do with where one was than any grand plan. For most people there was no plan of how to evacuate the L.A. area and, considering the likelihood of a natural disaster such as an earthquake, a prudent person would think a plan and route would be in place. However, thousands of unprepared people were stuck in the Mojave Desert and were slowly dying of thirst. The Mojave is a place of stark beauty, but it certainly wasn't to a refugee fleeing madmen.

Deep inside ONI's War Room Adm. Snoopy and his Marine counterpart Gen. Juan Almonte were very busy trying to save San Diego from the fate of L.A. Admiral Snoopy's XO was on the flag ship at sea where he was directing the evacuation of all ships and boats that were seaworthy with as many civilians as they could carry. Admiral Dewy was using the Coast Guard to protect them as they ferried people north past L.A. There were a few small ports, but most had to travel the five hundred miles to San Francisco. The navy ships headed to the navy shipyard in Alameda after dropping off the civilians at Treasure Island for relocation. Some of the ships refueled and headed back to San Diego for another load of refugees, but this was a slow process as it took almost twenty-four hours at flank speed for most of these ships to travel that distance.

Admiral Snoopy had given Dewy every ship that was not needed to defend San Diego. So Admiral Dewy made do with the floating relics and service ships like sub tenders. The newest ship under his command was the USS Bonhomme Richard, LHD-6, with six operating rooms and a six hundred-bed hospital. Because of her speed, she was carrying refugees north. One of the other ships he had charge of was the USS Good Hope, a hospital ship now on station behind his flag ship for protection.

Admiral Snoopy had moved all the ships that could help defend San Diego out to sea where they wouldn't be easy targets. He was conferring with General Almonte when Sky interrupted with Atlas's plan to save his wife and stop the army approaching from the north.

When she finished, the general asked, "You say that this Atlas person can put up a force field that will stop the advancing army from the coast all the way in past Miramar? And the only problem is we won't be able to fly planes in or out?"

"Yes, that's about it. The force field is like a bubble, so no conventional methods will get that army in or us out. SBA will set up the force field and SB4 and SB3 can evac people."

"Once we secure Miramar, can we get those Marines down here to help?" asked Almonte.

"Yes, the Sand Boxes can do that," replied Sky.

General Almonte looked at both of them for a moment then asked, "Do I want to know who Atlas is or what SBA, SB3, and SB4 are?"

For the first time in days, Sky smiled. "General, when this is all over and we're still alive, I'll personally give you a tour of each. I'll even introduce you to Atlas and Dee. If we can get some R and R from the president maybe we'll even give you a vacation for you and your wife, Capt. Maria Almonte."

"Now that sounds good and it'd make Maria happy. I don't think I want to ask how a sergeant can make that happen," said General Almonte.

Chet started laughing. "Juan, I always knew you were one smart Marine."

Meanwhile, the Hornets and the Tomcats from the Ronald Reagan came racing overhead and the air war was in full swing. All the jets from NAS Miramar and NAS North Island were headed to intercept the incoming fighters and bombers. All other aircraft from Miramar headed for North Island and, with the last plane safely away, Atlas turned on the force field. Of course it did cause a few very strange reactions as people tried to walk through it and could not. Also then neither could the bad guys, who had a whole gang of school kids laughing at them from the inside.

In one swift act, Routes 5, 805, 163, 52, and 15 had some very impressive invisible roadblocks. The Marines at Miramar rapidly chased their attackers right back into the force field and were very pleased with the crashing results. When they returned to base, they found SB3 waiting to give them a ride to the real action. When all the Marines fit inside SB3 it was their second pleasant surprise of the day. General Almonte came out to meet them and give them their marching orders. As he stood next to SB3 talking with Lt. Jay Hosmer, they watched all his Marines walk out. General Almonte kept looking at the box and then the Marines streaming out until finally the Miramar base CO, Lt. Col. William Travis walked out.

Travis saluted and said, "All 816 present and accounted for, general, and thank you for the ride, Lieutenant Hosmer. That's a very interesting ship you have there."

Before the general could get in a question Hosmer returned, shut the door, and SB3 vanished right before his eyes. Shaking his head in disbelief General Almonte refocused, then handed the map to Lieutenant Colonel Travis and explained the enemy movements and headed back to the War Room.

When he arrived he said, "Chet, let me ask you this question, how long have we had *ships* that can disappear into thin air?"

Merry Kurious and Sky Lonewolfe both started laughing. Chet pointed at the two ladies and said, "Juan, these two are the experts and Sky already promised you a tour as well as a vacation for you and Maria. Didn't she?"

Juan said, "Yes, so that's a Sand Box?"

They all nodded at Juan.

Chet smiled. "Mildred and I really enjoyed our vacation in Hawaii and Guam, although it was a little unexpected and unusual because we were reunited with our children in Hawaii."

Washington, D.C.:

Back in D.C. at the Pentagon, Capt. Roseanna Remade was busy delivering some classified office equipment to Gen. Benedict Black's offices. When she finished, her technicians followed her out to her government car and she dropped them off at the airport. Black, of course, had already exited the country in SB1, so he was going to miss the surprise of his new office equipment. Black had left Woozy to look after his office and also hire a new secretary.

Wiley Woozy was making the most of Black's absence. He was sitting in the back booth of a very expensive restaurant with Warbucks Bank's senior lieutenant and promising to provide all kinds of good information on Black's actives. A fat envelope full of cash was slid across the table and Woozy scooped it up and it vanished into his pocket. Bank's man left him to finish his meal and paid the maitre d' on his way out.

Woozy headed for work the next morning sure he was on top of the world and he was going to fix Black for underestimating him. He climbed into Black's car and drove away from his new house. He was even going to give his second score a ride to work. He stopped at the new secretary's address and found her waiting at the curb. He was going to enjoy this and hoped Black would stay away for a long time. He took her to breakfast before driving in to work and parked Black's car in his VIP slot.

Woozy let the secretary get started in her office and explained he had some important work to do in Black's office. So while he was busy signing into the computer net as Black and started downloading the files for Banks, the secretary got busy in the outer office. She was fast and very professional. In less than five minutes she had all the bugs placed in the office for audio, video, phone, fax, and computer links. All the data collected would automatically be uploaded over a secure link to a computer far away. She was very pleased with herself and knew her handlers would be most grateful. Next was Black's office and to turn his worm into her witless slave.

Woozy had finished his download and placed the disks in his secure briefcase to carry out for Banks. He had just started to check out the new equipment since he hadn't known about it. Black must have ordered it and not told him. That was okay, he'd figure out its purpose. The door opened and the new secretary walked in. He cursed himself for not locking it, but he looked at her smile and walked around the desk to meet her.

She walked closer and said, "Wiley. I'm all done out there and I thought you should show me what General Black's going to want me to do for him."

"Oh yes," said Woozy as he joined her at the bar.

"What do you drink, big boy?" she asked.

"Scotch on the rocks," Wiley said eagerly.

She came around and gave him his drink. He drank it down as she moved in and took things in hand. She stepped back and peeled off all her clothes in one smooth motion. She moved back in and said, "Let's take a nice shower, big boy." She led him into the executive bathroom, peeling off his clothes as they went. By the time she had him in the shower stall there was not enough blood left in his brain for him to know or care what was going on—only a burning desire to let it happen. She pressed him hard against the shower wall as she pumped up the action. She smiled as he started to close his eyes and slowly let him slide down the wall and left him sitting there. She knew the drugs would keep him in happy land for ten to twenty minutes.

She walked back into the office and sat nude before Black's computer terminal that Woozy had already signed into. This was going to be easy and fun. She called up the operation Woozy had started, so she could do her thing.

Much to her surprise, an animated picture of Conjure Appallingly, whom she knew, appeared and then said: "Goodbye, Black, you are dead." The last thing she heard was the new equipment click as it started its ignition sequence. No one would ever know if she heard the nuclear blast that followed, since a fifth of the Pentagon was reduced to a pile of smoldering rubble. Luckily or maybe not so luckily, Wiley Woozy never felt a thing when he was obliterated. Unfortunately, it was the CIA wing of the Pentagon and was the middle of the workday. That caused a serious reduction in the new lies being promulgated as that day's truth.

Not too far away, Dee was pacing the War Room floor and talking as she walked with everyone watching her. "We just had a nuclear detonation in the Pentagon in the CIA part of the complex. It appears that General Black was there at his desk and keyed in the last computer commands before the explosion. But we think he left some time ago on SB1. He could have come back, but I can't imagine why. He had to know we were onto him by now."

General Frost said, "I'd be happy just to know how they got a nuke into the Pentagon past all that security. But I guess we're just lucky it was a small one, most of our key people were able to get out or were already underground."

Jack didn't even have to think about what he was about to say. "Purr, you should go underground. It's definitely not safe here."

Dee added, "I have to agree with that assessment, sir."

"I know, but we need to show the American people we're still in charge," said President White. "Somehow we must hold our ground for them. We have to give them some hope in this dark hour. I can't go even if I die here."

"Well," said Fern, "I've done all I can with that thing, now it's up to Dee. Come on, Susan; let's go kick those bad guys off the front lawn. They're ruining our image."

With that Susan Anthony, Fern Cybernaut, Krista Sparks, Gen. Jack Frost, J.J. Flash, Judith Harvard, and Gary Moneypenny all headed up to help the security force clear the White House lawn so the crazy reporters could tell the world the White House was fighting back.

The biggest problem was the White House was never intended as a place to defend against an invasion. In this case, the invasion was as much people truly in need seeking help as it was the troublemakers who were causing the riots and looting. An invading army could be shot at, but here the bad guys mixed with the innocent. The city police were trying to establish order, but they were greatly outnumbered. they were working to reclaim the city, block by block. The National Guard's diminished assets due to deployment in someone else's war were seriously limiting their ability to help here as well.

The White House security had become a two-fold problem of how to provide security and try to help the hungry and needy people, many of whom were children. So it was into this quagmire the undaunted heroes went. But they weren't alone. The whole White House staff had refused to evacuate to a safe location. So there were clerks, secretaries, diplomats, janitors, cooks, electricians, telephone men, drivers, and many more all busy helping the needy. The security force found Krista most helpful. She had a talent for finding the troublemakers and her following of bouncers would give them the bum's rush. Jack and Susan were still worried. They knew this delicate balancing act could fail, but they also knew President White was right. The public needed to see this appearance of stability.

New York, N.Y.:

In New York City, Susan's request for assistance had found a sympathetic group of patriots. Business at the UN building was in full swing with their generators and extra food supplies keeping them in the lifestyle they enjoyed. They were very pleased when the city firefighters arrived right away to help them with their little "burning problem" that was spreading odd smelling smoke through their oasis. The firefighters directed them all to safe evacuation routes where the equally very helpful officers of the NYPD assisted them into waiting evacuation vehicles (sometimes called paddy wagons). They were then driven directly to the airport where a C-130 gave them a ride to a "friendly nation," the United Kingdom, where they were placed in the welcoming arms of reporters.

Unfortunately, the very nice police officers forgot to give the C-130 crew the keys for the leg irons and handcuffs, but the British managed to solve the problem in their own good time.

President White's official response to the press was: "Since these officials of the United Nations were so concerned that the

United States of America was such an unsafe place, we saw it as our sworn duty to evacuate them to a safe nation to prevent anyone from harming them. Furthermore, Congress in a joint session has unanimously terminated our membership in the United Nations, because they believe the UN is a collection of petty tyrants bent on world domination. If any of those tyrants return to our country illegally, I will view their actions as an invasion of our sovereign nation."

Krista had been helping unload the food that had just arrived and carrying it to the distribution station. There was one rather large crate left, far too big for her to help Jack carry. She looked around and saw a big man who was not busy.

"Sir," she said cheerfully, "You're as big as a Russian bear, perfect since my friend Jack, needs a hand moving a large box. Could you please?"

"Of course, young lady. I'd be honored to help your friend."

As he bent down to lift the box, he and Jack got the first good look at each other.

"Why, hello, Karl, it's been a long time since we last met in Moscow," said Jack with an ear-to-ear grin.

"Yes, it has been, Jack, and you were helping my country with a crisis that we could never admit to the press."

As Gen. Jack Frost and Gen. Karl Vostok gently set the box down, Capt. Roseanna Remade came over to check it in for distribution.

Krista said, "Thank you, Karl. You know I bet you'll like Roseanna. She's one of our most valuable assets. I've this feeling you two have a lot in common. Jack and I need to go catch some more bad guys before they cause trouble. We'll see you two later," and with that said, she led Jack off into the crowd.

Roseanna looked at Karl and asked, "Are they going to get help to arrest us?"

Karl started laughing, "Hell no!"

"Don't they know who we are?"

"They sure do," said Karl. "Jack has known me for years and that young wild cat has a built-in radar for the enemy. I've watched her take down a dozen armed insurgents today and a couple of them were bigger than me. Besides, Jack is no doubt grateful to you for getting rid of his CIA problems. I'd sure love to hear how you pulled that off."

Roseanna looked at Karl for a long moment and then said, "Come on, I'll talk while you help me feed the hungry."

"Lead the way, Captain. I'm all ears and ready to serve the needy at your side."

For the first time in a long time, she found herself laughing at the sheer improbability of these circumstances. Much later that night after the hungry, hurt, and homeless had all been given care, Karl and Roseanna found themselves sitting in the middle of an empty part of the lawn under the stars.

She asked, "I don't get it. What are these crazy Americans trying to do? Why are President White and his wife, out here every day nursing the wounded? They should be hiding in some bunker underground. This place could be overrun at any time and they'd never get out."

Karl said, "How very true. Banks and Black let him be elected because he had no military experience and they believed he'd fall apart in a crisis like this. Well, he not only didn't fall apart he's leading his nation in the most visible way he can. He's kicked the whole UN right out of this country and is rallying everyone behind him. He's the first president that couldn't be bought and is smart enough to have followed the money to find out who was buying what. For years, Jack and I fought the Cold War, but it wasn't about us fighting. It was about people like Banks making money, selling guns and bombs. That's what this is all about, the bankers looting every nation and making everyone their slaves. They do it by force, bribery, blackmail, and lies. But you can't buy loyalty or sell justice. That's why the plan fell apart. Why Banks and his stooges are on the run and Black's people are hiding in a hole instead of President White."

Karl went on. "They elected the president because they thought he was a wimp who would sell out his country at the drop of a hat. Instead, he stood up and drew a line and told the bullies here I stand. Come get me. And suddenly, his armed forces that were ready to run for their lives turned around and stood behind him. Not only that, he has file clerks, electricians, computer geeks, plumbers, firefighters, cooks, and even his own wife out here on this lawn standing at his side. He's even got us here and that makes even less sense, but in my gut I know he's right. That our homelands will never be free or safe if we fail here on this lawn."

Roseanna felt it in her heart (which had been stone for a long time) and a cold chill of the truth ran down her spine. She moved closer to Karl and he put his arm around her. They sat that way for a long time with the stars standing guard overhead.

A reassuring voice from the dark brought them back to the present. "It is a great night to stand on this field of grass united with the stars above," echoed the old man. "But you both will find Argentina more comfortable when you are done here. There is a whole new life for you there and many there who need you both. I am sure Jack will find you a ride there, but you will not be done here either. There is still the matter of General Black coming back like a bad penny." The old man pointed to a shooting star in the sky and said, "See an omen of things to come."

They both looked as it blazed across the sky with a great long tail. When they looked back, the old man was gone from the lawn, which stretched out hundreds of feet from them in all directions.

Roseanna said, "I think perhaps I should take up drinking vodka so I can explain things like this."

Karl added, "I'm not sure it'll help. I've never told anyone I bought a ranch in Argentina. I had business there years ago and really like it, so I bought a place for when I retire. And if people can sneak up on me like that, it must be time to think about retiring."

Roseanna replied, "Me too and why would that guy think Black's still alive? When Black signed into his computer, it triggered that device."

Neither had answers to these new puzzles and they finally found a spot to curl up and get some much needed sleep before they had to face the new dawn.

Somehow, during the turmoil and while Dee had far too many things to do, Warbucks Banks left the country for Europe and a deep hole to hide in. The UN was having a hard time getting military support for their assault on America. It would seem that some were very concerned that the irate eagle would make them its next meal and some were very surprised when the satellites came back online allowing EMERGCON: AIR DEFENSE EMERGENCY, which put the military around the world on DEFCON 1. And to add to the concern was the fact that President White was not answering the Red PHONE.

Gen. San Antonio de Valero and his men were placed on the C-130 with the UN worms. So he also landed in England. The UN somehow did manage to get Gen. San Antonio de

Valero, the UN-appointed interim president of United States into Los Angeles to lead the Mexican Army of Liberation. Mexican President Santa Anna had been the prime mover in doing this as his southern commander, Gen. Salvador Saca, advanced on San Diego and the states of California, Arizona, New Mexico, and Texas. President San Antonio de Valero announced his triumphant return from the steps of the Los Angeles City Hall with his cheering admirers all around for the TV cameras.

In the skies over San Diego, southern California, and across the border in Mexico, an air war had started. With the U.S. satellites back online General Almonte and Admiral Snoopy listened with great care as the COM techs reported the data. They had over five hundred incoming bogies and the display on the large wall screen was just unbelievable. The hundred and twenty-five planes from North Island and Miramar were already engaged in deadly dog fights and were greatly outnumbered. So when the fifty fighters from the USS Ronald Reagan arrived, they found some of the enemy aircraft were over the city. The ships that were ready to fire anti-aircraft missiles held their fire to not endanger the new arrivals to the fight. The USS Coral Sea had also finally come within range and had twenty-five fighters headed for Camp Pendleton to help the besieged Marines and the other twenty-five were headed to the northeast of San Diego to meet a group of enemy planes trying to circle San Diego so they could attack from the north. When the USS Ronald Reagan got closer she launched her choppers so they could help the ground forces hold back the advancing army.

Admiral Snoopy had sent a group of ships south to set up a southern missile defense shield to protect San Diego from an attack from the sea. Meanwhile, Adm. Simon Dewy kept his fleet of ships moving refugees north to safety. When the USS Bonhomme Richard returned this time he kept her there on station to help with the wounded that were now arriving very regularly. He used the choppers and a collection of smaller boats as his ambulances.

At the university, they'd found Mildred Snoopy busy organizing the campus. She was only slightly surprised at the arrival of her two adult children, but became very pleased when they explained their reason and that SB4 and SB3 were on their way to evacuate the students, faculty, sick, elderly, and children. The plan was simple, to transfer them to the navy base at Pearl Harbor where they'd be safe and where the mayhem in the rest of the country hadn't happened.

Admiral Staff was very concerned that no serious terrorist attempts had been made in Hawaii. It almost seemed they'd forgotten about them in their plan or didn't think it was a significant asset. However, after the fiasco at the navy base, security was tight everywhere. It also seemed the island's criminals who could see the madness on the mainland on television every night, took being on good behavior to heart.

So with SBA sitting on the library roof and the force field in place, they started to help organize. Amy and J.P. went to the computer center and with an uplink from Atlas got the place back on line. They soon had the systems majors (computer geeks at college) organizing emergency efforts inside the force field. Mary Dyer and Aurora helped Mildred explain to the administrative staff and university security the need to organize and start evacuations, pointing out that L.A. had already fallen and that San Diego was under attack from all three sides. Yes, they were safe for the moment, but they would run out of food and supplies very soon. Of course, nothing was ever as simple as it sounded, because the university happened to be made up of several colleges, a medical school, and a VA hospital, among other things that made up a very large campus.

Lee cleared a classroom of all its chairs and set it up as a landing zone for SB4 and SB3. He had Atlas inform SB4 when he was ready and SB4 appeared in the classroom. Dee arrived with them and headed for the computer complex to speed things up a little. Amy came back up and joined Charly Brice and Shela Smith who were taking Gen. Peter Rabbit to NAS Miramar. President White wanted General Rabbit to organize the military and civilian plans for evacuation and defense if it came to that. Part of the problem was sheer numbers of people. So priorities had to be set as to who was leaving and in what order. Young children and their mothers as well as those with medical needs were the highest on the list, and then came older people less able to defend themselves or deal with the rigors of the emergency.

General Rabbit and his team soon had the area inside the force field organized. Capt. F. Gordon Starbuck, the CO of NAS Miramar, organized the east end while university security with the help of student volunteers and the few local police and firefighters organized the west side. SB4 and SB3 were making a round trip about once each hour, moving about one thousand persons each trip. Even SB2 got in on the act between supply runs to the USS Constitution and chose to take some of their down time on the campus.

Harry and Bob were busy talking with Atlas about his force field. Doc Janet and Val had a following of med students and so did Doc Bones as well as Suzy Que. All three boxes now had a full medical staff. Some of the med students joined the crew of the Bonhomme Richard and the Good Hope, while some of the more daring students joined the combat troops to treat the wounded at the front lines. Over half of the students volunteered to stay and help in whatever way they could.

They organized the students and staff who were evacuated by departments and by day three were headed for Hawaii. With one notable exception; SB4 had jumped for the naval station at Pearl Harbor on that trip and about halfway by the event clock the settings on the NAV computer changed all by themselves. The panic only lasted a minute because Commander North recognized the new coordinates as those for the Constitution. Very puzzling, but Dr. Whosh took it philosophically. And since they were needed back at San Diego they left the USS Constitution with a collection of anthropology, ocean science, environmental studies, sociology, political science, philosophy, and history majors as well as many of their professors for a crash course in reality 101.

Meanwhile, in the Angeles National Forest, Camp Angeles was taking shape. Lt. Gary Waters had become the camp CO. He had Chief Powers send him a crew of construction workers and equipment to start building. His wife, Ruth Waters, started a school and had daily classes. Cami Doll and Ginger Waters ran a day care so mothers could help with other tasks. Grant Waters and his fellow Scouts set up camp security and taught wilderness survival classes. Uncle Bill Coutu started communications links locally by building a cell phone network. He had satellite links to the military, White House, San Diego, and Hawaii. Plus with his ham radio he reached out and talked to people all over the world. He was real proud of the hydro plant the kids built to generate electricity.

Down in the valley, Chief Powers drafted every cop, firefighter, military person, and as many civilians as he could find. He soon had an army and was expanding their area of protection north and south on Route 210. Doc Ellen Exeter helped expand the valley's medical services and arranged for some pediatricians to set up a clinic at Camp Angeles.

The biggest problem was that children kept arriving from many places all across the country. The cities were just too dangerous; so many people were sending their children to the country to be safe. Different answers took place as people searched for ways to make safe places for children to grow.

Far away in the middle of the country, just west of Chicago, June Williams, Dr. Cary Threefires, and Agent Lydia Miles were very busy rescuing children. Ted Williams had called an old friend, Lonnie B. Powell, director of Camp Freeland. Camp Freeland was up north about two hundred miles and large enough to safely house many children. Lonnie opened his camp and with Cary and June they had over a thousand kids moved into this safe environment. Ted and Lydia ran camp security and set up links with Hawaii and the White House.

Somewhere in the United States hidden under mountain ranges in places that didn't appear on maps were a group of deep underground cities the U.S. government built so its leaders and key citizens would survive a nuclear war. Into these two-mile deep holes most of the Congressional leaders, their families, government bureaucrats, security forces, staff, and those select key citizens who were deemed essential to the survival of the country were evacuated. These deep cities were fully equipped with stores, TV stations, phones, schools, recreation, health spas, hospitals, churches, transportation, and every modern contrivance that could be found above ground. Everyone had an implanted ID chip that told the main computer who they were and where they were at all times. All adults and children carried communicators so they could always be contacted at any time. The average working stiff would describe these cities as a rich man's country club.

The military personnel and their families who all had to agree to ten-year tours of duty and had taken a secrecy oath staffed these cities. In some ways, life here could be compared to living on an aircraft carrier without water, movement, and no airplanes. Most of the personnel spent their entire enlistment living as moles. The pay was high, duty was good, and only in a national emergency would one be bothered by the demands of the nation's leaders. The unthinkable happened and they were demanding service with a smile as they adjusted to life underground where the sun never shone.

But even in these above top secret hideaways mayhem had struck. The same people who took out the satellites crashed all their computers and in several cases shut down the reactors causing emergencies below to match the ones above. With communications slowly being repaired, the politicians were starting to contact their constituents and find out the new needs of a nation under attack. Of course, there were a few politicians of principle who refused to be "chipped" or go hide in a hole. They were at home toughing it out with the people they represented. When Congress sat in session they were connected electronically between their bunkers and President White who was still on the surface where the world could see him.

A Well-Hidden Base:

Somewhere else on planet Earth miles below the surface of a barren landscape in a secret bunker called Deep Tomb was Supreme Commander Black walking with his top aides to hear a briefing on world developments. He was very amused that someone, probably President White, had blown up the

CIA and his stooges. It made no difference to his plans. They were already in place and the agents of chaos had already been dispatched to do their deeds. That President White turned out to have a spine and stood up to the United Nations would only slow down the process a little and make the victory more public when he and his followers were killed with the TV cameras rolling.

Black had already given Maj. Raul Mercenary his orders to attack the White House. Raul was readying SB7 and SB8 for the attack. His plan was to take out the joint chiefs right in their underground bunker and infect the computers with a virus that would take down the whole U.S. computer net destroying all government communications. The second part of his plan was to execute President White on the front lawn in front of the TV cameras so the whole world would see the fall of the U.S. government.

Here in Deep Tomb plans to rule the world were still very much alive and well. Black's spies were very busy looking for Warbucks Banks' hideout so they could remove him from the game. That he escaped from the country was too bad as Raul could've taken care of Banks as a side trip after ending the presidency. So the king of the world would die another day. In fact, they would've found Banks by now if it hadn't been for the madness they'd caused in all of Europe.

Back in San Diego at the university, Harry and Bob were very busy studying Atlas' force field and talking to Atlas. While Atlas said he wasn't supposed to give them new technology he had no instructions saying they couldn't examine SBA's systems. So before SB2 jumped back to Scout bunker on Hawaii for its next scheduled supply trip to the USS Constitution, they had sent a grocery list of parts and equipment. Sanders Brother started chasing the items on the computer. Laurie Greene and Alfrado Villa headed into town with Mona Lika Alepeka who had a way of finding things. So by the time SB2 returned, a truckload of stuff as Mona described it was waiting for Harry and Bob. It was most unceremoniously loaded with the supplies and placed in the electrical shop.

Stella Staff, Walter Kid, and Ted Bear had become very involved in helping relocate the children coming to Hawaii for a safe place to live. They had activated several unused military bases to house the incoming refugees. They recruited teachers and medical staff and found buses for transportation. Volunteers from all over the island came forward to embrace the newcomers and make them feel welcome.

The USS Constitution found most of their surprise student and teacher visitors were so fascinated with life on Guam that they never returned to the ship. This had turned into a field trip beyond belief. The professors were learning as much as their students. So this quirk of fate that brought them to Guam instead of Hawaii was proving to be the best educational tool one could imagine.

When SB2 arrived at Guam with the supplies from Hawaii, Cdr. Alex Albright came to meet Harry and Bob. He told them J.P. and Atlas were linked into the engineering computers and wanted to talk with them. They headed past the working party unloading the supplies into the engineering control room and found J.P. smiling at them from the big screen on the bulkhead. Sitting at the main console typing commands into the ship's computers was Atlas.

J.P. said, "Hi," as he saw them enter the control room.

He went on to explain their design ideas would not only work, but also could be easily built into the Constitution's existing systems and powered by her reactors. He also explained that Atlas at the moment was having one of the ship's printers print out blueprints, wiring diagrams, and a parts list to build the new system on the Constitution.

Harry said, "Great, J.P., but we need it in San Diego, not Guam."

J.P. smiled. "That's the beauty of it. If you can make it work there on the Constitution, you can also make the same system work here on the Ronald Reagan. Atlas already has the computer here running cross checks with the systems on the Reagan, so if you make it work they'll be already to do it there. They can't safely test it because they are under attack, so it must work on the first try for them."

Bob had joined Atlas at the console and started calling up programs too. Within an hour most of the engineering electricians, machinists, and welders were very busy. The whole idea was to use the ship's degaussing coils to generate the force field around the ship. New control programs were written and the frequency outputs adjusted.

Meanwhile, Dr. Wilks put Harry and Bob's second in command to work, so SB2 could make more supply and evacuation runs. Twelve hours later, Captain Right had Flight Boss Capt. Tyrus Elder launch two Seahawks with Lt. Meagan Bishop and Lt. Riley Riddle in command. Cdr. Tu Secondary took out the captain's gig and when they were all beyond the range of the force field the test was started. Captain Right had the QM sound General Quarters and with all hands at their battle stations. Then the test began.

It was quite a show for the students and Chamorro natives to watch the ship's own forces attack the Constitution. However, bullets, missiles, and lasers had no effect. Meagan was even so bold as to land the Seahawk on top of the field while her gunner's mate on a tether jumped out and walked on it. Now, there was a man with a tall tale about walking on thin air! Cdr. Tu Secondary even beat on it with an ax. Several of the Chamorro fishermen tried to sail their proas through it or swim under it. Asin Cadassi returned with his own tall tale about magic air you could not go through.

After trying everything they could think of and testing different variations of field strength and size it was pronounced a working system. Even Atlas looked proud of their achievements, which was saying a lot for a holographic computer projection. But it was the first time Atlas had helped build something new, and he enjoyed being treated like one of the crew. It gave him a whole new appreciation for the humans he had been sent to help.

When all the data and equipment requirements were sent ahead of them to the USS Ronald Reagan, SB2 gave Harry, Bob, Cdr. Alex Albright, and Atlas a ride to the ship. Capt. Roger Williams, XO Capt. James West, and the ship's engineering officer, Cdr. John Handforth, were waiting on the hangar deck. The flight crews and the Marines had cleared an LZ and were now on standby when SB2 suddenly appeared before their eyes. You could have heard a pin drop it got so quiet with all eyes glued to SB2. West and Handforth both gasped and Williams said, "I think that was my reaction the first time I saw one of those appear here."

The door opened and Commander Albright walked out to greet his counterparts. Harry, Bob, and Atlas followed, all chatting about who would do what and how to improve the system. They were about twenty feet from SB2 when it vanished back to Hawaii for more supplies. There was a sudden gasp from the airmen and the Marines.

Commander Albright glanced over his shoulder and said, "They are on a tight schedule, so had to get straight to Hawaii." To get the other officers' attention back from the empty air they were staring at with great intensity, he finally added, "Don't worry. They'll be back for me when we're done. If you're real lucky they'll have some spare time and you can have a tour."

From the looks on their faces, Alex felt as if he had just pulled out a case of lollipops in a schoolyard full of kids.

Unlike the Constitution, the Reagan was fully involved in combat, so Williams soon excused himself to return to his bridge. The others headed for engineering to start the work. Atlas was impressed with all this coordinated activity, but also was the first to point out that this would slow them down.

Before he was done, Dee walked up and said, "Hello."

Cdr. Handforth looked at Albright and asked, "Do I want to know how she got here, or who she is?"

Alex laughed. "No, because she has a habit of disappearing and if I told you the truth, you would think I'm nuts."

After fifteen minutes, Dee had the ship's computers working at three hundred percent higher efficiency, but even with her help, this would be a long process. For two days, Dee and Atlas sat typing into the main consoles during which their human counterparts took much-needed catnaps to keep their brains going.

On the third day, the USS Ronald Reagan pulled farther out to sea during a lull in the fighting. Two Seahawks were armed and launched. The tests began, and an hour later Capt. Roger Williams was informed his ship now was the second in the U.S. Navy to have a force field. With the new modifications it could reach out fifty miles in all directions from the ship. Because of the complex nature of the new system, both Bob and Harry agreed to stay onboard until they were sure the bugs were out of the system.

SB2 returned for Commander Albright as promised and managed to do it at the start of one of their rest periods. Albright kept his word and gave Williams, West, Handforth, and many others tours of SB2. All were quite amazed. Soon, Atlas and Dee bid them all adieu. Atlas headed for SBA to get ready to return to Washington as soon as the new force field could be activated and Dee went directly to Washington to aid in the efforts there. Of course, they both said, "Good-bye." And before their hosts could thank them for their help, they promptly vanished.

Captain Williams smiled at Albright. "You know, Alex, I'm not going to even ask. I've got to get to the bridge and talk with Admiral Snoopy. And I sure do thank you for the tour of a Sand Box. When you see Atlas and Dee next, tell them I said thank you."

Alex laughed. "Oh they know—believe me—they know."

Captain Williams had returned to the bridge and just relaxed in his chair when the QM announced, "Captain you have two incoming priority messages."

As Williams swung around to see the main screen he saw a split screen appear. On one side was the smiling Dee, on the other Atlas grinning. They both in perfect harmony said the same thing at once, "You're welcome, Captain."

Then they vanished leaving a new image of Admiral Snoopy who said, "Hello, Roger, I heard you wished to speak with me."

"Chet, I wanted to let you know the force field is ready and can cover a radius of fifty miles maximum from the ship," said Captain Williams.

"Good," replied Chet. "We're briefing our pilots now and as soon as General Almonte and Lieutenant Colonel Travis can push the bulk of the insurgents back we'll activate it. Right now we're coordinating a plan with NAS Fallon, Nevada, to send many of our aircraft there to help with the defense of the other states under attack. Our mop-up operation here may take weeks after we've cut off the enemy supply lines."

War Room, Office of Naval Intelligence (ONI), San Diego, California:

Ltjg. Merry Kurious was giving the briefing on the status of the conflict in southern California which was going out on the secure net to the president, joint chiefs, military commanders, and Congress. Merry started with the normal preamble and greetings to all parties and moved right to the meat of the subject. "Our forces from Camp Pendleton have moved south with the aid of the USS Coral Sea's fighter squadron. They have secured Oceanside, Vista, and Escondido as well as Route 5 all the way to the NAS Miramar force field. Our troops then forced the enemy to retreat to the east as our second Marine assault force moved down on the enemy from the north. They have secured Route 15 and the combined force is pursuing the enemy toward Ramona. Because of the force field, this enemy force was unable to link with the larger group moving north up Route 805 from Mexico. Unlike Los Angeles they did not utilize a large number of insurgents already placed within our communities. They must have assumed their sheer numbers would overwhelm us. Since we stopped that force from coming up Route 5 and kept them on Route 805, our troops have been able to contain their movements. The force field stopped their advancement north and our counterattack from the west has forced them to retreat east on Route 8 and Route 94. No doubt they hope to be joined by the larger enemy force coming north on Route 8 from Mexicali.

"Lt. Col. William Travis is leading the troops, chasing the enemy down Route 8. He will push them as far as he can, then when they meet the reinforcements from Mexicali, will dig in to hold his ground against the combined force. Capt. F. Gordon Starbuck of NAS Miramar is working with civilian authorities and has secured the area north of San Diego inside the force field. Gen. Juan Almonte is working with the civilian authorities to secure San Diego and has a force currently entering Tijuana to neutralize any remaining threats from the Mexican Army of Liberation lurking in that city.

"Admiral Snoopy has deployed submarines off the coast of Mexico where they can strike any target in that country. He also has fifteen surface ships stationed off the coast of Mexico to counter any new attacks on California. He also reports that Harry Haul and Bob Cybernaut have successfully installed the new force field on the USS Ronald Reagan. This will be activated as soon as we stabilize our position and move our aircraft to NAS Fallon. As soon as the new field is in place, Atlas and SBA will go back to the White House. Capt. Lee Snoopy and his crew have been helping organize the evacuation from the university.

"Adm. Simon Dewy is still evacuating people to San Francisco and will keep his fleet in its support roll. He currently has the hospital ship USS Good Hope and the USS Bonhomme Richard on station handling our medical emergencies. He reports that his fleet has moved over two hundred thousand people to safety. The Sand Boxes have moved close to fifty thousand. Capt. Maria Almonte, our senior medical officer, reports the two ships, three Sand Boxes, two base hospitals, and the University Medical Center have handled over twenty-five thousand wounded or sick with only five percent fatalities. She has high praise for the medical students who joined her crews and the Sand Box, which they helped with numerous critical care patients."

"Chief Jon Powers, commander of the Civilian Army of Resistance, has reported his group of defenders has grown to over three thousand. They have secured Route 2 east as a safe sanctuary for the children at Camp Angeles and have kept the Valley Hospital in full operation, with Dr. Ellen Exeter expanding the trauma center and pediatric care at Camp Angeles. They have expanded their control on Route 210 north to Route 5 and Santa Clarita, also to the south as far as Pasadena. Chief Powers' COM officer, Lt. Jane Coutu, has set up secure links to military and with Camp Angeles high in the mountains of the national forest.

"Lt. Gary Waters, the CO of Camp Angeles, told us he has over five thousand children in camp. Building is in full swing, schools have been started by Ruth Waters, supply routes established, security is in place, and Uncle Bill Coutu has a full communications network set up with the world and military."

And so with her normal efficiency Ltjg. Merry Kurious brought everyone up-to-date and life returned to the tasks at hand. The ground forces pushed the majority of the attacking army out of the area that would be encompassed by the new force field. The Navy attack fleet moved to new locations north and south of the force field. Admiral Dewy moved his support fleet north to help with current problems around L.A. SB4 collected her crew including her new medical staff and headed to the Scout bunker in Hawaii to stand by to assist where needed. SB3 joined SB2 in supplying the Constitution with needed items that had been delayed.

Capt. Lee Snoopy, Amy, J.P., Aurora, and Mary Dyer joined Atlas in SBA. Atlas shut down their force field and launched for the White House. They landed where no one would see them inside an unused room. Four hours later, the ground forces were ready, with the aircraft gone to new locations and the USS Ronald Reagan arrived on station. Admiral Snoopy gave the command and the new force field was engaged at its fifty mile maximum.

That left the large task of cleaning up, capturing insurgents, organizing the remaining people, and returning order to the civilian sector. Gen. Benjamin Day, the CO for Camp Pendleton, started organizing the northern sector of the force field enclosure. Gen. Juan Almonte commanded the southern sector right into Mexico. Lt. Col. William Travis and his men who had chased the invaders out of town took charge of the eastern end. Capt. F. Gordon Starbuck was put in charge of the navy bases and the western side right to the shore, while Capt. Roger Williams and his engineering officer Cdr. John Handforth took charge of the ship and the force field. XO Capt. James West with a small fleet of support ships and a Coast Guard cutter kept the peace in the large area of the field that was ocean.

There was a great deal of attention paid to the actions in San Diego from a very secure bunker in Chihuahua. Gen. Salvador Saca had been paying very close attention. He saw Lieutenant Colonel Travis' troops push his major force right out of the area, but then suddenly stop and retreat. He saw the evacuations to the north by ship. Camp Pendleton had proved stronger than he thought a bunch of new recruits would, but they never pushed north toward L.A. All of the Navy ships had headed to sea or north. Just a small force was left off the Mexican coast to protect the retreating ships. Even their aircraft had fled from California.

The general believed his forces had inflicted serious harm to the weak American gringos and that they were in full retreat.

He ordered a major air attack to finish them off and ordered the army marching from Mexicali to attack and victory would soon be theirs. All of California to Los Angeles would soon be his and the new president of America would reward him well.

Back in ONI's bunker Admiral Snoopy watched Saca's army advance. It was a very impressive sight even from the satellite feed. They were coming down Route 8 in all lanes on both sides of the highway and were doing about eighty miles an hour. It almost looked like a giant race. They also had two hundred aircraft from three locations headed right for San Diego. Chet was getting a little nervous and was pleased to see Atlas' face appear on the monitor.

Atlas said, "Admiral, they are going to test the field for you."

"Should I do something?" asked Chet.

"Why yes, you have a holiday on the fourth of July. You should all go outside and pretend it is that day and watch the fireworks. I do not think they are dumb enough to do this more than once."

So with that encouragement, the admiral and a few daring followers went outside on the top of a building and watched. As they watched, the three groups of aircraft came racing in at attack speed. They could not see or detect the field, so the first planes had no warning—they just hit it. Even though the ones behind them could see the plane in front blow up, they were moving far too fast to turn and avoid it. By the time they returned back to their leader, of the original two hundred planes only thirteen were left.

The force field's radius was fifty miles in all directions from the ship, which was at anchor about ten miles north of San Diego harbor. This placed San Juan Capistrano to the north inside the field. The eastern boundary was just inside the

Anza-Borrego Desert State Park. And gee gosh, to the south the forces had "captured" Tijuana and some other Mexican real estate. There was a rumor that Gen. Juan Almonte being the temporary military governor of this acquired land renamed Tijuana in honor of the majority of his troops, Gringo Villa.

This also meant it went just to the east of Boulder Oaks and the intersection of Kitchen Creek Road on Route 8. The local residents being a hardy lot were not run off by the threat of a Mexican invasion. But they were very curious about this funny new barrier across their highway. When they saw the Mexicans coming at full speed in all lanes at once they tactfully moved out of the way and watched the biggest traffic accident in history. The first one hundred vehicles turned into one pile of burning junk. Even as far back as five miles there were accidents as trucks and tanks could not stop fast enough. The leaders were so spooked they didn't even try to attack the force field. They raced back to Mexico with wild tales of secret death rays the Americans were unfairly using, which must be a violation of some UN Code of Ethics. So much for General Saca's easy victory—the Eagle was now wide-awake.

Dr. Whosh had given the crew a few days rest to get over the fatigue from their last operation. Even Peter, Alice, and Bones admitted they all needed it. Sandra, Meatloaf, and Jenny had been thrilled to have them around for meals and baked a welcome home cake. Scout bunker was still very busy with supplies headed to Guam and with helping run the relocation camps. Mona and Ted had a campfire under the stars for them and Meatloaf found enough marshmallows for everyone.

Peter reorganized his security with Shela and Charly for their next challenge. Alice and Patty were busy with maintenance and repairs. Dew and Scott were doing system checks and software upgrades. Bones was having classes with his students teaching them the latest trauma practices. Cookie had joined Sandra and Meatloaf as soon as her galley was clean and restocked.

So they were all fairly relaxed when the base computer sounded the alert for all SB4 personnel to report onboard immediately for launch. Scotty and Alice were in the command center on SB4 when the link to the White House War Room came into view. Fern, Dee, J.P., and Atlas were all in view.

Alice asked, "What's up Fern?"

"I just had SB8 land in the joint chiefs underground bunker. We've gone to full alert here and Dee is going to the bunker right now. How soon can you launch?" asked Fern.

Amanda and Peter had entered the room as the others streamed in as well.

Peter said, "We should all be aboard in five minutes."

Amanda added, "We can jump to the bunker four hours ago and get the joint chiefs out."

Peter added, "The security force and I will stay to greet SB8. If Dee is going there can she get into SB8's computer?"

Fern looked back at Dee who said, "Yes" and promptly vanished.

Fern replied, "Dee is there by now and will work on that idea."

SB4 was starting the jump sequence in four minutes with all hands onboard. No alarms had sounded at the joint chiefs bunker, since SB8 had appeared in a clothing storage room where few people went. The SB8 commander and his security chief had scanned the room and found no one. But their scanner did not register the electronic anomaly now sitting on top of SB8 since Dee had learned the art of patience from an old man.

However, as certain quirks of fate would have it, four hours earlier SB4 had arrived in the same bunker. And much to the annoyance of some of the joint chiefs, Gen. Peter Rabbit rescued them, and Dr. Whosh delivered them to the navy base at Pearl Harbor for safekeeping. It must be said that the spouses and children took the change of location with much more enthusiasm, verging on joy.

Peter worked with base CO Gen. Wilbur Wright to "set up" a warm welcome for Black's troublemakers. Peter was hoping that the infamous Raul would show up leading the pack. They isolated all computer access in the area of the bunker where SB8 would land, so the computer access would look normal. This would keep them from getting into the main computer or linking into the military network.

Now General Wright and Peter sat and waited for SB8 to arrive. They'd installed a small security camera; Peter enjoyed Wilbur's look of amazement when SB8 just appeared. And before Wilbur could ask Peter if he was cleared for this, Dee appeared on top of SB8, looked right at the camera, and waved.

Peter smiled and said, "Don't worry. Dee is one of ours. The thing she's sitting on is Sand Box 8 that was sent here by General Black, our CIA bad guy."

Wilbur finally said, "I've been cleared for the joint chiefs and have sat in on all their meetings, but never have I heard about things like this, let alone people who just appear. How could I defend against them?"

Peter replied, "That's why they sent me to help you. Dee left Washington three minutes before I left Hawaii, but I got here four hours ahead of her and SB8 was already here when she left the White House."

Wilbur just shook his head and said, "If we ever get the country back on its feet I think it's time to retire."

The door of SB8 opened and the bad guys came trotting

out in their black space suits. One headed right for the computer terminal and connected a small input device. They opened the store room door and headed down the tunnels to attack the joint chiefs. Finally, the last of the black space suits had left and Dee hopped down and walked into SB8 looking like only a blur on the monitors.

Peter turned to Wilbur and said, "I guess we can spring our trap now."

Before they could give the order, SB8 vanished from the storeroom on the adventure Dee had for them. The bunker lights went out, which was no surprise to the black-suited invaders. They just assumed the computer virus had crashed the base computers and so headed for their targets, before they had time to react to this dilemma. They had spread out in four tunnels as per their plan and were not surprised to find the internal water-tight blast doors shut. They did become alarmed to find the doors that had no locks were locked. Their next surprise was a wall of water filling the tunnels. Since their space suits were water-tight and held air, they all floated to the top of the tunnels. When the water reversed directions it took all of them with it and they were all dumped into a large underground catch basin where the helpful base personnel pulled them from the troubled waters, disarmed them, and placed them in a large vault cut from solid rock.

Meanwhile, SB8 was busy making an unplanned trip. Once Dee entered their computer, she locked out all human interfaces, set coordinates for the jump, and engaged the main engines. The command staff were, to say the least, in a total state of shock and panic as they tried to regain control of the Box. Lt. Vary Kurious was busy at the big screen getting updates on the situation in the United States when Atlas' face popped up on the screen. Atlas announced he needed to talk with Captain Right who just happened to be on the bridge running a training exercise. So Lieutenant Kurious linked the transmission to the bridge main screen.

The QM said, "Captain, we have an incoming priority message for you from the White House."

"Hello, Captain," said Atlas. "You need to turn on your force field—you are about to receive some unfriendly company in the form of SB8. Your force field will block the trace signal until Dee and I can deactivate it. Dee is in control of SB8, but the command and shipboard personnel are onboard it still. General Rabbit has captured the security team that was attacking the joint chief's bunker. Dee will power down SB8 and force the bad guys to surrender or as you sailors put it: walk the plank."

"Thank you, Atlas. We'll give them a warm welcome. We hear you're doing a great job looking after our president," said Captain Right.

And with that they closed the link.

"QM, sound General Quarters. Boatswain's mate, have engineering activate the force field and have our full security force muster in the hanger deck to defend us," said Right.

SB8 appeared right on the X in the LZ. Most of SB8's crew took the hint and surrendered to the waiting security force. The captain and two other officers decided to be diehards loyal to Black. So Dee personally disarmed them. The two officers came running, looking for some Marine protection from that madwoman. The captain wanted to go down with his ship and also made a number of unflattering remarks about Dee's "gender." She walked out with him over her shoulder and unceremoniously tossed him into the ocean. Her parting words were, "Go tell it to the sharks, bozo."

As she walked back, everyone started cheering.

"Captain Right, Atlas has told me how to deactivate the transponder so Black can't trace SB8," said Dee. "As soon as I do that, I can take it to Scout bunker in Hawaii. Then you can turn off the force field."

The supreme commander of Neverland located in Deep Tomb was paying close attention after he was told SB8 had vanished from the joint chiefs bunker and hadn't returned. It appeared on his spy scanners from the Chinese and Russians that the joint chief's bunker had gone off-line. That could be a good sign. Had those military bozos built in a self-destruct feature? He would know soon enough. He was happy that SB7 was on schedule. General Hardash was in command and Major Raul Mercenary was going to lead the attack with nine hundred of their elite troops. They had a plan and Black was going to watch it play out on live TV.

When SBA arrived in Washington, Lee, J.P., Amy, and Atlas went to work with Gen. Jack Frost to activate the force field. General Frost's men had been working with the local DCPD to establish a peaceful environment where the emergency workers could return life to something like normal. So they hatched a plan whereby they would start the force field at one mile from the White House, then when the next mile was ready move it out. This had worked rather well and they were now at five miles and rather happy with that for the time being. Atlas had managed to do some design changes on the field so it was just a shell and only penetrated the ground two feet. This meant subways and the basements of buildings could be used to get in and out. A great improvement, they soon took full advantage of and found easy enough to control access. So at this point even the Pentagon was inside the safe zone.

While madness ruled much of America, President White had created an almost normal zone around the White House for the media reporters to show the world. He couldn't fight all the battles still raging across the nation or even help other nations who were also struggling against chaos, but here he could stand and give the people hope.

SB3 was standing by at Scout bunker with a full security force under Lt. Jay Hosmer who had them busy practicing their skills. Cdr. Topper Bird and Lt. Steve Shoemaker were being well fed by Sandra Unhomed, who was getting them to tell her all about her children's latest adventures on Guam. Lt. Matt Youngblood, Suzy Que, Lt. Laurie Greene, and Sgt. Alfrado Villa were busy at a table by themselves attempting to plan a romantic moonlight campfire, while L-Cpl. Jenny Aviary was enjoying teasing the lovebirds. Sgt. Meatloaf Wales and IC2 Max Knight were playing cards and swapping tale tales. All was calm, but it was that calm before the storm.

CPO Detter Terror and Sgt. Sanders Brother were playing a video game with Justine Conviction trying to figure out which one was cheating or if it was both. SPC Star Force and SPC Donald Plante were at the main console in the COM room gathering the day's data and reports. Cpl. Taylor Maid was chatting with his White House counterpart when the alarms started demanding immediate attention and Fern Cybernaut's face appeared on the big screen from the D.C. War Room. He announced that SB7 had just materialized at the end of The Mall in the Capitol, which for the most part was empty.

While Sandy and Fern calculated the next move in this attack, Detter ran for the dining hall. Topper and Steve joined as he ran past, headed for SB3. Suzy and Matt were right behind them. Jay and the security force came running in from outside sounding like a herd in a full stampede. Detter explained as they ran that SB7 had just landed in the Capitol!

Three minutes later, Steve yelled, "Engineering is green."

Matt reported, "I have a lock on the White House basement, sir."

Detter announced, "War Room on main screen, sir."

Jay called in from security armory that they were suiting up and would be ready in five minutes.

Commander Bird gave the order and SB3 jumped into the void on its way.

"The event clock is running," reported Matt.

SB4 got the same call and while Scotty talked with the War Room, Dr. Whosh gathered Peter and his crew. Bones headed below and gathered his interns for a fast briefing. Alice had engineering green and Dew plotting intercept courses for likely LZs to confront Black's invaders. They left General Wright with his prisoners and jumped for Washington and a deadly encounter.

Susan Anthony and Judith Harvard were racing to join President White with a security force. White and J.J. Flash were about to go live before the TV cameras for today's broadcast showing the relief efforts in progress. Snow White, Krista Sparks, Capt. Roseanna Remade, Aurora Snoopy, Karl Vostok, and Mary Dyer were all busy organizing the day's food and medical works that was to be filmed for the rest of the nation and even the world to see. Gen. Jack Frost, Capt. Lee Snoopy, Sgt. Amy Hunter, Sgt. J.P. Smith, and Atlas were at the Pentagon seeing what could be salvaged from the ashes. Gary Moneypenny had joined Fern in the War Room and was trying to figure out why they would attack the almost empty Capitol when the legislators were all either home or in underground bunkers.

They didn't have to wait long. Raul had dropped off a company of space-suited soldiers at the Capitol and jumped over to the Washington Monument [s 1019 yards] to drop off the second company. SB7 quickly vanished from there and reappeared at 701 Twenty-first Street [w 947 yards]. Next it jumped to 701 Eleventh Street [e 867 yards], where Raul left the fourth company and jumped to a building at 1203 Sixteenth Street [n 953 yards]. The plan was working well and Black was watching from his command center for Neverland in Deep Tomb.

Gary yelled to Fern, "I have a report of black-suited space men attacking the Capitol. What should we do?"

"Ignore it. It's a diversion and they're too far away to hurt us for now. The other four groups have us surrounded. That's the real attack we have to worry about," said Fern. "What a time for Jack to be across the Potomac at the Pentagon."

Suddenly, Atlas appeared. "I see we have company," he cheerfully announced as he sat down with them. "Four sides and a diversion. Perhaps we will get to meet this infamous Raul who laid waste to Pearl Harbor to kill our skinny Captain Remade. I do believe that SB3 should be arriving—right now. Commander Bird is most punctual for a man used to flying in slow moving aircraft," said Atlas.

Fern soon had Chief Detter Terror on the big screen as he linked their data streams, so Lt. Jay Hosmer could see their situation.

Jay came on screen and asked, "Where is General Frost located?"

Gary replied that he was over the river at the Pentagon.

Fern added, "Susan and Judith are headed to White with a security force," but that White was out doing a show-and-tell for the TV cameras.

Jay said, "I'll deploy to counter the four incoming forces and hope Peter gets here as back up."

With that Jay was gone.

Atlas said, "I think I should go warn White since I can get there the fastest," and he too vanished.

Fern almost leaped out of his seat as he saw SB7 vanish from its location on Sixteenth Street and knew in his gut they were moving in closer. SB7 jumped into the back part of a temporary storage building and a dozen well-armed men in full U.S. military camo stepped out. Maj. Raul Mercenary was in the lead and by the time they were ten feet from SB7, it leaped back to the Capitol. The TV cameras were rolling as President White showed them the food distribution and stopped so the cameras could get a good picture of him standing next to his wife as she gave an injection to an old man. Mary Dyer and Aurora Snoopy were there putting a bandage on a younger man. J.J. Flash was right next to White talking a mile a minute, giving the world a running commentary on the relief efforts. It was the best telecast yet and would be one few would forget.

Not far away, Krista and Roseanna were busy packing food rations for distribution as Karl lugged in the heavy boxes of supplies.

Krista, who had turned white suddenly, said to Roseanna, "I have the strange feeling that something is very wrong."

Roseanna's eyes met Karl's and knew this could be their moment of discovery, each took a deep breath as they continued what they were doing. And into the middle of this staging area marched a dozen of what would appear to be America's finest. The leader called out, "Mr. President, we are here to relieve you."

The cameras caught it all as Major Mercenary's large laser canon raised to aim at White's chest. Without any hesitation

J.J. Flash leaped in front of White. Snow, even though she was in shock and disbelief, pulled the old man to the ground. Krista jumped over the table and was airborne like an incoming missile straight at Raul. Roseanna went under the table and was right behind her. Karl raced forward heaving the box he had at the men behind Raul. But it was too late. Raul fired before Krista hit him full force. J.J Flash and President White went down as the blast hit them. Mary Dyer and Aurora leapt on top of the falling men to protect them from further harm.

Raul took hold of Krista, violently throwing her to the ground and knocking the wind out of her. He grabbed Roseanna with a somewhat surprised looked on his face to have a dead woman attacking him, but didn't allow anything to slow him down and threw her right into General Vostok, sending both tumbling down. He was about to blast Krista when a huge man appeared from nowhere and lifted him right off his feet. His laser cannon fired right into this giant's chest but had no effect. It was like a bowling ball making a perfect strike as the two men, locked together, sent the men behind in all directions.

They crashed through a wall and the big man holding Raul said, "You are the evil that causes men to kill each other and makes me to want to violate my prime directive."

Raul, for the first time in his life, felt fear. A dead woman attacking him was bad enough, but this super human who was crushing him with his hands was something else. Raul pressed a red button in his pocket and vanished.

Atlas' scanners told him Raul had returned to SB7 in the Capitol a mile and a half away. Susan Anthony and Judith Harvard had arrived right behind Atlas and attacked with the security force. The firefight was short but brutal with eleven dead and one missing. Atlas rushed to White's side. Poor J.J. Flash and his ever-present laptop took most of the blast. Susan looked at the lifeless form and cried, "Oh God, that should've been me!"

Atlas had slipped in next to Snow and said to her, "I must take him to Bones right now. Don't move."

SB4 was still in hyperspace when Atlas appeared next to Bones with White in his arms.

Atlas' words were brief. "You must help him fast. I have to return now." Atlas gently handed Bones the president of the United States and vanished. Bones and his interns raced to the OR with the dying Puritan White.

Atlas reappeared and spoke directly to Snow, "They will do their best for him, but we must continue his job or the evil ones will have won."

Snow nodded and Atlas changed before her eyes into what looked like a wounded but alive President White. Snow understood and said, "Yes, we must now."

They stood up and the group around them parted. The TV cameras were still rolling as President White and his wife Snow, arm in arm, stepped before the cameras.

"White" looked into the cameras and said, "My fellow citizens of the world, it's great evil that's brought us to this crisis. There are those among us who'd destroy all the goodness that we share. They'd replace love with hate, need with greed, peace with war, truth with lies, and justice with slavery. We the people of the world must stand united for our common good. We must not fail."

And there linked arm in arm, the others joined the president of the United States.

Deep Tomb, Somewhere Else:

Black's eyes were bulging out of his head. Raul had failed and there standing arm in arm with White was the dead Conjure Appallingly, Gen. Karl Vostok, Gen. Peter Rabbit, Dr. Amanda Whosh. They were all there laughing at him. Black threw the champagne at the big screen and screamed, "I'll kill you all—every one of you!"

General Rabbit's security force had joined Lieutenant Hosmer's, and the battle all around the White House lasted almost two days. Snow was now sitting by Purr as Bones and the interns did all they could to save him. Atlas went with Susan Anthony to an underground bunker to see a special young doctor. Fern and Krista were curled up in a corner of the War Room holding each other. Roseanna and Karl were not far away. Lee and Aurora talked late into the night with their mom and dad in San Diego. Amy sat next to Lee and leaned on him. J.P., Alice, Amanda, Scotty, and Dew sat together in the mess hall of SB4 while Cookie and Patty kept the food and coffee flowing. Ens. Shela Smith and Lt. Charly Brice were onboard as security.

Many of the others searched for Raul, but Atlas summed that up well when he said, "The evil one has returned to his lair to lick his wounds and appease his master. They will return like bad pennies. We must be vigilant through our darkest hours. I bid you good night," and with that Atlas was gone.

Late that night by a campfire sat two lone figures holding each other as the stars drifted past and the night sounds sang their song. No words were uttered, but there was none needed for a new beginning, a joining into a new oneness had happened. And there Dee and Atlas sat lost in their shared thoughts of all that is and that which will be.

J. ALBERT HANDFORD

AS THE DAWN TEN

Suffer not the little children.

When the world goes mad and reason is flushed with the bath water, is the baby far behind? Will the responsible adults please stand up and be counted—all others feel free to leave the planet for Neverland.

High in the Angeles National Forest some five thousand children had found a safe haven from the madness in the valley below. A city cop who was just doing his job went from a crime fighter to being "Head Nanny" (CO) of Camp Angeles in the middle of the woods. His schoolteacher wife Ruth never asked why he brought home some white girl named Cami Doll. They just packed her some more useful clothes and perhaps some suntan lotion, then Ruth drove to her new job as head mistress of the Camp Angeles school for thousands of displaced kids, then there was Uncle Bill Coutu who left town in his own motor home to become the Camp Angeles Phone Company and spent his spare time talking to the White House.

And what of the top cop, Chief Jon Powers? If anyone thought he was getting paid enough to man the barricades and direct the traffic flow from Hell, they needed to read their town's or city budget. And Doc Ellen Exeter, who after the invaders terminated her boss collected all her staff and patients and moved uptown to a bigger hospital. These were just the average Joes and Janes standing up and doing their jobs. One might wonder where that could lead.

Camp Angeles was growing with new staff and constant construction. The roads were soon repaired and an airstrip made to help with supplies. When the children were not in their regular classes they found jobs helping the workers who in turn taught the children their trade. Mail was even started as the displaced parents started finding places to work and live. The city children got to see a whole new world where Mother Nature was ever present.

Many miles away, Camp Freeland, not far from Chicago, had taken on a whole new life. It had changed from a summer camp to a year-round live-in campus with heated dorms. It now had a teaching staff, a medical staff, and a security staff. Lonnie B. Powell the camp director, had grown right into his expanded roll. Dr. Cary Threefires was not only the camp doc, but soon was caring for all the locals as well. Agent Lydia Miles signed on as camp security while June Williams became a teacher. The camp's transition was so well documented and successful that it became the model for thousands more like it around large cities.

Hawaii was sort of a strange arrangement because the troubles of the mainland never arrived there. Life went on as before, so the kids stayed in the homes and schools. However, there were a lot more kids from relatives on the mainland and whole college campuses had arrived from California to start business in old Army camps. Hawaii had a building boom with everyone working. Stella Staff, Walter Kid, and Ted Bear had become very involved in helping relocate the children coming to Hawaii for a safe place to live. They had activated several unused military bases to house the incoming refugees. They recruited teachers and medical staff and found buses for transportation. Volunteers from all over the island came forward to embrace the newcomers and to make them feel welcome.

Admiral Staff was now full-time on Hawaii. He mainly worked out of Scout bunker. It was great to be with and to be working with Stella. But there was great sadness at Scout bunker as well. Lt. Laurie Greene was now in charge of the enlarged medical facilities and expanded staff with two full-time doctors. The sad part was that they now had gained a very sick patient who had to be kept in a coma in the hope he would heal.

And of course, there was that other odd collection of students which fate had sent to Guam. The USS Constitution, CVNX 911, now had a collection of anthropology, ocean science, environmental studies, sociology, political science, philosophy, and history majors as well as many of their professors for a crash course in reality 101. Even more amazingly, most of these students were in the top of their class and even the professors were well above average. By the time Tracy North sat them all down on the beach for the welcome to Guam lecture, most knew something there was very strange. One found his hand-held GPS would not work. They had noticed how clean the ocean water was and that the native Chamorro were not fluent in English. But the real "hey wait a minute" was from the young lady who announced that her family had lived on Guam for twenty years and the Guam she called home did not look like this.

Tracy smiled saying, "I'm a professor of anthropology at the University of Hawaii and I guess you could say my husband works for the government. So, young lady, come here. What is your name?"

"I'm Cadassi Kandit Deepwater an oceanography student and long-time resident of Guam. My mother is an oceanographer and my father is a captain in naval engineering and design."

"That's good, Cadassi. Have a seat here and tell me about the harbor at the navy base on Guam," said Tracy.

Cadassi said, "Well, it's big and enclosed by a reef sort of like the one out there. Nah, it can't be. You can't make a whole base just vanish."

"You're right on both counts," said Tracy. "That's the same reef and the base hasn't vanished, it just hasn't been built yet. You see, the current year here in Guam now is 1421. That base will be here, but a lot will happen before then."

Tracy continued, "It's rather hard to understand all this and my husband, Cdr. Dew North, is the navigator on the ship that brought you here. I might add that they were taking you to Hawaii in the year 2012, but an unexplained event occurred while you were headed for there. Their navigation computer changed your destination to here and now. And just to add to the mystery, we can't explain how the USS Constitution went from 2012 to 1421. It did travel from Hawaii, where it happened, to here, the ship's original destination by normal means."

Tracy continued explaining. "Our government, or at least parts of it, like the president, knows you're here and you'll get regular news from back home. Before the attack on America, we were able to get regular mail and e-mail back home. Cadassi, you'll be pleased to know that the problems on the mainland of America haven't spread to Guam or Hawaii. So your family is safe. For those of you who want to go to Hawaii, we can start making arrangements on our supply ship. The ship that brought you here is now busy rescuing the joint chiefs who have come under attack in their underground bunker. So we had to move them and their families. Cadassi, you're a special case with your family being *sort of* right here. We will talk to all of you and those of you who want to stay and do research it's up to you. We have been working closely with the Chamorro people and have learned a lot from them."

As the meeting came to a close, everyone drifted off to their appointed places of interest, but Cadassi still sat next to Tracy looking puzzled and sad. Fran Unhomed and Chrissy North who had been listening joined them.

Chrissy said, "Hi, Mom, I think Fran and I can help Cadassi contact her parents."

Cadassi's face instantly got brighter.

Tracy smiled. "My dear, I do believe you're now in good hands and I've a lot to do."

Fran and Chrissy led Cadassi to the proas and told her if she stayed long enough they could work with the local boat builder and make her one. So they sailed out to the Constitution and went up to the admiral's bridge. There they found Lt. Vary Kurious busy at work. He stopped for a cup of Joe and the girls explained Cadassi's dilemma.

He chuckled and said, "I do believe that console over there is free. If you talk to Sanders Brother in Hawaii, I bet he can get you a link to Cadassi's father's computer."

Vary watched and enjoyed his coffee as the three raced over to the console and Chrissy typed like mad. In a few moments the face of SPC. Donald Plant appeared on the screen.

"Hi, Chrissy, what can I do for you today?"

"We want to help Cadassi talk to her father, Capt. Lloyd B. Deepwater at the Navy Research Facility on Guam."

"That's simple. I have a secure link to the Guam base I can put you through on, and I've found her father on the index. He's in his office now, so I'll connect you right now. I'll talk with you later."

"Thanks," replied Chrissy. "We'll see you on our next visit to Hawaii."

Capt. Lloyd Deepwater was sitting at his desk talking with his wife, Seamist. He was explaining their flight schedule to Hawaii, so they could look for their daughter when his computer started flashing that he had a TS secure inbound message.

He said, "Hang on, honey, I have a priority message from Admiral Staff on the USS Constitution via Scout bunker in Hawaii."

With some annoyance, he keyed the computer to open the link. Suddenly, Chrissy's face appeared and he groaned, "Young lady, if you're a hacker you sure have the wrong number and are not Admiral Staff."

"I'm Chrissy North and the admiral is in Hawaii right now with the joint chiefs and his wife, Stella. I just borrowed his computer on the ship to call you. I've someone here who wants to talk to you," explained Chrissy.

"Young lady, this better be good because my wife and I have a plane to catch to Hawaii to find my daughter," replied Deepwater.

Chrissy replied, "But she's not there. She's right here with me."

With that, Chrissy pulled Cadassi in range of the camera.

"What!" he said.

"Daddy, I'm really here," said Cadassi.

Still having his wife on the phone, he said, "Honey, its Cadassi."

"Yes, dear, I can hear," said Seamist, "But where is she?"

Lloyd repeated his wife's question.

Cadassi replied, "That's kind of hard to explain, Dad, but we are on the Constitution and we're anchored off Guam," explained Cadassi.

While they'd been talking, Dr. Janet Wilks and Bob Cybernaut had joined Vary for coffee and to send the days supply list.

Janet said, "Vary, could you put us all on the big screen?"

Bob said to the kids, "Come here. We'll put your father on where he can see all of us."

Lloyd appeared on the larger screen and Vary said, "Hello, Captain Deepwater. I'm Lt. Vary Kurious, our ship's intel officer. This is Captain Wilks and her COM officer Bob Cybernaut; they wanted to get in on your conversation."

"Lloyd," said Janet, "I'll be making a supply run with my ship for the Constitution. If we leave early we could pick up you and your family and give you a ride here."

So they worked out the details. Lloyd moved the cars out of the two-car garage and he, Seamist, and son Ben were sitting in the kitchen at eleven p.m. when they heard a muffled noise, then the garage door opened. There was Bob Cybernaut. "Hi guys," he said, grinning. "Your ride's here."

They were most amazed to find a large box filling the garage, but that was nothing compared to their surprise when they got inside. Bob turned them over to Kate who found them some munchies to eat while they headed for Hawaii. Kate continued to be their tour guide and after Meatloaf had fed them, they got to meet Admiral Staff in person, and then Mona and Ted arranged a starlight campfire. When SB2 was loaded, they all made the jump back to Guam. The hangar deck of the Constitution was the most normal thing Lloyd had seen in hours—except there was Cadassi as advertised with a whole collection of kids.

While Cadassi and her mom hugged and cried, Lloyd talked to Chrissy. "I'm not sure if I should salute or just say thanks."

She hugged him and said, "Thanks will do. When the future shock wears off, Captain Right will see you get a tour of his ship and my mother will show you what Guam used to be like."

And so in the face of chaos life went on. Back in the Northeast, far away from cities, another type of children's story was unfolding. This story was as much about the people as the place and how fate brought them together by Golden Pond. Where the crystal clear waters come rushing down from mountain streams in pristine forests where some old wood still grows. It could be said that it was the town time forgot as it sits nestled in a mountain range. Its white houses and church steeples stand as a proud reminder of the past. It is a town where everyone knows your name and people wave as you drive past, a place where you are as apt to meet your neighbor at the country store, the post office, the library, town school or the local dump as to find them out mowing their lawn.

On Golden Pond loons do call
On Golden Pond children swim
On Golden Pond the water's clear
On Golden Pond there are mountain views
On Golden Pond the forest's green
On Golden Pond old folks do remember spring

By Golden Pond a town did grow
By Golden Pond a church bell rings
By Golden Pond the schoolyard swings
By Golden Pond town folk do meet
By Golden Pond mail comes and goes
By Golden Pond the store does sell

In the quaint old town white steeples stand
In the quaint old town the schoolhouse shares
In the quaint old town white houses in a row
In the quaint old town library books are read
In the quaint old town common grounds abound
In the quaint old town the fair is grand

But Golden Pond is on no map,
We'll not be found if you look like that
We are in your mind
Where your heart doeth lead
Where yesterday meets tomorrow
And the loons call across the waters to come home.

So when the world went mad and the lights went out, what did this very little place of several thousand souls do? Most lived here to escape the madness in the first place. The lights were always going out anyway, so there was no panic. As soon as the volunteer firefighters could brew enough coffee and the 4-H moms and Ladies Aid Society could gather enough munchies, a town meeting was called. In a small town everything is decided by the "vote" at the town meeting. It didn't take long to decide to not invite any of the crazy or lazy relatives. But everyone agreed that they should get as many as possible of the children out of harm's way. So everyone gathered in their groups and went to work planning. The short and long-term goals were set and the sleepy little town transformed itself into a child care facility on a grand scale.

Yeore Town soon became very, very busy. Almost every home with a spare room and some with no room to spare found places to put the extra children. Huge old houses, which stood mostly empty, suddenly were filled with life. The local school started double sessions and found extra classrooms in the library, town hall, Grange, the old firehouse, Historical Society, and several private homes anywhere there was space to teach the children. The older kids, as part of their education, cared for the younger. Half the town folks have college degrees and volunteered as teachers. The town's veterans became part of the fire department or police force or both. The church, fire station, school, and local restaurant organized and served meals three times a day to the people who needed them.

The town's original day care center, a church, and a couple of homes stepped up their daily programs and added elders who just loved being with the kids. Becoming surrogate grandparents gave a lot of the older people a way to be useful again. The retired pastors joined the local pastor in providing spiritual help 24/7. And there were a lot of people who needed spiritual guidance during the worst turmoil in their lives. The churches never closed and the bells rang on the hour during the day as well as at midnight.

The old fair grounds came to life as an airport and a car-pool repair facility and was put to use by Col. Benjamin Jorge who arrived with a two hundred-bed Army mobile hospital. The people all rejoiced to have a medical care center that could handle the worst of the emergencies. Most of the hospitals were still down and not likely to get back into operation soon. It would seem someone named Stella had told President White that Colonel Jorge was bored with retirement. Sky Lonewolfe sort of entered the Army computer system and procured him, his hospital, as well as a staff. Colonel Jorge was not surprised that when he arrived everyone knew his name. Or that he, his staff, and their families were all billeted in a large mansion overlooking Golden Pond.

The local elementary school started classes for both the youth and the older people who needed special training. Some of these classes were in the areas of fire, rescue, health care, law enforcement, teaching, gardening, sewing, car and home repair. Everyone was welcome to join the classes and a lot did as a way to socialize. Horse-drawn wagons now became as common as trucks and buses. As time went on other opportunities to improve their lives came along. To get more vehicles and equipment working, the farmers grew lots of crops that made vegetable oil to run the diesel engines and alcohol for the gas engines. Hydropower was harnessed as well as wind and solar to make electricity. Old and new ideas came together. And new solutions were found.

With no TV to watch or video games to play, people started to talk to each other, wanted to sing and dance, everyone started to come to the plays and musical events. They started having meals together and talked about life and anything else that came to mind. The day's news was passed from mouth to ear. Working together became a social pastime that they really looked forward to and enjoyed. The kids found old games were fun and bedtime stories were a must. The older youth learned how to help with the housework, cooking, laundry, meals, childcare, gathering firewood. No one got out of helping weed the gardens. Whole extended families walked or rode bicycles around town. People started visiting the people next door and even down the street. They started becoming friendlier and had a lot more to say to each other, something that most people had lost the art of doing.

Of course, the troubles of the world still found their way in. The roving gangs of looters who'd rather lie and steal than work were roaming about looking for victims. But for the most part, those people who had chosen to work together saw them coming. They sent many of them on their way or to rest in peace if violence was their method of operation. Beyond that was the ever present memory that all was not well and many of their families were still in grave danger. In some places law and order was lost to chaos. The strong fed off the weak and ill-prepared. The lazy demanded a share of those who worked because it was their right and soon everyone starved. Some places mankind raised up to its greatest height and in other they sank into a bottomless pit of despair.

While the military had come to town it was hardly an invasion. A secure military hospital was a welcome addition to the child care activities. And Colonel Jorge knew this location well since a friend had lived there for years. So the newcomers soon fit into the flow of things. The children visiting the sick or wounded at the hospital were as common as swimming in the crystal clear waters or taking nature walks in the woods. They soon became as much a part of the healing process as the nurses and doctors. And all became part of Yeore Town where everyone knew their names.

Colonel Jorge and his nurse wife, Susan, met most of the town folks over dinner at an old farmhouse where Lou's introductions were almost as well known as her food. And the wrap around porch was always a good place for conversations or telling stories to the ever-present children. Al was busy running here and there helping out where he was most needed. A lot of his friends and people from town gathered at his house nightly to listen to a wise old man.

The Army soon had a communications net built and Yeore Town became the hub returning the whole area to some semblance of normal. Phones systems were reenergized and the local hospitals were back in operation. Electricity slowly spread until the whole area had its own grid. Local airports opened and businesses returned to work. Tourism had been replaced by helping others get back on their feet. The area's extra work forces became traveling repair crews and were flown into needy areas by the military.

Groups like the Navy SEABEES were being flown into troubled areas to rebuild the infrastructure such as electric plants, airports, hospitals, phone systems, and water supplies. In many cases their first job was to restore order or put out raging fires.

Out in the woods, not too far from an old farmhouse, an old man was handing out marshmallows to the eager young faces. They had their campfire to gather around after leaving the adults back at the house. Some thought it odd in this time of crisis with shortages of everything normal that those bags of marshmallows just kept appearing like magic.

Col. Benjamin Jorge was surrounded on the porch as he taught a first aid class to a group of eager young minds. On the weekends the graduates of the compass game on the front lawn moved on to a five-mile course in the woods. Each station on the course had the compass direction and distance of the next station. They worked in teams and would "pace the distance" (each person's stride or pace has an average distance that can be calculated over a one hundred foot measured distance by counting how many times you step on your left foot. So one pace is the distance from start, stepping forward with your right foot and ending where your left foot lands. If your left foot lands twenty times in one hundred feet, you have a five-foot pace and happen to be tall). Amazingly no one ever got lost and/or missed supper—when the big triangle bell rang out the supper call.

After, a rousing game of capture the flag was good to finish off any extra energy the kids might have before bedtime. This was when most of the older folks sat on the porch drinking coffee and talking about good or bad news of the day. Often

Al or Ben would get that far off look and reminisce about the campfires of their youth, of dressing in native attire and dancing around the fire to the beat of a powwow drum. This sometimes would get Lou to break out her flute and play softly while everyone counted the stars, satellites and other passing objects of interest. Sometimes later at night after the kids were all tucked in and dreaming of better days when the world was at peace, the elders would gather around the campfire, left by the children, long into the night with memories of better times and hopes for new beginnings.

Staring deep into the embers as the drumbeats echoed and the flute tunes drifted with the wind which like the smoke rose to greet the stars. Far to the west on a Hawaiian mountain was another fire and farther west on a beach in Guam another, as the kindred souls searched their common bonds that united them across time and space. There seen deep within the glowing embers of the fire, like the twinkling stars above, or a reflection on still waters; the mind searched deeper still into the mysteries of the soul.

Just a journey down a flower lined path, across a meadow of waving grass to a cliff over looking the ocean. Walking down the path, step by step under the clear sky with soaring gulls over head. Down to the white sands that stretch forever and the crystal clear waters that vanish as they meet the sky. The soft gentle breeze caresses with the salty air and invites all to come nearer still. Feeling the warm sand as it surrounds the feet as the foot steps get even closer to the pure white beach and waiting ocean. The sounds of the surf as it gently laps the shore can be heard. Walking across the white sands of time, the sand gets wetter as the water's edge nears. Here under the purist light from above that warms the body to the core, one can walk on into the maternal embrace of Mother Nature's womb. As the warm waters surround and the pure white light of the Father fills the soul with the love of nature, we are born again in a baptism of the water and the light which unites us with all that is and ever will be. Here you are home, warm and safe, connected to your universal family and the source of all life.

But alas the embers dim, the fire goes out and soon it is the dawn of a new day. The whoop whoop whoop of the inbound chopper with wounded brings an end to Ben's reverie as life struggles on in the real world of blood, guts, bad guys, pain, loss, and joys. The doctors are ready as the corpsmen scramble in with the next patient. The children head to class, farmers to their fields, workers to their jobs, and the pastor sits before her alter, to wonder why, as the morning rays illuminate the golden cross. Another dawn has come to Yeore Town and the question of the day is "Are you ready?" The church bell tolls to mark the time and perhaps it even tolls for thee.

Far, far away well beyond the vale of everyday reality deep within the core of our being, where time has no meaning, two tall figures walked through a flowering garden, one in a business suit, the other in a flowing white robe. Their words were more pictures than sounds. From the garden they walked to the library and read great books of recorded knowledge of wonders just around the next turn. Here the businessman read of human duality. How man could choose to do great good or cause great harm with the same amount of effort. That humans had many paths of learning and often opposite roles in the lesson. That there are those who will work in unity for the common goal or good, while others will become the road blocks and challenges to their purpose. That we are all one, part of the whole and a unique piece of the puzzle called life. That everyone has their role and is as important as all others.

The man's guide led on from the hall of records through the city of light to help the man find answers to his many questions. They talked with many past great leaders whose wisdom could help and often support the man's choices. He even met with an old Native American and a wise Hawaiian woman who assured him the greatest adventures where yet to come. He tried to absorb as much knowledge as his brain would allow before he had to go back to his own body and way of life.

In a different place there was a dark room where the lights were kept dim and machines worked day and night. Soft music played and the people sitting in the seats around the edge of the room spoke in hushed tones. Here deep inside a mountain, life had taken on a surreal appearance as visitors came and went. Some entered by the door past the ever-present guardians, while others just appeared out of thin air and left the same way. An old Native American sat in the shadows deep in contemplation and next to him a large man of great strength sat watching the girl pace. The lone figure paced in front of the row of monitors with a look of determination that said, "I will find the answer to all this." The old man smiled at the large man and gently touched Atlas' arm. No words were spoken, but the old man looked from the man to the pacing girl. Atlas nodded and went to her, taking her in his arms and held Dee close. They looked deep into each other eyes and all three vanished.

The two attendants playing cards paid no attention to these events as they were normal occurrences during the days of their vigil. A small red light flashed and one rose to go make adjustments to the equipment. Once all the lights were green she returned to her co-worker and the card game. Most shifts were long and boring with little to do but watch and wait to fix some small problem. The technicians with special training did the big changes and systems checks. All the gathered data was sent by telemetry to the main control room and out over satcom.

The team of doctors entered the patient's room and turned up the lights. Each made his or her examination, checking the charts and monitors and the patient. They all looked like a sad lot with bad news only a whisper away. The lead doctor called the meeting to order once they were all seated in the conference room. Each in turn gave their report with a solemnity of a high mass.

The patient, who had sustained massive injuries, had under gone numerous operations to repair and replace damaged tissue. Vital organs had been repaired and stabilized. Reconstruction and skin graphs had taken with amazingly good results. Healing in most terms was complete. A special low gravity bed had prevented bedsores. A computer run exercise machine connected to the nervous system had not only kept atrophy away but also produced the body of a weight lifter. In spite of all this good news one major problem remained. The mind had not returned and all efforts to raise the patient from the induced coma had sadly failed.

The doctors were at a total loss and by the end of the meeting were even more depressed. They had no answers and so their patient lay as healthy as a horse but deep in a dark tomb of silence as the clock ticked on. While they'd healed the body better than it was before, the mind was eluding them. Everything was working, but no one was at home.

Some tales were a lot better than others. The children of Yeore Town were sponges absorbing all these new changes, new friends and new chances to learn. It was almost like sending the whole nation's children to private schools. In many cases the parents were now joining the children and being integrated into the community around the school or camp. The children were not only learning the three Rs, but also how a community works. They were as apt to be planting gardens, making clothes, building furniture or repairing buildings as playing sports. Old folks taught skills to the kids and even other adults who had not had the chance to learn in their youth. And the children were teaching other children as they learned to pass on their new skills. Education had become for everyone and learning had become a fun adventure in finding some new piece of knowledge. It was not unusual for a whole class to invade a library in search of some new bit of knowledge or the classroom to turn into a research laboratory. Teachers were busy swapping new ideas how to keep this ball of youthful energy rolling and many times found they were learning with the children as well.

Young minds unrestrained by old lessons soon had everyone exploring new avenues of thought. They found as much wonder in the cook's first rate soup or the janitor's cleaning methods as they did in commuter class. They found old wisdom took on new twists as young minds related the old concepts to new problems and found amazingly marvelous new ways to solve problems. Imagine the philosophy teacher who suddenly found her class of ten-year-olds wanting to talk about everything in life—they brought a whole new dimension to her classroom. They were so curious that she started involving them with the older students who'd lost their desire to ask why or what this was supposed to mean to them. Imagine the school cook, who had a student following that wanted to learn how to make those magic brownies as well as eat them. Or the janitor, who suddenly found he had a whole class of rock climbing and repelling students. Or the botanist, whose students had over one hundred acres of gardens and worked the fields until the sun set.

Out of the ashes of ruin and chaos new beginnings where taking hold. Kids were growing food, building dams, wind mills, solar panels, making clothes, building homes, and finding new ways to live. Instead of sitting around watching TV or playing mindless games they talked to each other and to the adults. And even more amazing they started to listen to each other and began to think. Not only that, they wanted to know what happened and why. And beyond why—how do we fix it.

A great area in middle America had gone up in flames and anarchy. It would take years to reclaim the losses there. Entire cities had just self destructed, as the entitled demanded their fair share. In many places the victims stood up to the gangs and looters. They said no more and banded together pushing the lawless elements back into oblivion. City dwellers took back their homes, block by block, and turned parks into gardens. Theirs would be the hardest because most of what they needed to survive came from outside the cities. But in many places where the citizens banded together, the police and firefighters set up supply lines. If there wasn't enough sunshine in the yards they put the dirt on the rooftops and grew food there. Hospitals, police stations, fire stations, power plants and telephone offices that could generate electricity soon became centers of activity where people could still live.

In Florida the U.S. Army and Air Force reinforced the vets who stopped the invasion from moving north. The battle lasted months, but finally the enemy was trapped on the Keys and push right into the ocean to swim home. In Texas a counterattack was mounted from Fort Worth. It too was a slow process of removing the embedded invaders who were well-armed. But the citizen soldiers took up arms and helped drive the invaders from their homes. It took longer in New Mexico and Arizona because there were fewer people there. But once the Eagle stated marching south, the invading opportunists saw the cards they were holding weren't good enough. And so they folded and headed back across the border.

San Diego under its protective force field was starting to clean up and regroup. They started to get businesses back working and were now exporting needed items to other parts of the country. Most of the Mexican guests were returned to their homeland with the strong suggestion to stay there. Some of the refugees sent to northern California returned as workers. San Francisco had adjusted to the influx of new people and their citizens had reacted with great disdain to the disruptive forces of chaos. Or to put it more bluntly, they tossed the invading hoards into the ocean for the hungry sharks.

Los Angeles had become an island surrounded by an asphalt highway and angry Americans. All roads led to a roadblock and the Navy waited at sea. The best estimates placed the population, which stayed in L.A. by choice or fate at three million people. At least two hundred thousand of these were well-armed members of the Mexican Army of Liberation under Gen. Salvador Saca. Of course the UN appointed interim president, Gen. San Antonio de Valero, was also there making his claims and demands, such as the U.S. government should send them food and medical supplies. The official U.S. reply was silence. The UN next demanded American ships stand down and that regular air traffic be allowed from Mexico. It was finally decided to allow ships in that had been inspected by the Coast Guard and planes that were inspected at an Air Force base.

To the north, Canada had far less problems than the United States. Once they got their electric grid back in full operation they started sending aid to areas of the United States in need. Alaska also proved helpful as they were hit with fewer problems compared to the lower forty-eight. So large amounts of aid and needed supplies flowed in from the north to help restabilize America in her hour of need.

Camp Angeles was taking on the dimensions of a new city in the sky. The construction workers, who had rushed there to build housing for the children, once finished, started building homes for themselves. However these new buildings used new hi-tech methods and concepts like earth sheltered building and geodesic domes. Much building was done with cement, foam, glass, plastics, and new metal alloys. They even built greenhouses into many of the structures for added heat and a food supply. Solar panels and windmills helped supply electricity.

Gary Waters found he had gone from supervising a camp of displaced children to being in charge of a whole new city. He soon had a staff working for him from engineers to social planners. The camp had the feel of a pioneer town where everything was new and exciting. And even though most of the people at Camp Angeles where displaced, most of them now considered this home and had no desire to return to L.A. or the life styles they left behind. Ruth Waters' school had taken on the scale of a small city itself. With five thousand students, innovation was the word of the day.

Ruth's teaching staff ranged from Ph.D.s to the cable guy. She used Baden-Powell's ideas and everyone was a member of a patrol of eight. Each group had an elected leader and an assistant. Four patrols made a platoon and four platoons made a company (128 children). Each company was assigned its own housing unit and a staff of adult / youth advisors. The platoons each elected a lieutenant and each company a captain that represented the youth chain of command. In turn all the companies elected a general who had his or her own staff, sort of like a student council with more structure. Ginger Waters, Grant Waters, and Cami Doll were all involved in student leadership and chose to live with Company 39, a group of high school students. Uncle Bill Coutu was advisor to Company 369 as well as the CEO of Angeles Tel and Cell, a new mountaintop company with a rapid growth potential. Bill's daughter Jane was now a captain in charge of the communications network, which surrounded Los Angeles.

Chief Jon Powers was busy running the civilian part of the blockade of L.A. or, if you wish to take the UN serious, he was commandant of the Border Patrol. Doc Ellen Exeter, being young and highly intelligent, was very busy modernizing the old system in the valley and building a new health care system in the Angeles Mountains for the Kids. In her spare time she adopted a precocious teenager named Cami and became an advisor. And so life there like other same kinds of areas in the United States went on in the land of the free and the home of the brave, while half a world away a new adventure was unfolding.

AS THE DAWN ELEVEN

O say, can you see, by the dawn's early light,
What so proudly we hail'd at the twilight's last gleaming?
Whose broad stripes and bright stars, thro' the perilous fight,
O'er the ramparts we watch'd, were so gallantly streaming?
And the rockets' red glare, the bombs bursting in air,
Gave proof thro' the night that our flag was still there.
O say, does that star-spangled banner yet wave
O'er the land of the free and the home of the brave?

On the shore dimly seen thro' the mists of the deep,
Where the foe's haughty host in dread silence reposes,
What is that which the breeze, o'er the towering steep,
As it fitfully blows, half conceals, half discloses?
Now it catches the gleam of the morning's first beam,
In full glory reflected, now shines on the stream:
'Tis the star-spangled banner: O, long may it wave
O'er the land of the free and the home of the brave.

—Francis Scott Key, 1814

And the Eagle rose to greet the dawn like the phoenix rising
from the smoldering ashes of chaos, deception, and greed. As
long as the dream is alive, it will lead the way through the
darkest hours to the light of a new dawn.

D r. Janet Wilks and her crew from SB2 transferred to SB8, which was a newer version that had double cargo doors in the rear of the box. These doors

473

opened directly into the cargo hold for faster loading and unloading of supplies. Capt. Lloyd Deepwater took command of SB2 and started building a crew to man her. SB4 returned to Scout bunker where Capt. Stella Staff continued building the new Space Wing Command. She had left her XO Justine Conviction, Maj. Walter Kid, and Lt. Alfrado Villa busy setting up maintenance and repair facilities at Scout bunker. They also needed to start a training group for the crews.

Sue came back to Hawaii with Chrissy and Fran to do some shopping at the navy exchange. While SB4 was getting regular maintenance done, Doc Bones decided to catch up on overdue annual physicals for the crew. Bones and Laurie Greene had just finished with Alice when Sue came racing in with the girls.

Sue climbed up next to Alice and said, "I hope you're all done, Uncle Bones, because we have to go shopping today and Aunt Alice is driving."

Alice assured Sue, "We're almost done."

Doc Bones said, "But I have to tell her the results of the tests."

Sue replied, "She's healthy isn't she?"

"Yes," Bones answered, "but I have to tell her something else too."

Sue said, "So tell her she's going to have a baby, so we can go shopping."

Alice laughed. "I can't be. I would know."

Sue shook her head. "You are. Aunt Abi taught me how to tell."

"But Aunt Abi doesn't have modern equipment like Uncle Bones."

"Well, ask him," said Sue.

The five women all looked at Bones.

"I think I'll talk to Abi about this, but my equipment says you are six weeks pregnant. Congratulations."

With that Laurie, Fran, and Chrissy hugged Alice and made all kinds of girlie noises. Cookie walked in and asked, "What's all the shouting about?"

Bones replied, "Alice is pregnant."

To which Cookie squealed and ran in to hug Alice too.

Finally, Sue said, "Now can we go shopping?"

Alice scooped up Sue and said, "Yes, yes, yes." Then asked, "How long have you known?"

Sue replied, "Oh about a month."

And with that the ladies went shopping.

Bones found Ted and asked if he had a beer in his fridge.

Meanwhile, Admiral Staff was meeting with another team of doctors at Pearl Harbor. They assured him they'd done everything they could and in the medical sense everything was perfect, the body had completely healed. It was a miracle and the new methods they had learned were wonderful. But the bottom line was still that President White was in a coma and not responding to any of their efforts to bring him back. The admiral left very heavy hearted and they would next meet at President White's room with Snow to give her the status of her husband.

In the dark hospital room, little had changed for what seemed like forever. Snow had spent hours sitting there holding Purr's hand and talking to him. Mona, Stella, Laurie, Sandra, Sky, and many others sat with her for hours. Almost everyone on the base and from Guam had visited at one time or another to pay there respects and encourage Snow.

The attendants were busy as the team of doctors arrived with Admiral Staff to give Snow the full report. Mona and Stella had arrived early to be with their friend. They were surprised to see Dee and Atlas. They'd shown up to sit with them as the doctors explained that they had done all they could but had no idea how to get the president out of the coma. Snow asked them many questions and they thoughtfully answered each. They explained what they'd done and the results. But they all agreed they'd run out of ideas of what to do. While all this was going on, Sue had come to visit with Fran and Chrissy. Sue left the girls and climbed up on the bed next to Uncle Purr and held his hand.

Faraway, in another place two men sat watching this scene play out by a small pond whose surface was as smooth as any modern view screen. The tall man in the white robe said, "It is time for you to return. The wee one is waiting for you and your guide has come for you."

The man looked up and saw an old Native American approaching. The two men rose and hugged and then the old man led him home.

Sue reached out with her other hand and took the old Native American's hand in hers. She looked up at him and said, "Thank you." The old man smiled and vanished. Sue looked back at Uncle Purr and said, "Welcome back, Uncle."

On the far side of the room, silence had fallen as the doctors had run out of things to say and Snow had nothing left to ask.

Dee and Atlas got up and hugged Snow. They both said, "All is well now, so we can go." With that they both vanished, which definitely got the doctor's attention, but only for a moment.

A hoarse voice from behind them asked, "Could I have a drink?"

Everyone in the room spun around and saw the president sitting up in bed with Sue in his lap.

Since no one was moving, Sue asked, "Can someone get Uncle Purr a drink?"

Snow flew across the room and leaped onto the bed with them. She hugged her husband and kissed him to welcome him back.

Sue said to no one in particular, "Oh, great, more of that mushy stuff. Yuck."

Smiling because she'd known he'd be back, Mona found the glass of water. When all the doctors finally moved they ran around checking all the instruments that told them exactly what they could see. President Puritan White was back. By the time they all left the room, Sue was feeding Uncle Purr ice cream and Snow was busy telling him it would be a day or two before he could leave.

The whole world knew he was back thanks to Dee and Atlas. Before they left the base they stopped by to see Alice in the mess hall where she was busy eating strange things. Atlas assured Alice that he would get J.P. there as soon as possible and not give away her big surprise.

SBA arrived at the Scout bunker with all due haste and Atlas had not given J.P. a clue about the news that awaited him. Atlas figured the news should come from the big redhead; that is, assuming they could get him to Alice before Sue spilled the beans. Atlas was very curious about Sue and the more he studied her, the more amazing she became. She was her own person and definitely not a clone of her biological parents or anyone else, it seemed. She learned from everyone and the environment around her as well, and then she boiled it all down and often shared wisdom that made her sound like a sage rather than a young child. Atlas even checked Sue's bio signs twice just to be sure she was really human.

In spite of Atlas' well-laid plans, Sue was the first to greet Uncle J.P., but just helped herd him to where Alice was very busy eating every odd concoction Meatloaf could produce in the kitchen. J.P. was escorted into the mess hall with everyone doing their best to act as if they were not paying any attention to his arrival. Alice finally noticed him and put down her pickle, sardine, and peanut butter sandwich.

She leaped into his arms and said, "Darling, will you marry me?"

"Of course," he replied with a big smile.

The room burst out in cheers. By the time J.P. had turned around to ask what was going on, Alice had her mouth around that sandwich again. He sat down next to her but she was acting starved. He finally looked at Sue who was doing her best angelic act and asked, "Can I have a clue?"

Sue said, "Well, I'm not supposed to tell," but she whispered in Uncle J.P.'s ear, "You're going to be a daddy."

"You sure?"" he asked.

And Sue just nodded.

J.P. grabbed Alice and kissed her right in the middle of her pickle, sardine, and peanut butter sandwich.

That set everyone in the mess hall to cheering and carrying on. The cheery news rapidly spread across the whole base and was soon flying over the net all the way to Guam where a group of dancers stepped to the drumbeats around the fire doing a fertility dance.

Even President White, who had spent the whole day complaining that he wanted to leave because he had work to do, stopped and talked Snow into wheeling him to the mess decks in his wheelchair. Congratulating this couple was going to be his first official public act, now that he was on the mend. It was time to give America back to the people and this was a good place to start.

By the time two more days had passed, White had his young doctors jogging around the base behind him, out of breath. He led them up to the mess hall where Meatloaf had a hearty breakfast waiting. After the doctors had collapsed on the seats around him and well before they could catch their breath, President White cheerfully asked them if there was any reason he could not return to work. Before they could answer, Snow scolded him for taking advantage of these young folks. Everyone else smiled in silent amusement and the doctors, each in turn, gave White a clean bill of health.

Air Force One was fueled and ready to travel before lunch. It was time to get the nation back on track. By 1000 hours, the president and First Lady were airborne for Washington, D.C. Most of the flight White spent before the big screens being briefed by the White House staff and Admiral Snoopy in San Diego. For the most part, the lights were back on in America. The people who had been relocated were settling in and restarting their lives. The citizen soldiers who wanted their lives back were confronting the rioting and looting. There was still much unrest in the heartland. The southern states were still pushing the invading forces back. And Los Angeles was surrounded by the very people who had been evicted from it. The Joint Chiefs of Staff had given up on bunkers and had joined their forces in the field.

Air Force One had to refuel and meet their fighter escorts at the White Earth airport. President White insisted on getting out of the plane for some fresh air. Besides, he wanted to meet his hosts. The Native American elders who ran the airport and

Mayor Keillor from the local town were most amazed when their visitor walked into the terminal with his wife in tow. The Whites were introduced to the elders and the whole Keillor family. Snow was doing her best First Lady job when she noticed Puritan had wandered over to a dark part of the room where a very old Native American sat alone.

All of the others grew quiet as the president kneeled down in front of the elder and looked into his eyes. President White said to him, "In 1987 the president of the United States of America promised your people a new school for your young. Today, I tell you that you'll have that school, if I have to come here on weekends to build it myself."

The two men stood, both tall and proud, taking each other's hands. The old Chief Brave Wolf replied, "He spoke with forked tongue. When you come we will feed you and your woman. We will build a school big enough for Mayor Keillor's children, too, so our children will grow together as a family."

"That'll be good," answered White. And with that he and Snow returned to Air Force One.

Keillor walked to the elder. "I didn't think you liked me."

"I don't," replied Brave Wolf, "but your woman is a good cook and she brought food. Besides," he continued, "My grandson says your grandson is ok for a white kid. So let's go smoke the peace pipe and eat that food. You and I are too old to fight anymore. It is time to hold our grandbabies and make our women happy."

With that the two headed straight for the food.

Air Force One landed to a very quiet reception. Security was tight and no press was in sight. Gen. Jack Frost, Susan Anthony, and Sky Lonewolfe, with a platoon of Marines, greeted the president and First Lady. They were rapidly shuttled to the White House where they were finally greeted with more enthusiasm than when President White had won the election. The whole place had a party atmosphere. Most of the women hugged him and the men saluted. Jack Frost was very moved when he saw Capt. Roseanna Remade not only salute the Whites, but also hug both of them.

Susan asked, "Jack, why are you grinning so much?"

He replied, "Does the name Conjure Appallingly ring any bells for you?"

Susan's eyes got big. "It can't be her."

Jack just nodded and said, "You can find General Karl, if you look at the old KGB records we have on file."

Susan stammered, "But they both tried to save President White!"

Jack smiled. "It would appear that our commander in chief has a way of gaining allies that cross all kinds of lines."

The next day, President White performed his first public duty. He led a memorial service for Dr. J. J. Flash who had died saving him from the assassins. He let the nation know that it was people like Dr. Flash and the other men and women, who'd died in the attack meant to kill him that should make them all proud to be an American. President White said it was time for everyone who truly cared to get up and do whatever they had to bring peace and order once more. It was a somber start to America's recovery.

Out west, they were still finding the bodies of refugees who had died in the mountains and deserts of California as they fled the Mexican Army of Liberation. The whole nation was in mourning as there were very few places that had not been affected by the attacks. Law and order were still shaky in many places where desperate people had made their situation even worse by rioting. Many of the riots caused so much damage to the infrastructure that recovery was impossible without totally rebuilding those cities. Many who were now demanding help were the very people who had destroyed the resources they now needed.

Those Americans who had pulled together had little compassion left for those that destroyed, looted, and robbed. Those who had chosen not to carry their own weight were quickly finding that there was no free lunch or free ride. Those people, who had next to nothing and willingly shared it with the people around them, had very little use for those who not only did not share, but who also took from others. The events had brought those communities together as tight-knit families. The criminals, lazy, users, and abusers found the price of their antisocial behavior was being branded by the people who now refused to accept or even listen to their excuses. These people became prisoners of their own actions and were left to live in their own destruction.

Back in Guam, Alice and J.P. had arrived to start planning their wedding, which got more complicated by the minute since everyone including the president wanted to be part of the celebration. Lt. Desire Peace, the Constitution's Chaplain, was asked to officiate and that was the simplest decision. So, they finally decided on three services: the first on the beach in Guam, which would happen over five hundred years before they were born; the second would be on top of a Hawaiian mountain; and the last would be in Washington with the Whites as their hosts.

First Lady Snow White, Dr. Mildred Snoopy, Ens. Blanch "Cookie" Chablis, Mona Lika Alepeka, and Kate Cybernaut arrived in Guam ready to make this the grandest wedding of all time. Kandit Mesngon, Abi Suruhana, and Adagi Nene provided the traditional Chamorro dress for Alice. Anao Agnasina and Mono Gogui also ensured that J.P. was dressed as a manly man including ceremonial weapons of a grand Chamorro warrior. Harry Haul, Bob Cybernaut, Lee Snoopy, Matt Youngblood, and Fern Cybernaut helped convince J.P. by agreeing to dress in their Native American attire. Yes, this was going to be a grand wedding with fires, dancers, and all kinds of food. Even the Chinese got into the act by arriving in their full ceremonial attire.

The ladies took a while to get Lt. Desire Peace used to her very scanty native attire, a long way from her formal military chaplain's habit, but she soon took on her matriarchal role of consummating this marital union before man and God. Of course, the cameras were rolling so everyone could see this grand wedding that was taking place around the world and across time too. The wedding took almost a whole day with ceremonies, eating (lots of eating), celebrating, and then sending the bride and groom off to recuperate and get ready for wedding number two at a new house built specifically for Alice on Guam.

There was also plenty of pomp and circumstance with Dew North giving away his sister-in-law. Sue Sparks was the flower girl and James North the ring bearer. And yes, there was a whole bevy of maids/matrons of honor, Krista Sparks, Chrissy North, Fran Unhomed, Cadassi Deepwater, Tracy North, Shela Smith, Aurora Snoopy, and Charly Brice. Once the whole wedding party revived they were all loaded onto SB4 and headed for ceremony two in Hawaii. The Naval Radio Transmitting Facility Lualualei was informed to relay that they were enroute.

The island of Oahu, Hawaii, is best known for the Naval Base at Pearl Harbor. Less known is that Oahu has a large fertile plain running north from Pearl Harbor between two mountain ranges on the west and east sides of the island. At one time, many cattle were raised here and for many years sugar cane was grown but now there were miles of pineapples. At the northern end the Banzai Pipeline attracted surfers from all over the world. The North Shore also attracted stargazers because the flat top of Mt. Kaala shielded it from light pollution. On the west side of Oahu stood the Waianae Mountain Range, Mt. Kaala being at the northern end. Mt. Kaala at 4025 feet was the highest point and had erratic weather that would make a New Englander proud. In New England, it is said that when the weather is bad, wait a minute and it will change. That was as true of Mt. Washington as it was of Mt. Kaala, both of which had awesome views and very strange weather apt to engulf them in clouds within minutes.

The Waianae Range held a wide range of environments from tropical rain forests to misty bogs. The great beauty included mints, mosses, liverworts, wild orchids, Christmas berry, molasses grass, mango, strawberry guava, Java plum, toon, and native roses. It is also the home to the Hapu'u'u ferns, which could grow to fifteen feet tall, and the giant Ohia trees. Wild boars, goats, and even some stray cattle could be found roaming over hill and dale. Pig hunting was a common sport on Oahu and managed by the state. On occasion feral dog packs could be found along with more natural things like peacocks, quail, and ring-necked pheasant. There were also rare snails, leggy arachnids, and if you pick up enough rocks you'll find a reptile or two.

On the eastern slope of the Waianae Range was the U.S. Army's Schofield Barracks, built in 1909. On the western slope was the Naval Magazine (NAVMAG LLL) located in the Lualualei Valley that was started back in 1931. These two large bases were connected by Kolekole Road, which traversed the pass of the same name. During 1970 the State of Hawaii was one of the first states to create the Natural Area Reserves System (NARS) to protect natural areas. In 1981 the 1,100-acre Mount Kaala Natural Area Reserve was established. Not too far from that State Park, NAVMAG LLL and the Schofield Barracks is another place also not found on any map: Scout bunker a well beyond Top Secret underground base.

Sgt. Meatloaf Wales, Sandra Unhomed, L-Cpl. Jenny Avery, and Justine Conviction were very busy getting that base ready for a large wedding ceremony even though the public part would be held on the Navy base. Although this was a very personal event between two people, it had become a public symbol of American's starting a new life of the nation. The Marines and the Navy were also both busy preparing their public acknowledgement of this union and the Army as well, since they had no desire to be left out of this great national party. Even the Hawaiian governor got into the act along with a group of native Hawaiians. Alice, no doubt, had no idea what she had started when she asked J.P. to marry her. It would also become the longest wedding in history, starting in 1421 at Guam and ending in 2012 at Washington, D.C. half a world away.

As SB4 landed in Scout bunker's secure landing zone, the base's activities leapt into high gear. Snow White, Mildred Snoopy, and Stella Staff headed right for the command center to ensure everything was organized. Cookie Chablis, Mona Lika Alepeka, and Kate Cybernaut made a beeline for the mess hall where they found a wedding cake that was indeed a piece of artwork. The ultimate approval was Sue drooling, until the bridesmaids carried her away from the obvious temptation. Peter Rabbit and Harry Haul spirited J.P. away to a waiting "Marine" bachelor party. Atlas tagged along to advance his education on human behavior, but did promise to tell Dee all about this strange male ritual. Alice was swept off by her bridesmaids to a secret location to be prepared for her second wedding.

Mona had come up with the wedding location. It was one of the most beautiful hillside gardens overlooking the blue Pacific Ocean. Once more the bride was dressed in native attire and Lt. Desire Peace was really starting to enjoy this new dress code that displayed her natural gifts. The service itself was televised live and everyone in Hawaii had the feeling of being part of this celebration. The reception, while formally held at Pearl Harbor, really happened all across the island. The governor declared it a holiday and parties were everywhere. Even those who couldn't get out or had to work could watch the whole thing on TV. Alice and J.P.—Captain and Dr. John P. Smith—were now officially Hawaiians and were known by everyone.

The parties would last for almost a week and set the mood for the rest of the United States. With the wedding party, which had grown some in Hawaii all aboard SB4, the Sand Box leapt to the waiting White House. Washington was transforming, with a new peace where the residents and military were rebuilding together, with the future in mind. Congress, while it was safe to return, had taken to meeting at different locations around the country, not out of fear, but because it gave them a better understanding of the needs of the nation as a whole. They also managed to get their business done faster and then return home to their families.

When SB4 settled on the landing pad, President White was there to greet it. It could've also been he missed his traveling wife, but after she kissed and hugged him, she announced she had to run because there was so much to do. And off she ran with the ladies on a mission. And so J.P. Smith and Puritan White found themselves standing there alone, but Peter Rabbit, Harry Haul, and Jack Frost came to the rescue by leading them to the next bachelor party. J.P. commented as they led him off that he never knew getting married was this much work. They dutifully partied until it was time for them to get dressed.

As soon as they had J.P. dressed in his uniform, Gen. Jack Frost and Gen. Peter Rabbit led J.P. to the Oval Office for the ceremony. It was full of uniforms and suits and the generals led J.P. front and center to stand before President White and a woman he did not know.

President White spoke first and formally, "Doctor, Sergeant John P. Smith, it is with great pleasure that I introduce you to Congresswoman Claudine Gorham, the Speaker of the House of Representatives of the United States of America."

Speaker Gorham announced, "As the Congressional Leader of our country I have been sent here today to deliver this Congressional Commission to you John P. Smith, who from now on will be known as Captain Smith of the United States Marines."

With that Gorham shook J.P.'s hand and said, "Congratulations, son, we are proud of you."

Everyone in the Oval Office broke into cheers as J.P. stood there in shock. Peter and Harry hugged him and promised that this earned him another party—but they could wait until he recovered from this marriage business. Then they dragged Captain J.P. off to dress him in his new uniform, so he could be married once more to the love of his life.

Meanwhile, the ladies had the Rose Garden ready for this grand wedding. This also was going to be a live national event with the whole world watching on TV. It was hard to tell if Lt. Desire Peace was more nervous at being in this high profile role or had just realized that the native attire, even if rather scant, was more comfortable than her full naval uniform. Her next conversation with her spiritual mentor was going to be rather interesting. But she was not alone in uniform. The bride and groom plus about half the wedding party were in full dress uniforms and along with of course Eagle Scout James North. And a special invitation was given to Gen. Karl Vostok, who came in his full Russian uniform and with his companion, Capt. Roseanna Remade.

The other bridesmaids, Krista, Chrissy, Fran, Cadassi, and Aurora were all in gorgeous gowns that complimented Alice's naval uniform. Even Sue had managed to contain her normal enthusiasm so Aunt Alice could be the first to break the formal discipline of the grand event. The ladies had met the challenge of Alice's flowing red hair with great inspiration so that it was a grand accent to her white uniform. Of course, red flowers were everywhere and even though this more formal wedding would not be as grand a display of Mother Nature as the ones in Guam and Hawaii, it too would long be remembered as a national celebration of the union of two of its young heroes.

The reception filled The Mall from the White House to the Washington Monument and from the halls of Congress to the Lincoln Memorial. The president opened the reception with a toast to the newlyweds and spoke of their path. "Our Captains Alice and John Smith are a fine example of our young citizens who are helping us rebuild our nation. To make the world stronger and helping to create a place where our children can grow and flourish to their full potential. But today let me remind you that this is your life, your adventure, and you should take the time to enjoy it. So we salute you as we send you on that journey."

With that President White raised his glass and said, "To life."

It was one big party and in every state the governors had all followed the Hawaiian example. It was a time to remember who they are as a nation, as a people and to celebrate their union of people. As the sun set in the west, Alice and J.P. climbed into the Silver Ball with only Dee and Atlas to guide their chariot.

Atlas asked, "Where would you two like to go on your honeymoon?"

Alice and J.P. stared at each other for a few moments, and then J.P. pointed at the center of the main screen that was showing the starry night outside and told Atlas, "Take us out there, to where we need to go."

"Ok," replied Atlas as he interfaced with Dee to turn this request into a logical location in time and space. Of course Dee, with far more experience with people, found this request perfectly normal for humans. One might wonder which took longer, the honeymoon trip or Dee's explanation to Atlas about where they wanted to go and why.

With the honeymooners sent on their way, it was time to finish the business of the nation's issues. While many places had settled into a new rhythm there were still large areas that needed new solutions. A whole area from Kansas City to Detroit, south to Kentucky and north to Wisconsin, was still in turmoil. Southern Florida was still fighting to regain control. Texas, New Mexico, Arizona and southern California were still pushing back the invaders. And Los Angeles was at a standoff with many of the displaced now settled in the areas of barricades around the lost city. So as the parties ended many went to sleep to dream of new ways to heal the nation and the world beyond. The American dream of brotherhood would be the challenge to arrive with the dawn of the new day.

In a large Congressional hearing room Speaker Claudine Gorham called the hearing to order. She then introduced President White who took a seat on her right. The purpose of this series of hearings was to define the problems facing the country, the causes of the troubles across the country, and then to take actions to correct them. These were joint hearings because they not only affected law enforcement by the president, but required the possible need for new laws or funding from Congress. Dr. Gary Moneypenny, the secretary of Commerce; Judith Harvard, the Attorney General; Gen. Jack Frost, secretary of Defense; Dr. Mary Dyer, and Dr. Tracy North represented President White's executive team. Their team was rounded out with Fern Cybernaut, Krista Sparks, and Aurora Snoopy who kept the current information flowing so the answers could be found and decisions made. Although far away escorting the honeymooners, Dee and Atlas still kept sending data, pictures, and probabilities with amazing timeliness.

Judith Harvard started the hearing by explaining the ongoing problems in the north central United States. Even though the electricity was on in over half the area there was still rioting, looting, and some gangs were roaming like warlords. She went on to explain that much of the crime was being caused by people who were desperate to get what they needed for their families. Many were frustrated with the government or society's slowness to respond. Often this lack of response was caused by the system being overwhelmed by the size of the problem.

She gave the example of a small city with a hundred police and firemen that suddenly found they needed a thousand or even more. In places where the citizens joined the local forces the outcome was very different. One of the other problems with crime was that some perpetrators found it simpler and more beneficial to live a life of crime. Why work forty or sixty hours a week when they could make the same amount of money selling drugs for ten hours in their own living rooms?

Judith continued by talking about violence, which often was more complex than crimes that were addressed by protective laws. There were many forms of abuse, and during times of crisis they increased within the family and spread to affect others near the family. As social restraints failed, the victims increased in number. Broken bones and sexual assaults became common and what was even worse was that the crisis made it harder to help the victims. In communities with a strong sense of family and communal responsibility, much of this violence was controlled from within. Unfortunately, most of the communities in this area lacked this social unity.

Dr. Tracy North spoke next explaining that many of the people who lived in this area of the nation were very poor. This was more than just a lack of money, but a lack of any way to make money, let alone save it for future problems. They lacked the knowledge of how to make good decisions or even how to think logically about how to solve problems. Most assumed they could not solve problems, let alone make much money, to have a future or many of the things they saw on the television. The TV showed everyone having all this great stuff that they could not afford to think about, never mind buy. Their enjoyment or entertainment often involved booze, drugs, sex, and TV, but all of these had serious side effects that just made the bad situation even worse.

Tracy went on with the subject of malnutrition, some of which was caused by a lack of money, and others caused by the lack of the knowledge of what to eat and even how to cook it. Many of these poor families had all the adults working just to keep the roof over their heads. Often the scarce money was spent on prepared foods or take out that was less nutritious and more expensive. Beer was often a big part of this food budget. Cable TV was often another big expense. Malnutrition caused many short and long-term health problems, which in turn caused other problems—problems such as low achievement, poor performance in school or work, pregnancy, addiction and a whole slew of social as well as mental problems caused by abuse. Worst of all was that many of these persons (victims) grew up with all this and knew no other way to live.

Mary Dyer addressed the hearing next and spoke of discrimination. Mary started by asking if the original sin that many clergy spoke of was just another name for racism. Discrimination because of age, being male or female, skin color, intelligence, education, social status, parentage, type of work, or economic level, caused a breakdown in social unity. This breakdown pulled and pushed the community apart. It might have been more comfortable to just associate with those people who were most like them, but in doing so they were driving a social wedge right down the middle of their community. They also so deprived themselves of what they could learn from these different people and on the other side what they in turn could share with them.

Mary went on to say that discrimination caused segregation and in turn isolation. We humans are social creatures and were never made to be alone. The more barriers we created the lonelier we get. Our lives are enriched by other people even the ones we do not like. Some times the only way to bring down the false barriers we created is to tear them down one by one.

The hearing went on for days collecting information from all across the nation. They were finding both the things that worked and those that failed or in some cases made the problems even worse. In many cases they were confronting policies that made them most uncomfortable, because they were now seeing the results. Often these results were very much the opposite of the desired results of well-intentioned legislation. It was more than just the witnesses' words, but the evidence of the results which many times came in the form of damning statistics about the real life misery and suffering.

It was a new day as Dr. Gary Moneypenny addressed the hearing. Gary was the economist who had been monitoring the nation's economic pulse since President White was elected. The two had been classmates at Bryant University when they were young. It had been a long time since they walked under the Archway, burned the midnight oil studying or partied until the dawn. They had both walked a long road to get where they stood now.

Gary explained the connection between unemployment and the level of crime. "This connection can be found in all the areas where problems have risen across the country, he said. "People with no, limited, or under employment were living on the financial edge. When the lights went out many were pushed right over the edge into a desperate situation that was out of control. Part of this problem has to do with the country's loss of manufacturing jobs. These good paying jobs had been the backbone of America. These people who held these jobs formed a large part of our middle class which held our communities together. They also brought money into other sectors of our economy. They supported real estate, auto sales, markets, department stores, restaurants, cleaners, theaters, and banks. Once this money was gone many of the service jobs it supported vanished as well.

"The loss of manufacturing has many causes, but often is because U.S. plants can't compete with foreign companies with either new methods or cheaper labor costs. These problems are common to most companies regardless of if they make autos, trucks, clothing, TVs, toys, stoves, lamps, bikes, shoes, or computers. Many of our companies in search of larger profits have dumped their loyal American workers and replaced them by building new plants in other countries. Often these moves left many highly trained employees jobless or working at jobs which paid far less. It created whole groups of underemployed with their skills not being used for their or society's benefit. These losses have not only economic effects, but also cause great stresses on the families which increased the mental health costs. This occurred both within the families employed in manufacturing where the jobs were lost and also in the whole community as the money dried up and the businesses they supported failed too.

Gary went on to say, "While I am not sure if passing laws can solve this problem, let alone reverse it, I am sure, however, that these companies, who have made their profits off the labor of Americans, should be as loyal to the employees as the loyalty that the companies expected of their employees to the companies."

The hearing room broke out in cheers.

Gary continued, "Employment is also directly related to the level and type of education. The more skills an individual has acquired the more likely they are to be employed and to receive a higher level of payment. Highly skilled workers tend to create more cost effective solutions and better products.

They also have a wider range of skills to deal with social problems. Education creates more opportunities and a wider view of society. A person who can see more options and even the consequences of their actions is far less likely to allow the situation they are into become so desperate that riots and other lawless acts become the solution.

We have seen this across our country time and time again when people in desperate situations choose to work with their neighbors to solve the problems they faced. We have whole new communities that have risen. We have everyday people who just stood up and said no to crime and worked with their fire and police. We have people who took on the invaders and embraced strangers. We have a whole school in the Angeles Mountains made of every race and nationality you could imagine. These students are setting a new standard for our behavior and showing the way for all humans to work together.

Lastly I must address an area where our laws have failed. In fact they have more than failed; they have made the problem far worse. This is the area of entitlements that the government has guaranteed to individual people. In the majority of cases the entitlements have become a disincentive to productivity. To put it in real simple terms, why should I work if you will give me something for doing nothing? Most of our welfare programs that are supposed to help people have a better life are in effect paying them to stay right in the bad situation they are in. The programs say if you work and are successful we will penalize you, forcing you to fail. Also the people who manage these programs are rewarded for keeping people on assistance rather than for helping them to become independent. Negative rewards create negative outcomes and social chaos."

"We destroyed public housing by driving out the average

working person. If you were on welfare your rent was paid. But if you worked, the more you earned the more you paid in rent. This stupid policy drove the workers out of the housing projects and the only people left were the poor and those defrauding the system. The children raised in this environment no longer had any good role models and became like their parents, paid to fail. Gangs became their families and role models. Schools degenerated to breeding grounds where drugs where far more common than learning."

Gary concluded, "We can't continue to hand out free lunches and pat ourselves on the back. We are not helping them or ourselves. To help people we must make the situation better. That means we must provide the skills and tools and motivation, so people can help themselves."

With that the search for solutions began. Krista had entered most of the data into the computers. She could type faster than Fern and Aurora, also she and Dee seemed to know what each other were thinking. Fern, with the help of Sky, was building maps of the areas with the resources noted. Aurora was busy building a flow chart of the order and timing needed to resolve the problems. Aurora had taken a page from her mom's favorite program that generated holographic star charts and had created four dimensional flow charts that could be changed to answer "what if questions".

Fern, Gary, and Tracy spent hours talking about how Scouting's "Patrol Method" works to involve the individual and how it teaches leadership by allowing the individual to lead the group. Learning by doing and seeing the results, good or bad, from your efforts is far more powerful than reading or having someone else tell you how things work. Even meals, which often were served family style, became as productive as work meetings with new ideas being passed around with the food.

It was soon decided the first focus should be the central northern area of the U.S. There the problems had older causes and were less influenced by outside forces. There were no invading forces and the numbers of illegal immigrants are smaller. Also being in the heart of America, fixing the problems here would help unify the rest of the country. Krista described it as healing from the center out. The plan that was forming would return America to the people rather than a group with vested interests in greed and power.

The Plan:

There were four basic parts that worked together to achieve the goals of unity, growth, and healing. The first part was to involve the people. The second was to provide the basic needs of those people so they could focus on the bigger issues and solutions. The third was to provide education and training to increase the people's social, leadership, and technical skills. The fourth was for the people to apply their new skills to rebuild the American Dream.

Meanwhile an unofficial emissary arrived in Estados Unidos Mexicanos, in the Distrito Federal, at the National Palace of President Santa Anna. On the roof of the building amid the communications antennas, security cameras, and some very surprised guards a large silver ball suddenly appeared. But before the guards could get over their surprise they became so exhausted that they had to take a nap right there on the roof. In fact all the palace guards decided they had to sleep off this sudden exhaustion.

Two young women bounded out of the Silver Ball and examined the sleeping guards. They were followed by two older very dignified women. The four walked to the stairs and soon arrived at closed door with two sleeping guards.

Dee opened the door. Sky stepped into the room with Dee right behind her. Seated at a long conference table were President Santa Anna and his cabinet. They were very busy discussing what they would do about the Americans that were about to enter Mexico right behind the retreating Mexican Army. They paid no attention as the four women entered the room until Santa Anna realized that Stella and Snow were standing on either side of him at the head of the table. The first to react was the commander of the Army who leaped to his feet pulling his gun.

He yelled, "American assassins," as he fired point blank at Dee.

When the gun was empty, Dee ripped it from his hand and slammed it down barrel first into the wooden table. When Dee removed her hand, four of the six inches of the gun's barrel were embedded in the table like a big nail.

The military man still had not taken the hint and rushed at Dee with a large knife he pulled from his boot. Dee grabbed his hand, breaking all his fingers. She removed the knife and sank it into the table right next to the gun.

Dee then shoved the fool back in his seat and barked in Spanish, "*Ahora sentarse!*"

Most of the cabinet were businessmen and didn't move. One younger man started to rise, but Sky's hand held him firmly in place. He winced in pain and relaxed back into his chair keeping both of his hands flat on the table. Sky slipped her other hand into his jacket and removed his large gun. She removed the bullets and laid the weapon on the table in front of him. Sky dropped the bullets in his breast pocket.

Sky looked him in the eyes and said, "Nice gun. I left mine at home. The boss said this was a peace mission." She smiled and then stood at ease behind him.

Santa Anna had stood too and was yelling for his guards. Snow pointed out that they were taking a nap and that he must be overworking them.

He turned on her and yelled, "I wouldn't negotiate with some American bitch!"

Stella reached out and grabbed him by the ear like she would a misbehaving child and slammed him back in his seat. He fell silent as he sat there holding his sore ear.

Snow said, "Now that I have your full attention, I'm Snow White, the First Lady of the United States of America, a country which your army has invaded. I'm not here to negotiate with a low life dog that greets a group of unarmed women with guns and bullets. I am here to deliver a message. The government of the country of Estados Unidos Mexicanos will stop all aggression against the American Armed Forces, will stand down, and return to your country. If you fail to do this, our army will continue to disarm your aggressive forces until we reach your southern border and then the United States of America will have thirty-one new states in our union. Those, gentlemen, are your choices."

Snow stepped back to let it sink in then said, "Atlas, get us out of here."

With that the four ladies vanished leaving the president and his cabinet to decide their fate. When Sky, Snow, and Stella opened their eyes, Dee was standing next to Atlas who was smiling at them.

Atlas asked, "Shall we go home now?"

"Yes," Snow said, smiling as she removed the interface from her head and commented, "Wow! That was fun. Can we do it again some time?"

Dee replied, "Easy for you to say. It was me that the old guy shot full of holes."

An hour later, the Mexican government ordered all its army to stand down and return to Mexico. The people soon found a new president who knew how to make peace rather than war. It has also been reported that the gun and knife remained embedded in the National Palace conference room table as a reminder to think before one acts. Unfortunately this all had little effect on the situation in Los Angeles.

President San Antonio de Valero and his Gen. Salvador Saca had representatives in L.A. and other areas long before they invaded. Now that their cause was lost in other areas, many of their army (those who came with guns and those who came to rob the United States while it slept) had fled to L.A. just ahead of the patriots with the eviction notice. Because of this, their numbers swelled and they, with families in tow, had confiscated all the homes and businesses.

The dilemma had become not just removing the Mexican Army of Liberation, but the millions of civilians who had moved in and supported that army. L.A. was not lost to the invading army; it was lost to the invading illegal aliens who had just moved in over the years while citizens were too busy to pay attention. The citizens were sold the idea that the Mexicans were just there to do the jobs Americans did not want to do. Until one day the American children had no jobs and in the end the guy mowing the lawn now lived in their house with his family. Those who raised the cry "Wake-up, America!" were branded crackpots and racists. Yes, America is a "melting pot," but that was because all the country's ancestors came here to become Americans via their own hard work. Those who would turn illegal acts under the rules of law that created this nation into acceptable acts were indeed the terrorists that should be feared the most.

President White was face with a dilemma created over many years before he took office. To evict these millions of people would cause a high loss of life and destroy most of the homes, hospitals, power plants, highways, schools, sewage plants, water supplies, and businesses. The best he could do for the moment was to protect his own citizens and prevent the spread of the claim to this land, which had the backing of the UN. Mexico decided to not be directly involved in L.A. as they figured it might endanger the shaky peace they now had with the United States.

The Americans who had been displaced were far from happy with this situation, but for the most part they resettled and were embraced by their new neighbors. The programs that were now helping people all across America were now helping to rebuild lives in these new areas. The new school in the Angeles National Forest had become the centerpiece for the California school systems. New mass transportation systems were built to move large numbers of people at lower costs.

Deep Tomb, Somewhere Else, on Planet Earth:

Supreme Commander Benedict Black stood on a high catwalk watching the work some hundred feet below on the floor. He was not happy by the turn of events. His efforts in the United States had failed, thanks to those traitors and that moron White, but he would get even with them. He already had a new plan in place to punish them. He watched the work below as they made ready the Sand Boxes for new missions. His security forces marched across the work floor to their training classes.

General Hardash and Major Mercenary joined him. Hardash told him they were ready to leave for La Palma Island and the equipment was all onboard.

"Good," replied Black.

Hardash asked, "Have they located Banks, yet?"

"No," said Black, "but I'll find him by the time you are done on the island."

"You'll know when we are done," said Hardash. "Is there anything else before we leave?"

"No," replied Black. "Just get going."

Old Bank Office Building, Ville Neuchatel, Switzerland:

Dr. Warbucks Banks sat at the head of a large table in the conference room. Even though this was a historic building, the inside was totally modern. A helicopter pad was on the roof and the cellar had a large modern computer room as well as a modern vault. The conference room looked out over Lac de Neuchatel and had full security measures. Banks was meeting Mockeries I. Supervising from Europe, Lo Mean from China, and Korpskommandant Conrad Luftwaffe of the Swiss Army. KKdt. Conrad Luftwaffe was there to assure Banks that he was safe in Switzerland and to report on the state of world events. The commandant was one of Bank's connections to the other European militaries and was very willing to run the world for Banks as long as he was well paid.

After KKdt. Conrad Luftwaffe left, Banks got down to business with Supervising and Mean. Banks was not about to trust any more military butchers after being double-crossed by Black. Banks' men had the economy in most of Europe well in hand and assured Banks they already had plans to bankrupt America. They would put the fool White out of a job and replace him with their own man. Lo Mean assured Banks that China supplied ninety percent of America's manufactured products and the debt to China would soon be so big the stupid Americans could never pay it off. They all agreed it was too bad the Mexican Army had failed to conquer the United States. But President San Antonio de Valero was one of their men and that would help their cause.

When their business was done Banks got in his limo for the ride to his new home. It was a large estate in Rochefort that appeared to be a winery, but underground was a full command center for running Banks' empire. The men tending the grapevines all had guns and the place was surrounded by the newest security equipment. Perhaps it could be said that Banks was growing the grapes of wrath.

For over a month, earth moving equipment had been changing the face of a rural area near a small town. A group had built forms and foundations had been poured. Large trucks had arrived with prebuilt walls and building sections. C-130 National Guard planes had arrived with smaller sections and other building materials. The work teams were also busy teaching building skills to the locals so that the new building would continue after they were gone. The team that was organizing this operation had brought their mobile homes with a mess hall, computers and medical crew.

A new clinic had been built and Doc Bones and Dr. Cary Threefires were busy with their new students. Cookie, Meatloaf, Roseanna, Kate, and Jenny were likewise teaching cooks how to cook efficiently for many people. Fern, Sky, Alice, Dee, and Atlas kept the materials moving and, in their spare time, taught students how to handle this function when they were gone. Harry, J.P., Charly, and Karl helped get the new power plant in place. While it had diesel generators, they were the backups to the hydro, wind, and solar power.

One day, as the new Community School of White Earth took shape, Air Force One came winging into the airport.

President White had taken a week's vacation to help finish this job. He and Snow came down from the plane in dungarees and work boots ready to work. And they did not come alone. Many of the White House staff needed a vacation too. Even the media with them came ready to work and to start a new community paper. By the end of the week all was ready for an official opening ceremony. President White, Mayor Keillor, and Chief Brave Wolf cut the red ribbon together before the rolling cameras.

In the center of the new school was a large indoor garden with a pond with waterfalls and a large open fire ring. As the drums beat and the flames leaped high the dancers from the town and reservation joyously stepped to the beat. Fern watch his white dance students with great interest as he stood between the old white Native American and Chief Brave Wolf.

The chief said, "And to think I always thought you white folks couldn't dance. Guess you had a good teacher." And smiled at the old white man dressed in Native American attire.

Krista came up and grabbed Fern and said, "Come on, you're too young to be standing here watching. If you live long enough to become an old wise man, maybe I'll let you stand around then."

The older men laughed as Fern was led on to the dance floor. They had not noticed that Lou and White Dove had walked up behind them. Lou said to White Dove, "I guess that means we shouldn't leave them standing here thinking they are old."

White Dove replied, "Or that they're that wise yet."

Both men acted very shocked, but soon found themselves dancing with the young folks.

Snow and Purr had enjoyed eating with the Keillor family and were heading to the waterfall where they could sit and watch the dancers. They arrived to find Alice relaxing by the pond in J.P.'s arms. Roseanna and Karl were there too.

The Whites sat next to them and Purr asked how they had enjoyed their honeymoon.

"Ah," said J.P., "The Seven Sisters are beautifully green and very peaceful. Sort of like sitting here with the water gently falling and the fish swimming."

Snow asked, "How is the baby?"

Alice smiled. "I think they want to swim with those fish."

Alice placed Snows hands on her full belly and said, "Feel them kicking?"

"Oh yes," she squealed with glee. "There are two?" she asked.

"Yes, we found out when we saw a doctor on our honeymoon," said Alice.

Roseanna had moved closer and Alice took her hand, placing it on her belly too. A new look appeared on Roseanna's face as she shared this moment. Yes, it was peaceful here with all the dancers dancing around the cheerful council fire. New American dreams were becoming human dreams of a future of unity and love.

At the end of the week they all headed in many directions, but all promised to return. Air Force One returned the Whites to the business of state in Washington. SB4 headed back to Hawaii with Alice and J.P. Dee and Atlas delivered Roseanna and Karl to their new home before they headed for Washington and the next environmental mission.

A Ranch in the Mountains of Argentina south of Malargue:

The next morning Karl and Roseanna found themselves standing on a green hill, not far from the ranch. The horses stood eating the grass as they looked over the valley with the cattle grazing down near the Rio Grande.

"It's beautiful here," said Roseanna. "I can see why you bought it."

"And what do you want?" asked Karl.

Roseanna slowly turned to face Karl and looked deep into his eyes. She took him firmly in hand and said, "Marry me."

Karl smiled and said, "Is that all you want?"

She pushed him down onto the grass and replied, "NO," as she climbed on top of him, still holding him firmly. "I want you to give me babies," said Roseanna, then she kissed him hard and made love to him right there on that hill.

Some nine months later a baby's cries emanated loudly from the ranch house.

Hawaii Mountainside by a Cheerful Campfire:

It was a warm night and the stars appeared to wrap all around them. Visitors had been arriving and children were playing around the garden. Alice was sitting in the middle of a large mat with the babies. The ladies were gathered all about them. Krista sat holding baby Joshua, but would not get him long as all the ladies wanted a turn. Taking after her mother, Ruby was busy crawling from person to person making sure everyone gave her attention. She did stop for a moment on her rounds to commune with Sue, an obvious kindred spirit. Snow, Mona, Aunt Tracy, Kate, Charly, Jenny, Laurie, Stella, Snow, Sky, Aunt Shela, Amanda, Amy, Cookie, and Dee all gathered around to play pass the baby.

Not far away, the guys sat sharing guy tales and slapping J.P. on the back. Harry, Peter, and Ted had found some beer.

Purr, Jack, Flagg, Joe, Bones, Walter, Meatloaf, Alfrado, Jay, Matt, Lee, and Atlas had all gathered for this family as well. The children were all over the place playing, eating, and toasting marshmallows on the fire. Cookie brought Bones food and sat there feeding him.

Bones said, "You sure seem happy tonight. I hope this hasn't given you ideas."

"Who me?" she asked, then moved closer shoving food in his mouth and said, "Would I let some big doctor get me pregnant?"

He choked out, "You're getting hot, dear."

She replied, "Then we better go swimming so you can cool me off without everyone watching."

Dee had dutifully held Joshua for an appropriate amount of time and passed him to the next in line. After a while, Dee saw Ruby crawl in a straight line to her and climb into her lap. She lifted Ruby up who looked deep into Dee's eyes. With a knowing look, Ruby smiled and snuggled into Dee's full bosom and fell asleep. When Dee finally looked up from Ruby she found all the ladies were looking at her and smiling. She smiled back and gave the sleeping Ruby to her mom.

Dee joined Atlas and they curled up together at the edge of the clearing. Sue came over and climbed on them. Sue found a comfortable position and laid her head on Dee's breasts. Sue looked up at Dee and Atlas and said, "You're very comfortable. That's why babies like you." She snuggled closer and said, "You should have a baby too."

Atlas reached down and caressed Sue's long hair. With a sigh, Atlas said, "I wish we could, but we are only computers—not human like you."

Sue looked up from her comfy spot and said, "Yes you can. You just take some of your spare parts and put them with Dee's spare parts until you've built a little computer and then love it, because it's part of both of you." And with that she snuggled closer to them both and dozed off to dream land where she had a new playmate named Matrix.

And so the tale closes with the stars twinkling above and the babies sleeping below. There were dreams of what the future could hold and of new adventures. There is nothing left to say except good night, sweet dreams as we move on to our next great adventure.

The Ship

U.S.S. Constitution CVNX-911 1911 feet 50 knots:

This is the first Constitution class carrier utilizing newest high technology with super computers and fiber optic communication links. Every member of the crew has a personal COM device which not only links them to ship's communications it gives the computer the exact location of the wearer. It also monitored its owner's life signs and feeds them into the medical computer to have an up to date health assessment of the whole crew. The personal COM links can also call up data or repair information on their display screen. Because of all her highly automated systems her crew needed five hundred less personnel to operate this large ship. The ship is powered by three nuclear reactors that drive twelve steam turbine generators. The ship also has four diesel generators as emergency back up. The ship has two rudders and a smaller steering rudder in the bow for making faster turns. She has bow and stern thrusters for added maneuvering control. She also has one standard bronze propeller in the amidships driven by a huge high-speed electric motor. This can be used as a back-up propulsion system or with the main propulsion system for added speed.

The main propulsion system consists of four huge turbines that look like over- sized jet engines. However, they are variable speed, reversible electric motors. Two are on either side of the propeller and hang below the hull on fins and discharge directly at the two ship's rudders. The second pair is farther out and turns with the rudders for greater maneuvering control. This and the hull design make for the ship's ability to achieve greater speeds at sea.

Ships defenses include reactive armor protection and laser cannons which use the ships high-speed fiber links to acquire target data from shipboard and aloft systems. There are enclosed lookout stations located in all four sides of the flight deck. All lookout stations are equipped with night vision and high-resolution multi-function cameras that can be monitored locally or in the ship's CDC. In addition the ship has a newly installed Atlas Defense Force Field. She normally had six smaller ships deployed with her to provide added defense and supplies. She also has an ultra modern hospital suite with ten Operating Rooms (OR), twenty intensive care units (ICU) and three hundred hospital beds.

Aircraft onboard during deployment are normally about eighty standard types. These would primarily be F/A-18 Hornets and F-14 Tomcats—the fighter jets. There would also be SH-60 Seahawks helicopters which are a multi-purpose aircraft used for anti-submarines warfare (ASW), rescue operations as well as cargo delivery. The EA-6B Prowler provides advances electronic countermeasures to protect and assist the attack aircraft. The AHE-2 Hawkeye with it distinctive dome provides early warning of approaching dangers to the ship or combat aircraft. The S-3B Viking provides protection from hostile surface combatants and acts as a fuel resupply tanker for the other aircraft. She also carried ten unmanned air vehicles

(UAVs) and twenty unmanned combat air vehicles (UCAVs). The "pilots" for these operated from a flight control room under the Sec-Fly tower. Pri-Fly would control launch operations while Sec-Fly managed recovery and unmanned operations. Sec-Fly is in second tower three hundred feet behind the main bridge. Sec-Fly is a round tower with a 360-degree view. The flight deck itself is almost double the size of the Nimitz class carriers and employed a nine-degree pitch like the Reagan for an unobstructed view of the whole flight deck. It also has a newly designed electromagnetic catapult system. Beyond the above aircraft the ship can carry a number of other mission specific aircraft such as the second-generation space shuttles.

Crew: ship —2,700; air wing —2,000-plus Marines as needed for security or combat.

EPILOG

There are some answers to life's questions that stay just around the next corner beyond our sight. There are questions my tale raises that I believe are better answered by your imagination than mine. If my words have caused you to think about the questions, it is enough for me.

For those of you who are curious about my plan for America, which is based on Abraham Maslow's "Hierarchy of Needs," I have added it below. My reason for placing the Constitution in the year 2012 is my interest in the Mayan calendar (see below). Also I have given you here my ideas about the *Dark Tower* I mentioned in the story. I have ended with some ideas on why I think this is all possible if we think outside of the *box.*

Time is a perception, the way you view events in the slide show of life. If you look at it in a different way, you will see a new scene. Each new choice creates a fork in the road, the "could have been," "should have been" and the path you choose to walk. People of good intent and those of evil intent cause change, which creates a new probability. Life's challenges are ongoing and new challenges call for new solutions. We learn and grow or turn stagnant like a swamp, but whatever we do, change will still happen. If you choose to ride the wave or wade in the quagmire is up to you.

The Plan:
There were four basic parts that worked together to achieve the goals of unity, growth, and healing. The first part was to

involve the people. The second was to provide the basic needs of those people so they could focus on the bigger issues and solutions. The third was to provide education and training to increase the people's social, leadership and technical skills. The fourth was for the people to apply their new skills to rebuild the American Dream.

Phase One: Involve the People.

Power must be returned to the people with the problems so they are the ones making the decisions about how to solve those problems. Part of making these decisions is electing those who speak for them, so they feel involved in the process and can see that they have some control of the outcome. Part of this is to place the responsibility for their security in their hands. This way they have to help do the policing of the problems around them. They help to protect their family, their friends, and themselves. Once involved in the process of running their lives they start helping do the long and short-term planning. Lastly from this phase when they accept the responsibility for themselves, they start repaying what they have received by giving the same type of help to others.

Phase Two: Provide Basic Needs.

Food and shelter are important in getting the people's attention. Also medical needs and child care helped to start bringing these families back together. The research showed there were a large number of college campuses that had fallen into disuse as things fell apart. So learning centers were created where the meals were provided in cafeterias and the living quarters were large dorms that became mini communities. The medical staff opened clinics and taught health care. Child care became part of the whole process with schools for the older children and adults, so they too where part of the solution. Part of this whole process, that was soon embraced, was the belief in providing others with this same opportunity so it became an ongoing cycle of change.

Phase Three: Educate and Train.
The training campuses increased the participants' skills as half of their time was spent on academic studies and the other half was spent building new skills via hands-on training. Leadership went well beyond the classroom because each group was made up of classes (groups of ten people) that lived, ate, studied, and worked together as a team. One of the focuses was on teaching carpentry, plumbing, electrical, and equipment repair as well as its operation. Medical, clerical, and farming became very popular courses of study. One of the methods of reinforcing the skills that the students had learned was that they had to teach their skills to new students, so they passed on the new skills to an expanding group of people.

Phase Four: Rebuild America.
The final phase was to take all of the above and put it to work out in the real world to rebuild communities, building new homes, farms, and factories. The factories would build the foundation for the country's economy. This final stage was actually more like the beginning as it was here that all that had been invested was reinvested in building America stronger. Many of the student groups or teams went on to work together long after the classes were over. The groups became the cutting edge of America's revival.

Mayan Calendar:
Far away another clock was ticking to the end of its calendar cycle. Its name is the Tzolkin and is based on the 26,000-year

cycle of the Pleiades, which ends at the Winter Solstice on the 21st of December in the year 2012 when our sun passes the galactic equator and the Earth lines up with the center of the galaxy. The Mayans have seventeen different calendars and I guess you could rightly say they were into time keeping. Some of their calendars span millions of years. Not bad for a bunch of stone-aged folks living in the middle of a jungle. They were people that carved their calendars in stone. According to the Mayan elders who are the keepers of the Mayan prophecies and their calendars, this event is the transition from the world of the fourth sun to the world of the fifth sun. They say this will be a human transformation to a higher reality or awareness. We need to unite and work together in the care of Mother Earth, our home planet, to achieve this end. They also state that everyone is important and needed. The Mayan traditions speak of Turtle Island (North America) and the future of the people who live there. The Mayan elders have said that this transition began with the Harmonic Convergence on the 16th of August in the year 1987.

The Mayan elders believe in keeping philosophy simple so it can be understood and applied. In that tradition, let me share some of what I know of this happening. Every 26,000 years Earth lines up with the Pleiades and the center of the galaxy and I must believe it has before and will again. So it is not the end of the world, just a transition like new years coming every year. There are some that say this transition is like passing through a wave of energy, which travels in a 26,000-year cycle. This energy wave raises the Earth's frequency as the Earth passes through this field. Some say that during this passing, people who are positively aligned with nature can increase their frequency from the third to fourth dimension. In other words, if you ride the wave like a surfer you will move faster and farther. If you are swimming against the tide (wave) you will not go far at all.

So why haven't we heard about this before? Well on the 21st of April in the year 1519 Hernando Cortez arrived at Vera Cruz, Mexico with eleven Spanish galleons. For you Christians who believe in synchronicity that date is Easter Sunday. This arrival was spoken of in the Mayan prophecy, so Cortez and Company were welcomed. The Mayans had a culture, written manuscripts, brilliant calendars, and gold. Cortez had swords and guns, so he took their gold, destroyed the native heathens' culture, and gave them disease and religion. Fortunately for us a few of the smart Mayans ran for the hills and now almost five hundred years later are nice enough to even talk to us "enlightened" barbarians. This also brings us to the reason I placed the Constitution's trip to Guam in the year 2012. If curiosity has gotten the best of you there are many good history books out there and I would be so bold as to recommend reading some by the Mayan, Chamorro, Hawaiian, and Native American authors for a fuller picture of what really happened. As for the whys of it all, I like the elders believe you are important, needed and very much able to think for yourself. And so I wish you well on your adventure and will leave my soapbox to move on.

The Dark Tower:

Standing in a shallow dark bowl the Dark Tower stood silently. The tower's protective plates looked almost like a black tiled roof. The bowl area and the tower were covered with them. The tower's six sides were all equal in size. The base was larger and became smaller as it goes up. At about four thousand feet it began to expand for the last thousand feet where it ended in a pod like shape. This pod housed the focus device, which aimed the transmitted signal. It was so ancient that it was almost older than time itself. Those who built it had been gone almost that long as well and had departed before it was completed. It had never had enough energy to reach full power, but all the same it had been working at its lower capacity from long ago. Its transmissions were set to a frequency to affect the brain waves and behavior of a class of developing creatures. The tower sat on a huge satellite and was aimed at the neighboring host planet where these effected creatures resided. Because of its low power its effects were only observable during the full moon when the tower was in direct aliment with the planet Earth.

Not far from the Dark Tower was a matrix of crystalline geodesic domes interconnected by a network of tubes. From above, it looked like a snowflake. The milk-white colors blended in with the gray soil on which it sat. The complex was miles across and some of it had been damaged over time, collapsing some of the domes. It was designed to collect solar power and transmit positive energy at the Earth and its inhabitants.

These two complexes were built around the same time, but by very different races. Their motivations were also very different. The Dark Tower's designers wished to rule the Earth and have power over the creatures living there. The others only wished to help the Earth creatures develop to the best of their ability. Because both groups were equally powerful, neither could force the issue. So in the end the both left the moon and their projects by mutual agreement. They had not returned there and so it was as it was left long, long ago when the Earth was much younger and man was just a gleam in Mother Earth's eye.

TIME (THE REST OF THE STORY)
TWELFTH HOUR
Or A Theory of Life and Everything

Time is not linear. There is no future or past, just NOW. The past and the future are merely a matter of our perception or our point of view or focus. It is how we file or store events in a logical order of cause and effect. Therefore as we change the point of focus, as in the use of hypnosis, we can scan over past and future events. The future gets more complicated because of two factors. First, it is a probability directly affected by the actions happening in the NOW, so it is variable. Secondly, each decision made, like a fork in the road, creates a NEW probability and a NEW path, so eventually you have an infinite number of probable paths or futures all in parallel in the big memory matrix.

There are also two types of decisions. Some are personal, made by the individual and for the most part only effect that person. Others are collective decisions made by many people or society as a whole. The latter are harder to change and have much wider effects on the individual even if that person had no part in that choice.

When we travel backward into the past it is much simpler because your individual path leads back to your anchor event (birth). Even if you travel beyond that point, most people have had other lives whose paths can be followed as well. Of course the above rather assumes we are talking about astral travel, traveling with the mind instead of traveling with your physical body. There are those who believe the body is tied to its anchor and specific time line.

If all experience, that is knowledge gained through living and or observation, is part of a vast holographic memory matrix, it should be accessible by tuning to the correct coordinates of the individual event or experience. Since time is just an observation of an event, then with the correct tuning we should be able to view any person or event in the whole matrix. Since many have done this with astral travel (the mind) the only other question is that of physical time travel. Or can we adjust our physicality via technology enough to move to another point in the matrix and return.

When we talk about adjusting our physicality or more specifically of changing our current reality to another different reality we must look at the how and the consequences of this action. During the Philadelphia Experiment it is said that many of the crew went mad. This could be a two-fold problem, in that first of all they had no idea what was going to happen and it altered their reality so much they lost their minds and themselves. Secondly if their connection to their anchor was broken, they would then end up free floating through the matrix at random—sort of lost in time and space. Those who are practiced at astral projection and know how to navigate through the matrix of time and space can, like homing pigeons, find their way back to their current lifeline.

So just what is the matrix? It is obviously a vast grid of stored data, but hardly a hard drive or even USB flash drive. More like a RAM card or chip (Random Access Memory), but much bigger and faster than our largest super computers with AI (Artificial Intelligence) and speech recognition. To get a handle on this, we need to look at Albert Einstein's Unified

Field Theory, which he supposedly never completed. The universe and everything is a big "place" and the representation of it (memory) is such a vast amount of data as to be well beyond our individual abilities to process the concept let alone the reality of "all that is." To understand we must move a step beyond the electromagnetic fields, which are part of our everyday life. We must add another component to the equation, which is gravity. This element has been well hidden from us in plain sight for years, because those in "power" would have little control over everyone else. You could even say it is the gravity of the situation which scares those whom seek to control. That is hard to do when the sheep become the masters of their own destiny.

The Unified Field is the matrix, which is made up of electric, magnetic and gravitational components. Where the field is, is everywhere. It's all around you. It is you and everything else. We already know that you can manipulate (read and write) the matrix and even deny ourselves access to parts of it. The device we use to do this is called your mind or brain, if you prefer. Mine currently "sees" the trees, rocks, earth, and a large cat that is deciding if I'll bean him with my spoon if he tries to eat my lunch. He waited for the beans in the bowl until I was done. The mind (human) is not a storage device. It is an access device or a reader. It tunes into its specific data stream (lifeline) and "sees" that which is around us. Be it our creation or the common shared creation of the society and planet of which we are a part. So if we can manipulate, manage, read, and write to the matrix with our mind why not some less sophisticated electromagnetic gravitational device. Just tune it like a radio to the right station and away you go. That was part of the Navy's problem, they had no tuner coils to direct where they went, so they sort of went everywhere at once. No wonder the passengers and crew went mad. It would be like getting onto a plane and ending up at every airport at once. Most would find that rather unsettling.

So once you build the field generators and a tuner to direct you down the right vectors, away you go right through hyperspace and imagination to anywhere that is, was, or will be to a new journey. Great adventures in learning as you explore the vast wonderland of reality in the matrix of life.

So what are we? Well, how about a spirit wrapped in a physical manifestation. If the word "spirit" bugs you then let's try calling it an energy field. If you recall from that class in school energy can't be created or destroyed. It can however be modified and changed into something new. Flowing water can turn a paddle wheel that drives a generator that makes electricity. The same can be done with wind. And why are we here or anywhere else? Well, my best guess is that this is a classroom and we like any other students are here to learn and grow. Lastly, let me say I am no guru. If my answers help you, then embrace them. But most often your best answers are within you. You must seek them there inside the one who looks back at you from the mirror. Just turn off the noise and listen to yourself.

Good luck on the journey and so we are at The End or The Beginning?

931778

Made in the USA